D1061425

12/26 - 42

From O. M. Nortie

SIGNED WITH THEIR HONOUR

JAMES ALDRIDGE

Signed with their Honour

NEW YORK

THE BOOK LEAGUE OF AMERICA

1942

COPYRIGHT 1942, BY JAMES ALDRIDGE

ALL RIGHTS RESERVED, INCLUDING THE RIGHT
TO REPRODUCE THIS BOOK OR PORTIONS
THEREOF IN ANY FORM

PR6001
.L45S5
1942
OMN

CL
PRINTED IN THE UNITED STATES OF AMERICA

TO
SQUADRON LEADER "PAT" PATTLE
SQUADRON LEADER T. S. HICKEY

Both killed in Greece

127864

Near the snow, near the sun, in the highest fields
See how these names are fêted by the waving grass
And by the streamers of white cloud
And whispers of wind in the listening sky.
The names of those who in their lives fought for life
Who wore at their hearts the fire's centre.
Born of the sun they travelled a short while towards the sun,
And left the vivid air signed with their honour.

—STEPHEN SPENDER

COPYRIGHT 1933, BY STEPHEN SPENDER

SIGNED WITH THEIR HONOUR

Chapter 1

All summer had been filled with dust. It had been so bad at times that everybody had gone around wearing gas-masks. It had clung to everything in the camp. It was always in the food, on the dishes, in the clothes . . . everywhere. It was in the bunks at night, in the morning and all day. In your mouth all day and night too. In the water. On the surface of anything that had a surface. It became synonymous with heat; the grittiness on your face and body was the same as being hot. You had the idea in your head that if you could wash all the grittiness off and get into some ungritted clothes, you would be cool, despite the high temperature and humidity.

And if it wasn't the dust, it was the sweat, and the flies, and the wet nights and cold mornings. The flies and the sweat were the same too, like the dust and heat. If you could get rid of the flies, you figured you wouldn't sweat. The wet feeling of humid sweat mixing with dust to a paste on your face was unpleasant. The wet irritating grittiness of your shirt against your back was continuous, even when you took your shirt off.

Even if the dust, flies and sweat lifted for a while, there were the Italian raids. They were always in the early morning around one o'clock when the moon was high. To have sleep interrupted like that was like a sigh that kept being drawn into your breath and never getting out. You would feel fine in sleep, then the raid. You could not stay in your bunk because of the incendiaries, so you fell into the slit trench. When you got back to bed, there was the extra grittiness and plain dirt of the slit trench on your body.

It had been the Italians' round in the summer war. It started to go

3

their way when Graziani took over. He used C.R. 42 biplanes, equipped with cannon using armour-piercing shells, against the Hussars' armoured cars.

It had been the Gladiators' job for a while to go hunt the C.R. 42's and keep them off the armoured cars; but it was a forlorn sort of job. The C.R. 42's were never around, and they were too near home when you found them anyway, and you were too far from home to chase them. But it was unsatisfactory combat because the Italians had orders to give up after the initial attack. It was very sensible, though it didn't make them feel good having to run away. They were never very good in combat because of this.

Later, when Graziani and Malletti invaded Egypt, the war had changed again. The Italians were using about every 79 they had strafing and low-level–bombing all the bases and airdromes. The Gladiator squadron had to leave everything it owned, except the cars, and evacuate from BuqBuq way back to Martin Magush.

The Italians came on as far as BuqBuq. They stopped there and started to build up their supplies. So they operated from Sollum and kept bombing Mersa Matruh with 79's and Cants, and brought in Macchi monoplane fighters for the first time.

It took some time to get used to Macchi tactics after the 42's, which were about the same as the Gladiators. The Macchis weren't so manœuvrable, but faster. It was even more difficult when Macchis and 42's were mixed. It was a matter of deciding whether the plane was a Macchi or a C.R. 42 before attacking, so that you would know just how to attack it. The Gladiators were a few down after this.

And then the Hurricanes came in. There were three at first. They took a turn at patrol over Mersa Matruh around midday of one Wednesday. They were way up around fifteen thousand when about fourteen 79's and ten Macchis came in from the sea. In their first dive they got two 79's and one Macchi. They didn't even break formation when they got up again. The Macchis spread out, however, and the 79's were left wide open. The Hurricanes got two more in the next dive. Then they chased for a while and went home.

The Italians didn't come back for two days. Then they got their

4

bombing over in a hurry. They were waiting for fighters that could keep off the Hurricanes. So it became quiet again.

Sometimes the Gladiators did some strafing of Italian positions and columns. The Italians were building a road atop the escarpment from Sidi Barrani to Mersa. It was long straight for twenty miles. Twice the Gladiators flew bumps up and down it, strafing the sappers working on it. A few were killed, but it didn't do anything more than delay the work.

After that it got so quiet that the Gladiator squadrons were sent back plane by plane for overhaul, back to Heliopolis. The pilot flew his own plane down to Heliopolis and, while it was being re-serviced, he had two days' leave or more to spend in Cairo; then he would fly the plane back to his squadron. This was going on in the last days of October when Italy invaded Greece.

Because most of Eighty Squadron were in Heliopolis being re-fitted, they were ordered to Greece. After the C.O. came back from surveying the Athens airdromes, the first five Gladiators went over, stopping off at Crete for refuelling. The next five followed two days later. The last five were delayed because they were new planes and had to be tested at Heliopolis. They drifted over in twos and odd singles. The reserves, when there were any, were to be flown over as they came.

The summer was ending. The dust and the east wind were tired before they got anywhere. The desert was getting colder at night, and staying colder longer in the mornings. There was no moon, and the Italians had stopped raiding. The flies and grit were never-ending, like death. But you forgot them a little because there was less humidity, and sweat seemed absorbed internally. The winter quiet spread soft over the desert's breadth.

5

Chapter 2

"Do we stay around twelve thousand?" the young man said.

"We'll stay around there." John Quayle nodded his head. "The Greeks claimed they were at ten thousand. But you can't be too sure." The two men walked across the green mud of grass and earth in the general direction of the biplanes at the end of the field.

"Keep well behind young Gorell, Tap. Don't let him get wide."

"I won't."

"And don't get wide yourself."

"I won't," Tap said again. "Do you think they've got escort?"

"Not from the report. And not this far down anyway."

"I don't know, John. The Italians were bringing in those new F. 5's when we left Egypt." The boy named Tap zipped up his Irvin suit and started pulling on his thin gloves with their worn fingers and split seams.

"They're not long-range fighters. But if there's any around, get young Gorell out of the way."

"I don't like this business of tailing the flight. You can have it on your own," the boy said.

"You'll get used to it. Just keep looking behind. You'll be the first to see anything chasing us. And keep Gorell following me. He'll be all right if there's no escort."

"All right, but don't make your turns too tight. I can't keep height when I'm back there trying to keep up with you."

"Well, keep Gorell in tight then."

The two men separated. Quayle walked towards a plane that was taxiing downwind to the perimeter of the field. He held up his hand with his helmet in it. The plane taxied towards him. The boy in the plane swung it around and throttled down.

"Say, keep in close to me, will you, Gorell?" Quayle yelled.

"Sure."

"They're Savoias, I think. So if you get a bead on one, get it on that hump over the trailing edge of the wing."

Gorell pulled at his harness.

"Tap will be behind you." Quayle lifted his hand again and walked towards a plane that was being warmed up by two aircraftsmen, two hundred yards away. He looked up as he walked and saw water blue in the sky and streaked chalk in the clouds. He was thinking they would be too high to hide in. Probably at fifteen thousand, and not much of them anyway. Maybe twelve thousand wasn't height enough for the fighters. The Greeks said the Savoias were around ten thousand feet. They might climb a little to get over the anti-aircraft and the Greeks ought to keep their anti-aircraft quiet. Quayle thought this as he walked across the field.

As he approached the squat, khaki-camouflaged biplane, an aircraftsman climbed out of the cockpit. The plane's engine was making a hard soft noise.

"All right, Sergeant?" Quayle asked the short figure who stood by the plane.

"Fine. There's still a bit of oil floating around the cockpit. I wiped the rudder bar clean, though. Keep your feet off the floor and they won't slip off."

The slight young man pulled on a fur-lined waterproof flying suit and a parachute harness, stepped onto the wing of the biplane, eased himself up and down into the cockpit. He pulled on his helmet, buttoned the microphone across his mouth, plugged the cord in, held the brakes of the plane tight as he opened up the throttle lever. Quayle released the brakes, pressured the right rudder bar. The plane swung around and, in short bursts of engine laughs, moved in a boy's swagger over the green bumps of the airdrome. There were three other planes taxiing down the field from different directions. They were all Gloster Gladiators, like the Flight Lieuten-

7

ant's. The young Gorell was already turned around and facing up-wind waiting for the others. One by one they came around him and formed an arrowhead. Quayle moved in last and became the apex of the group, keeping his engine opening in gusts and closing in sighs.

Taking one look behind him on both sides, Quayle moved the control stick, then opened the throttle and moved forward. The five planes bumped slowly over the field, gathered speed until the tails lifted. Lightly the wheels were unweighted until they were touching only the prominent surface and picking up the greensward which made them spin until they left the ground completely. The planes climbed easily, with their noses on the horizon. In a great curve the five fighters uncurled themselves from the basin of mountains around the airdrome and began their climb over Athens.

Quayle could see the new city below him sometimes as they climbed. There was no traffic on the streets, because there was an air-raid alarm over the city. The Acropolis stretched white and without height between the city and the sea. And around it were the green earth of the Pnyx and the woods whose good fists were closed.

It is so simple to be here, Quayle was thinking as he looked around at the flight close-flying behind him. It is simple because this is the simplest way of being anywhere. Hickey had said, one day at Fuka when there was a dust storm blowing across the desert — he had said: "Looks like we're going to Greece." And that had started it. It was not sure, though, even when Quayle and Hickey left Fuka and flew down to the Heliopolis airdrome near Cairo. Hickey was the Squadron Leader, and because he was going down to Cairo and the remainder of the Gladiator squadron was already there at Heliopolis being refitted, it meant something was in the air.

There had been a station wagon waiting to take Hickey to Head-quarters. Finn and John Hersey had been there, too. They said they had been having a wonderful time while waiting for their planes, which were due to go back to Fuka when H.Q. told them to wait. Now they wanted to know what it was all about, and one by one the remainder of the squadron found out that Hickey was in Cairo also.

In the afternoon they had waited in a Cairo bar where they usually drank beer, waited for Hickey to come back from Headquarters across the city. When he came he had shrugged and said "Greece," and they had separated their thoughts to think about it. They had wanted to talk about it but couldn't because it was still secret. But later, when Quayle and Hickey were walking back to Headquarters, Hickey had told him that Eighty Squadron was to be the only fighter squadron in Greece. "It's only going to be British air forces in Greece," he had said. "No military, except supply. Two-Eleven Squadron is there, the Blenheims. There's a Wellington squadron there, too, doing night raids on Italy. The Blenheims are bombing Albania. We'll be doing escort for them. We'll be at a place called Faleron near Athens for the first couple of days, then we'll probably go to Larissa. That's inland somewhere. They tell me the weather's hell and the mountains high."

And Hersey had said that night, "Athens is fine." But nobody had believed him, so no one took any notice when he said that it was a new city and not old at all. . . . And he was right, it is new, Quayle was thinking. . . . Hersey had gone on — Nobody speaks English, but they speak French and German, he had said. There were good cabarets, too, with Hungarian girls; they were all over the Balkans. "We'll probably get there in time to see the finish," Hersey had said. And he, Quayle, had been optimistic and replied, "They might surprise you." "Who, the Greeks?" said Hersey. "As fighters they're good cooks."

They had left in groups of three the next day. Hickey had taken Gorell and Finn over. Hersey had brought over Vain and Stewart. Tap had brought over Constance and South, and Quayle himself had brought over Brewer and Richardson. The others had straggled over.

It was a long flight, and they had put down at Canea on Crete to refuel, then had come on to Greece. Hickey had been waiting

9

for them at Faleron with the station wagon, which had been sent there by ship with the ground crew. And they had driven into Athens.

There had been those surprising scenes: People calling to them as they speeded the two miles into town . . . The wagon was still desert-camouflaged a dust-colour, and this made it distinctive as British and military. When the Greeks recognized it they shouted happily at them, everywhere. And the great crowd that had suddenly gathered as they lifted their kit out of the wagon to carry it into the Athinai Hotel which they were billeted in . . . His own bag had been taken out of his hand. He had been slapped and patted on the back and his head knocked. He had to fight his way with Hickey to get in the door of the hotel. It had been fine; he had heard them shouting, *"Inglisi, Inglisi airoplanos!"* It was very happy for everyone, and they all felt the Greeks were very fine people.

And every time they had walked down the street, people had followed them and talked happily to them in Greek. When there was an air-raid alarm on the first day and they had not taken cover, the police had tried to push him and Hickey into a shelter, but they wouldn't go. The people had been puzzled that they were not up at that given moment keeping the Italian planes away. But no Italians had come over the city and the Greeks were even happier, and a well-dressed Greek had said to Hickey: "They, the bastards, will not come now. No. We can be happy now. You are fine fellows. We are glad you are here. They, the bastards, will not come now. Oh, no!"

And at night in the wild cabaret, which was bright and expensive and filled with fliers from the two bomber squadrons who had been here a week, they had gone wild. It had been filled with Hungarian and Greek cabaret girls who tried to put on their floor show, but the idea was abandoned as the fliers took liberties with the girls, who liked it and crowded more closely and made grand public love to everybody. And as the place had filled there was no room to move and no silence to talk into and no single sounds to hear; so that it was all right what the girls did and it dominated the place.

Particularly the wild girl with a tiny scar over one of her wide glassy eyes. "*Inglisi, Inglisi!*" she had shouted.

She had poured beer over the cabaret floor to make it slippery and smell good. Her dress had been torn down the back; it was a smart and expensive dress. Her body was very brown. Someone had shouted, "She wears polka-dot underwear." She had said "No . . . no . . ." in English; she got hold of Hickey, pulled his red hair, pointing to it, shouting, "It is red, see," and pulled his head down to her breast and pointed to her slip in the valley of her breasts and said, "It is the same — it is for him — see, it is for the same." And Hickey, who was usually aloof and unbending, had not been embarrassed, because he was warm with drink — though not drunk enough to be embarrassed by it, when he tried to be dignified.

It had been mad and like a moving picture; but the next day and night had been as mad and fantastic, and it was still fantastic.

The squadron had not left the airdrome, because of the low cloud, until to-day. This was their first flight. Hickey had gone to Larissa to see what its airdrome was like, with Hersey and Stewart. They all might move up there in a couple of days. He would not be sorry; it didn't make much difference where you were so long as there were warmth and cinemas.

He looked at the instrument board with full consciousness, without other thoughts, and realized suddenly he was very cold. He had kept some of his consciousness receiving his eyes' registration of the instrument panel as he had climbed. His eyes had not stopped roaming around the skies and flicking to the instrument panel and behind him to the flight.

The five planes had climbed in a wide circle over Athens area without leaving it; they were a few miles north-west of the city now, over low mountains, at fourteen thousand feet.

"Say, I'm getting cold. How much higher are we going?" It was Tap he heard in the bulging earphones.

"We'll stay here," Quayle said into his microphone. "And no talking. They ought to be somewhere around by now."

There was no answer from Tap and Quayle looked around at his

11

flight. They were shining now in the white-blue background to high sunlight. He could see Gorell, Brewer, Richardson and Tap below him. He never got used to seeing Gladiators with camouflage; it made them stumpy and more dangerous. They were small and shorter-looking. And he never got used to the idea of biplanes like Gladiators fighting in this war. It was more by good fortune than calculation that there had been numbers of Gladiators in Egypt when Italy entered the war. It was good fortune that the fighter plane the Italians relied upon was a twin to the Gladiator. The Fiat C.R. 42 was a biplane and manœuvrable like the Gladiator, with a top speed around three hundred, which was a little faster than the Gladiators. Hurricanes were too fast and not manœuvrable enough to shoot down C.R. 42's. And the Italian equivalent of the Hurricane, the G. 50, was too fast and not manœuvrable enough to shoot down Gladiators.

Gladiators were only good for shooting down C.R. 42 fighters. Seldom could one Gladiator alone shoot down a bomber unless he got in two or three attacks, which wasn't often. A squadron or a flight of Gladiators had a chance, because one by one they could concentrate on a single bomber in a formation and get the pilot or an engine, but it had to be at close range. The Gladiators' four 303 guns had short range — up to five hundred yards — and a small cone of fire. The C.R. 42 was the same. The two were good for shooting down each other and that was about all. They would die out quickly, like the Fairey Battles after the fall of France.

The flight was at fifteen thousand now, and it was very cold. Quayle looked around. The Savoias would be along any minute. They would be hard to see against the variable colours of the Greek hills. He pulled his transmission switch and said, "What do you see, Tap?"

Tap came back immediately. "I thought you'd seen them. There's six of them at about 170, around ten thousand all right, and no escort."

Quayle looked at his compass. The flight was heading around 180 degrees on the compass. He pulled around to 170 and looked for the

Savoias. Suddenly he saw them, slow and dark in wide line formation, caught in the light background of a Greek field between two mountains.

"Keep in close, Gorell, closer." Quayle turned his head to see if Gorell was pulling in.

"We'll take them going down first," he said into his phone.

"Broadside on, John?" the Australian, Vain, asked.

"Yes. Don't lose me. And no isolated attacks. Keep on the one plane."

Quayle knew he could trust Richardson. He was a steady person and a steady flier, and always kept a level head in a fight. Quayle knew he wouldn't have to watch Richardson, but he would have to watch young Gorell. He was the newest member of the squadron. His face was very simple and clear, and Quayle could not picture him giving deliberate and complicated thought to the pattern of things that evolve in a dogfight. It was the same with Tap. Tap just went in carelessly and smacked at anything that got in his way, and if anything got on his tail, he did the first thing that came into his head. Vain, the Australian, was all right. He was clear-headed, like Richardson. That dark lean face was always carefully set in expression, though his youth was deceptive.

The Savoias seemed way below and were still five or so miles away. Quayle headed in their direction, keeping the nose of his plane a little off course so he could see them all the time. They must have seen the Gladiators because they appeared to be climbing. They were still far enough from Piraeus, where they were heading, for the Gladiators to catch them while they were leveling to do the bombing.

The flight neared the Savoias, which were definitely climbing. They were heading straight for Piraeus, which was about two miles from the city. From this height it looked all the same place.

As the bombers came right over the port, Quayle brought his plane into a position where he could nose straight down onto them broadside on. He took a quick look around and saw the flight was packed close behind him, waddled his wings as a signal, then pushed the stick forward. The nose of the plane dipped, the flat drop of the first part of the dive faded, and he was heading like a spear, with his eye ahead of the Savoias, which were flying level and bombing.

Down; fourteen thousand went by on the meter, thirteen thousand; the speed had gone up beyond three hundred; and suddenly, as if two seconds had been passed over in time, he saw the tail Savoia in his mirror sight. He pushed his rudder quickly, slightly, so that the plane slipped in its steep dive and the hump at the head of the Savoia came into his sights and he pressed hard on the thumb trigger on the stick.

He felt the shake of the guns and kept his plane heading for the Savoia, which was blurred now, and held his finger on the gun button until the whole of his sight was filled by only a portion of the Savoia; and he pulled back on the stick and felt his stomach rise, and the black mass of Savoia underneath him and white tracers from the Savoias' guns passing beside him.

He rose two thousand feet in flat climbing and looked around quickly to see the flight. It had broken up, it always did. He saw two Gladiators way to his right behind him. He banked to come back at the Savoias and suddenly saw the white smoke with black edges coming from a plane that was falling quickly. He couldn't see whether it was a Gladiator, and the Savoias had got way ahead now and he could see their bombs bursting below. They were good, at least they went on with their bombing, but they had split up, which was dangerous for them.

He saw one Savoia alone to his left ahead of him and a thousand feet lower. He pushed the stick forward again and calculated his rudder and stick movements so that he knew for sure he would come across the Savoia's blind spot at the tail.

He did not feel his way as most do; he calculated his stick and rudder movements like a series of chess moves, and he came down flat behind the blind spot of the Savoia. He kept his speed and pushed the gun button. He had the port engine in his sights. The guns shook. He took a quick look behind him to see if anything was on his tail, and pushed the gun button again and the four guns shuddered to his feet. He pulled up and banked tight just as a Savoia moved in from the starboard to pick him off. He saw the tracer bullets from its gun amidships streak up beside his tail.

As he climbed again he looked around for the flight. He could see one Gladiator moving down on the plane he had just attacked. From the way he was going at it Quayle thought it must be Gorell, because he was coming down too fast and steep. He banked and watched the scene, way ahead of him now and out of reach. The Gladiator came down on the Savoia and Quayle saw the tracers dragging past the Savoia, and the Savoia's bullets passing into the Gladiator, but the Gladiator pulled up and nosed over to the left. Smoke was coming from the port engine of the Savoia and it was losing height. He watched it turn and could see it was out of control. It fell faster and went into a flat spin. He half looped and banked so that he could see it lose height and head-crash into the sea.

He looked around for Savoias or Gladiators. The Savoias had a good lead now and were out of sight. He could see one Gladiator far below him. He turned and realized he was about ten miles from Athens over the sea. He kept looking around for Gladiators, then called into his phone: "Make for home. Come back if anyone hears me. Come back on the phone."

"Hullo, Quayle — how many did we get?"

"Was that you coming down on that Savoia, Gorell?"

"Yes. We got him. I kept following you."

"Where's Tap, and the others? Did you see them?"

"Tap's heading home. I think the others are all right. I didn't see Richardson. I saw Vain. He got the first one. Say, two bombers is good."

"Come on home," Quayle said.

And they went back to Faleron. Young Gorell landed first. Quayle could see three Gladiators on the field as he came down and rolled low over the field. He always felt foolish doing a slow roll over the field, but it would be snobbish if he didn't, since they had brought down one bomber for sure. He put his flaps down and fish-tailed in. He taxied to a corner of the field and saw Jock and Churchill, the fitter and the rigger, walking over towards the spot. He pulled the sliding cockpit top back and unbuttoned his microphone. As the plane stopped he pulled off his gloves, beat his cold hands together and eased stiffly up and over the top of the cockpit and landed heavily with cold feet jarring on the ground.

"Who isn't back?" he said to Jock as he came up.

"Mr. Finley." That was Tap.

"Did I get any punctures?" Quayle walked around the plane.

"No. I can't see any. Mr. Gorell did."

"Yes. I saw him get it."

Quayle unhooked his parachute and walked towards the hangars. Young Gorell and Richardson and Vain, and the doctor of Two-Eleven Squadron, were walking towards him.

"Did you see Tap?" he asked them.

"Vain did," young Gorell said. "He saw him heading this way. It was Tap who got the first one. I thought it was Vain."

Quayle looked up to see whether Tap was around. There was no engine sound and he couldn't see anything.

"We got two of them. I watched the one Tap got. Young Gorell says you and he got one," said Richardson. He rubbed his fluffy hair and spoke very quietly.

"Did you see it hit the water, Gorell?"

"Sure. Say, there's something now." He was excited, but keeping it down. They were almost at the hangar when they heard an engine. They looked around but couldn't see a plane. Quayle listened for a moment, said "It's a Gladiator," and walked into the operations room. He heard Tap do a ground loop as he came in, then throttle down as he put his flaps down to land.

Quayle had started to write out his report when Tap walked in.

"What happened to you?" Quayle said, without looking up.

"I went to make sure I got him."

"You certainly kept young Gorell in close. He stayed in the flight and you didn't."

"Gorell was all right. I could see this Savoia break off when you got him. I climbed and got a wonderful burst into him. He went

16

down straight away. I chased you and Gorell for a while but you were too far away. Did you get that second one I saw you go after?"

"Gorell got him. You can't keep clearing off like that, Tap."

"Well, I could see young Gorell was all right."

"It's nothing to do with him. You would have looked fine if those G. 50's had come out of the blue."

"I would have looked fine anyway — sitting on the tail of the flight."

Quayle finished making out his report. He folded it up and pushed it in his coat pocket. The other four were already sitting in the Squadron Leader's station wagon. It had been recamouflaged a light green-and-brown earth-colour.

"We're going into the King George for a bath. Do you want to come, John?"

Quayle asked young Gorell where he could bathe in the King George Hotel.

"You can pay fifty drachmas and go to an empty room."

"That's a swanky place to have a bath," Quayle said. "All of Headquarters live there." Quayle spoke flatly and evenly and he raised his eyebrows when he spoke.

"I know," young Gorell said. He was showing teeth too even and white to be real, but they were. "But it's the only place with hot water to-day."

So they went to the King George Hotel, after Quayle had put in his report at H.Q. The King George was next to the Grande Bretagne, now the Greek Headquarters. There were Evzone guards in white skirts standing at the entrance, and two cars filled with thugs and machine guns. They were Metaxas' bodyguards. There were groups of people, and young Fascist E.O.N. youth in their blue ski-looking suits with white gaiters, waiting for Metaxas or Papagos, the Commander-in-Chief, to come out. When they did the people waved and shouted, because they were paid to by the E.O.N., and if you wandered down Acropolis Street any morning, you could see people who needed money being told by the young E.O.N. Fascists where to go and cheer. Sometimes Prince Paul and his Bavarian wife went in there, too, and there was little cheering, and no shouts from the E.O.N. Once, when the first public hero from Albania was brought down to be made a spectacle of, there were many more people and much more cheering.

Around the door of the King George there were always groups of Metaxas Secret Police, who were not secret at all but just grim men in civilian clothes. It was easy for Quayle and the others to get into the hotel, because they were in uniform; but they were watched, and the little porter with the black moustache and the white hands kept a notebook with the names and ranks of all the passers-by and what they did.

They walked into the hotel, bumping the Secret Police as they went in. There were people sitting around in the long lobby, women in expensive clothes and British army liaison officers, and wealthy Greeks and French, and Germans — because Germans were not at war with Greece, so they came into the King George lobby to watch the British coming and going and the general activity, and there was none to stop them because the Secret Police were German-trained and pro-German.

"We want a bath," Tap said to the porter with the white hands.

He looked at them for a moment, then said, "It is impossible. We have no rooms."

"You had them this morning," young Gorell said. "I rang up and asked you."

"We cannot give you a room," the porter said.

"Why?"

"The manager has said no. He said no."

"What's wrong? We pay you, don't we?" Tap said.

"The manager has said he must keep the rooms for other gentlemen."

"To hell with him."

"It is impossible, impossible. He said no."

"Is Mr. Lawson in?"

"I do not know."

"Well, Jesus, find out," Tap said.

18

"He is not in," the porter said immediately.

"Come on, Tap. Can't you see we're not wanted around here?"

"We'll go up to Lawson's room."

"Who's he?"

"He's a war correspondent."

They walked to the lift and the porter called something after them. He was telling them they couldn't go up, but the lift door closed.

Lawson was not in, so Tap went to get the maid to open the door. She came, was stout and pretty and wore a wedding ring, smiled when she opened the door and said "*Inglisi*," then, "*Monsieur Lawson est parti.*"

"Yes," Tap said. "But we want a bath. A bath." Tap pointed to the bathroom.

"Oh . . . *pour tout?*" the maid said.

"*Oui.* Sure. All of us."

She said something else in French.

"What did she say?" Tap was pulling off his shoes.

"She's gone to get some towels," tall Richardson said.

"Fine." Tap had already turned on the water and was taking off his coat. "I'm going to the Argentina to-night. I'm going in here first," he said.

Quayle sat down on the low bed and looked around the room. On the mirror at one end was drawn a face in blue and green and black crayon. It had been drawn with soft pencil that will surface on glass. It was put on thickly to give depth, but the streaks where the mirror showed through gave the face more depth and shape, because the light reflected from it. There were large War Office maps of Greece, and a picture map of Albania over a desk. There was a small typewriter on the desk and a number of folders. In the bookcase there were books in German, French and English. Quayle pulled out a book called *Exiles in the Aegean.*

The maid came in with an armful of towels, gave them to Tap with some soap, and went out again.

"Who is this war correspondent?" Quayle asked Tap.

"He's an American," young Gorell said. "They're attached to the army."

"What's he like?"

"Oh—he's like you. He's all right, though. He talks like you."

Tap was already in the bath. Young Gorell and Vain were pulling out magazines from a cupboard. Richardson, the tall boy with fluffy hair and a steady manner, was trying to operate a small radio. As Tap was getting out of the bath, a tall blond figure in khaki uniform stepped into the room. He looked around for a moment, then Tap said, "Hullo, Lawson. We were borrowing your bath."

"That's all right," Lawson said.

"This is John Quayle. He's our Flight Loot," Tap said.

"How're you?" Lawson said. He saw the slight, fairly square young man who stood carefully and was careful in exactly the way he stood. He saw quickly the rather dull face collectively, but individually split into features, the keen nose, the regular shapeliness of his features. He could hardly see Quayle's eyes because they were so far back in his head under the two ridges above his nose. His top lip was thin and without expression, but the bottom was full and shaded, the curve leading to his chin. Finally, he noticed the brown, silky hair that was soft but somehow regular and not very wild. He liked it all immediately, and liked the slow smile that spread around Quayle's lips when he shook hands. Tap introduced the others and Quayle sat down on the low chair.

"Are you an American?" Quayle asked Lawson.

"Sure. Say, you must have known Anstee."

Quayle thought quickly, not deliberately. It was easy to remember Anstee. He was an American that had been in Eighty Squadron and was wild and too reckless to fly Gladiators and had finished up with a score of twelve 42's and crashing head on into a Savoia and never getting out.

"Yes. Did you know him?" Quayle said.

"I went to school with him."

"Are you from the Middle West, too?"

"Yes."

"Anstee used to get mad when he heard them talking about its being isolationist."

"So do I. It's got a slab of isolationists. But what the hell."

"Where are you going to-night, Lawson?" Tap asked him as he put his coat on.

"Nowhere. I'll probably have to do battle with censors."

"Why don't you come with us? We're all going to Maxim's."

"I might drop around later," Lawson said.

"What about you, John?"

"I might drop around later, too. You fellers go on."

Lawson sat down at the small desk and rolled some paper into a typewriter and started to type. Richardson had gotten out of the bath and young Gorell went in there. Quayle read the book while the others had their bath and Lawson typed. When Vain, the young Australian, had finished bathing, Tap and the others, who had been sitting around reading magazines, got up.

"Thanks for the use of your bath, Will," Tap said to Lawson.

"That's all right. Any time."

They all thanked him and went out.

"See you later, John," they said to Quayle.

Quayle nodded and stood up. He asked Lawson if it was all right if he took a bath. Lawson went on typing and laughed and said, "Go ahead." So Quayle took a bath and wiped himself on the only dry towel left and piled the wet ones into a basket and pulled on his clothes. Lawson had finished typing when he came out.

"Were you up to-day?" Lawson asked Quayle.

"Yes."

"Did you get any?"

Quayle hesitated.

"It's all right," Lawson said. "We'd never get it past the censors, anyway."

"We have to be careful," Quayle said. "We got a couple of Savoias."

Quayle liked this blond American as quickly as Lawson had liked him.

"Do you have much trouble with the censors?" he asked Lawson. "They're the curse of this war."

Quayle was pulling his flying boots on.

"How do you get on with the Greeks?" Lawson asked him.

"All right. Pretty good. We don't have much to do with them."

"They're funny people," Lawson said. He was folding the paper in his hand and pulling out the carbon paper between the slips. "They're about the toughest people I ever ran into. They're fighting a war with bare hands. But God, they've got no idea of system."

Quayle smiled.

"They'll listen to Metaxas now. They have an idea that he's systematic. They love system when they can get it. Yet they hate Metaxas' guts, really."

"What about the British?" Quayle asked him.

"That's different." Then Lawson saw that Quayle was pin-pricking him and he had not suspected it of Quayle and he laughed.

"Will you walk down with me?" he said to Quayle.

"Sure. Where are you going?"

"The Post Office."

"What do you do, just put the cable in?"

"That's all. Then the censors get at it."

Quayle laughed.

"I get pretty good treatment," Lawson said. "I take them all out to lunch sometimes."

"You certainly have the Greeks taped."

"Don't get me wrong. I like the Greeks. There's a wonderful guy you ought to meet. He's pretty typical of the average Greek. He's a newspaperman. He was exiled by Metaxas for running a liberal paper in Salonika."

They had walked into the streets and were bumping their way along in the black-out.

"Do you know any Greeks at all?" Lawson asked him.

"No."

"Would you like to meet this guy? He's married, got a son and daughter. I was thinking of going out there later. Do you want to come?"

Quayle was silent for a moment.

"Thanks, I will," he said.

"It's an interesting family. The old man thinks that Metaxas is good for the present situation, because he's a good general. But the boy says he isn't deceived. He says that Metaxas didn't want to fight when the Italians started this invasion. He says they were all going to sell out. It was just those goddam Greek soldiers up there who had rifles, so they fought, and the Metaxas crowd just had to fight whether they wanted to or not."

"Do you think that's right?" Quayle asked him.

"Sure. So does the daughter. She's that way, too."

They walked along in silence and they felt the friendliness towards each other without expressing it or needing to.

Chapter 3

They were in a ramshackle taxi heading out of town towards Cephisia. They passed along the great road with the street-car track in the center which was heavy with traffic. The dull khaki of crumpled Greek uniforms on soldiers was spread around every street-car. They were coming in from the Cephisia barracks, which spread along the great roadway; a white wall perimetered it and white eucalyptus hung over the low buildings within the yard. Darkness was shadowing the fields that flanked the road as they went farther out, until there was nothing to see either side but quick passing deep light and moving shadows of trees, fields, then houses, then fields and trees again. They passed through a black quiet village with empty streets, and pulled up along a dirt road to a two-story white stone house.

Lawson paid the taxi driver and they went up the stone path. The door was opened by a dark girl in a white dress with a peasant blouse.

"It is Will," she said in English.

"Hullo," Lawson said.

The girl was almost as tall as Quayle when he stepped inside. His hair looked fair beside hers.

"This is John Quayle. He's a Flight Lieutenant. This is Helen Stangou."

They shook hands. Helen Stangou took Quayle's cap and hung it up, led them both into a low-ceilinged room. She introduced a thin boy with glasses as "Astaries, my brother."

A woman with white hair came in and said "Hullo, Will," to

24

Lawson, smiled at Quayle, said, "You are very welcome here," when Lawson introduced Quayle to Mrs. Stangou.

"I cannot speak English very well. You must forgive me," she said.

"I'm sorry, but I do not speak Greek," Quayle said to be polite.

Then Stangou himself came in — thin, like his son, with grey flecks in dark hair, and brown eyes above red, transparent cheeks over a dark complexion — smiling eyes and mouth as he spoke. He shook Quayle's hand vigorously and was very happy with Will Lawson. He was a man with happiness as part of him, but strain that belied its easiness. But he was very warm, and Quayle felt warmly towards him. His conversation was quick, and one moment he was talking about his appetite and the next about the two bombers he had heard were brought down to-day.

"I saw one fall," Mrs. Stangou said.

"Yes," Helen said to John. "We were out at Glyphada. We saw a small plane come down on it."

"That was probably Quayle here," Lawson said.

"It was probably young Gorell — it was his first plane down."

"Were you up there?" Helen said.

"How many Italians have you shot down?" Stangou said.

"About twelve," Quayle said with correct casualness.

"And the Italians aren't any good?" Stangou asked.

"They're good when they want to be."

"Why do you shoot so many down then?"

"They don't get enthusiastic about it. They're all right in a good fight."

"The Greeks say the Italian planes are no good," Stangou said.

"They're all right. They're just not enthusiastic. They're all right in a good scrap. They can fight all right."

John was bored with what was going on. He could not keep watching the girl because every time he looked at her she smiled or caught his eye. Her black hair fitted in with her round face and Turkish eyes. She wore a cut bang that rounded her face even more and softened her face when she smiled.

They deliberately discussed non-political subjects while they ate. They were not sure of Quayle. They did not know how far to trust a person in uniform, and you were never sure of the British. The British had this strange streak of cold patriotism that was really not cold but overdone. You could never be sure of them. So they kept off talking Metaxas and politics, though that was why Lawson had brought him out here. He didn't mind, because of the girl. She was very important to Lawson too; Quayle had noticed that earlier. Her father and brother knew what was going on. The father was amused and Astaries was cynical about it. He said nothing all the time the empty conversations between Quayle and Helen went on. But he started an argument with his father in Greek which ended when Mrs. Stangou said something.

"You must forgive them. They argue all the time about the war," she said.

"It is good they argue," Quayle said.

"Not always. They disagree too much, and they are still father and son."

"What do you disagree about?" Quayle asked. He was fed up with the complicated pattern of avoiding political discussion.

"It is impolite to discuss it before you," Astaries said.

Quayle said that was political cowardice, and they were more scared of the effect than the injury.

"You cannot say that in this country," the girl said. She was angry.

"I apologize," John said.

"We cannot take chances and don't intend to," Astaries said. He didn't look thin now, but vigorous, because he was standing up for the first time and walking around.

"I agree," John said. He wanted them to see he was not antagonistic.

It stopped there because they did not acknowledge what Quayle said. The girl got up and went out. Quayle watched her slow slight swagger and the movement of her shoulders and the proportions of her figure. There was silence, then Lawson asked Stangou what the Greek Communiqué to-night would be.

"They are getting near Koritza — we have captured a mountain which will give us the town in a day, or, just as they said yesterday . . ."

Quayle looked up then and saw the girl coming down a stairway to the hall; she had a scarf around her head, or it was a peasant shawl, he did not know.

"I am going down to ring up," she said in English to her mother. John got up immediately and walked to her.

"I will walk down with you," he said and got his cap.

"It doesn't matter. It is not far," she said. She was still angry and she was not scared of him.

"I will go" — ignoring the excuse.

She shrugged her shoulders and he could see the others looking at them as they went out.

"Do not put your cap on," she said to John as he pulled it on his head.

"Why not?"

"We have been told not to be with British soldiers. Undo your coat too."

He put his cap under his arm and undid his coat.

"I know your father has been in exile," he said to her.

"Yes," she said.

"I'm just telling you that I know why you have no discussions."

"You are *Inglisi*. We have to be careful. We do not know who you will tell things to."

"It's all right," he said.

"We are always watched. Astaries is always being arrested. They leave my father alone now. They don't put him in jail any more because he signed that he was for Metaxas, but Astaries won't."

"You shouldn't talk at all," Quayle said.

"If we do not, we are cowards, as you said. But they shoot, now there is a war. We are prudent."

They had walked down the stone path and through the gate. It was very dark now and no moon was above yet. He took her arm as they walked, ostensibly because the path was earth and without

27

surface. She did not draw away but accepted it and he could feel the warmth and the firmness of her arm and her waist. They turned into a narrow tree-lined path with wind down its sides and no ceiling of sky because of the trees. There was a small kiosk at the end of it which marked a bus stop. The boy who sat in it gave Helen a hand phone. She rang the number, spoke in Greek, then hung up.

"I was telling the post I will go there to-morrow," she said politely as they walked.

"You are a nurse?"

"No, I help in a First Aid post."

"What did you do before the war?" he asked her.

"I was at the University. I was a student."

"Have they ever touched you?" he asked. He tried to put even pressure on her arm.

"They cut off my hair because I was with Astaries once when he was caught."

He involuntarily looked at her hair in the dark and said, "When?"

"It was long ago. But I do not do anything like that any more because of my mother. With a family it is two struggles. My mother turned her hair that colour when my father was away. He signed for Metaxas because she was ill. I do not do anything any more because of this."

So they walked along quietly after that and deliberately slowly. It was difficult to do anything while he carried his cap because it was in the way and he felt awkward. It was bad trying to be gracious. He had not any approach to this girl. He knew she did not object to the firm arm pressure, but he knew she would resist if he did anything more. He did not want to take the chance.

"Where do you work?" he asked her. "In Athens?"

"Yes."

"I will come and see you," he said. It was awkward conversation.

"I work in a small place behind the University. It has a Red Cross, so you cannot miss it. I will not be there long." She paused.

John didn't say anything. She went on. "I am going to Janina, which is near the front. But you will be fine for the girls there at the post. You must come. They talk about the blond *Inglisi*. But you are not blond like Lawson, who makes the girls anxious about him."

"I will not make them anxious. When do you go?"

"Next week. I will be glad. It's bad to be here when there is a war. It is not the place to be because we do not feel anything, we do not know it."

"Don't be anxious to get in a war," John said. "It is dirty, the dirtiest thing there is."

"I know. It is not colour like rainbow to me. It is essential."

They turned in the wide gate and up the stone path into the house.

"I will come to see you to-morrow. Is it all right?" he said to her as they waited at the door.

"Come at lunch hour. We do not work so hard then and we could eat something."

Mrs. Stangou opened the door and they went in.

Chapter 4

He did not see Helen Stangou the next day. He never knew when he could do anything for sure the next day, unless it rained. He was standing-by all day at Faleron in case there was a raid. Hickey was not back from Larissa and Gorell's plane was not fixed, a cross-section support in one wing had been torn by a Savoia bullet. So Tap and Richardson, with Vain and Quayle, were standing-by from early morning until late at night.

That same night they were ordered to Headquarters. The Wing Commander was waiting for them in the large white building that had been a school. Hersey was there and they were surprised to see him. Hersey said he had come back by road from Larissa to look at the route for supplies. He said it was very bad country for flying. There were the worst mountains he had ever seen between Larissa and Albania. The roads were so bad, too, that it was going to be hard to get supplies up by anything but Bombay transports flying them up.

Then the Wing Commander, who was short and vigorous in his speech, said: "I thought you would all like to hear you're going up to Larissa. Gloomy Hersey has just come back. He and Hickey seem to think the drome there is all right. I looked at it myself yesterday. It's a bit wet but you'll be all right. There's only one thing — you'll have to rely on Greek ground staff for a couple of days. It's going to be impossible to get large supplies over those mountain passes by road. We'll fly the skeleton ground crews up on the Bombay. We've got one for the squadron now."

Nobody asked any questions when the Wing Commander paused because there was more to come.

"The Greeks are getting badly knocked about at the front," he said. "The Italians have up to thirty bomber and twenty-five fighter squadrons covering three sectors, so they get hot water. They're pushing the Italians back near Koritza, but along the coast it's more difficult. We think the Italians are going to concentrate on road and railways leading to Larissa and along the coast. That's why you're going to Larissa. Later you will go up farther, I think. But you will go up to Larissa to-morrow and wait for the Italians to show up. You'll be patrolling the road and coast areas, but they're so far away you won't be over target areas long. We want the operation kept secret, so just move out quietly to-morrow. We want to surprise them one day without escort. We want bombers down. They're worrying the Greeks to desperation because they've lost most of their fighters. But we want this done quietly, and concentrate on bombers, but don't risk your neck getting bombers if there are fighters around. You'll always be outnumbered about ten to one with fighters because the Italians are just not taking any chances. Every Italian flight that comes over has a swarm of C.R. 42's along with it. And they've got some G. 50's we think, but they haven't been checked yet. Hickey will tell you everything when you get to Larissa to-morrow. You can leave before dawn. It will be better and quieter — and do not tell anyone anything about it, even other squadron members. This may be win or lose for the Greeks."

"This is going to be fine," Tap said as they walked down the stairway.

"Yes." Hersey was the oldest so he was allowed to say that. "So we just get picked off by the 42's as we pick off the bombers," he said. No one took much notice, because he was a grouch.

They went out and walked towards the King George Hotel. Quayle wanted to find Lawson so that he could talk with Helen Stangou. There was some sort of party going on at the King George, and there was a new porter. Lawson was not in and the porter did not know where he was. Tap and the others had disappeared below to the bar. Because they were leaving so early, Quayle knew he would have to get them out before they got going. He went down too.

There were a half-dozen bomber squadroners there. They were talking with Tap and the Australian, Vain. Richardson was at one end of the bar drinking beer and eating peanuts. Quayle pulled Tap by the coattails and said: —

"We'll be late. Come on before you get started here."

"Wait a minute, John," he said. "You know Davies of Two-Eleven?"

"Sure. Hullo, Davies."

"Hullo, Quayle."

"He's telling us about swarms of C.R. 42's that get at Blenheims over Valona."

"Have a drink, Quayle." Davies turned to the bartender.

"No, thanks," Quayle said.

"Are you working to-morrow?"

"No. I'm just not drinking."

"Well, go on, Davies. What about these 42's?" Tap said.

"They just come down on you. We come low over the target. They've always got height. We usually get one or two, but we lost Phil Calhoun yesterday. They kept coming after him when he got behind the formation. When are you fellers coming up to do some escorting? What are you doing down here anyway?"

"We don't know ourselves. You can survive until we get up there," Quayle told him.

"I hope you find it as hot as we do," he said, and went back to his drinking.

Quayle got Tap, Vain and Richardson out and they went back to the Athinai Hotel, to their quarters. Hersey, who had remained with the Wing Commander, came in as they were going to bed in the long suite that was their dormitory.

"If you leave your bed-rolls here in the morning, I'll take them up with me in the Bombay."

"What sort of quarters have we got?" Richardson asked him.

"Lousy. Cement huts. Tents at the airdrome to stand-by."

"Any gals in Larissa?" Tap was sitting on his bed turning the pages of a Penguin book about insects.

"Sure — but they've got a wall around them."

"A detail — a detail," Tap said.

He was still reading about insects when Quayle went to sleep.

Chapter 5

Rutger, one of the ground crew who drove the station wagon, woke Quayle next morning.

"It's five-thirty, Mr. Quayle," he said, and Quayle was half-conscious of having to do something and then realized what it was.

"What sort of day is it?"

"It's raining cats and dogs."

"Did you bring the weather report from the operations room?"

"Yes." He gave Quayle a slip of paper. It said cloud on Athens ten tenths, at five thousand feet, visibility nil, wind 40 m.p.h., storm center moving east across the Pindus from Missolonghi. It might pass over by midday.

The others were getting up. They had noticed it was raining.

"Are we still going?" Vin asked. He was rubbing his dark jaw. His black eyes were blacker with sleep.

"We'll go out to the drome and stand-by," Quayle said. "It may lift by midday. I want to pick up the maps anyway. Come on."

They had breakfast and went in the station wagon under the quiet dawn to Faleron. The rain was so heavy it was flat. The cloud had depth and none of them thought it would clear up. They went into the operations room, dumped their flying kit and sat down to wait for the weather to lift. Tap lay on the camp bed in his Irvin suit because it was still cold. He was soon asleep.

They waited all morning for the clouds to lift or the report to change. The storm center kept widening and it spread north along the Pindus towards Larissa. At midday Quayle said he was going into Headquarters to see the Wing Commander. It was too dangerous to phone him. The others wanted to go with him, but Quayle wanted to see Helen Stangou, so he told them it wouldn't be wise to leave the airdrome because they still might have to leave in a hurry.

When he talked with the Wing Commander, he said to call it off for a day but to make it an hour earlier the next morning so there would be more chance of good weather. They had to get there for certain to-morrow.

So Quayle went out to see Helen Stangou.

She was sitting at a table rolling bandages with a small wooden machine. She stood up when he came in and smiled. She was dressed in a pale yellow overall and her long hair was serrated against it on her shoulders. She was firm-cheeked when she smiled and her forehead was tight. Her eyes were low and dark, their shape made clear by her face's proportion.

She said, "It is you. Come in. You are very wet."

Quayle said, "The water will drip." Then, "I couldn't get here yesterday. I'm sorry."

She said, "Yes. I knew."

He stood there with water from his damp great-coat dropping around him.

She said, "I cannot go out now."

He interrupted her. "I know, but I'd like to see you to-night."

"It is difficult." She spoke very softly so the other girls could not hear her.

"It may not be possible to see you for a while. I'd like to see you to-night."

"I will be here late. Can you take me home?" she said.

"Yes, I think so. What time?"

"Ten o'clock. Will you wait over near the University?"

"All right," he said. He shook her hand with firmness. She smiled and he went out.

The others were impatient when Quayle got back to Faleron, but glad when he told them that they did not have to leave that day. There was nothing to do so they went into Athens to see a movie.

Life always felt good in a cinema. The film was a portrayal of Robin Hood by Mr. Errol Flynn. There were fine colours and wonderful ideas of Sherwood Forest that made Quayle want to believe it was Sherwood, though he knew Sherwood was not like that. There was small time for nostalgia when the late Mr. Herbert Mundin, with other actors, dropped out of trees. It was very good for Quayle and the others because there was no rain and they were not unclean and damp because they had forgotten it. There was no finer feeling than real excitement without nervousness and some physical connection to it. It was excitement without responsibility and threat. It was good for them now, but would not be if what they were doing every day were constructive instead of destructive.

After Mr. Flynn had taken Miss de Havilland's hand, there came news-reels about Greek soldiers at the front. They could not understand the Greek commentary but saw the crumpled cold Greeks marching in no formation and tiredly. They got up and left.

Quayle went at ten o'clock to the University steps and waited for Helen. It had stopped raining and the cloud was high and light. He knew it would be fine to-morrow. He did not want to think about it because he did not want to leave the city. Larissa would be like the desert, but with wet and mud instead of sweat and dust. It would be colder, which was worse than heat. And Athens was light with plenty of people and new buildings. It was not a place to leave. He knew Larissa would be a village with old buildings and quiet, good people who were wonderful to you, as all people are; but it was not smooth and slick, which was what you wanted to fill in time with.

"It is you." Helen touched his arm as he watched a car slipping on the road.

"Hullo," he said.

"We will walk down here to a bus stop." Helen took his arm.

He said, "No, we'll get a taxi."

"Soldiers cannot afford taxis," she said with some gaiety.

"I am a Flight Lieutenant and I'm not married. I can afford it all right."

"How big is a Flight Lieutenant?" she asked him.

"The same as a Captain in the army."

"You have enough money?"

"Yes."

"As you wish then. But be careful how you talk in the taxi."

They walked along easily in the wet darkness and felt the cold reflection of water from the leaves of the trees and the concrete road. They found a ramshackle taxi. Helen told the driver in Greek where to go and he hit his meter with a small ball-peen hammer and started. They went through the dim white and black wet streets to the Cephisia road, and Quayle could see Mount Pentelikon dark and above sight stretching before them, as if they were driving right into it.

He put his arm around Helen's shoulders and grasped her wrist with the other hand.

"Not here, please," she said softly. "Not here."

Quayle took his arm away and slumped down in the seat. She leaned over and gently took his cap off and he could feel friendliness in what she did and not resistance. But it was bad to be rebuffed.

"Am I poaching on Lawson's territory?" John asked her quietly.

"Do not talk. And that is silly. I am not earth. If I was I would not belong to Lawson." She put his cap on the seat beside her and took a firm grasp of his arm, but kept away and sat silently while the bulk of the old taxi fell over the surfaced road in jolts. She stopped the taxi long before they were at her home and they got out. Quayle paid the driver when she motioned him to do so. When he had gone she said: "We can get you another to go home. We will walk. It is not safe for taxi drivers to know what you do."

As they walked along the muddy earth path, Quayle put his arm in hers. She took his hand and both were warm.

"Why will you not have a possibility to see me again?" she asked him.

"Does it matter?"

37

"Yes," she said. "But if you can't tell me it does not matter. It is better you do not tell me in that case."

"I just want to make sure I'll know where you are," John said to her.

"If you write to me at the Red Cross. Someone will write in Greek for you."

"But you are going away. When are you going anyway?"

"I think next week," she said.

"And what about this new place — can I get you there?"

"At Janina? Yes. Do not forget Janina. Janina."

"I won't forget," he said.

John stopped her by pulling her arm. Then he pulled her firmly around to him and kissed her full on the mouth. She did not hold back. Her mouth was closed tight and was very warm. He couldn't feel himself any more. He could only feel heat in his head and even warmth spread from her all over him.

When he took himself away they turned around and walked on slowly. He did not say anything. He did not say anything because he knew it would be clumsy. And he felt again that he didn't want to be clumsy with this girl.

"It is foolish," she said as they walked.

"Nothing is foolish," he said.

"You go away. I will go away. And we do this now," she said.

"Nothing is foolish. We will see each other." He didn't want to talk.

"I am not worried like that. I have concern because we start something that cannot go further."

"Why not?" Quayle tried to stop again but she walked on.

"Because it is too difficult," she said. "And because you will go away."

"I'll be back," he said.

"No! I mean you leave Greece." She was not hysterical and was behaving very calmly. He wanted her to be weaker in her reactions.

Quayle stopped her again and this time he could feel her lips beating like a tight blood pulse. He could feel her arm with flesh warmth around his shoulder and he was excited and kissed her harder, then very softly. She drew away.

"It is bad if we cannot do this for a long time yet." She was still speaking calmly.

"You will forget?" he said.

"Perhaps. But I know it is bad for a long time to pass."

"It may not be. Please — it may not be."

"I don't know," she said. "I don't know."

They were at the entrance to her home. Rain had started sifting in a mist downwards and he kissed her again. He put his hand on her head. Her hair was fine and wet. He could feel how thick it was and long to her shoulders, and the quiet fullness of the fringe over her forehead.

"You will not forget?" she said fiercely and quietly.

"No." He was mad. He felt it. He felt mad.

"No," she said and pulled his head roughly.

"I will let you know where I am. Don't go away," she said.

"No," he said, but he knew he would.

"Do not come farther," she said, as they came to the gate.

"Just as you say."

He kissed her once and she touched the side of his head with great tenderness and held her mouth slightly, softly, open. Then he swung around, and walked away wondering how he would get home — because she had forgotten to get another taxi for him.

Chapter 6

It was fine the next day. The flight took off before dawn and climbed high to get over the Parnes. It was bumpy from the start and Quayle kept climbing to get above the weather, but at twelve thousand it was still rough with a twenty-mile-per-hour headwind, and it was hard on gasoline. It was very monotonous, and it was hard to keep awake. The flight was sitting back with throttle settings and a set course. Quayle did not want the flight to get ragged, so he was always looking behind to see that Tap wasn't straggling and Vain and Richardson were keeping up. You never actually lost the habit of continuously looking behind to see if there was an Italian on your tail, even as now when you knew that the chances were a thousand to one against Italian fighters being in this area.

Below there were great colours as mountains rose and valleys fell and kept falling until they had the mountains tied up from below. There was low cloud hiding the peaks and beneath them the shadow of green timber that rolled heavily over the mountains and made more great colours. It was very fine from here at twelve thousand. But some day, Quayle was thinking, he would like to come back and see it from below. Or see any of the country from below. And get back his normal sense of distance and time between places. But this particularly would be country to be over on foot. After the war it would be swell — after the war . . . He tried to veer off any thinking about after the war. He was looking at the instrument panel to confuse the thought about after the war but it was there. After the war . . .

What would Gorell or Vain or Tap or Richardson or Stewart —

Constance, South, any of them — do after the war? What the hell were they doing before the war? He didn't know. He didn't know because he didn't ask them, because he had a rough idea that would give them liberty to ask him questions, and he did not want that. Why? What if they did ask? What would he say? He was at London University, being an engineering student; that was all right, but what the hell, what had that to do with any one of them? Take Tap. Quayle knew what he had been doing before the war. He had been sitting around in London spending his money because he had plenty of it. He had seen Tap's name in the papers, but was surprised the first time Tap had come to the squadron, and he had taught Tap a few extra Gladiator manœuvres — and Gorell.

Gorell would be very young when the war started, maybe eighteen. He had been at King William's College after Quayle had left. He must have been there the same time as young Gorell, but he couldn't remember the simple face, the clean teeth, the wavy hair. He will be all right if he survives this, Quayle was thinking. He will grow into a large simple fellow, thoroughly honest and without any complicated thought. Something like Vain, only Vain was Australian and more real. Vain was conscious of what went on around him and he reacted quickly to circumstances. He was like his dark, angular face, very quick, and his broad accent seemed like Cockney at first. But Vain had been indignant when Tap had said that once. He's young too, but he seems to have had a practical background; he's always talking about the sheep station he was brought up on; what the hell got him into flying? Australia must be a place like that, it would be a place to see after the war.

And Richardson, with his fluffy hair, rather cynical and always arguing with Tap because he took things seriously and Tap didn't . . . He was steady-headed and was always good in a fight because he was reliable. What the hell was he before the war? He never spoke about it either, and Quayle suddenly liked him for not talking about it. This was a separate life and had nothing to do with the life before the war.

Also Brewer — he never spoke about what he did either. Brewer,

41

tall, gangling, easy-going Brewer . . . He should take more notice of Brewer, Quayle was thinking. I should take more notice of them all. I always think that at this stage, when I'm up here. But it all falls through when I get down there. Restraint is good in this business. It is essential. But you ought to notice them more, Quayle. South, for instance — Does anyone ever notice South? That medium-faced boy . . . He's always there, but he never says a thing. He has no personality, or not enough to get above his quietness. If he had something of Constance's sense of humour . . . That had been fine, the day Constance had climbed out of the Gladiator and he had been laughing so much he couldn't tell them about it and he said that he had been leaning forward to see a 42 and his hand had slipped and his knee knocked the stick and he had rolled and there he was upside down without knowing where the hell he was and he had accidentally pushed the gun button as he pulled the stick over and nearly shot Tap's tail off, and everybody laughed highly about it except South.

Old Hickey had been like Richardson in the old days too, but he had grown quieter as the squadron got bigger and the new ones came in. Hersey and Tap and Hickey and Quayle himself were the foundation members of the squadron. All the others seemed comparative strangers. Hersey was the oldest member in the squadron. He was appropriately cynical, but Quayle remembered the time Hersey had got excited in a bombing raid at Fuka and nearly pulled Quayle's arm off to get him on top of the control tower to watch the bombing.

The two others were Finn and Stewart. Finn was very blond, like Lawson. He is like Lawson to look at, Quayle thought. He's always with Stewart. Stewart is dark and medium and they fit together. They usually go off on their own. They are both very young.

"John," he suddenly heard, "I'm getting sick back here. Can't we get up a bit?"

It was Tap. Quayle realized how bumpy it was and saw the high clouds ahead. The flight was at thirteen thousand feet.

"How about going up?" Tap said again.

"Up to fifteen thousand then," Quayle shouted. "But come in, Tap." Quayle was checking the time they had been out for their position. They were over the last range and could start coming down in half an hour.

"We'll be going down in half an hour, Tap. So we might as well stay around here," Quayle said into his mouthpiece.

There was solid cloud beneath now, too solid to break into. He was trying to contact Larissa.

Quayle kept the flight up. They cruised around over the clouds for half an hour but there was no break. He told the flight to keep in close and not lose sight of him. Quayle cut the mixture and nosed down easily into the cloud. It was thick and white and as the flight came down in wide sweeps like a mountain road, the cloud didn't show any break. The flight was close behind and kept there until they were at six thousand. It got too thick in one place. A down draft hit Quayle and he lost five hundred feet. He could see two Gladiators still behind him, but the other two were missing. Vain and Richardson were not around. At two thousand the cloud broke up and Quayle was under it.

He found the airdrome easily then, and the flight landed in formation over the wet heavy mud.

Hickey had found an old house in Larissa township that was empty. Quayle, Vain, Tap and Richardson and young Gorell all took fibre suitcases and kitbags, which they carried in the Gladiators. Hickey had a large Packard car that he had got from the Greek General Staff at the Larissa garrison. They went the two miles into town. The house was bare and wet. It was depressing because it was a house and it was so wet. It was all right its being wet outside, but to have it damp and cold inside a house like this one was very depressing.

They saw that this was a peasant town. It was mostly old white stone buildings spread into square blocks over cobbled streets. There were new buildings along the highway that passed through the town There was a new hotel and a restaurant on the square, but it was locked from the inside and they could not get in. Small, dark, heavily clad Greek peasants and crumpled Greek soldiers and small traders smiled quietly and happily at them as they walked along the street, and some patted their arms. They were peasants, and young Gorell said, "I always used to think the Greeks were not like this."

Richardson, Vain, Gorell, Tap and Quayle went into a restaurant that was dismal from the outside and had thick painted wooden shutters. It was dully lit by bare electric globes, and ancient marble-topped tables were uneven across the dirty wooden floor. They sat down at a table and a wide-headed waiter came up. He was dressed like anybody else, so they didn't know for a while. Then the waiter disappeared, after nodding and smiling to them, and came back with five small glasses with white water-like liquid in them. He put them before Quayle and the others, nodded his head quickly and said something in Greek. Quayle picked up the glass and smelled it. It had a liquorice odour.

"*Oúzo — Oúzo,*" the Greek said.

"All right," Vain said. "We'll drink." He lifted his glass.

They all lifted their glasses, turned to the whole room and then to the waiter, and said, "Your health" and drank it.

"Christ," Tap said, "oh, Christ." It was very strong.

The drink tasted of aniseed. The Greek waiter brought a bottle and filled the glasses. Then he brought small cups of Turkish coffee. They drank again. It spread all over you inside. A priest came in the door and walked to Quayle and the others. He had long hair, long beard and black robes with a square-topped cassock.

"*Messieurs,*" he said.

"*Monseigneur,*" Quayle said.

The priest said no more but smiled and called for another bottle of the drink. He got a glass for himself and kept filling their glasses as they drank. Other Greeks in the room, heavy-clothed workers and the peasants with their baggy pants and turned-up shoes, came over; and the flight widened the circle and kept drinking, and the Greeks patted them on the back and spoke happily among them-selves, during which Quayle heard "*Inglisi*" mentioned a lot. Quayle could feel himself getting very warm and happy. Vain was having a wonderful time with the priest, drinking glass for glass with him, patting him on the back. There was a lot of animated talk among the peasants and the workers. One man was gestured out of the place. They kept drinking the white drink out of the small glasses. Some of the peasants were drinking it out of larger glasses and mixing water with it, which made it cloudy. All the time the Greeks were talking excitedly and the flight would pass remarks among themselves in English. It would break up when they turned on the Greeks and they beamed at the flight and the flight would beam at the Greeks in great friendly silence. It was great silence and they didn't need explaining to each other.

Soon the Greek who had been gestured out of the place came in and Quayle had another with him. He was dressed in a European suit with brown shoes and a grey hat.

"You English?" the new Greek said.

"Yes."

"You fly. You fight. Ha! Welcome here. You fight?"

"Yes."

He turned to the others and spoke in Greek, then said to the flight: "You are wonderful, boys. We saw you to-day come in. Oh my — "

The others were talking to him and he listened. "They want me to say you are welcome to here. At Larissa, they welcome you and drink your health. They all do. Yes."

The others were nodding and smiling and lifting their glasses. Vain got up and bowed to them and raised his glass. "*Ellás*," he said, and hearing that one first Greek word from any one of them, which meant "Greece" and which Vain had learned at the Argentina, made them stand and stamp around him — and they all drank.

"I am Georgius. I'm Aussie — see." The Greek had taken a passport out of his pocket which had British Passport marked on top and Commonwealth of Australia under the Australian coat-of-arms. Everybody turned to Vain. He was an Australian. This was terrific.

"Vain. He's your countryman. Australian, see." This was wonderful, a Greek countryman of Vain! They all roared because it was so good.

"Your health," Tap shouted and laughed and drank quickly.

45

Vain was very happy about it. And he and the Greek both started talking about Brisbane. Then Vain was starting to sing "Waltzing Matilda" for the Greek, who joined in.

"You bloody Tommies," Vain shouted. His dark chin was sticking out.

"Bloody Aussie yourself," Richardson said to him.

"Listen to this song," Vain shouted again. He was leaning back in his chair and started singing "Waltzing Matilda."

"Quieter!" Tap shouted.

But Vain went on singing and Georgius was leaning on him and singing too. He was happy because Vain was looking to him for this mock national support.

"To hell with you," Vain shouted. "Look," he said. "There's two of us. We'll take the whole lot of you on. Two of us, uh?" He turned to Georgius, who was smiling broadly.

Quayle was laughing at Vain because he was standing up now and was trying to look belligerent.

"When we get near the Italians," Vain was shouting, "they run like hell, don't they?" He looked around him.

"This is wonderful," Richardson said. He wasn't quiet-looking now.

"You will beat those bastard Italians," Georgius was saying.

"We've come here to lick hell out of them," Vain said.

There was quick talk in Greek again and Georgius said, "They want me to tell you that you will save Greece. We on land and you in the air. They say that we hate the Italian Fascisti more than you do because we got some of it inside. And that's why we fight so good. They say to tell you that you will shoot every Italian in the air and we will do it on the earth."

"Tell them that you are all the greatest living land fighters and that we are very proud to clean the air for them," Vain said. He was punching the priest with his fist as he said each word—and he tapped the priest harder and nodded his head as Georgius told them in Greek in twice as many words and gestures.

The priest raised his glass and said one word—"*Níki!*"

"Victory!" Georgius said.

This was wonderful. They laughed loudly and drank, because they had never drunk to victory before; and the Greeks took it so seriously that they laughed.

"Can we get something to eat here?" Vain asked Georgius. The priest was looking at Vain's Byronic features with obvious pleasure.

"No — but I show you a good place. I know a place."

"Ask them how much all this is," Vain said. He was delving into his pocket. Georgius asked the waiter in Greek, but the others all spoke loudly at once and Georgius said, "They say it is not for you to pay anything. You are their guests. We are so happy you are here — you are our guests."

"Oh no."

"They will be insulted," Georgius said. He rubbed his hands.

"Ask them if we may buy them all one drink, then. It is good that way."

Georgius asked them and they all laughed and smiled again and nodded. "Yes, they will be very happy."

The glasses were filled again and they raised their glasses to all the Greeks and the Greeks raised theirs with seriousness and drank in a gulp.

"They want you to drink again," Georgius said.

"Tell them we have not eaten," Quayle said.

Georgius told them. The Greeks nodded and the flight stood up.

"How much is it?" Vain asked.

"Oh, leave twenty drachmas. That is plenty," Georgius said. "I will show you where to eat." They stood up and the Greeks started shaking hands with them. They shook hands with all the Greeks and the Greeks clapped them on the back as they put their great-coats on.

John Quayle had trousers tucked inside his sheepskin-lined knee-boots and a peasant pointed to them and nodded. Quayle nodded back.

"They want you to come back to-morrow and drink with them," Georgius said.

"Tell them we will be glad to."

The flight went out with Georgius and the Greeks shouted *"Zíto i Inglisi!"* after them. They shouted *"Zíto i Ellás!"* back to the Greeks as they walked across the square. It was only then that Quayle realized how drunk he was. His co-ordination was slow, and his reaction uncertain.

They went to bed early because the drink, which Georgius told them was called *oúzo,* started to react an hour after they had taken it and they were more drunk than ever. Hickey was not very pleased. They were all going on full patrol to-morrow because the Italians had started their expected bombing attack on the coast towns and roads. The Greeks were getting hell and unless the squadron beat off the attacks the Greek Army would probably fall back instead of going forward.

They were all very serious and aware of what they were doing the next day because they were self-conscious about being laid out by the white liquid. They went out to the airdrome and Hickey got the maps out of the cement hut, one half of which was a Greek operations room. The maps of the area were too small at one to one million. They were all the squadron could get unless they had Greek-named maps. The area they were covering was directly west-south-west to the coast town of Arta, which was the port entry and west road route supplying the coastal front. This meant flying over the Pindus, the mountain range splitting Greece from north to south. They would patrol the road area between Arta and north to Janina and between Janina and Metsovo, which was atop the Pindus.

They took off in threes. Hickey, Hersey, Quayle and Tap were leading the flights. They climbed rapidly to about one thousand feet to get safety, then pulled their formation to a stagger running right.

They climbed over the low range and got height, following the Peneios River that flooded the plain between Karditza and Trikkala. They hoped to hit Arta about the same time that the large flights of Italian bombers had bombed it yesterday.

There was snow on the tips of the Pindus, and that made Quayle feel colder than he was. He wished he had Irvin suit pants, but

48

they were hard to get outside England. The non-operational officers seemed to have a monopoly of Irvin suits anyway. It was bumpy and he wondered if Tap was getting sick. Quayle had Gorell and Richardson tight behind him. Tap had Vain, the Australian, and young Finn.

When they could see the Pindus from the west side, it was getting time to climb. Hickey didn't like to use phones because any Italian planes near by might pick something up, and surprise was the best chance they had in a scrap. So they had to do some good formation flying to keep in close. But Hickey's flying was so perfect and so simple that he made it easier on the others.

The squadron got over Arta. There was a degenerated cloud sheet spread over the small town which only gave Quayle occasional glimpses of it. The cloud formations were too low to make any use of, but the sun was good and strong. The squadron turned north from Arta and followed the river which flanked the winding road, and this was the bombing target for the Italians. The flight was all looking around now waiting for something to happen. They had opened up its formation for attack and were holding height at fifteen thousand feet. Quayle didn't like the idea of scrapping over this area because the peaks were too high and too sudden and topped with cloud. Hickey rocked his machine and Quayle looked around and down. Below, heading toward the squadron, was the biggest flight John Quayle had ever seen. They were strewn out for ten miles. There must have been a hundred and fifty planes. Quayle couldn't see the bomber–fighter proportion yet, but he could see the separate groups that were probably fighters and he said "Christ" out loud because there seemed to be fifty fighters at least.

They were directly above the Italians very quickly and Quayle didn't know whether the Italians knew they were there or not. When the Italians had passed below the flight, Hickey dipped a wing and Quayle knew it was beginning. God, this was always happening. This was hell. Fifty of them. He had a stomach-ache now because there was so much tenseness. The flight had winged right over and were now directly behind and three thousand feet above the Italians. And it started.

Hickey put his nose down and the others followed. Quayle could see them disappearing from in front of him. When Richardson went down Quayle followed — and he could see nothing but Savoias and C.R. 42's and was thinking, this is going to be miraculous.

By the time his nose was down far enough, Quayle could see that Hickey was going on to the bombers, right through the fighters. The others were following. Tap and his flight had stayed up top to get the squadron out of trouble when they got into it. So there were nine of the squadron — nine against this flock.

And then Quayle passed the fighters.

He was going a billion miles an hour, and passed between two C.R. 42's and saw both the pilots turn their heads to look at him. He knew they would follow, and he kept going in a hell dive right abeam of a Savoia. He would get this bastard anyway. He was right on him. . . . Quayle couldn't feel his ears. His head was high and the Savoia flashed into the ring sights, and he pushed like hell on the gun button and yelled as he pulled out of the dive, and scraped the Savoia's back as he started up, and he was screaming. . . .

Quayle pulled upward and came over in an Immelmann turn, and saw tracers dive past him. There was a 42 coming up after him. Quayle did a snap-half-roll and came down contemptuously over him, across his beam, gave him one burst which he knew got him, then kept going in a wing-over, and came back on a Savoia bomber and got a burst into him, and climbed again — looked around — and the other 42 and a hundred others were around him on his tail and he saw the tracers around him.

Quayle pulled up with the throttle wide open and he knew they would think he was going to Immelmann out of it. But he pushed hard on the right rudder and pulled the stick back. He stalled into a falling leaf and two 42's shot right over him. Their guns were red and still firing. Quayle started after one and the Italian went into a hell dive. Quayle followed him down and his ears were roaring again and he kept winging the tail around to get his sights onto the 42, but the Italian was getting farther away because his dive was faster. So Quayle gave him one burst and pulled hard on the stick and felt the wrench on his stomach and blacked-out as he came up in a wide normal climb and stalled at the top.

And he came out of it again.

The sky was filled with 42's and he couldn't see a Gladiator any-where, but two 42's were coming beam-on at him and he could see another one diving on his tail. He pulled up quickly and there were inches between the two 42's as they passed under him. The other one was still on his tail. Quayle dived hard and pushed the throttle open, and kept pushing it because he was crazy for speed to get away from the Italian. He didn't look around. He pulled the stick back and roared screaming up in a loop, straightened out at the top of the loop, then dived. He pushed hard on the throttle again but it was wide open as he dived and he knew he would get the 42. It was Hickey-trained calculation and he came down right on the 42's tail. Quayle was less than fifty yards from the 42 when he straightened out and the 42 didn't know Quayle was there. Quayle had the Italian's head in the sights when he pushed fanatically on the button, felt the vibration, saw the tracers cut the Italian in half and his hand push through the glass panel.

There were still 42's all around. Quayle suddenly saw a Gladiator zooming with a 42 firing close at him. He winged over and didn't look behind but pushed down on the 42 and ripped a burst into his tail. The 42 lifted his nose too suddenly and stalled and fell. As Quayle came out level he could see a parachute burst way to the right and wondered if it was one of the squadron.

But it stopped there because he looked below and was almost wing-to-wing with a 42 a little above him but closer than if they were deliberately formation flying. Quayle could see the Italian's face and its puzzled look because he didn't have a mask on. The Italian could see Quayle's look. They were so close and both instinctively looked behind to see if anything was on either of their tails and kept level flight, each waiting for the other to move and looking at each other.

51

It seemed a long time but it was seconds. . . . Then Quayle pressured the right rudder and closed the throttle until his right wing stalled. He slipped in a falling leaf under the 42. He pushed the throttle wide open and pulled, straining up, and got the 42's belly in his sights and swore aloud as he pushed the gun button and knew for certain that he hit him. He nearly crashed into it as he banked and winged-over out of the way as the 42 burst into flames and fell.

Then Quayle seemed alone.

Way to the right the sky was filled with mixed-up planes and he could only see 42's until he saw one Gladiator hurling down on two 42's and saw the guns' red-and-yellow streak and the tracers cut into the 42. The 42 hung, then fell over, but Quayle saw a Gladiator on the left losing height and it seemed to be in trouble. Quayle looked around for the others, but he could only see three Gladiators other than the two he could see near him. He could see Tap's machine because it had a grey patch on the upper right wing.

And it was then he saw the Gladiator go down in flames right past him. He could see the figure still in the cockpit but couldn't see who it was, but knew he was done. He looked up, and saw the 42 that had got him winging off, and he was going after him when Tap winged in, because he was nearer, and climbed after the 42. But the 42 did an Immelmann and was nearly on Tap's tail when Tap did the tightest, fiercest loop Quayle had ever seen — came out over the 42, and clung to the side of him, pouring burst after burst into the 42, which was burning and falling off. Quayle knew Tap had run out of ammunition because he saw him loop again, come in behind, and put his hand up, a signal.

And they headed for home. The two of them were all Quayle knew about now. He felt very tired, and didn't look to see what had happened to the 42's which were way out heading north. He didn't care whether they had stopped the bombers or not. He didn't care about anything, but was very tired. The strain had given Quayle a tight belly-ache so that he wanted to relieve himself right then and there in the plane. But he just set a course for Larissa and climbed because they had come down from fifteen to three thousand

52

feet. He had forgotten about the mountains during the scrap —
and now they were there, and very frightening.

Quayle plugged in the phone, pulled the switch and said: —

"Tap, come in."

"Yes," Tap said. "Say, that was a shaky-do. Who was that going
down?"

"I don't know," Quayle said.

"It looked like Hickey," Tap said.

"No, Hickey wouldn't get like that."

"Did you see young Gorell? Did you see anybody else get it?"

"I saw someone losing height," said Quayle.

"Jesus — what a mess. You should have seen young Gorell. He
went mad."

They didn't say any more and dragged on back to Larissa. They
dropped carelessly when they were over the town. Tap came over
the drome in a perfect slow aileron roll and Quayle followed him
with a snap-roll though he was tired and sick and he knew Tap
was sick. Quayle pulled up at the other side, climbed out and saw
the big Bombay transport. Two figures came across the field
at the double, and Quayle saw it was Jock and Rutger, the fitter
and rigger. They had come up in the Bombay while they were scrapping.

"Who's back?" he asked them.

"Mr. Hersey, Mr. Finley, Mr. Richardson and Mr. Stewart," one
of them said.

"Christ, is that all?" Hersey, Tap, Richardson and Stewart and
himself . . .

"Yes, sir. Mr. Finley is lucky to get back at all. His plane's in
bits."

Quayle had pulled off his parachute and was undoing the harness
as Jock walked around his plane.

"Not a hole. But look at those stays," Jock said.

The stays were loose and almost flapping in the slight wind.
Quayle glanced at them and walked away.

Only four, and Hickey not back; that must have been Hickey

53

down in flames as Tap said, he was thinking, as he walked across to the Greek cement hut. No, it couldn't be — Hickey, Gorell, Constance, South, Brewer, Finn, none of them back. Brewer and Finn . . . What a scrap for them to get into! Brewer — Might have been Brewer . . . And South, quiet South . . . Five back out of twelve . . . There must have been a hundred 42's. There were some others somewhere. He wondered what had happened to the bombers. He had forgotten to look for them again. God, what a mess. This was everything.

"Hell, would you believe it?" Tap said to him as he came in the operations room.

"Do you know what happened to the others?" Quayle asked him.

"No, nobody does."

They heard an engine and went out. They all looked up. There was more than one plane. He could see three, coming low from the narrow valley. They were very low. They came in straight and landed as if they were anxious to get it over with. Anderson, the squadron doctor who had come up in the Packard, drove over to the three planes because they didn't spread out over the field but kept together and pulled up. Quayle saw Hickey get out of one. They ran over to the planes. He saw Constance get out of the second. Both Hickey and Constance went to the third plane and the others rushed there along with Anderson. It was young Gorell they were pulling out when they got there. He was being sick as they got him out and he was dead white. Young Gorell kept his eyes strained closed tight and kept being sick as Anderson pulled him onto the ground. . . . He had blood all over his face and down his jacket, and Quayle saw the clean bullet-hole in the neck when Anderson pulled off the Irvin jacket. Anderson opened a small case and started swabbing the neck with gauze and ether. Quayle saw Tap turn grey and step back and they were all talking as two of the ground crew came up with a rough Greek stretcher. Hickey and Quayle carried him over to the Packard as the doctor kept swabbing the blood and avoiding young Gorell when he turned over to be sick. Young Gorell didn't open his eyes at all but kept them closed very tight.

"This is no good," Anderson said finally. "He's lost enough blood. This car is no good."

"Can you wait until we see if we can get an ambulance?" Hickey said to him.

"No. Get him in. Keep him flat. Keep his head up," Anderson said.

They put young Gorell lengthwise on the back seat and Hickey got in the driver's seat as the doctor sat on the floor in the back holding his medical kit.

"I'll come back. Wait here," Hickey said to the others.

"We'll go in with the crew," Tap said.

Hickey said "All right," and roared the Packard to a start and went slowly off.

The others walked over to young Gorell's plane to see what had got him. His tail unit was just about shot away completely. The bullet that went through his neck had come in the back of the cockpit and finished up smashing the turn-and-bank indicator. There was blood covering the bottom of the cockpit and the seat.

"He was going mad when I saw him," Tap said. "When he went down to get at the bombers he pulled out too slow and got slap bang in the middle of them and a 42 was on his tail already. He just seemed to forget about the 42 and hung onto the tail of the Savoia, and I could see him pouring stuff into it. The 42 was pouring stuff into him. I don't know how he held out. He just kept onto the bomber's tail until it fell off and burst into flames. It was fabulous. He was just wandering in and out of the scrap and I was just waiting for something to finish him off. He must have been hit already because he couldn't have known what he was doing."

They walked away from the plane. Now that young Gorell was gone they didn't delay the sorting-out of the fight any more and everybody started talking at once. Tap was listened to because he had seen the beginning of the fight from above.

"How many did we get anyway?" Richardson asked.

"I saw about two go down in the first twenty seconds," Tap said.

"What about Vain and Finn?"

"I think that was Finn that went down in flames," Constance said.

"No. I saw Finn getting hell from about ten 42's near me and I was away from that," Richardson said.

They heard the engine then and looked around. "That's a Glad," someone said. They couldn't see anything yet. They could hear it, and were physically straining their eyes to see where it was. It appeared low, coming from the north. There was a second one way behind it.

"Two of them, two."

When the first plane landed they stood and watched someone get out. . . . They couldn't see who it was until he pulled his parachute off and walked towards them.

"It's young Finn."

The second one landed. "That's Vain's plane," Constance said. But they waited for him to walk towards them.

"It's Brewer," Tap said.

Now, only Vain and South to come . . . And one had gone down in flames, one by parachute.

Brewer was beating his hands together as he came over.

"I'm frozen. Who got back?" he said.

"Everybody but Vain and South."

"I saw South bail out," Finn said. "I followed him down awhile."

"Well, Vain came almost on top of me, on fire," Brewer told them.

So it was Vain. Somebody in Australia would be feeling pretty low in a couple of days. Quayle thought: We are three pilots and four planes short now. Probably five planes, with young Gorell and one of the others shot up as they were. I wonder what the chances of replacements are, or of the remaining three Gladiators in the squadron's getting here. We aren't much good with only seven planes against swarms of 42's like to-day. And trying to get bombers . . . And Vain . . . Oh well.

They went into Larissa in the big truck the ground crew had been given by the Greeks. They didn't talk, mainly because it was too difficult in the truck. When they got to the empty new hotel they had taken over, there was no hope of getting the feeling of warmth back because there was no light, no movement, no warmth in the building. They were cold because everything around them looked cold and was cold, and hiddenly damp. Hickey came up just as they were getting out of the truck. They asked him how young Gorell was and Hickey said he thought he would be all right.

He smiled quietly when he saw Finn and Brewer. "That leaves only Vain and South," Hickey said.

"It was Vain that went down in flames," Tap told Hickey.

"South — he must have bailed out. Was that him?" Hickey said.

"Yes; Finn saw him," Quayle said.

"What got Vain?" Hickey asked.

"They got him when he pulled out under a Savoia, I think," Tap said. "I didn't know it was him. But he must have got it when he followed me down under the Savoias to help you out."

"Well. Let's go up to my room and clear this all up," Hickey said.

They would clear it up. They would all talk about their portion of the fight and what they had seen go down. One by one they would tell what they had got. Sitting there they looked at John Quayle and waited for him. When Quayle was around they were subject to him, not because of any seniority or pressure by Quayle. It seemed natural to all of them. Hickey noticed it, which none of the others did. Tap ignored the whole thing. But Richardson and the others were quietly waiting for Quayle's version before telling their own. It was Constance, waiting to laugh when someone told him an amusing incident of the scrap. And Brewer, sprawling out on the bed with his big feet up waiting for someone to start. He did not seem to care about the whole thing. But Quayle usually knew what had gone on so he might as well wait for Quayle to have his say. It simplified things. Finn was talking

57

to Richardson, while Quayle and Hickey sorted out their end of it.

"Did you see Vain?" he said to Richardson.

Richardson turned his wide eyes on Finn and shook his head slowly.

"No, I didn't. That might have been him way over us. I don't know."

Hersey had been sitting on the floor knocking a nail out of the sheepskin boot. He had folded his face up in a quizzical expression and he looked much older than any of the others when he did that.

"He was on the other side of you," Hersey said.

"Come on," Hickey said to them all. "Let's get this straightened out. Quayle here got two Savoias, one probable, four fighters, two probables."

And that started it. One by one they said what they had got. Richardson said he got a Savoia. He might have got a 42. Finn got two C.R. 42's and one possible. Hersey said he got a Savoia, he thought, certainly two C.R. 42's. Brewer quietly said he thought he got a 42, and Quayle said, Yes, he did, he had seen the one Brewer got go down. Brewer also said he saw South get one before he bailed out.

They all listed their individual claims, then they talked about it all until they let Hickey finalize it. Hickey had got one bomber and two fighters.

"That's good," he said. "Five bombers, ten fighters, with a possible eight more."

"What's the damage?" Hickey asked Hersey, who stood up.

"Well," Hersey said in a flat voice, "South's and Vain's planes are gone. Young Gorell's is all right, but Tap's isn't. There's a couple of ribs gone aft of the cockpit." Hersey was pulling off his Irvin jacket. He suddenly noticed he was bleeding at the wrist.

"I wondered what was wet," he said.

"Tough guy," Tap said to him.

"A mere scratch, Tap my boy," Hersey mocked him.

"Say," Tap said to Hickey, "how long will young Gorell be out?"

"Quite a while," Hickey said, looking up from the book he was writing in. "He'll probably be shipped back to Egypt."

"How did you pick him up?" Quayle asked Hickey. He knew Hickey would not tell that unless someone asked him.

"I just saw him wandering off and losing height. I steered him in."

"Well, how about something to eat? Has anybody got any money?" Tap asked.

"We can go to the place we were at last night," Quayle said.

Between them they had enough money to buy a meal each. Hickey went to Greek Headquarters to send the operations report back to Athens. The others went to the restaurant to drink the white *ouzo*. When they came in, the waiter went out and got the Australian Greek, Georgius.

"My fine pommies," Georgius said when he came in. "They want to know if you shoot down any Italians to-day."

"About twenty or thirty," Tap said and drank the *ouzo*. "Have a drink."

"Thank you," Georgius said. He was looking around. "You cleant the air, certain." He looked around again. "Where is my Australian?"

Tap looked at Quayle. Finn and Brewer were arguing at one end of the table and they stopped. Quayle looked at them all and their expectant faces.

"He got shot down," Quayle said to the Greek.

"Yes? He gets shot down?"

"Yes," Quayle said.

Georgius turned away. Then he looked around and at all the squadron sitting there and said quickly, "He was all right. That he was."

"Yes," Quayle said quietly. "He was."

"I have sorrow," Georgius said. He turned his back to them and walked quickly out of the room. Quayle could see in his back the argument between emotional Greek and careless Australian, and he never knew which really won because he never saw the Greek's face.

Chapter 7

Hickey had not come back from Janina that night. He had gone up there to inspect the airdrome and facilities. They patrolled again at two o'clock the next day but they didn't see anything again. The weather was clear too. At night the report that the Italians hadn't come inland for two days was sent to them, and the note added that this was the direct responsibility, in the General Staff's opinion, of the fight, of Eighty Squadron's victory over the Italians. But it didn't mention Vain or Gorell or South. Quayle could not find out anything about South. He had not been found so far as he knew.

When Hickey came back he said the squadron would move straight up to Janina which was a hell of a town but was nearer everything. So the nine good planes left on Thursday morning for Janina. Tap's plane was being fixed by the riggers and could be used as a spare. The remaining three planes in the squadron had arrived at Athens from Egypt and were coming up in a day or so.

It was straight flying over Metsovo Pass, which from that height looked the worst country Quayle had ever seen. He was thinking of Helen. He remembered the name Janina, and her telling him not to forget it, that she was going there. If this was the place — you could never tell with these Greek names, they all sounded the same — it was going to be fine. If this was only the same place . . . The earth was ridged with close-packed mountains in confusion. There was snow on the two highest that must have been nine thousand feet. There was a road that wound up the mountains and through the valleys which could be seen occa-

60

sionally. The hell was pouring softly in rain when they landed, coming down in the basin of slow mountains under the cloud to the field that Hickey had chosen. It just looked like an ordinary field even from three hundred feet. There were no runways, no hangars, and a flock of sheep in the middle of it which Hickey almost ran into. It was worse than Larissa — thought Quayle — this is the worst of the bunch. . . .

There was a large camouflaged bus waiting to take them into the village, which was sprawled around one side of a lake set in mountains. There was a Greek driver in blue Greek Air Force uniform, with blue puttees and very muddy. There was a tall Greek in an army uniform near the bus.

"I am Captain Alexander Mellass," he said to Hickey.

"My name's Hickey." Then he introduced the others.

"I am to look after you," Mellass said. "I will take you in my bus into town."

So they got in the bus. Mellass said there was fine feeling in the town about there being fighter planes around at last. . . .

They went along the muddy road that was not surfaced and passed through the damp narrow streets of a satellite village that had many people waiting at each side who shouted as they passed by. There were long streets that widened and narrowed, filled with soldiers and mules and small Greek peasants turned traders in the village. They all shouted to the squadron as they went. Mellass was talking all the time with Hickey. They passed a solid rock wall that rose to a hundred feet, turned when its shape turned and came to a thickly treed road that flanked the lake. The bus stopped near a series of stone steps that led up to a cave in the side of the solid rock.

"This is Headquarters. I will take you in," Mellass said. They got out of the bus and went into the dimly lit cave that was strewn with people in uniform over paper-littered tables lit by bare globes. The atmosphere was thick with smoke of Greek cigarettes. The squadron stood around and everybody looked at them. Some shook them by the hand while Mellass disappeared into an anteroom in the big cave. He came out with a fat Greek with a wide wiry moustache that curled like General Budenny's, but he had not Budenny's face. He was pock-marked and had liquor in his nose.

"This is General —— " And Quayle never remembered his name. Mellas introduced them to him. He didn't talk English but he answered the salute they all offered him with a short salute and clicked his heels very well. He had gold braid on his chest like General Sir Edmund Ironsides. He was very dirty and muddy all over, which made him real. The squadron was all dirty and hadn't shaved for two days, and the mud from three airdromes was high on the men's worn boots.

The General offered Greek cigarettes all around but was glad and put them away when Tap produced a package of American Chesterfields that had cost him half-a-crown at the NAAFI.

They then went to the Acropolis Hotel, which was on the corner of a bombed block of buildings. The hotel had shrapnel marks strewn over its new cement front and half the windows were broken. Mellass had a long argument with the big porter, who was drinking coffee behind his table. They finally got three rooms between nine of them. They could get the first bath since they had left Athens, but none of them had any clean clothes. They gave a pile of laundry to the maid, who was small and not pretty but with a wide laughing face. Tap said he had her lined up already. But Quayle doubted if she would do anything about it. She prepared a bath on each floor for them and while Tap had a bath the others went down to a restaurant.

There was the largest number of Greek soldiers in this town that Quayle had ever seen. Mules kept coming through the streets too, and everything stopped when the squadron walked through because they were the first *Inglisi* the people had seen. It had got around that fighter planes had come to keep off the Italian bombers from Janina. The squadron was very conscious of and somewhat embarrassed at being the only English up here, because the Greeks were expecting an English army too. Mellass had asked Hickey jokingly when it was coming, but they knew he was serious about it.

The restaurant was like the one in Larissa. It was crowded with Greek army officers and soldiers in dirty muddy clothes, unshaven and without any class look about them. But it centered on the squadron when they went in there. A table was found for them when two Greek Colonels threw out a group of hungry-looking, very small, muddy Greek soldiers — though the squadron protested with English democratic demonstration. Mellass went out into the kitchen, and the soldiers passed the squadron slapping their backs with a demonstration that was Greek. Mellass came back and said the food would take a while and he would come back. He wanted to do something.

Mellass was tall and had a fine moustache on a long oval face shadowed by thick hair which made him handsome, and his uniform was the cleanest and the smartest in the town and everybody spoke to him.

Quayle was thinking about Helen. If this was the place she would be here by now. He would not give too much thought to working-out whether this was the place or not. He had a hunch it was. Janina . . . Janina . . . Mellass said it like Helen. This is the place Helen said she was going to. I've been away about a week. Maybe she's here already — at a First Aid post. That would be the hospital — this is the place. I certainly fall into things. I couldn't do much about it in the hotel. No, that would be bad. This is fine. I hope this is the place. I don't want to be clumsy with her.

It was good to eat meat again and eggs with watered cabbage over them. The Greeks cooked their food more than the English but it was fine and hot. Tap came in looking fresh from a bath. Quayle took the next turn.

He went back to the restaurant afterwards and asked Mellass where the First Aid post was.

"There's hundreds of them," Mellass said.

"Where's the head one?" Quayle asked him.

"At the hospital, I suppose," Mellass said. He told Quayle it was right up the street, the only building standing over on the hill.

So Quayle went there. The girls at the entrance were being

anxious about him when he went in because of his English uniform. There was a fine lot of nurses and other girls around. Quayle asked a girl at a desk where the First Aid post was. She shrugged but touched his arm and led him along a passage. She knocked at a door. There was an elderly woman seated at a table. The girl said "*Inglisi*" and the woman stood up.

"How do you do?" she said.

"Is this the First Aid post?" Quayle said. "How do you do?"

"No. I am the Matron. This is a hospital."

"Excuse me, Matron," Quayle said to her. "I'm looking for the First Aid post."

"There's none here," she said and smiled.

"I am sorry. I was told there was," he said.

"There's an office here. Where they all come in," she said.

"That must be the place," Quayle said. "Thanks. I'll find it."

"What is it you want? Perhaps I will help you," the Matron said.

"It's all right. I want to check up on somebody, that's all," Quayle said.

"You have injured somewhere?"

"No." Quayle was getting embarrassed because the Matron was too attentive.

"Well?" She sat down.

"It's a friend of mine who said she was coming up here."

"Oh." The Matron looked up. Quayle looked solidly at her.

"What's her name?" the Matron asked.

"Helen Stangou." He spelled it in English. "I don't know if she's here or not yet."

The Matron picked up a phone and spoke to someone.

"We will find out. You sit down. You are an aviator?" she said.

"Yes."

"You have come to keep the Italians from our town?"

"In a way," Quayle said slowly.

A small girl came in with a tray that looked like scales and gave Quayle a small cup of Turkish coffee. She gave another to

64

the Matron, who gave her a coin, and she went out. Then the phone rang and the Matron spoke for a while in Greek; she turned to Quayle and smiled.

"Your young lady is not here yet. She will be here to-morrow perhaps, perhaps the next day. We have always loved Englishmen. We have made Byron a patriot. He is a Greek hero. Your friend is political?"

"No, her family is."

"That is good. Every Greek is a poet and a dictator. He is not a Greek if he isn't. The women are different."

"She's political enough," he said.

"Then you have something real." The Matron was drinking her coffee while she talked and was blowing into the small cup to cool it. She wiped her hands on an apron as a woman does in a kitchen. Quayle stood up.

"Well, thank you, Matron. Thanks for the coffee too. I'll come back to-morrow to see if Helen is here."

"You bring her to me. It is good for you to mix blood. Will you marry her?"

"I know her only slightly," Quayle said.

"It is not a study. If you feel you feel. When you don't have to excite yourself any more, so it is time for marriage. It is real though when a woman is political."

"Yes," Quayle said noncommittally.

"You change her," Matron said, "or she changes you."

"Or you don't change at all." He laughed quickly. He liked this woman.

"No one is that strong, particularly a Greek woman with politics."

"I'll be back to-morrow, then, Matron. We will talk more politics."

She laughed. "All right. You will keep the Italians away."

"I'll talk to the C.O. about it."

"Who?" She didn't understand what "C.O." meant.

Quayle explained. "The Squadron Leader. Good-bye," he said. "*Au revoir,* my *Inglisi* . . . Good-bye."

John went back to the restaurant where the others were still talking. They told him about a British advance.

They had heard the news on the radio. The British had pushed forward from Mersa Matruh and had taken back Sollum. They had captured twenty thousand Italian prisoners.

"Now we're getting somewhere," Tap said. They were all excited about it.

"I don't know what they did it with." Richardson was sceptical about it. So was Quayle. There were not enough troops to make any push against the Italians. Seeing both sides from the air gave you a rough idea of position and supplies, and the British Army didn't have enough, but Hickey said the news was confirmed at Headquarters.

"Someone will get back our old Mess," Brewer said casually.

"Well, it won't be us," Tap said. "We're here forever. We're going to fight the whole Italian Air Force ourselves. In fact we'll be fighting the Italian Army too. We've got to hold them back and push them over," Tap said.

"Come off it, Tap," Hickey said. Mellass was listening.

Tap was silent. They paid the bill and walked back to the hotel.

It was early-morning patrol next day. They were all out at the airdrome before sunrise. It was wet, and the basin of high hills around couldn't be seen for the breath of thick mist that was a stratum flat over the field. The Greeks had put trees over each of the Gladiators and the squadron was surprised when they pulled the camouflage away. They had to wait an hour for the Greek truck with the gasoline in drums to refuel the machines. Hersey went around with them to make sure they did it all right. The others walked around stamping their feet and looking at an old French Bréguet, a 1918 model, that was weighed down by Greek camouflage.

When the Greeks finally got the refuelling done, they took off into the mist, and above it met low clouds and bumps. They hit out towards Delvinakion right on the Greek-Albanian border, which was the front line at the moment in this sector. They crawled around the mountains following Hickey, because it was too thick to try getting over the clouds. Once you got above them you would never find your way back through them again. So they bumped down low through the valleys, banked around the snow-tipped mountains, climbed over sudden peaks and then got as high as they dared over Delvinakion.

They were over the area for an hour. Twice Greek front anti-aircraft guns opened fire on them but they didn't take any notice. They never knew whose lines they were over because there was no indication by either side where they were.

There was just thick timber and a road that slunk around the mountains. Quayle could see a thin stream of transport coming southwards along the road. . . . When it was about time to be going back he heard Hickey say, "We'll do some strafing. Keep your eye on that motor column and come off after me. Only one attack, then we'll pick up formation and go home."

They came low into a slight cloud and Hickey shook his plane, then winged over through the cloud and came out along the valley machine-gunning the surprised Italian motor convoy. One by one they came off, and Quayle put his nose down after Brewer. He pushed his gun button the moment his sights caught a truck, and as he levelled out with his sights blurring along the line of trucks, men, faces, objects, he kept it down and kept his nose down as long as he could and the gun shook. He pulled out of it. He blacked out for a second, then remembered the sides of the valley and the machine-gun fire from the convoy and he pulled way up again, until he saw the remainder of the flight ahead. He could see some of the trucks burning and small figures at the side of the road.

They headed back to Janina through the valleys. Again they more or less followed the road because it was too difficult to keep check on positions for navigation. Quayle was feeling pretty sick by the time they got back. They had eaten no breakfast because the staff of the hotel didn't get up until seven o'clock.

They were in the restaurant waiting for coffee when the stomach whine of the air-raid sirens started. People passed quickly through in a crowd to the back of the restaurant where there was a shelter. They tried to get the squadron there but they waited for their coffee until the cook went down to the air-raid shelter too.

They went out in the streets and across to an open stretch from where they had been digging sand. In a bombing raid the open was better than an uncertain shelter. A bomb had to be close to hit you in the open. The debris always got you in the shelters. So they waited around in the white mist. They heard the echo of an engine from the mountains . . . several engines . . .

They sat down waiting for the planes to appear. A flight of low-flying planes came out of the mist from the north-east. Immediately, two Bofors Pom-Poms which the squadron knew nothing about opened fire somewhere out near the airdrome. As they got nearer the three planes widened out and they came over very low.

"They're Fairey Battles," Finn shouted.

"Don't be cockeyed," someone said.

"They've got our markings. We've got no Fairey Battles around here," Tap said.

"They're Italians," Brewer said.

"They're Greek markings. We sold ours to the Greeks," Quayle said. "They're Battles."

"Only brave men fly Battles," Tap said. "They can have them. Thank Christ they've got them, otherwise we might have them."

They walked back to the hotel still arguing about Fairey Battles.

By midday they were all sleeping except Hickey. He was at Greek Headquarters trying to get the Bombay up from Larissa with the ground crew and some equipment. He wanted the three Gladiators in Athens up in Janina too. When he came back he said the squadron was due for another tour over the lines at three o'clock that afternoon. They got up, had dinner at the restaurant and went out to the field. The Greeks had not shown up with the refuelling truck, so they stood around in the mist waiting.

68

The Greeks meanwhile wheeled out the old 1918 Bréguet observation plane that had been weighed down by a couple of trees. They pulled the boughs off the fuselage, uncovered the cockpit, and a tall Greek climbed in. The other Greeks wheeled up a great wooden triangle and a stepladder. One of them climbed up the stepladder, attached the apex of the triangle to the airscrew and another began to wind a handle on it. This turned the propeller so that it primed the engine, and tightened a spring on the winder at the same time. When the Greek got down off the ladder, the one in the cockpit shouted "Contact."

"Contact," the other shouted and pulled a release of the spring. There was a great twang, the spring released and the airscrew turned, coughed the engine, then stopped.

"What war is this?" someone said.

"My father used to talk about these things in the last war," Brewer said.

A Greek was putting two rocks under the wheels to serve as chocks as the engine was primed again.

"Contact."

"Contact." There was a long *ttt* in the Greek version.

They had to repeat what they were doing several times before the engine burst open and started, with great chokes of flames shooting out the ejector exhaust, and nearly lifted the plane off the ground. The engine was metallic and the fitter was giving it short bursts of fuel which made it roar then die softly. The squadron was laughing when the two Greeks came up from nowhere. They both wore Greek Army egg-shaped steel helmets. The smaller of the two had no uniform on. He was wearing two heavy overcoats and knee-boots that laced up the front.

The tall one had a great beard and was laughing at them when he came up.

"You fly, you fly this?" Tap pointed to the Bréguet. He didn't know how much English the Greek spoke.

"Yes, I fly. Observe. I have pictures, take pictures. See?" He pointed to the little man with the laced knee-boots, and laughed with a great head-shake. The little man grinned and pulled on a parachute harness over the two overcoats. The big bearded Greek tapped his tin helmet, opened up a hemp bag he had been carrying and pointed inside. There were old boots and empty cans and bottles. . . .

"We have no bombs, these we use. It is enough to make fear for the Italians." And he roared laughing into his beard and threw his head back. He put his arm around Tap's shoulders when Tap slapped him on the back. . . .

"You come this trip with me, you take pictures, huh, *Inglisi?*"

"In that . . . ?"

"Nay. Yes. It is good. We come low. No one sees from above. They shoot badly from underneath. Only the Greeks' shoot get close to us. The Greeks shoot at everybody."

"No thanks," Tap said and the bearded Greek laughed again.

"I am Nitralexis. I am pleased you *Inglisi*. We fly together. You come."

Hickey, who was silent till then, smiled so that his blond moustache stretched almost to his ears. He introduced all of the squadron to Nitralexis and the little Greek who said his name was Papagos. "My great General . . ." the big Greek had said, alluding to General Papagos, when the little Greek mentioned his name. Nitralexis clicked his heels to each of them. Then pulled on his parachute and climbed into the forward cockpit. He was laughing as Papagos tried climbing up the high cockpit. He roared when two of the ground crew pushed him up and he fell in.

One of the ground crew handed Nitralexis his hemp bag and without revving his engines Nitralexis called something in Greek and someone crawled in the mud and pulled the rocks from the wheels. He taxied straight down the field and they all expected him to turn and take off into the wind. The plane roared, speeded, floated for a while, then rose shakily into a down-wind climb. They could see little Papagos stuck way up in the air holding the machine-gun steady. Its barrel stuck up in the air like a mast. . . . They dis-

70

appeared quickly in the mist, though Quayle heard the engine for a long time straining in low climb — and once heard Papagos, the observer, clear his machine-gun.

"That is the end of him," young Brewer said — and the others were laughing at the idea of Nitralexis.

"He's crazy," Tap said.

Quayle said, "The more I see of the Greeks, the more I'm convinced they're winning because they are crazy."

"What chance have the Italians against him?" Richardson said.

"A thousand-to-one chance," Tap said. "What about a fleet of 42's on his tail?"

"He wouldn't care a goddam," Richardson said.

"He'll get it in the neck, though. In fact if he gets back in this weather with that crate I'll believe anything."

"Where the hell are those Greeks with that fuel?" Hickey said.

They waited around until the Greek truck finally turned up with a bunch of laughing Greek aircraftsmen hanging on the side of it. Mellass had not turned up either, so Hickey just looked mad and said, "Get a move on. Get a move on. Come on." Hersey went around with the truck during the refuelling, but it didn't seem to hurry the Greeks, who were more anxious about the drums and the cans that were emptied. They always left a small amount in each can for themselves.

By the time the refuelling was done the mist was lower than before and the light failing. Hickey said, "I wish to Christ we had some weather reports. We can't take off in this stuff at this time of the day."

"Come on," Tap said to Hickey, "we ought to follow that mad Greek just to see what happens to him."

"No — we'll call it off to-day. Those goddam Greeks. What the hell kept them so long?"

Tap put up a mock argument with Hickey for a while about going, but he was as glad as the rest of the squadron when Hickey said it was off. He wouldn't have the flight going into that mess. So they got into the bus and went back to the hotel.

Chapter 8

John went straight up to the hospital and asked the girl at the desk if he could see the Matron. She shook her head and Quayle guessed the Matron was busy. He was going out when someone called. He turned around. It was Helen.

"Hullo," he said. "You got here."

"Hullo," she said. "So it is you."

Quayle felt the warmth already when they shook hands firmly.

"You did get here," he said again.

"Was it you asking for me — from the principal? Yes, I got here all right."

"I came up here looking for you. I got talking to the Matron," Quayle said. He was smiling very fully at her because she looked serious.

"You should not have gone to the Matron."

"Why? The Matron's a friend of mine," he said. "Come on. We'll go see her."

"What did you say to her?"

"Nothing." He took Helen's arm and walked towards the Matron's room.

"She asked me about my father." Helen said this with seriousness.

"I told her your father was political."

"That is dangerous," Helen said.

"The Matron is all right," Quayle said.

"You do not know in so short a time. Do not talk of such things."

"Come in and meet the Matron. She's all right."

Quayle knocked on the Matron's door. She called *"Embros"* and they went in. She looked up from a table full of large white cards.

"Hullo, Matron," Quayle said to her. "I have something."

"Ah. My *Inglisi* — "

"This is Helen Stangou," Quayle said. He indicated Helen.

Helen said something quickly in Greek and the Matron nodded.

"Excuse me," Helen said. "I was apologizing to the Matron."

"She is a fine girl," the Matron said to him. "She apologized for you."

"Thank you. I hope you do not think me impertinent."

"What does Miss Stangou think?"

"I haven't asked her," said Quayle.

Helen was looking puzzled because she did not know what they were talking about.

"You are fine, the way you both look. She is very good Greek in looks. She has some Turk and she is very dark — and you look so light beside her."

"The Matron thinks we should mix," Quayle said to Helen. He knew she was embarrassed, but he felt this was easy-flowing conversation that would connect him with her more directly than what he would normally say.

"We are too busy," Helen said. She smiled to cover her embarrassment.

The Matron laughed and said, "Go on out and walk in the muddy streets."

"I am still working," Helen said in English to the Matron.

"Go on. I will explain," the Matron said in English. Then she said something in Greek. Helen replied in Greek, but the Matron said something quickly and Helen touched Quayle's arm and they went out.

"Good-bye," he said to the Matron. "And I'll look after her."

"She will look after you, *Inglisi*. She will. Good-bye."

"*Au revoir,*" Quayle said. They walked down the passage and he heard the Matron laughing quietly as they were silent.

73

There was quiet mist and darkness making dismal the brown mud on the streets. It was quiet and without lights because of the black-out. There were low mud houses and spaces that disappeared into the fields. Thick and heavy trees were low over the mud walls.

They walked slowly towards the town. She had taken his arm, the first time she had done it easily and familiarly, but she did not speak.

"How did you get up here?" Quayle asked her to break the silence.

"With Lawson. He came up in his car to see the front."

"I see."

She looked at him quickly.

"What do you see?"

"Nothing." He was jealous and felt unfriendly.

"You take everything too seriously."

"I hope you do."

"I take the right things seriously," she said. "Not these things."

"These are the right things," he said. He pulled her around and kissed her warmly and brutally.

"We will get put in jail if anybody sees you doing that."

"Great Christ! What sort of people are you?"

"We are all right, but our Fascisti are not. Please be careful."

"I apologize."

"Now you get serious. Please be with sense."

John knew what she was saying was right. He knew that it was not good to have anything serious between them because it was very temporary. He would be leaving soon. No one believed that anything was very permanent about the war. The Greeks were winning. They had pushed the last Italian out of Greece and were getting well into Albania. But something would happen, particularly if the squadron was ordered to go after bombers. She was right, he knew, but it was in the way of what he wanted and he would not acknowledge it.

"All right," Quayle said. "But if I get serious I will do something about it."

She leaned over and put full lips on the side of his unshaven cheek.

Quayle took Helen to the restaurant where the others were. When he walked in he saw them make cracks to each other. They would meet Helen sooner or later, so it might as well be now. He took Helen's arm quietly and walked to the table. Hickey stood up first, after looking hard at Helen and noticing her yellow overall. The others stood up too and it was conspicuous in the whole room, and Helen did not feel comfortable about it either. Quayle could see the surprise on all their faces.

"Helen," Quayle said. "Here is the squadron. This is Hickey, our C.O. This is Helen Stangou," he said.

Hickey smiled quietly and put out his hand. Helen was used to Greeks, who merely bowed, so she was behind-time in putting her hand out. But she laughed a little and it pleased Hickey.

Then Quayle introduced Tap, Hersey, Richardson, Brewer, Constance, Stewart who clicked his heels and bowed, Finn who said, "You surprise us, Quayle," when Helen smiled. Someone got a chair and they all sat down and there was silence.

"You speak English?" Tap said slowly.

"Yes, in a strange way. I lack grammar," Helen said, and Tap was surprised and looked at Quayle.

"Are you a nurse or something?" Brewer said.

"No. I'm in a First Aid post here. That's the letters on my uniform."

Quayle let it all go on because Helen would fit in her own place with them. It was no good trying to tell them what and who she was.

Quayle ordered something to eat, through Helen, and she ordered something for herself; and he knew it was merely coffee because she knew she was on exhibition and eating would be too difficult under the circumstances.

"Do you live here?" Hickey asked her politely.

"No. I have been here only last night. I live in Athens."

"Hickey . . . I think she ought to be attached to the squadron,

75

don't you?" Tap said. Quayle knew something like that was coming and he knew Helen would not be pleased about it.

"Yes," Hickey said in his quiet voice. Quayle didn't like it at all.

"Miss Stangou, would you join our squadron?" Tap was being very jovial.

"What can a woman do?" Helen was trying to be jovial.

"Can you cook? Well, we get shot up sometimes too. It would be a pleasure with you around."

"Then I will not come. I would not want to encourage you to be shot."

"We don't need much encouragement," Finn said. He was sitting next to Helen and was looking at her full in the face.

It went on while Quayle ate his dinner and Helen drank her coffee. Tap was the worst of them because all women were anybody's property and had only one thing in mind and Tap worked on it quickly.

"Where do you live?" Tap asked her.

"At the hospital," she said.

"May I come up and see you?"

Helen looked at Quayle. He didn't indicate anything.

"It is difficult," she said.

"Well, then, you must have dinner here with us," he said.

"I will try," Helen said. "And now I must get back."

Quayle stood up with Helen. He asked Tap to pay his bill. They all stood up when Helen left and Tap shook hands with her and smiled carefully. When Quayle and Helen had said good-bye and were outside, Helen said, "It is hard to believe."

"What?"

"They are young."

"The younger you are, the better the flyer. You've got to be young."

"Do they know what they are doing?" she said.

"No. That doesn't make any difference to them."

"Do you know what you are doing?"

"Yes," Quayle said.

They walked on through the yellow mud, and light rain was making night more dismal. At the door to the hospital he stopped and said, "Will you come out later on?"

"No," she said, "I can't. It is too difficult."

"Everything is too difficult."

"Some day you will see."

"All right," he said. "Good night." He didn't touch her but turned and walked quickly away. He heard her open the big door and go inside and he kept walking into the now heavy rain.

When Quayle went into the Acropolis Hotel he saw Lawson. He was standing with a pair of muddy boots in his hand talking to the porter in French.

"Hullo there," he said. "So this is where you got to."

"Hullo," Quayle said tersely.

"You certainly disappeared. We wondered what had happened to you all."

"We've been around," Quayle said.

"Was that your crowd that got those fifteen Italians the other day?"

"Yes."

"They went mad down in Athens. You're heroes down there."

"It doesn't seem to do us much good up here," Quayle said.

Another war correspondent came down the small steps from the first floor and nodded to Quayle.

"This is Milton Woll. He's a correspondent," Lawson said. They shook hands. Woll was a small dark American with Indian features and a vigorous body.

"Say, who did you lose that day when you got all those Italians?"

"Vain."

"Vain — the Australian?" from Lawson.

"Yes. Was he a friend of yours?"

"I knew him," Lawson said. "But I know a gal in Athens who is going to feel pretty bad."

"Wasn't there someone else?" Woll asked Quayle.

77

"South," Quayle told him. "He bailed out. We think he's all right."

"That must be the guy we passed in Larissa," Woll said.

"Short, medium sort of person?"

"He had a beard. He was medium though. He had bailed out. That was him all right," Woll said.

"Was he all right?"

"He had his arm in a cast. The Greeks had picked him up, I think."

"Will you tell our C.O. if you see him?" Quayle asked of him.

"Sure," Woll said.

"Say, Quayle," Lawson said. "I brought a friend of yours up."

"I know." Quayle looked casually at Lawson and nodded. "I know."

"She was worried when you disappeared."

"We couldn't tell anybody about going."

"I told her that. I thought you had gone back to Egypt for the new push there."

"Is that true about getting Sollum back?"

"The last I heard they were on their way to Derna," Woll said.

"I guess the Greeks shamed us into it," Quayle said.

"The Greeks are about as excited as when they took Koritza," Woll said.

"Did they take Koritza? We never know what's going on."

"Yes. That's the way it is with us too," Woll said.

"Well—what are the Germans going to do?" Quayle asked them.

"Nothing—not yet," Lawson said. "They'll wait for the spring. I doubt if they will invade England before."

"I don't think they'll ever invade England," Woll said.

"I guess they'll hold out," Quayle said and went back upstairs.

"See you to-morrow," Quayle said.

"Sure. . . . Good night," they said.

"Good night." And he went slowly to his room and lay down on the bed with his clothes still on. He wondered what the hell he was doing here and . . . about his boots; why was he here wearing those boots? He was thinking that he would probably not see London again . . . one way or another. He sat up quickly and began undressing because that was no way to think. He thought about Helen instead and he was sorry he hadn't kissed her when they were on the hospital steps. And then he was wondering if Nitralexis and little Papagos had got back in the old Bréguet.

Chapter 9

Nitralexis and Papagos got back all right. The war would have stopped if they had not got back. Because it was the crazy thing they did and the way they did it that was keeping them going. If it didn't succeed there was no continuation for them. It was because, and only because, they did these things that they could keep fighting.

The war went on like that into the rising winter. It came with malice. The snow began early. There was always low cloud on the mountains. At first the snow was only on top of the mountains. They were wrinkled with it. Then it came lower. And sometimes there would be sun and the snows would melt and the roads to the front would be impassable from Janina anywhere north. But they became passable in a day, and more mules came up. So many mules passed through Janina that Quayle wondered where the breeding went on. But it was all mule country beyond Delvine towards Aryyrikasha where the Greeks were flying then, and trucks were no good. The Greeks were fighting out of the mountains, not from the roads as the Italians were. It was all climbing and manhandling. The artillery was the worst. It was fortunate now that Venizelos had built up the artillery. With what the Greeks had to use, they had no equal. It was their artillery hanging on the side of the mountains and the gun-layers who sighted angles by merely crooking their arm at the elbow and calculating the angle that way. They got artillery all over the mountains, when the Italian artillery seldom left the area of the roads and clear spaces.

And as it went on Janina became wet with more rain and mud

and the squadron's patrols were limited. Lawson and Woll had gone to the front. Only Nitralexis and Papagos went out to observe. When the Greek General Staff told them to go out and get some information, the weather had nothing to do with their flying. They just went out and got it — and came back again. Nitralexis came to live with the squadron at the Acropolis. And his laugh was fine for them. Until one day he went away and they did not know where he had gone.

Everything passed through Janina. The wounded began to come in after a while, and one night there was disorder in the town when fifty ambulances that had once been buses came in with full lights and got jammed up in the narrow streets and they had to carry the wounded from the ambulances to the hospital. And the hospital was too full so they put them in the houses.

Janina was never raided during those months. Nobody could ever understand why. This was the feed town to the whole west and central fronts. It was the squadron's operational base and sometimes the Blenheims came up and operated from the military airdrome the other side of town. The Greek Headquarters was enough to go after and the fuel dumps and the road bridges. There was one long bridge that crossed a swamp that was the only way out of Janina to the front, but it was never bombed. There would have been chaos and it would have been serious if Janina had been bombed. The Italians came up and down the roads each side but never touched the town. It was a big mistake.

An increasing number of the wounded were frost-bite cases. The Greeks did not know what to do about frost-bite. They did not have extra socks. They had no change of clothing. They had no blankets. They kept warm by drinking cognac and putting on every item of clothing they carried.

And there was treachery too. The officers were taking too much of the supplies. They were not going forward with the men. The work was being done by the non-commissioned officers. There was no leave for the soldiers. They had to walk all the way to the front. It sometimes took them six or eight weeks to get there and they were so tired when they did get there and sick and their boots so worn that they were no good for fighting, but they did fight.

Sometimes the men got very sick. They argued among themselves and with the officers who were bad. Sometimes they shot their officers because they suspected them of treachery. The officers were not so used to discomfort as the soldiers, who were peasants and workers. They just wanted to end the war and get back to lighted cities where there were buildings and no physical fear and less hunger. So they would compromise and the soldiers would shoot them.

Quayle was walking through a rain storm in Janina with Helen towards the hospital when he saw the squad of Greek soldiers being marched through the rain. Their coats were undone. They had no hats on. Their heads were shaven. They were grey and without sight, though they looked forward as they walked. Their hands were bound behind their backs with crude rope, and a thick piece of rope strung the nine of them together. There were nine other Greeks with rifles on their shoulders each side escorting them. Neither did they see though they looked forward and screwed their eyes up to keep out the beating rain. Quayle asked Helen where they were going. She looked at him and took his arm.

"They are going to be shot," she said.

"Shot. Are they spies?"

"They shot their officer."

"What for?"

"They tried him themselves for treachery and shot him. So now they will be shot."

"Where are they taking them?"

"Behind the hospital," Helen said.

"Christ," he said.

"It has been going on for a long time," Helen said slowly. "They shoot the men behind the hospital because the wounded are always talking about how bad their officers are and not wanting to go back to the fighting under the officers. They hear it when the men are shot." Helen spoke very softly and looked around in the dim light of exhausted day.

Quayle watched the squad as it moved through the wide river of mud and open space, moving ahead of them to the hospital through the rain. He could see the yellow-brown of the Greek uniforms after they had disappeared across the wet field behind the hospital. When he stood on the steps with Helen he could still see them in the dimness. He left her suddenly and quickly, and crossed the field to the stone fence. He saw the Greek soldiers tying hemp around the eyes of the others. He could see they were not talking, and he could see their grey faces as they did it. They lined the nine up, and the nine shuffled awkwardly because they could not see what they were doing, and the firing squad led them by the arm into line in the open field. He saw one fall over and stumble up again. One of the firing squad wiped the mud from his face and put him in line. He could barely see for the rain. They did not untie the nine's hands. They just stood there in an uneven line and were trying to see death through the hemp bandages but only the rain met their eyes. And they were just out of their mothers' wombs.

Quayle felt the overpowering thing that was making these men shoot these others, because it kept them there against the wall just looking instead of trying to do something about it. He also felt the quiet acceptance and the surety of the Greeks with the bandages on their eyes. Because they knew they were right — and Quayle knew they were right without going into the details of anything. He knew they were right and he could not take his eyes off them because that was something of him there. He had forgotten where he was but he knew what part of him was there and he could not go away. He just stood and watched the nine walk back from those in the line. He watched the rifles go up to the shoulders and the darkness of their hunched forms and the death of the uneven line that stood awkwardly waiting for what was theirs, and it came suddenly and unevenly in cold shots. He had lost consciousness of the act going on until he saw them fall on their stomachs and their arms tight behind.

And Quayle saw the one man not fall but stand there. The shot had missed him. Though Quayle could not see that, he could see the Greek's puzzlement and what was the blankness of his mind — just standing there after the noise of the shots; because the Greek was the most puzzled man on earth for a second, and he did not have time to become unpuzzled because the Greek who missed reloaded and the single shot was all the noise on earth at the moment and the man fell very simply straight down without gestures — and Quayle felt what was of him in there, and of him in the firing squad, because it was bigger than he and they, but it would not be always.

Quayle knew that was what it was all about. It was bigger than he now and bigger than those over there but it wouldn't be — not always. He had no recollection of turning around and walking back across the field to the hospital, and the first thing he remembered was Helen there on the steps.

"What happened?"

"They shot them," he said.

"What do you want to see it for?"

"I see a lot of things," he said slowly.

"You see — about the Greeks?"

"Yes," he said.

"That is what you should see," she said.

"I see it," he said. And he knew what he was saying. She leaned over and kissed him.

"Good night," she said and turned to open the door.

Quayle saw with her what he saw with the ones that had been shot, and he knew he could do nothing about it. He opened the door for her. She stood a moment, then went in without saying anything more. He closed the door and walked down the wet steps, and he knew the way he felt for her. And he did not want to believe it. He would not believe it — but it was there, and he knew. He knew.

Chapter 10

He did not see Helen the next day, or for about a week. The wounded were coming in so fast that she could not leave the hospital. And Quayle took Tap and Brewer in a flight up to Koritza. They operated from there, escorting Blenheims bombing Italian front-line positions and bridges because the Italians were making a counter-attack. It was easy and there was no opposition.

The front gradually froze into a sort of stalemate with a big Italian counter-attack, then a Greek counter-attack. But no one knew how the Greeks were holding on, because the supplies were getting scarcer. They were relying on captured Italian transports to get the supplies up as far as the road would go. The British sent some trucks, but everything was held up for spare parts; and a wise old Greek, who regretted the war and was an engineer, whose responsibility the spare parts problem was, said there would not be a car on the road in six months' time. But they kept going.

The squadron was grounded for a week because it rained or snowed every day. Even Nitralexis did not go up. And they all sat around in the restaurant drinking *oúzo*. Hickey had been trying to get three planes up from Athens. South, who had parachuted in the Larissa scrap, was going to fly up in Tap's Gladiator that they had left at Larissa, but he had not come. It had been patched and was good for flight again. But it would have to act as reserve. Gorell was all right too. He was in hospital in Athens, and he wrote a letter to Hickey thanking him for bringing him back and asking what was going on. . . . And they were being sent back to Egypt.

Mellass kept them amused with his stories about when he was

85

in exile, though they didn't believe him. He told them too about the special squad of raiders he had that dressed up as peasants and went behind the Italian lines and set fire to camps and stores. He would disappear for days, and when he came back he would tell them that he had been on a raid. But they did not believe him. He seemed to be answerable to no one, and he had a fine time with Nitralexis, who laughed at his stories and said he had never heard such stories even in Baron Munchausen's biography. But he went away, too, and they didn't know where he went.

It was a good let-up. They shaved every day and got clean for the first time since they had been in Greece.

Quayle went up to the hospital every day. When Helen was not busy they would walk through the mud and snow behind the hospital and through the village out towards the high Mitsikeli range. They did not argue very much now. They were very cheerful instead. They laughed deliberately and easily at each other, because they had kept off arguing since the day the Greeks were shot. And sometimes he would go into the Common Room at the hospital with Tap and Hickey or the others. The First Aid girls and the nurses would sing with seriousness and harmony which astonished them because of its naturalness and spontaneity. They were discordant peasant tunes with a limited range which made them easy to follow and quickly likeable though they seemed without melody the first time you heard them.

The two of them were very fine with each other during that time. He still avoided being clumsy with her and only once did his resolve break down. Helen came to the hotel to give Lawson a letter to take back with him to Athens. Quayle tried to get her to come up to his room, because he had one to himself now, and Tap and young Brewer had got some of the First Aid girls to come to their rooms. Quayle had avoided the atmosphere they were in, but now he felt the warmth spreading into him and he asked her. She merely shook her head and went out. She was feeling his reticence about most things and knew he liked that in her too, so she was never deliberately too familiar with him.

But he went through the mud streets almost every day and he learned some words of Greek, and she asked him about England and told him about the days when her father was in exile, and he did not comment — but she would dismiss it all quickly and teach him Greek words and laugh with tight cheeks when he made an error in pronunciation. And they were warm at night for brief seconds, but it was unsatisfactory when he had to leave her with the warmth still spread in him and nothing done about it. But they were very fine days — and they were relaxed.

Chapter 11

All that ended with the bombing raid on Janina. Quayle heard
the siren about five o'clock in the morning. He did not get up because the sirens went every time there was any plane in the vicinity.
He drowsed off, but the hotel shook with the first bomb and he
heard Tap in the next room shouting to Brewer to put his boots
on because there was a raid. Quayle pulled on his flying suit over
his pyjamas and put his flying boots on as the hotel felt the shake
of more bombs. He could hear the planes now and wondered how
far away the bombing was.

They got out on the open field towards the hospital. He could
see the bombs spilling out of the first plane, which was high in the
new light. He flattened out with Tap and Richardson as the bombs
came down and burst somewhere down in the village. He felt the
noise and the earth shake—and then came the rest of them. He
turned on his side to look up and saw the whole flight of Savoias
and the small fighters winged on top of them and Tap said, "Jesus—
this is going to be a dose." It had come down thick. The string
of bombs came right along near the hotel and a hundred-pounder
hit the mud between them and the hotel. Quayle felt the whole
earth throw up and its mess come down all over them, heard only
the earth shake in its tracks and the end of silence forever until
there was the individual sound of shrapnel winging off the cement
front of the hotel and coming around in great high cries.

And it moved forward from them towards the hospital, and
another landed farther up, and then farther as the earth shook
again. He could see the hospital through mud going up and coming

down, and green grass of the field high in the air with the boom and the high cry of shrapnel.

The next lot came on the right and pieces of timber and rock from some of the buildings were moving around in the air above them. He looked up and saw the thirty or forty planes winged high over the air field and saw the string and cluster of bombs come down on the air field. He knew they had found it. They had not camouflaged the planes or the big tent where the ground crew lived in any way as the Greeks camouflaged. In the bright morning the Italians couldn't help seeing it.

"They're getting serious," Tap said when he got up. There was a wide one hundred-pound crater in the mud road about twenty yards away, but because the earth was so soft the bomb had gone deep and blown high instead of flat, so they had missed it. Quayle heard a plane and flattened out again and Tap came down quickly beside him. But it was a fighter and they could hear some casual machine-gun fire as it strafed. So they stood up again.

"They finally know the town exists," Tap said.

"They didn't drop much stuff," Richardson said. He was laughing and rubbing the dirt out of his fluffy hair.

Quayle turned around and looked toward the village, but there was only white smoke and still the same lines though there was a lot of damage. The hospital had got a lot of new scars on the side of it and a black powder mark. The hotel was looking dilapidated.

"I wonder about the field — I hope the crew got out of that tent," Quayle said.

Hickey was coming out of the hotel. He had not got up during the raid and he said as he came out, "It sounded as if something dropped over near the field."

"Stop in the middle of it," Brewer said. He was red with the earth from an explosion farther down where he had been lying in the field.

"We had better go out," Hickey said. They got in the station wagon and drove down around the craters and saw the people being carried out of some of the smashed buildings and some crying and others mad with anger and running in an unknown direction for unknown reasons and twisted wrecks of cars piled high over a wall and the smoke from a white burning house near the restaurant which had two of the veranda posts blown away and all its windows smashed. It was like that all the way down and there were craters along the empty road to the fields.

Whiter, who was a Flight Sergeant, came up to Hickey when the cars stopped. "Are you all right?" he asked them.

"We're all right. Did anything happen here?" Hickey asked him.

They got out and looked around.

"A couple came pretty near. They strung across the field and we got a few punctures in the tent. But we're O. K. They can't hit the side of a barn."

They could see the black craters across the field but the Gladiators were way to the right of them, scattered out.

"We got a couple of sheep out of it," Whiter said. "They killed a couple with the blast and they landed almost in our lap. The old shepherd here nearly cried himself sick so we bought the carcass for a hundred drachmas."

"How are you doing out here anyway?" Hickey asked.

"All right. We could do with some blankets. When are those stores coming up?"

"They promised them to-day."

"Are they coming up by plane?"

"I don't think so," Hickey said. "Are you low?"

"We haven't any. We've got to buy our bread and meat from the village."

"Hell — that's no good," Hickey said. "I'll talk to Athens about it to-day."

"Those desert sores are giving Masters some trouble," Whiter said.

"Is he around now?"

"Yes, sir." Whiter called Masters. He was a pale-looking boy with lank black hair and quiet features. He looked very sick. His hands were bandaged roughly and his movements with them were awkward as though his whole arm were affected.

"How do you feel, Masters?" Hickey asked him.

"All right. I can't move my arms very well," he said. He was a Cockney.

"Do you want to come in and see Doc Anderson?"

"Now?"

"Yes."

"How will I get back here?" he said.

"We'll get you back. I'll see about those stores," Hickey said as he got back into the car.

Anderson was up at the hospital when they got back to the town, and there was a lot of people stringing their way up the road towards it. They took Masters up there and tried to find Anderson in all the mess that was going on as the wounded from the town were brought in and laid on the floor at the entrance. They found him working on a Greek and told him about Masters.

"Look what I'm in," he said. "Bring him back after breakfast."

They left Masters in the restaurant, and went with Hickey to Headquarters to get the orders for the day. The orders were waiting for them when they got there.

The squadron was to head for Elbasan and wait around there for bombers. Reconnaissance showed Italians were operating from there, and about three new squadrons had come up for a big counter-attack the Italians were starting in the central front. The Italians seemed to be going about this one in a big way.

The squadron took off in between the bomb craters and climbed into an easy stretch heading north into the high sky that was without cloud except the white around the peaks caused by the sudden rising warm air. This was like going back to school after the summer vacation. The flight was hard to keep in tight because they were all feeling lazy.

Hickey kept them over behind the mountain in a wide circle. They waited around for fifteen or twenty minutes, but there were no bombers coming up and none coming back. Then Quayle saw

127864

two planes taxiing down the field like ants crawling. Hickey had seen them too because he winged around and came over towards the airdrome again.

There were about twenty bombers and a group of fighters lining up to take off in groups. It was miraculous that nothing came up at the Gladiators as they came lower over the town. They were at eleven thousand before anything started and then the black anti-aircraft started bursting around them. And between Hersey's wings Quayle saw Hickey shake his plane and nose over. Quayle took a quick look below and saw the first flight of bombers just leaving the ground.

The Gladiators came down through the black anti-aircraft which twice was near enough to bump Quayle's plane, but Hickey was leading them carefully and they were down through the barrage. Then they headed steeper and Hickey pulled out right on top of the first ten Savoias that were climbing desperately and were firing wildly at the Gladiators even before they were in range. Hickey held his fire until he was right on the bomber, then gave it and held it in a long wide burst of fire. Constance came after him on the same bomber and it was Constance hitting the pilot that crashed the Savoia. It went straight down without any preliminaries and crashed.

The Italians had come in close and the tracers from their guns amidships were wild because they knew they were trapped because they were so low.

Richardson came beam-on into a bomber and he almost cut it in two. It stalled as the nose went up and it fell quickly away.

The Savoias were waiting desperately for their fighters to come up and help them. The Gladiators were waiting for them too, because it would be no fun scrapping at this height. Quayle was less than five hundred feet, and with no pull left in his climb because Hickey had not climbed. He had winged around and at the bombers again as Brewer and Finn came down in their initial dive on them.

Tap was on top waiting for the trouble to get to the others. The

Savoias were firing everywhere wildly, and dropping their bombs on their own air field to get rid of weight, and one who got a hundred feet over the others was getting away when Brewer and Finn both went after him and came at him from both sides and poured everything they had into him.

By this time the 42's had left the ground and were in among the squadron. The first to get them was Finn, and Quayle came around and shot a 42 away from his tail just as he was about done. Quayle could feel another 42 on his tail as he levelled out, the most dangerous moment in a fight — when he levelled to get at the 42 on Finn's tail.

It was strange to see so much level flying in a scrap because everybody was so low. Two Gladiators were out of it above Quayle and another one was way to the right. Tap was coming up after his dive, with his flight still hanging onto him.

Quayle could see only one Gladiator down there after that. The Gladiator was trying to get height, but there were at least fifteen 42's around him and two on his tail. Quayle started out in that direction but Hickey streaked by him as if he had got some human element into his plane so that he got extra speed out of it.

But Hickey was too late.

The Gladiator suddenly turned over and fell in a left spin — quickly — then wildly — and Quayle waited without breath for whoever was in it to jump, but there was no jump and he saw it hit the ground and the black smoke and red flames spread over it.

Then Hickey came in over him and they all started on home. Quayle had not seen any other Gladiator go down, but he could only see five beside himself around and he wondered who it was that crashed.

It was always slow getting back. Quayle called into his phone a couple of times but no one replied, so he did not try again. It was cold now and he could feel his feet getting stiff. His neck was sore because he had bumped it when he pulled out of the first dive. He was thinking of Helen because he turned to that thought for escape. She was there wherever he was and he had something of her. He was remembering she had said, "Do they know what they're doing? Do you know what you're doing?" And he had said "Yes — I know what I am doing." But he did not, because he knew that it had nothing to do with him. He knew he shouldn't be here now. And should the others? And should the Italians in the Savoias? Nobody should be here. I care for nobody, no not I, if nobody cares for me. Should the Greeks? No. This was fine. So nobody should be here — nobody. Nobody should be on earth — nobody. The Albanians should be there, not the squadron — none of them. It had nothing to do with them.

And the Greeks that were shot — should they be there? No. Had it anything to do with them? Yes. . . . Putting it onto them, are you? What more had it to do with the Greeks than it has to do with you? You just aren't willing to be shot. So they were willing to be shot both ways and you care for nobody, no, not you. They got it because the odds were two to one against them — but it was their business being here — they thought so — they even thought so when they were shot. Helen thinks so too. She knows what she is doing. Everybody does but you. So my boy . . . do you know what you're doing? Yes. I do. So cut it out — you don't feel bad about letting fly at those 42's. It's just like shooting a plane that flies itself. If it's got a pilot in it, too bad . . . That's the way we all think. The Italians think like that too. So what's the difference? Do you know what you're doing? "Yes," he had said to Helen. "I know — and you know. . . . Yes. I know. It's just that it's a long-term policy with no immediate results for me that confuses me like this."

If you were a Greek you would be confused too. It's just a matter of fighting the worst of two evils. So you would be confused just the same.

There were four Gladiators in when Quayle got down. Hickey, Constance, Hersey and Richardson. None of Tap's flight was back. Brewer, Finn and Tap himself . . .

"There was quite a mess when I left," Richardson said.

"Who went down?" Quayle asked as he came to the four of them.

They were sitting on the running board of the station wagon with Doc Anderson.

"We don't know. Richardson says it was Tap," Hickey said.

"Tap!" Quayle was surprised at the big feeling within him.

"I saw him come out from about twenty 42's and when I turned around the next time I thought I saw him caught again, and then he went down," Hickey said.

They stood up and looked towards the north-west. There was still the engine undertone but they couldn't see anything and Quayle suddenly realized it was coming from somewhere east. He turned around and looked that way and saw the Gladiator coming through the valley. They all watched it flatten out and come down. It approached too fast and its flaps were not down.

"His flaps have been shot away," Hickey said.

The Gladiator came low very fast and hit the field. It bounced. The earth splashed from its wheels. It floated high and fast. The nose dipped a little. It came down again and slid very fast across the field. Quayle could see the pilot was scared to put his brakes on lest he tip nose-down. The Gladiator stopped just at the beginning of the rough area. The pilot climbed out — undid his parachute. Quayle saw, then, it was Finn. That left Tap and easy-going Brewer still away.

"Was that Tap that went down?" Quayle asked Finn.

"I don't know. I didn't even know anybody went down. Who's not back?"

"Brewer and Tap."

"I didn't see anything of them," Finn said. "I got my port aileron shot away way back and I've been crawling back. I lost my flap control somewhere too."

They waited around in the warm sun. The group of ground crew were pulling Finn's plane off the field over near the tent. They were shouting to another group who were cleaning out the empty shells from Quayle's machine.

"How many did you get?" Hickey asked Quayle as they sat down on the wet grass.

95

"One. A 42. I damaged a bomber but he stayed put."

"That makes six — and only three bombers," Hickey said.

The last Gladiator came low over the road through the village. There was no demonstration. It landed straight on. It came in downwind and the squadron did not get a good look at the plane until it taxied right up to them. When it was near enough Quayle saw the pilot ease up and out of the cockpit and land heavily on his feet on the earth — into the cold ground. Quayle knew when he looked.

It was Tap.

They accepted his being the one that came back and its being Brewer that had been shot down relatively and together. They were pleased that Tap was back, and it was this they thought of above what they thought about Brewer's not getting back.

"Hullo, suckers," Tap said.

"Hullo, you bastard," Constance said in the same way.

"We ran into it all right," he said. What he was saying was awkward.

"Yes — certainly did," Quayle said. He was looking at Tap's good features, now looking grey.

"Did you see Brewer get it?" Tap said awkwardly.

"Yes — I did," Quayle said slowly.

"Did you see me underneath him?" Tap said.

"No. Is that where you were?"

"Yes," Tap said. "That's where I was. That's why he came down. He took a couple of 42's away that were after me. That's why he came down."

"How did you get out of it?" Hickey asked him.

"They couldn't see me," Tap said. "I was so low. I kept underneath them and came out over their own airdrome. A couple saw me and chased me for a while but I got in the valleys and I lost them. Is everybody else back?" He looked around.

"Yes."

Tap was suddenly sick. He sat down on the running board of

the station wagon and unzipped his Irvin jacket slowly. No one said anything to him. It was Tap's affair.

"How many did we get?"

"Six without yours."

"I got a 42," Tap said. "Brewer got two, I think. I don't know. I didn't see the end of it."

"That's seven for sure. Only two bombers," Hickey said.

"Why all this about only so many bombers?" Tap said slowly. "Are we going to go after bombers forever?"

"They want bombers," Hickey said quietly.

"I wish those bastards could try getting bombers," Tap said.

"I know," Hickey said. He was being patient with Tap, and Tap knew it, so he felt madder.

They waited for the Flight Sergeant to give Hickey the rough check on the planes. He came over from Tap's plane and said that it wouldn't fly for some time because the support joints in the upper wing were shot away. The flaps on Finn's plane could be repaired. Hickey wrote it down and they all got into the station wagon. They went into town very fast. Quayle kept thinking it was late afternoon or evening, but it was only about midday. It was because the time element got confused in a fight. Incidents became the measure of time and it was confusing to find it always earlier than you thought.

They didn't say anything on the way into town. It was Tap's affair whether or not there was to be any discussion, because of the way he felt about Brewer. He was settling whatever there was to be settled. Hickey left the squadron at the restaurant and went on to Headquarters to put in his report. The others went into the smashed-up restaurant. The big redheaded waiter was sweeping up the mess of glass and wood splinters and broken tables.

"We want to eat," Quayle said in bad Greek.

The waiter didn't stop sweeping but said, "*Ohi. Ohi.*"

He said something in Greek that Quayle didn't understand but he shrugged his shoulders and swept his arm around.

"It doesn't look as if we're getting anything," Quayle told the others.

"Ask him when we can get it," Tap said. "I'm hungry."

"I'm good," Quayle said, "but not that good."

He tried all the Greek he knew on the waiter but it didn't get them anywhere, so they went out. The village was disturbed by the bombing. The squadron couldn't get anything to eat, so they went back to the hotel to get some more sleep.

Hickey was down at Headquarters talking to somebody in Athens on the phone.

"Hullo, Hickey," the voice said. "How are you up there?"

"Hullo," Hickey said. "We've just come back. We're all right. We lost Brewer to-day."

"I'm sorry," the voice said. "What happened?"

"We went where you told us and it was good all right. We got two bombers and five 42's."

"Two bombers?" the voice said.

"Yes," Hickey said. "Only two. We can't do better than that with what we've got. We did a suicidal thing to-day as it is. It's lucky any of us are back."

"I know," the voice said. "But we're after bombers."

"I know that," Hickey said; "but we need replacements."

"I'll try to give you the three from your squadron that are here."

"Thanks," Hickey said. "We'll need more than that."

"I can't get you any more," the voice said. "But about those bombers . . . The Italians are making the biggest offensive since they started. The Greeks up there say the bombers are giving them hell. You'll have to keep them away if you can. They'll tell you about it up there."

"They tell me about it," Hickey said. "But there's only seven of us. The Italians are flying in fifties."

"I know. I know," the voice said. "I know how you are, Hickey. But that's what they want down here. I'm sorry. But it's no good unless you go after the bombers. This attack the Italians are making is win or lose."

"That's what it was the last time," Hickey said.

"Can you do two patrols a day?" the voice said.

"If you can get us up some supplies. We're living out of restaurants."

"I will get the Bombay somehow and get you stuff up there," the voice said.

"Well, we need those replacements badly. If you want bombers, how about some Hurricanes?"

"I've tried for Hurricanes. It's hopeless," the voice said.

"All right. We'll do two patrols," Hickey said. "Do you want another one to-day?"

"Yes. I hear you got bombed. Is everybody all right?"

"Yes," Hickey said wearily. "We're all right."

"Fine," the voice said. "Well, put your report through as usual, Hickey."

"Yes, sir."

"I'll hear from you to-morrow. Good show to-day. Tell the others."

"Yes, sir."

"Good-bye, Hickey. Good luck!"

"Good-bye," Hickey said. He put down the phone and swore. He gave his written report to the English-speaking Greek lieutenant who had been standing beside him during the conversation. He turned without saying anything and walked out into the mid-day sunshine that should have been evening by the way he felt. He drove straight to the hotel and was surprised to see Tap and Richardson in the lobby trying to get some food out of the Greek porter.

"No food, Hickey. You just can't get any," Tap said.

"What about the restaurant?"

"They're bombed out."

"I'll go have a talk with the Greeks. Those supplies should have been here days ago. How the hell do they expect us to go on like this," Hickey said.

"We can get some bread around somewhere," Richardson said.

"I'm not that hungry. I'm really hungry," Tap said.

"We've got another job this afternoon."

"Where?"

"Same place. I'll tell you about it in the room."

"Jesus, what's happening?" Tap said.

"The Greeks are getting hell at the front, I suppose," Richardson said.

"We'll be after bombers. God, I'm going to make sure the next squadron I'm in has Hurricanes or Spitfires or Defiants."

"The Yugoslavs have just joined the Axis, so we might be getting them. Hurricanes, anyway. They'll *have* to have Hurricanes against the Boche."

"All the Greeks around here are just waiting for the Germans," Tap said.

"We'll probably get them too," Richardson said.

"I don't mind the Germans if there's Hurricanes around. But oh, mother — keep me earthed in a Gladiator!"

"Well, we'll know in a couple of days," Hickey said. "I'll go and get this food."

Hickey went out. Tap and Richardson went up to their rooms and slept.

Chapter 12

At two o'clock Hickey woke them all up.

"Come on, fellers," he said. "I've got some food."

"What time do we take off?"

"About an hour," Hickey said.

They went downstairs and Hickey had arranged for a table to be set in the hall. There was hard Greek bread, salami, cheese and coffee.

"Fine thing for heroes to live on," Quayle said.

"Who, the Greeks?" Richardson said sarcastically.

"No, for us. It's fine for the Greeks."

They ate the meal in comparative silence.

Quayle finished before the others and went up to the hospital. He looked in the Common Room for Helen but she wasn't there. He walked into the Matron's room.

"Hullo, *Inglisi* . . . Hullo," she said to him.

"Hullo, Matron. How are you these days?"

"I am very well."

"Sorry about the raid this morning."

"We were not damaged. We were only frightened. And you went into the air afterwards. Yes?"

"Yes."

"You shot down Italians?"

"Seven," Quayle said. "We lost one."

"I am sorry — that is always the way. It is equivocal."

Quayle looked at her when she said that and smiled.

"Who was it?" said the Matron.

"I don't think you ever met him," Quayle said. "Brewer — tall, easy-going, very young."

"What does it matter if I have never met him? I know them all."

"I'm looking for Miss Stangou," Quayle said to the Matron to change the subject.

"She was not in the Common Room? Just a moment."

The Matron picked up the phone and said something in Greek and put it down again.

"Do you think the Germans will invade us soon?" she asked him.

"I think so. They don't wait once they start."

"We cannot hold against the Germans. But we fight. You have Australians in Greece now, yes?"

"Yes, I guess so."

Helen came in. She apologized to the Matron for Quayle, but the Matron said, "It is all right. Look after him. He is very young and he is always in danger. Do not worry. Look after him and do not let him be unhappy."

When they went outside Quayle asked Helen Stangou what the Matron had said. She smiled at him in the tight way and said, "She said you were always in danger and to look after you."

Quayle laughed without thinking about it.

"That's the first time I have heard you laugh like that," she said.

"I like the way she treats everybody as her only son. Is she like that with you, Helen?"

"Yes. She is very kind. Everybody likes her. Did you get somebody shot down to-day?"

"Did I?"

"No. I mean did somebody get shot down?"

"Yes. Brewer. Got caught in a swarm of 42's."

"He's the very young one."

"Yes."

"It's so bad. You never know who it is. I never know about you."

102

"Don't worry. Don't think about it. I don't. If you get it, you get it. Say, what'll happen to you if the Germans come in?" he said.

"I don't know. We'll probably be sent back to Athens. The Australian troops are there now, aren't they?"

"Yes."

"I am glad. We would have no hope against the Germans alone."

They walked down to the field where the Greeks had been shot. They did not talk much — then Quayle said, "I'll have to go — we've got a patrol on."

"Now?" she said.

"Yes."

"It is getting worse. Please come straight up to the hospital when you come back. I'll keep anxious until you do," she said.

"Look, we spend all our time avoiding thinking like that."

"I am sorry."

"I'm not. I'll come straight up. I like you to worry."

"I worry, John." It was one of the few times she had used his name.

He took her arm. "We'll have to do something about this, Helen."

"About what?"

"You know — about us. We can't stand a mile off like this for long. I'm getting worried about it."

"Let me wait, John. I am afraid you will just go away, and then what will happen?"

"If I go — you're coming with me." He knew what he was saying.

"Don't think that," she said. "It is not as simple as that."

"I mean it. If I go, you go too. It is simple enough."

"I could not. We will not talk about it. Where would we go? No."

"I have to go now anyway." Quayle pulled on his cap and they walked up to the hospital. He left her there and ran to the hotel. The others were waiting for him there. They got into the station wagon and drove out to the field.

* * *

When the flight was almost over Elbasan village, Quayle began to feel sick. His stomach was tighter than usual. He could taste bile coming into his mouth and he wanted to be sick. They were cruising above the cloud at twelve thousand feet and it was not bumpy. Hickey had warned them about being surprised, but Quayle was very surprised when he saw the swarm of 42's coming in from about fifteen thousand feet on their starboard in a sweep.

"Hold it," Hickey yelled through the phones.

When the 42's came close Hickey pulled way up and the others followed. They had been struggling to get height. The 42's met them almost head on because Hickey had pulled them up and around. As the 42's came in their sweep Quayle could see the wing shadow of two 42's straight before him and could see the white flame coming from the machine-guns in the wing stubs. Just the white short spread — quick — then gone. And the tracers coming over his head . . . It was so long since the initial attack that he was slow in pulling up. . . . He nearly crashed into a 42 as it did the same. He gave it a burst as its tail crossed his sights — less than fifty yards away. He couldn't see anything but 42's when he levelled out and there was one making a beam attack. He winged over and got out of the way but he had lost height. Another 42 came at him from behind. He tight-looped out of the way and looked around for 42's or Gladiators. He saw two Gladiators in a mix-up with about twenty 42's way off to the right. He pushed the throttle way open and went out to them.

Quayle got in an initial attack on a 42 that was following a Gladiator down in a spiral spin. The 42 pulled out of it and kept going, going, flat to earth — and burst into flames. The Gladiator was flat-spinning too. Suddenly Quayle saw the pilot hurl out of the cockpit like a black ant and the white burst of his parachute spreading in a puff.

Quayle looked around, and then he saw the 42 diving towards the parachute. He saw the white burst of the 42's guns and the tracers. . . . He saw the parachute burst into flames and the sudden black smudge as its slow speed became a lightning streak of charred smoke and the black figure of the Gladiator pilot hurtling two thousand feet down into the black earth.

Quayle winged over and put the Gladiator into a straight drop. He didn't take his eyes from the 42 that had shot at the parachute. It had pulled out and was climbing. Quayle straightened out a little so he would meet it head on. As soon as he saw it in his level sights he pushed on the gun button hard.

He kept it down and kept the plane heading at the 42 with it shaking under the gun vibration. He kept it heading towards the 42 until his madness relaxed and he pulled up over it and tight-turned around and came in fury to get at it again. But the 42 was a black flame, on the way down.

The 42's pulled away and Quayle saw two Gladiators heading homewards.

Quayle wondered who it was that had gone with the parachute. He had been too far away to see what had happened to the others. He tailed the two Gladiators, who were way ahead of him. He was so mad about the 42 shooting down the parachute that he had white tears in his eyes. He felt helpless that he had only shot at the plane to bring it down. It was not enough. He wanted the personal death of the 42 pilot. If only I could have seen him close up and got him, he was thinking.

Quayle was the last to land. He came down after a tight loop over the field — with stomach pain when he got out of the plane and stepped on the ground. . . . Rutger and Williams, the rigger and fitter, took hold of him.

"Are you hit, Mr. Quayle?" Rutger asked quickly.

"No. I've just got a belly-ache. I'm O. K."

"Fine. We thought you were gone this time," Rutger said.

"You did? Who isn't back?"

"Mr. Hersey. They say he went down in flames. And Mr. Richardson."

"Richardson bailed out and an Italian shot his parachute up," Quayle told the others.

"The bastards . . . The unnameables . . . The sons of bitches," Rutger said.

"Yes," Quayle said without feeling.

He walked to the bus where the others were sitting inside waiting for him.

"We thought you got it, John," Tap said.

"No. Did you see what happened to Richardson?" Quayle said.

"Hickey saw it. Was that you that got the bastard that did it?"

"Yes."

"Jesus, fancy doing that — fancy shooting up a parachute! The bloody bitches, sons of bitches." Young Constance felt madder than Quayle. He spoke in a wide Oxford accent and it was absurd to hear him swear that way.

"How did Hersey go down?" Quayle asked. Hersey — it would be strange without old Hersey.

"Just got too many around him. Jesus, I was surprised when they came down on us," Tap said as the bus lunged over the bad road.

"I'm sorry, fellers. We should have been up top, too," Hickey said.

"You warned us, Hickey," Quayle said to him.

"How many did we get? How many did you get, Quayle?"

"I got two for sure. Maybe another one."

"That makes a total of six altogether and all 42's," Hickey said. "H.Q. is going to feel fine when I tell them."

"To hell with H.Q. What the hell are we supposed to do? What if the bloody Germans come in?" Tap said. "Fat lot of good we'll be."

Quayle was looking at Stewart, Constance and Finn. They were the only ones left of the new batch. He felt awkward thinking of it. With Hersey gone it left Quayle himself, Hickey and Tap as the only long-time members of the squadron. These boys were still strangers . . . To Quayle they were just new, bottom half in the squadron . . . and now they were part of the top half of the squadron. . . .

106

"Did you get any to-day, Finn?" he asked the blond boy, who smiled at him.

"One."

"You've broken your duck, then."

"Yes. So did Stewart."

"You did?"

"Yes," Stewart said. Quayle thought that must have been the first time he had ever heard the boy speak.

"How did you get him?"

"Came up from under him. I was surprised to see him as a matter of fact."

"I think you always are," Tap said. "I am. I'm always surprised."

"I'll shoot every bloody Italian that bails out from now on," Finn said. "Jesus, fancy Rich getting it like that."

"It won't help to do that," Hickey said quietly. "This Italian is an exception. We don't want to start a feud like that."

"I suppose you're right," Finn said.

"Yes, I am," Hickey said.

Quayle was still astonished because there were only six of them. Because there was only one conversation and they were all so closely knit now. Just as long as old Hersey had been there and tall Richardson, the squadron was still divided into groups — he and Tap, Hersey and Hickey, the old-timers, sometimes with Richardson; none of them taking much notice of what the others said. But now you couldn't help it.

Hickey got out at the Headquarters cave and the others went on to the hotel. Quayle took his flying gear into his room then went straight out and walked up to the hospital. It was getting the long light of evening. He was not going up to see Helen because she had asked him. He was going up because he wanted her now — when he thought of Richardson and Hersey and the conversation in the bus. It was catastrophic. He wanted something that would absorb what was in him. If he could yell his head off and eat the earth madly, that would be it. He had read that somewhere, but it would be fine. But he wanted Helen now. Just to know she was there as something real. He found her in the Common Room packing bandages in a small First Aid kit.

"Helen," he said abruptly, "can you get away? I want us to talk," he said. He took her overall in his fingers and tugged it quickly. She looked at him and saw that he was looking at her without thinking about it. She could see what he wanted. . . . It was too easily seen.

"Just a minute." She went into the small room at the side. She came out with her overall off.

"Come on, then," she said. "I've only got a few minutes."

They went outside. It was automatic that they walk to the field where the Greeks had been executed. They leaned on the wall that Quayle had leaned on that night when the Greeks were shot. He was thinking about it now. It was repeated in his mind — and it was Constance and South who were being executed instead of the Greeks. Helen didn't say anything — watched him carefully. He turned to her quickly and said: —

"We've got to get married."

She only looked at him.

"It's the only thing. I know what I want."

"Yes?" she said slowly. Then she smiled at him.

"We've got to, Helen. You know we have. I don't care what you say. I know it."

"You just can't say it and do it," she said. "It's very difficult, John."

"Why not? I don't care. We will. Why not?"

"You just can't, John. I don't want to get caught up in the air like that."

"We've got to. I know it will be difficult. But I'll get Hickey to straighten things out. You can go back to Athens if you want to. But why can't we?"

"Do you know what you're doing? You know what will happen to you if you marry a Greek girl?"

"How?"

"I am no child. I've watched what way you behave to Greeks.

It would be difficult for both of us. And when you leave here . . ."

"We'll be lucky to ever leave here," Quayle said viciously.

"I have a family. You forget. I want to, but I cannot."

"But why let moralizing hold it up?"

"It's not moralizing. You know that whatever you want of me you can get. But I've had to be careful. I've had to stop you from taking it. We've got to keep living in this way of things. It would be difficult if I just went to you like that. You know I feel for you. I know that you feel for me, but it isn't simple like that."

She said it so simply that he was surprised and looked at her.

"I can't say I love you. I do. But I don't like using that to say what I feel. But it's that way. I know that's right. I love you—I want to marry you now."

"I want to marry you, John. We should. It is right. But it is not simple. Let me think about it—Please . . ."

"Haven't you thought about it?"

"Yes—but let me think about it—now that you say you want it . . . Please, John."

"Till when?"

"I don't know. To-morrow. To-night. Just until I think it out."

"To-night," John said. "I want to know, Helen."

"All right. Please we will go back now."

"Yes."

They turned from the field and walked apart up the muddy path to the hospital.

"I'll come to-night," he said as she opened the big door.

"Yes. But think about it too, John."

"I have," he said. "And I know. You think about it."

"Yes. Good-bye."

"Good-bye," he said and turned away.

Quayle knocked on Hickey's door and walked in without waiting for an answer. Hickey was getting undressed to have a bath. He was sitting on the bed in a woolen short-sleeved undershirt with police braces hanging over his hips. He was pulling off his boots.

"Can I talk with you a minute, Hickey?" Quayle said to him.

"Sure. Sit down. Say, that was bad business to-day."

"Yes."

"I didn't think anybody would ever do that."

"Tough on Richardson," Quayle said.

Hickey swung the boot in his hand and half-frowned.

"He was getting pretty good too. You could always depend on him."

"Yes. Say, Hickey," Quayle said abruptly, "I came in to ask you about Helen."

"What about her?"

"Just formal. Is it all right with you if we get married?"

Hickey looked up quickly, then smiled broadly.

"Well! Who'd have thought it?"

Quayle smiled too. This exact moment indicated the warmth between them, and the similarity. Quayle saw Hickey as a mixture of sensible restraint and wild actions, like his red hair. Hickey in the air was always careful and always right. This half-smile of Hickey's now was something like his bright green eyes, and there was humour in him. Hickey could see Quayle like that too. Their thought of each other was almost identical. Hickey knew that Quayle did not do anything wrong in the air, that he was sensibly restrained on the ground, that he was older than his years. This medium figure with keen individual features was too sure of himself in the air to fail when he was on the ground. He looked at Quayle's quizzical expression.

"I know," Quayle said.

"Do you?" Hickey said and chuckled.

"Sure. It amuses me too."

"Well. You didn't have to ask me."

"It's in the book of regulations."

"Do you always stick so close to them?"

Quayle laughed at Hickey's banter.

"When are you getting married?" Hickey said.

"I don't know. To-morrow."

"We've been ordered back to Athens to-morrow," Hickey said

slowly. "The Germans are expected in, any day. The Hurricanes have moved up to Salonika."

"What are we going back for then?"

"I don't know. We'd be mincemeat up here. Six Gladiators."

"Will we get replacements?" They were talking easily and slowly.

"I don't think so. This looks like the end of the Gladiators."

"You mean we'll get Hurricanes?"

"I suppose so," Hickey said. "You know, I'll be sorry, John."

"For Christ sakes, why?"

"So will you be. Hurricanes are all speed and no aerobatics. You black out on every turn and you take a mile to do a loop."

"Don't be romantic about it. Gladiators are just finished."

"I know," Hickey said. "But you know as well as I do that flying Gladiators is about the last individual air-fighting there is. I'd sooner have it that way. Flying scads of Hurricanes is like being second pilot in a bomber."

"I suppose so," Quayle said.

"Yes. I'll be sorry," Hickey said. "I won't be sorry for these kids, though. They're better off in fast planes."

"Who?"

"Oh, Finn, Constance, the others. It seems funny without Hersey, with all these new ones."

"Yes," Quayle said, somewhat absently.

They were quiet for a moment, then Hickey dropped a boot and stood up.

"How are you going to get her back to Athens?" he said.

"I don't know," Quayle said. "I will somehow. Can you do anything?"

"I might be able to. I'll try. I suppose I ought to congratulate you."

"Thanks. When is the Bombay going back — if it's going back?"

"In a couple of days," Hickey said. "It will go after us."

"Maybe she could get down in that."

"I'll see."

"Thanks, Hickey."

"That's all right, John. It's all right." Hickey smiled broadly.

Chapter 13

Quayle went out and up to his room. He slept until after eight o'clock, then dressed and went downstairs. Hickey had ordered the table set up again in the hotel hall, and the others were eating.

He was struck again by the fact that there were only six of them.

He ate the hard Greek bread and drank the thick *retsína* that tasted like violin strings because it had resin in it. He walked out of the broken entrance to the hotel and up to the hospital. There was no moon and the streets were hard from the two days' sunshine. He waited in the Common Room for Helen to come. She was dressed in a long yellow coat with a small yellow First Aid cap on her head. Her cheeks were drawn in that tight-muscle way. Her eyes were long across from her nose to her cheek-bone and her roundness was slimmed by the cut of the coat. They walked down the steps and through the village out towards the bombed bridge at the foot of the lake. They were silent through the village. But on the white-misted road he spoke to her.

"Do you know now?" he said to her. "Before you say anyway, I'll tell you. I think I can get you back to Athens in the Bombay. That's the transport plane. We've been shifted back to Athens."

"You are going back. You're going back to Athens. When?" she said.

"To-morrow or the next day, I don't know. But you can get back in the Bombay. What have you thought about — "

"I don't know," she said. "It's different, you going back. It's different now. What will happen at Athens? I don't think I can go — I can't leave here."

"I'll fix that. The Matron will — "

"But even then, what is there ahead?"

"Not very much. Nothing definite. If I leave Greece, you would come too. It looks like I'll be here until the Germans come in. Then we'll go back to Egypt. You can live there or go to England. Just so long as we're not split by a war. What do you expect?"

"It's going to be difficult leaving," she said.

"That's what is on your side. But this is about the most important thing you do or don't do. I'm trying to be cold about it."

"I suppose it will be all right," she said. "But I don't think the Matron will let me go."

"We'll go back now and see her."

"No. I will ask her."

"No. It's easier for me to do that," Quayle said.

He pulled her around as he had not done for a long time. She was softer than she had been before. She did not hold him but just let him spread his body over hers. He pulled away suddenly and they walked in silence back to the hospital. He was very sure of himself. The Matron was surprised when Quayle and Helen Stangou walked in.

"Hullo, Matron," he said. "I'm sorry to disturb you — but I want to ask you for something." He noticed he was speaking with prepositions, as Helen did.

"Hullo — you look serious — what is it?"

"We would like to get married. I want Helen to come back to Athens."

"You are wanting to marry?"

"Yes," Helen said to her in English.

"Yes," Quayle said. "Can she go back to Athens to-morrow or the next day in our transport plane?"

"So you want to marry. We need everybody here. And the Germans — They will come in soon."

"I know that. Matron, she can go on helping in Athens if that's what you're worried about."

The Matron was quiet for a moment, then nodded and said,

113

"It is easy to arrange to go back. She can go. I will make it all right."

Helen smiled quietly. Quayle nodded.

"That's swell of you, Matron. Thank you for that," he said seriously.

"She can take some parts for a heating machine down for me. We have no parts down there. She can take them down for me and it will be fine."

"Yes. Anything. Thanks a lot," Quayle said again.

"I am glad. You are fine young people. You will be happy if there is to be any happiness. I felicitate you. You are right to do this. But you should look more happy."

"I don't know how we can get married around here," Quayle said.

"Have you some religion?"

"Officially I am Church of England. But isn't there a civil marriage?"

"No. It is for the Church."

"I don't care where it is."

"You worry about that to-morrow. Or in Athens."

Quayle and Helen went out and Helen said she would have to finish some work. So Quayle went back to the hotel. Hickey was sitting on his bed when Quayle passed the door. He called him in.

"I hope you fixed things up all right. The Germans are due in Greece to-night or to-morrow. Any minute. Your girl can go back on the Bombay to-morrow if she wants to. We've got a patrol to do before we leave."

"Where to?"

"Do you remember Nitralexis?"

"That crazy Greek flyer? I haven't seen him for a long while."

"He's been up at Koritza. We've got to take him out on a recco. Over towards Valona to see what the Italians are doing."

"That means low flying."

"Christ only knows what it means. I just hope the Jerries aren't in by then."

"What time are we up?"

"Six o'clock. You'd better get to bed."

"Yes. Well, I'll be glad to get out of this place."

"So will I," Hickey said.

"Good night, Hickey."

"Good night, John. I'll get the porter to wake you."

Chapter 14

There was no mist the next morning. The Gladiators were standing coldly in the blue dawn. One by one the fitters were starting them and the cold roar was warmth in the air. It had its definite place as a sound, in the morning. The Greeks had wheeled out the old Bréguet and were going through the pattern of starting the engine. The wet mist ran in rivers from the metal wings as the engine vibrated slowly then set itself into a mild roar.

Quayle and Hickey stood around waiting for Nitralexis to appear. Hickey showed the others on the map where the reconnaissance would take place. It was over a rocky high stretch of mountains way behind the Italian lines, where it was thought that large stores were hidden. Nitralexis came up with Papagos. He was already in his flying coat, and Papagos had the overcoats on. Nitralexis put his arm around Hickey as he greeted him with a wide smile. Hickey was not sure of his feelings toward the Greek. He thought him a little too mad but put up with his affection. "I am happy to-day," Nitralexis said. He laughed with his head back. "I have accompany from you. This is going good." He knelt on the ground and unfolded a crumpled Greek map of the area, much better than the ones the squadron had. Nitralexis in careful slow English showed what he wanted to do, and he knew his business very well, Hickey decided. He showed Hickey the approach he would make to the area, and Hickey was pleased because it was his choice also. They would come around a high mountain peak, Nitralexis would make the straight reconnaissance flight down the valley while his pictures were taken, would turn around for another run then climb immediately and head for home whatever was happening. Instead of keeping height and waiting in case 42's attacked the Bréguet, the Gladiators would fly along with Nitralexis at whatever height he was going to take his pictures from.

"We will wish each other good fortune, yes?" he said to Hickey as they walked to their planes.

"Yes, we'll need it," Hickey said.

Papagos was already in the rear cockpit of the Bréguet.

"What about the boots for the Italians?" Quayle called to Nitralexis.

"Boots?"

"The bag — you drop on Italians — the bombs — "

"Ho-ho. . . . I have some. I have some, yes — inside." Nitralexis threw back his black head and laughed loudly above the mild roar of the Bréguet's engine. He pulled on his tin hat, brushed his hand across his tremendous beard and strained up into the cockpit. To get warm Quayle ran across the field to his plane. He pulled on his gloves, strapped on the 45 Colt in the canvas holster on the canvas belt, did up the cumbersome parachute straps between his legs, clipped them into the circular release in his stomach, pulled his helmet on and climbed awkwardly into the plane. He eased open the throttle as he put his brakes on and pushed his stick forward. He liked the good even sound of his engine. He tested the rudder, eased the stick from side to side and watched the ailerons. Then he took off the brakes, swung the Gladiator around and taxied to the right of Nitralexis. Hickey, Constance and Stewart were on one side. Quayle, Tap and young Finn were on the other.

As Nitralexis opened the throttle he lifted his hand and they all moved insecurely forward. The Gladiators were off the ground before the Bréguet. As Quayle pulled his hood over he kept his engine back so that Nitralexis could catch up. The Gladiators formed a stagger around Nitralexis and let him make the pace and the height. They climbed over the Koming Oros and headed north-north-east.

The Bréguet was rising and falling in great jumps as they came down and around the mountain. The flight kept in close and Nitralexis levelled the Bréguet out at five hundred feet, bumping straight down the valley. The speed seemed increased because of the relative position to the ground. They made the straight run once and Nitralexis turned. He didn't wait for the flight to pick up with him, but pushed the old Bréguet flat along the valley again. Then the short bursts of anti-aircraft made black puffs around the sky and points 5's opened up with tracers. Nitralexis finished his second run and quickly started climbing. They turned back towards the mountains. All they had to do now was to get home.

They were almost at cloud level when the 42's came. Quayle saw them and was not surprised. It was like knowing what was next in a book. In such perfect conditions for a 42 attack, it was inevitable that 42's were around. There were sixteen or so in the first group. They were coming straight down in formation. There was another group coming beam-on lower down, about twenty. And Quayle knew this was the toughest spot he had ever been in. He looked behind him quickly at the flight. Tap was in close for a change, and young Finn was flying steadily.

The attack met them another two miles on. There was nothing much they could do about it except try to get height, hide in the clouds. But the Bréguet slowed them down and the 42's came down with full guns blazing. For the first time since he had been fighting Quayle got bullets in his plane. He felt them hit and knew they were 20 mm. explosives. He saw the fuselage tear from the under port wing, saw the 42 that did it wing over and climb to return and attack. He looked up desperately to see where the clouds were. They seemed a long way away.

Then he saw Hickey wing over and the flight follow him. They would fight. He came up immediately for an attack on two 42's that had tagged onto the Bréguet's tail. Quayle could see little Papagos way up in the air firing his gun at the 42's. He took a quick look at the batch of 42's coming back to renew the attack, decided to meet them head on.

He kicked the rudder, eased the stick and slipped into a glide coming in a slip right into the head of the 42's. He saw the white spread of ragged-edged flame from a 42 as he got the underwings where the Fasces emblem came into his ring sights. He pushed hard on the gun button, knew immediately that he had come in too close and that 42 shells were hitting his plane. He pulled hard on the stick to come up over the 42. There was slow action. The climb was too slow. He could feel the controls loose somewhere and the plane losing height again. He banked around — and suddenly caught a glimpse of the Bréguet crashing beam on into the middle of a 42, and a strange tangle of machines going down.

His controls were bad, there was something wrong with the elevators and he couldn't get height though the engine was still functioning. He turned on his side as a 42 came up from below and gave him a short burst. Quayle knew quickly that his machine was badly hit. The plane was suddenly loose in his hands . . . He had no control. He pulled on the stick and the plane straightened out, but it was losing height rapidly. He was going down too fast. He pulled the stick back and tried turning on his side and using the rudder as an elevator, but he kept falling. Quayle was afraid. He pulled desperately on the stick, took a quick look out, knew he was too low to bail out.

The plane was hurtling fast and the wind screamed high through the slits in the cockpit cover. He cut the switch. The ragged side of a mountain came up quickly . . . the green timber, red earth somewhere, rocks, speed, blurred movement . . . nothing before him but solid, solid . . . Goddam it Goddam it . . . this is it . . . this is everything . . . this is all the world. It's coming . . . it's here.

And Quayle crashed in a wide bump, skidded deep below the timber tops, came into the rocky earth. Spars, fabric, struts were torn to shreds, went flying everywhere. The weight of the engine carried the shambles of plane forward until it was crumpled into a tight ball. . . .

Quayle was conscious of the bump, the terrific tearing of the fabric, white sight and silence . . . and the great speed cut deep into earth like a razor into a finger. He was wild with fear. . . . He clutched the stick waiting for the movement to stop as it tore into the timber. He was solidly, terrifically thrown forward and his head crashed against the instrument board. It was all quiet, very quiet for a moment, then nothing.

Chapter 15

Blood had frozen on his head. Where the flesh had been broken by the metal, there was a hard crust of blood that stuck to his skin and to the object. There was blood down the front of the Irvin suit, and where his face showed through the mask there were blood and cuts. The mask had been pushed under his jaw, and had crushed against his neck. His hands had bent with the stick and were loose and bleeding at his sides.

It was dark evening when the greyness started moving into consciousness. He lifted his hands and pushed on the smashed panel. He was not conscious of what he was doing. He was not conscious of movement. It was slow coming to him. He was drunk and there was nothing definite. He pushed his hands against the panel again. His head came up, tearing the clotted blood from the flesh and the metal, and the pain got through to his brain. He made a quiet sound.

The face wounds started to bleed again and his first conscious feeling was the blood running into his eyes. He couldn't close his eyes, he didn't know how to do it, co-ordination of nerves had not come back. His eyes were open but not with focused sight. His head was back now and he moved his hands again. He was conscious of this movement.

Then suddenly he felt it all for a small conscious moment and it was with terrific pain but realization that he was jammed in the cockpit. He couldn't see clearly yet and he was intoxicated in his movements. He was conscious now of the pain and the fact he was in the cockpit but not clearly conscious. He wondered about his movements as he tried to push himself up and felt divorced from them.

When he could see, he could feel the indefinite pain and the concentration in his head, which made it impossible to co-ordinate what he was doing. He pushed his hands up because he vaguely knew that he would have to get the cockpit cover back to get out. His hands groped above his head which he could not raise to see what he was doing. There was no cockpit cover left, it had been torn off and there was only cold air above him.

He had a grip on the side of the cockpit and he pulled himself up. His parachute harness caught on something and he fell down again and his hand caught. He pulled up again until he was almost standing with knees bent. The air hurt him. He pulled harder on his arms and he got his legs up. He felt the weight of the parachute and fumbled to push the harness release in his stomach. The straps fell away and he got to the top of the smashed cockpit. He paused, blacked out, then fell hard to the earth.

Very slowly his co-ordination came back and the concrete pain came with it. It was indefinite, everywhere, at first, then it became separated and he could feel the soreness in his arms, his legs, and the wild stinging of his cut face. He lay crumpled on his side and fought off unconsciousness through the pain. He was scared he would stop breathing. He was scared with so much pain he would die, and he concentrated everything on keeping conscious and keeping his breath deep. He cried twice until his body loosened with the great crying, and then he stopped.

He became completely conscious without influence of pain in his mind when he saw the earth before his eyes. It was red and wet with leaves in many-coloured brown or purple — very purple. Too purple for this sort of leaf, was his first real thought above the pain. He looked at the earth and breathed for a while. It was dark but the moon was lighting up everything, he was conscious of that next.

Above the pain he was thinking it was the moonlight that made the leaves so purple-looking, or he was colour blind. But he couldn't be colour blind, because he had got in the air force.

"Christ," he said aloud.

"Christ almighty, I'm in a hell of a mess," he said. He could feel what he said vibrating in his ear heavy on the ground. He used his hands like an animal to lever himself up. He saw the Gladiator rolled and smashed in pieces in uneven wreckage in the trees. He wondered how he had survived, and was scared again to think about surviving because he was not sure he would, so he wouldn't challenge it. He moved his legs and they seemed to be all right. He knew his arms were all right. It was his face that was smashed badly, he knew that. He pulled at his helmet, and he could feel how it had been cut and was sticking to the blood in his hair, but he pulled it off.

Because he wanted to make sure he was all right so nothing could cheat him, he struggled to get to his feet. He stood up slowly and grasped the side of a tree. He could stand all right. He moved his neck and knew his spine was all right. He felt the white wind and knew he was well alive. He couldn't stand up for long. He sat down again. He was wondering what he was to do. He couldn't stay here. He was too sore to move far. He would have to get strong enough to move some distance before he moved. But he just couldn't sit here. He would have to get going. He was thinking that in a minute or so he would force himself up to get going — somewhere — when he fell asleep again.

There was plenty of day alive when he woke up. He was normally conscious immediately. He was quickly conscious again of all the pain and stiffness of his body, but mostly the swelling and cuts of his face. He sat for a moment and looked at the timber around him and the wrecked plane.

"That thing will never fly again" was the absurd thought there in his head. Quayle stood up and walked uneasily and unfirmly to the plane. He wanted the emergency rations, and the map. He unconsciously looked at his watch. It was smashed in, so he couldn't use that as a compass. He went around the other side of the plane wreckage and climbed up on a rock. He pulled out the parachute pack — saw that the plane's compass was smashed. He reached down and pulled out the tin of emergency rations. It was squashed but the rations were all right.

He got the First Aid kit and the maps. Then he sat down on the rock and rubbed the ointment from the kit over his face. He could feel it swollen and badly gashed. He pulled the release bar on the parachute and the pilot parachute sprang out and some of the big silk with it. He cut it with his pocket knife and tore strips off. He bandaged his neck and the top of his head. His hair was like hard mud, so much blood had soaked it. He took a long drink from the military water-bottle that hung on his waist opposite the 45 pistol. Then he stood up and with the maps under his arm walked unsurely up the slope a few yards until he came to a break in the timber and he could see where he was.

When he could see the landscape, he was surprised to see how high he was. He was on a high mountain and below to the east he could see a ribbon of road and beyond that a river that was big and wide and green with the birth of its own fertility. To the north there were lowlands and to the south high ridges, as high as the one Quayle was on. It was easy to see where he was, the ridges to the south gave him his position. The map marked the mountain he was on as Lap Martalloe. He was way behind in the Italian lines about twenty miles north of Tepeleni. He was about the same from Chimara, on the coast, and he did not know who owned the town. Whatever way he went back he would have to go clean through the Italian lines. It would be simpler to go to the coast; but the Germans might be in Greece already, and he had to go back through Janina so he could get Helen. He began to wonder about Helen. She may have gone down in the Bombay just the same . . . "But I don't think so," he was thinking. "It's going to be tough getting back that way. It would be simpler to go to Chimara on the coast. There was a river course that could be followed pretty easily." He knew because of Helen he would go towards Janina . . . He had to get back there before the Germans got in.

He would have to keep high in the mountains and travel at night, because he was sure to bump into patrols. He was in the thick of Italian support positions. If he travelled only at night it would take him weeks to go up and down these mountains. The sooner he started the better. He stood up and walked back to the plane. There was nothing he could take with him. He sat down and peeled off the heavy flying pants. It was cold without them but his ordinary pants were better for walking in. He pulled on his belt with the 45 and the water-bottle. He picked up the emergency rations, looked at the sun, held up the pocket compass and moved across the slope.

He was bending down to get under the low timber as he left the plane. He heard the noise of walking. It was suddenly near and heavy and above the quiet wind in the leaves. He fell flat and waited. The movement was close. He peered through the foliage. He knew there were more than one. He didn't think of his 45. He just lay there looking with his eyes long-focused. The figures came through the timber and stood for a moment. Quayle looked quickly. He crouched into the earth. Then he saw the beard, the wide face, the tin helmet. It was Nitralexis.

Quayle stood up and walked in the direction in which Nitralexis and the other figure were moving. He came in across an open stretch. Nitralexis stopped quickly, looked surprised and in mid-air for a moment. Then Quayle said, "It's me — Quayle."

Nitralexis frowned, then smiled in his beard — walked forward. "*Inglisi . . . Inglisi,*" he said, with a great laugh.

Quayle looked at the other figure. It was not Papagos, the air-gunner. It was a peasant in a long black beaten felt cape with a hood. He was very young with hair over his forehead and red full cheeks. He smiled at Quayle.

"Where's Papagos . . . Papagos?" Quayle said. Nitralexis was patting him on the back with his arm. He took it away and shook his head.

"We burn — we crash — we burn, fire. Papagos . . . " and Nitralexis shook his head.

"How did you find me?" Quayle asked him.

Nitralexis didn't understand at first, then said slowly:—

"He—" pointing to the peasant—"said another *avion*—airplane—we going back. He said another airplane. I wanted . . ." He didn't know what the word was. "Medicine," he finally said.

"You are hurt," Quayle said.

They were sitting now and the peasant boy was standing where he had stopped in the first place. Nitralexis undid his coat and showed a deep bruise and black gash in his arm to Quayle. Quayle pulled out his First Aid kit and rubbed the ointment on it. Nitralexis looked at Quayle's face and grimaced.

"You hurt very bad—very bad—it is sore."

"Not much," Quayle said.

When he had smoothed the ointment over Nitralexis' whole arm, Quayle took the maps out. He pointed to their position on the map.

"Tepeleni," Quayle said. "We'll go towards Tepeleni."

Nitralexis picked up the map, then put it down again and pointed to Chimara on the coast.

"Here—we go here—this is better."

"Tepeleni—near Janina—it's quicker," Quayle said, and pointed to Tepeleni again.

Nitralexis shook his head with certainness.

"Too many Italians," he said. "Too bad country. That's impossible."

"No, it's quicker," Quayle said.

Nitralexis shook his head.

"We are safer—Chimara—no Italians there many."

Quayle shook his head, folded the map. He knew that if he gave way to Nitralexis he would not pass through Janina, but go down the coast to Chimara and back to Athens. He didn't want to miss Helen. He had to go through Tepeleni to Janina.

"I'm going towards Tepeleni. I want to get to Janina," Quayle said.

"Is dangerous—Why?"

"Faster—it's faster," he said.

Nitralexis looked at him closely — shrugged his shoulders — then smiled broadly. He patted Quayle on the back with mock gentleness.

"Dangerous," Nitralexis said.

"No. We've got to go through the Italian lines anyway."

"Much climbing," Nitralexis said.

"So it is to Chimara. Ask your friend here." Quayle pointed to the peasant.

"I think you want, you must go to Janina. Yes?"

"Yes," Quayle said.

"Why?"

"Plenty of reasons. I'm going to marry a Greek girl. A Greek girl. Marry."

Nitralexis pulled his black beard and pushed his tin hat back. "You marry? Girl in Janina?"

"Yes. We were to marry to-day. To-day." John pointed his thumb into his chest.

"Ho . . . *Inglisi*." Nitralexis laughed, and said something in rapid Greek to the peasant, who smiled and nodded, and said something back to Nitralexis.

"We go — we go to Tepeleni . . . You will have the girl . . . The Italians will have us . . . Ho . . . *Inglisi* and love!" Nitralexis patted Quayle affectionately on the arm and chuckled into his beard.

"Fine," Quayle said. He picked up the maps.

Quayle looked at the map and started to take directions again. Nitralexis shook his head.

"It is no need, no compass. He — " Nitralexis pointed to the peasant — "will take us. He knows this. It is his country."

"Well, let's go then," Quayle said to them.

Nitralexis told the peasant what they were to do. The young peasant shrugged, turned around. Quayle picked up his belongings.

"What's his name? His name. Who is he?" Quayle asked Nitralexis, pointing to the peasant boy whose cheeks were the reddest Quayle had ever seen.

126

"Deus. You know — it is God, a God. Deus. He is a Greek of Albania. He is of the hills. He found me," Nitralexis said with his bearded mirth. The boy turned around when Nitralexis mentioned his name. His felt cape was majestic across his shoulders. The hood of the cape made it monklike. The fringe across the red forehead made his face the son of a god's. He smiled broadly and white teeth caught in the white sun and looked yellow.

Quayle put the emergency rations, the First Aid kit, the maps, into his cross-shoulder bag, and they started out.

Chapter 16

Deus led them through thick timber where the wind slapped and back-slapped the trees. The direction he took was around the crest of the Lap Martalloe. There were deep valleys all around and other crests. Occasionally Quayle could see the white road way down in one or another of the valleys and the river beside it.

"Which way?" Nitralexis asked him once.

"We're heading due east—" Quayle told him.

Nitralexis said something to Deus. Deus replied without stopping.

"Says we cross road—quicker," Nitralexis said.

"What about the Italians?" Quayle asked him.

"Plenty of them—be dangerous."

Nitralexis discussed it with Deus for a while as they walked, and Quayle dropped behind so they could talk more easily.

"We will cross it at night," Deus told Nitralexis.

"What about the river?" Nitralexis remembered it on the map.

"We cross that too. It is a wide flat stretch. It will be difficult."

"Do you know a place where there aren't many Italians around?"

"No," Deus told him. "There is no such place. They swarm over the road."

"How do we cross the road and the river, then?" Nitralexis asked him.

"At night. We will walk right between the Italians' legs," Deus said.

"All we have to do is get down to the road without being seen. To cross it according to you, God, is like crawling between Italians' legs. Have you ever crawled between an Italian's legs?"

"It will be difficult," Deus admitted. "The Italians are frightened people. They shoot quickly."

"That, I know," Nitralexis said to Deus.

"Perhaps I should have the *Inglisi's* pistol," Deus said.

Nitralexis knew that Deus had been eyeing the Colt 45. It would be worth a fortune to Deus, such a pistol. Deus would steal it if he couldn't get it by other means. Nitralexis knew that Deus would shoot them both, without malice, if it would get him the pistol.

"The *Inglisi* will give it you when you get us through the Italians to the Greeks."

"He will?" Deus said it as a question.

"The *Inglisi* has promised me. The *Inglisi* is very trustworthy, you know that."

"What is face like behind his blood?" Deus asked.

"He is like a calf, very young. He is the best fighter the *Inglisi* have."

"Why did he get fall then?" Deus asked.

"He was saving his fellows. He shot down fifteen Italians that day."

"He has a fine jacket."

"It is very poor. It has surface charm only." Nitralexis was afraid Deus would do something about Quayle's coat as well. He would have to warn Quayle to keep his pistol empty. Deus would be more dangerous than the Italians sometimes. But he was a fine boy.

"You keep pistol without bullets," Nitralexis said to Quayle over his shoulder. "This one . . . he would take the pistol. Keep it careful. If he gets it he will leave us. He will do most of things to get it."

"You can carry it if you like. It's bloody heavy. I don't want it," Quayle said.

"Keep to it. He will be doubting. I have promised to him you give it when he delivers us to the Greek."

"I'll give it to him any time he likes. It's too heavy."

"No. He will leave us if you do. Keep it."

They were climbing now and the path was difficult. There were great rock stretches, and the trouble was getting over them and through the thick timber. The high wind made all sounds confusing and they were always falling flat to earth when one or the other thought he heard approaching people. Quayle got hungry and chewed on one of the chocolate bars. Nitralexis was eating hard brown bread. The road below was getting more directly beneath them. Quayle saw by his map they were still travelling due east. Occasionally when the road did come into view, he saw movement of vehicles and men on it.

The three of them started to move down the slope in the late afternoon. Quayle was getting stiffer and they had to go slowly. By evening they were half-way down the slope and the road was in full view. Deus stopped in a tight clump of plane trees.

"We will sleep here," he said to Nitralexis.

"Aren't we near enough to cross the road to-night?" Nitralexis pointed at the road.

"We must observe first." Deus took off his felt cape. He looked at Quayle, who was sitting down with his head leaning on his knees.

"He is with pain," Deus said to Nitralexis.

"No. He's all right. That is the way the English rest themselves. He's all right."

Quayle looked up and asked what they were stopping for.

"We sleep. To-morrow we observe. The road is filled with Italians. We must wait."

Quayle lay down as he was. His head was heavy and thick again and he couldn't move his legs properly. He was weary but not tired. He looked solidly at the earth before him and fell asleep.

Deus and Nitralexis waited for each other to move. Finally Deus wrapped his cape around his shoulders and lay down. Nitralexis blew his nose with his fingers and did the same.

Quayle awakened suddenly. There was a purple moon again. He knew something had been happening. He looked around for

Nitralexis. He wasn't there. Deus was gone too. He thought suddenly that they had left him. He sat up. The pain hurt him. Nitralexis appeared.

"The Italians are near as your skin," he said in a whisper.

"Where?"

"Down below. Listen."

Quayle listened. He heard voices and laughter. He was suddenly drawing breath.

"Where's Deus?" he asked.

"He's looking at the Italians," Nitralexis said.

"Why don't we shift out of here?"

"We safe. We are safe, if we are still."

Quayle felt for his pistol. It was gone.

"Deus has taken my gun," Quayle said in a whisper.

"No. I have taken it. I took it. He tried to take it but I had already take it. I will keep it.

Quayle could feel that the little square pouch for ammunition on his belt was empty.

"Did you take the ammunition too?" he asked Nitralexis.

"In the gun?"

"No. I keep it in this little pouch," Quayle said.

"No. I did not," Nitralexis said. "Deus must take that. He did, uh?"

"How do I know? Yes — he must have. There's none in the gun, either."

"So we have the pistol. Deus has the bullets." Nitralexis laughed softly.

"How will you get it back?"

"We will not let him know about shot. He would then be afraid and leave us, but follow, and he would squash our throats in sleep. Oh no. We will be silent. He does not know where the gun is."

"What's he doing now?" Quayle asked.

"He observes the Italians. He will be back. He is a fine boy if he doesn't kill us."

Quayle could hear the Italians very plainly. He recognized a few words.

Deus suddenly appeared on his knees, very quietly. He was smiling.

"The Italians are small. We will be safe here until morning. Do you know what they say?" he said to Nitralexis.

"No. I know not. If we are safe we will sleep again."

"Yes. We will move higher up when the sun shows." Deus was already lying down.

Nitralexis told Quayle to go to sleep again. He was still feeling heavy enough to accept the idea carelessly. He went to sleep immediately.

It was Deus who woke him up. He was smiling into Quayle's face with wide-open eyes and a friendly expression. It didn't convey the idea that he would shoot them both for the pistol. But Quayle was not up to thinking it out. Guns in Albania were plentiful, he figured. With the Greeks and Italians fighting in it . . . But they would be hard to get for the Albanian mountain people. They were afraid of the airplanes, so they did not make raids on the Italians for guns, fearing reprisals.

"O. K.," Quayle said in English.

Deus beamed some more and said "*Horkai*" in imitation. Quayle nodded in friendship. Nitralexis awoke. In the quiet approach to morning light, they moved up the slope until they came to a prominent clump of timber on a rock hanging over the slope. From here they could see the road yawning in the now clear morning light.

"We will observe," Deus said to Nitralexis.

Nitralexis nodded and smiled broadly at Quayle.

"I am at work again. I observe. I wish for my Bréguet, though. How I wish!"

Quayle lay down again to sleep so that the pain would go away. Deus looked at him and asked Nitralexis if the pain was great in Quayle's head or his body.

"Both," Nitralexis said.

"If he dies you will give me the pistol?" Deus said.

"He will not die. You will get the pistol when we are with the Greeks."

"Thank you. I hope he does not die," Deus said and leant over the rock to watch the road.

When Quayle awakened again the sun was high above him and he felt warm. His pain was slightly better and he felt his legs were less stiff. He could see Nitralexis eating stale bread again. He smiled at Quayle and chuckled into his beard.

"You sleep like an Italian. The Italians are great sleepers."

"Thanks," Quayle said.

"You wish some bread?"

"I've got some chocolate. Where's Deus this time?"

"He is looking at the road and the river. He is very serious."

"He is a fine boy if he doesn't kill us," Quayle mocked.

"That is right," and Nitralexis laughed into his beard.

Quayle felt very unclean and wanted to tear off the tight silk bandages that covered his head and face. Instead he cupped water from his canteen in his hand and soaked the bandages. Nitralexis offered to do it for him. Quayle shook his head.

"You will not get poison, no?"

"That ointment will stop it — I hope," Quayle said. "How's your arm?"

"I had forgotten it." Nitralexis smiled, shrugged and patted his arm.

"When do we cross this road?" Quayle asked him.

"To-night perhaps. Deus will say. We will do what he says. If he doesn't kill us, he will get us out of this Italian warmer."

"I'm in a hurry," Quayle said.

"It is very bad for your girl. She will think you are dead. She will not wait?"

"She might not. I'll take a chance," Quayle said. "Just so long as the Germans don't get there before us."

"Perhaps they have started the war with us." Nitralexis was serious.

"Maybe. I hope to Christ they haven't. We've got to get to Janina before they do."

"Life has some dangers, isn't it?" Nitralexis said quietly.

"It certainly has." Quayle pressed his hands lightly on his face. It was still swollen massively and he could feel the bad places where the gashes were. The blood was hard and scratched the wounds when he turned his face. He knew that it would be serious if he didn't get to a hospital soon.

Deus came back in the late afternoon. He was muddy all over. His hair was wet and plastered on his rosy forehead. His cape had brown wet streaks on it. He smiled at Quayle. Quayle nodded his head. Deus held his head with his hands and rocked his head. Quayle nodded.

"We will be all right to-night. But there are many Italian camps," Deus said to Nitralexis. "Can the *Inglisi* walk quietly on his stomach?"

"He can walk all right. The pain is only his head. In his country he is well known for his stomach-walking," Nitralexis said.

Quayle offered Deus a piece of his bar of chocolate. Deus looked at Nitralexis.

"Go on," Nitralexis said. "It is chocolate. It's all right."

Deus took the chocolate and smiled broadly at Quayle. He bit the chocolate carefully and opened his eyes wide like a child.

"It has sweetness. Do *Inglisi* eat this always?" he said.

"No — but nearly always. Everybody eats it."

"It has much sweetness. It is very glorious."

Deus smiled at Quayle again and sat down chewing the chocolate. Quayle lay down again and thought himself to sleep above the pain in his head.

He woke up again with the movement around him. He did not want to move. He was still exhausted and his head felt thick. Only his legs were somewhat better. The night was open with moonlight again. There were deep white clouds to the south. There were dark clouds coming low from the Lap Martalloe. It would rain soon.

"We are going?" he asked Nitralexis.

"Yes. You are all right? We have to walk upon stomachs."

"Whose stomachs?"

"We will walk flat. You understand?"

"Yes," Quayle said. "It's going to rain."

"No matter. Come on."

Nitralexis helped Quayle to his feet. Deus was smoothing the surface of the ground where they had been sleeping. They started down the slope again with Deus leading and Nitralexis coming up behind Quayle. Deus held the branches of the trees he ran into, carefully, so they wouldn't swish. He walked slowly and quietly. They did not talk, but sometimes they stopped in their tracks when they thought they heard a noise. Quayle heard talking to the right of him once. Sometimes small boulders would slip ahead of them and the noise would key their nerves.

Then it rained. The moon had been closed by the clouds and the rain hit the leaves with that slight definiteness, then hit the earth with the round sound, and the rock with the quiet splash of its size. They were at the place where they slept the night before. From here on it was going to be dangerous.

They crept quietly from here and, using their hands, they levered themselves down the abrupt drops. Once Quayle saw a fire two hundred yards to the left in a clearing. They passed another Italian camp near by. He knew because he could smell it. It was a long time in his mind that they kept going down the slope. The rain was soaking him now and it cleared his head. He was far more directly conscious of what they were doing.

When the slope graded out, Deus almost stopped. He took every step carefully and very quietly, and often he stopped dead. They came to a clearing and before him Quayle saw the road. He could see the streaks of rain where there was no timber, and the road. It seemed to be clear and empty. Deus sat down in the little creek bed that ran from the road. The other two waited for him to move. He moved out on his stomach and slowly wormed his way up the wet grass in the damp rain. Quayle followed, peering into the darkness. His pistol belt kept sticking in the ground and he cursed within himself. Nitralexis was behind him and he seemed to be making a lot of noise. Deus stopped twice and Quayle waited for something to happen.

They were nearly to the road when they heard the engine. It came nearer and Quayle could see Deus flattening close to the earth. He put his head down as a truck with dimmed blue-painted lights came down the slight turn in the road and rumbled past them. There was another one behind it. They clung to the earth as the convoy passed. The faint blue light flicked over them and Quayle expected one of them to stop and find them.

When the convoy had gone, Deus crawled through the mud towards the road. Quayle eased his way forward on his elbows. At the road, which was built up, Deus got into a crouching position. He touched Quayle on the shoulder, nodded his head, and stood up slightly. Crouching he moved quickly up the rise and crossed the road. Quayle followed him and felt the hard gravel crunching under his boots. He fell into the ditch on the other side and Nitralexis came.

Deus started moving forward again. They crossed the wet grass and Quayle felt the rain getting down his neck. It seemed they were crawling for hours in the dark. They could hear voices all the time now. When they got to the river they were glad of its running sound. Deus stopped again and they sat crouching in a small circular dip in the earth.

Deus whispered something to Nitralexis.

"This is not deep," Nitralexis whispered to Quayle. "There are some Italians the other side. We must be careful then. If something happens we will keep going upwards. There is a dead river running upwards."

"O. K.," Quayle said quietly.

"*Horkai.*" Deus turned around and smiled. They moved off again.

The water was very cold and swift running. It was seldom above the knees. They crouched close to the surface. Sometimes the water seeped through John Quayle's Irvin suit and got into his stomach and almost made him utter sound. They got across it all right and lay down on the white-pebbled bank. Deus moved slowly forward then dropped quickly. The others followed. Quayle felt the pain in his head as he hit the earth. There was someone walking. He waited for something to happen.

They moved forward again into a rising crevice that was the dead river. They were making a lot of noise because the pebbles underfoot slipped. Suddenly there was a shout in Italian.

"Hola . . . Hola!"

They fell flat.

"Hola . . . Who's there?" again.

This is not right, Quayle was thinking. If he hears a noise and no one answers him, he'll suspect something. He tried to think of some simple Italian word that would answer him, but could not and knew there would be more questions and he could not answer them, so he lay quietly.

"Hola . . . Hey . . . Get up, Ansaldo — There is noise over there."

"Oh — be quiet." That was apparently Ansaldo.

"It is real noise, I inform you," the Italian said.

"If it's the Greek Army, shoot them and be quiet."

There was silence again. The three of them lay still and Quayle could feel himself moving above the earth when he breathed and the pounding and vibration of his tenseness hitting the earth and coming back into his body. They lay there for half an hour. It was one third of all time, to Quayle. . . . Deus carefully moved forward again.

Quayle lifted himself carefully and followed. He could hear Nitralexis behind him. Suddenly there was a quiet slipping of pebbles and a clear sound.

"Ansaldo!" said the Italian. Then: "I fire if there is no answer."

"Great sleepers, these Italians. I sleep like them. They're touchy — what the hell do they get het up about? Why can't they just let the sound alone? They're too jumpy," Quayle was thinking. Then came the three shots. . . .

They hit the earth way to the right of them. Then suddenly Deus moved. He picked up a large stone and hurled it down towards the river. It crashed into the undergrowth.

"Ansaldo," the Italian called. Then there were more shots. Deus moved quickly upward. Quayle followed close, stumbling over the slippery wet rock into the dark rain which beat heavily upon them. He could hear the voices again. Quayle laughed within himself because it was like playing games when he was young. You throw a rock to distract attention somewhere else. It is simple like that, he was thinking; danger isn't complicated as you think it will be. It is simple. This whole thing is simple. He was almost running now to keep up with Deus, who was crouching into a lope, and he could hear Nitralexis behind him. They could hear the voices way behind, then Ansaldo calling upon the Saints to get them some sleep. . . .

And soon they were out of earshot, and the three of them were crouching upwards along the dead river. They went on into the night.

Chapter 17

There was depth of sunlight above them. They were on the high mountain over the valley, where the road and the river were running almost due south. Quayle was lying on his back with the bandages off his face. He had bathed the wounds with water from his canteen. He wanted to get the air into them. The wind was cold, but the sun warmed his face without hurting his head. Deus looked at him from where he sat chewing at the hard bread he had produced from somewhere on his person.

"He is unlike the calf," he said to Nitralexis.

"He is unlike the calf because he is strong. But without the blood his face is like the calf," Nitralexis said.

Deus smiled at Quayle. The peasant's red cheeks were unmarked by growing beard. He was still smooth because he was young. Quayle had grown a beard through the wounds and it was black because of the blood.

"You are certain he will give me the fine pistol?" Deus said.

"The *Inglisi* can be trusted. He trusts you — therefore you can trust him."

Deus nodded.

Then Quayle looked up because he heard the sound of engines. He was doubtful at first, but then he was sure.

"What's that?" he said without thinking.

"*Airoplanos,*" Nitralexis said. "Yes! *Airoplanos!*"

They were both standing up now. They could hear the steady deepness of aircraft engines. It was regular and vibrating. Nitralexis and Quayle shaded their eyes and looked to the north. They could see nothing. Gradually the regularity of the engines was undecided and the up and down hum of multiple-engined aircraft became distinct.

"There," Nitralexis said, pointing to the north-east.

Quayle could see the large formation getting nearer. They were in three groups. There would be at least fifty planes in each group. They were about ten thousand feet and in good formation.

"Christ—Hundreds of them," Quayle said.

Gradually they came near enough to distinguish the details of their construction. Quayle shaded his eyes and looked at them carefully. He realized suddenly what they were.

"Germans!" he said to Nitralexis. "They're Dornier 17's."

The long pencil-shaped planes were solid in their formation and were carefully grouped. They were definite in their shape. Quayle could see the second large group clearly too. They were mixed Junkers 86's and Heinkel 111K's. The Heinkels' clear oval fuselage was massive-looking though they were smaller planes than the long thin Dorniers.

"So now we have the Germans too," Nitralexis said.

"I wonder when it started. Christ almight—"

"Somebody will have many bombs from that lot," Nitralexis said.

"We'd better get going. Ask Deus when we get through the Italian lines."

Deus was looking at the bombers. "*Inglisi*," he said to Quayle.

"Germans," Nitralexis told him.

"They fight too," he said.

"Now they do. We've got to get forward before they do."

"How long will it be before we are with the Greeks?"

"Perhaps to-morrow night we will see them. We must be careful."

"We must get to Janina before the Germans," Nitralexis said to Deus.

"Perhaps to-morrow night we can get through the Italians' legs."

"Well—let's go," Quayle interrupted them. He was winding the dirty bandage around his head. "What's he saying?" Quayle nodded to Deus.

"He says we may be within the Greeks by to-morrow night."

"Fine. Let's go. I wonder when this started," Quayle said half to himself.

Deus led them along the side of the high mountain as the bombers disappeared to the south. Quayle looked at his map, saw their own course was due south now. That would lead them to the road which went back to Janina. . . . That's probably where the Germans are going, Quayle was thinking. They'll go to Janina because it's the key town for this whole front. The Germans have sense that way. They would probably flatten it with bombers first. If they had not flattened it already. Quayle put the maps away and concentrated on the rough path that slipped down the high mountain towards the valley.

All that day they heard bombers going over. Sometimes they could see the planes, and they were always German. Sometimes they could not see the planes but they heard bombing. Quayle was thinking that if the Germans had started their advance into Greece, the Italians would be attacking too, so they would have to walk right through a battle.

During the second day from the high mountain they moved in a great circle around the level area, until at night they had reached a small plateau overlooking a wide Italian encampment and the road between Tepeleni and Klisura. They could hear the artillery from both sides somewhere to the south, and the Italian transport on the road never seemed to stop.

"We wait here," Deus said when they sat down on the small plateau.

"How long?" Nitralexis asked.

"Until darkness. We must cross the road again. It is difficult."

Nitralexis told Quayle, and they all lay on their stomachs and watched the activity in the Italian camp until complete darkness made only the sounds clear. Then Deus stood up and started carefully down the steep slope from the plateau.

"Do we go right through that camp?" Quayle said.

"No — we go around it."

They were moving very fast as Deus chose good footholds and kept the movement decisive. When they reached the end of the slope Deus motioned them to lie still. Quayle could hear the deep continuous boom of the artillery, much nearer now. He could hear the Italians talking in the camp to the left. Then Deus moved on his stomach out into the open. Quayle followed him.

Slowly they moved and Quayle could see the clear outline of big Italian Diesel trucks ahead of them. Deus stopped when he saw them. He's miscalculated, Quayle was thinking. He didn't expect those trucks to be there. This is going to be fine.

Deus had not expected the trucks to be there. He looked at them now and then wormed his way in a right-angle turn to a clump of bushes. The others followed him. From there they crawled parallel to the road and came to an open space.

"It is wrong," Deus whispered to Nitralexis. "We have come too far."

"Well —"

"You are in a hurry? There are chances to be taken."

"We take chances?" Nitralexis asked Quayle with mild humour.

"Sure — what's wrong? Let's get going," Quayle whispered.

"We take chances," Nitralexis told Deus.

"*Horkai,*" whispered Deus and patted Quayle on the back.

They crawled into the open space. Quayle noticed the bulk shapes with tree boughs on them. It suddenly struck him: Tanks. They were crawling through a tank dispersal area, only they weren't too dispersed. He saw the tracks of one when they crawled close to it. Deus fell flat as a guard passed along the road which was less than twenty yards ahead of them. It was too early for the moon to be very clear and Quayle couldn't see what was beyond the road. He kept close to the soft grass earth and followed Deus as he wormed inch by inch to the road. They stopped again when the guard paused up the road.

"*Horkai,*" whispered Deus.

"Come on," Quayle said to Nitralexis and together they crouched across the road and dropped close to it in a ditch on the other side. Quayle looked ahead and saw a wide clear space with shapes of big guns and limbers strewn around.

They crawled through a field of soft mud into a ploughed stretch and Quayle felt the dampness seep into his sheepskin boots. They crawled along to the timber clump that outlined itself against the clear sky.

"Wait," Deus said to Nitralexis. "I will see."

Deus moved forward and Quayle was restrained by Nitralexis.

"He observes," Nitralexis said.

"What's wrong now?"

"Nothing. We came too far. Those Italians sleep well. Yes?"

"*Shhh*. You'll wake them up and we'll do some sleeping."

"How comes your face, *Inglisi*?"

Quayle was surprised because that was the first time Nitralexis had asked him about it. It must be that we're both scared, Quayle thought.

"It's fine. Where's that young bastard gone?"

"He will be back," Nitralexis said. "I have the ammunition back. Here." Nitralexis handed Quayle the ammunition and Quayle put it back in the pouch. Deus came back without any sound following him.

"We have more such places to go through. It will be long," he said to Nitralexis. "Is the *Inglisi* all right?"

"He's fine."

"We go then, but be very careful. The Italians do not sleep well to-night."

"Go on then," Nitralexis whispered.

They crawled into the timber that was beyond the small clearing. They seemed to make a terrific noise when there was timber to reflect the sound. They kept stopping, and Quayle felt his vibration in the earth every time they flattened out. Soon they were in another open space that was a camp for Diesel trucks and motor cycles. Quayle became more amazed at what they

143

were doing as they crawled around the edge of the camp without being seen.

When they reached the river Quayle could hear its shallow water slow on the pebbled edge — also the quiet deep water that swirled in the center. He could see the moon now and the shallow light across the flat stretch of white water that was silver.

"It is deep," Deus said. "We will move together."

Nitralexis repeated that to Quayle.

They walked into the shallow water and the swiftness got dimensional as the water got deep, until Quayle was up to his neck. He could feel the Irvin jacket getting heavy but he could not take it off now. Deus was downstream from him, and Nitralexis was holding onto both of them as suddenly the depth of water was too great and they were swimming. The water rushed into their bodies and Quayle could feel Deus grasping him tightly on the neck. He was almost sinking as he struggled to move forward with breaststroke. Nitralexis was behind him, but Deus was holding on . . . until he suddenly let go. . . . Quayle saw him shoot down the current. He felt his kit bag tangling in his legs. He pulled it off his shoulder and went after Deus. Quayle could hear him splashing, then suddenly saw him in a white moonlight stretch. He pushed his arms wide and kicked widely until he got to Deus. He grasped him by the heavy felt cape and almost went under as Deus struggled to hold onto him. Quayle went under and felt his feet on the bottom. When he came up he found he still had hold of Deus. He pulled the water with his left arm and kicked and heard the splash of his kick and repeated it until he thought he could not do it any more and would be carried all the way downstream, and then his feet found the bottom.

He pulled Deus up into the shallows and lay there drawing deep breaths. He could hear Deus breathing. He wondered where Nitralexis was. Deus did not move, so Quayle leant over him and rolled him on his stomach. He pulled off the sodden cape and put his hands into the small of Deus' back. He leaned forward and then back. As the respiration worked it did not expel water so much as it forced Deus back into consciousness. He uttered a quiet sound and turned over on his side and was sick. He looked up at Quayle, and in the dim light of the white moon Quayle could see him looking. Quayle nodded to him. Deus was sick again and Quayle was scared that the noise would bring some of the Italians down on them. He heard a sound in the water and lay flat. He could hear the movement — then guessed it was Nitralexis.

"Hey — " he said in a whisper.

"*Inglisi?*"

"Yes," Quayle said quietly.

"You got him?"

"Yes. He is here being sick."

Nitralexis came out of the shallow water to the bank.

"Ho — he looks he is finished," Nitralexis said in Greek.

"You will say I am grateful to the *Inglisi?*"

"Yes," then, "He says he thanks you," Nitralexis said to Quayle.

"I had visions of our trying to get through the Italian lines without him," Quayle said.

"He says he has grown to like you. You are his friend. He could not let you see the bottom of the stream for a deathbed," Nitralexis told Deus. Deus nodded and said nothing. He pulled his wet cape and stood up. He wavered, then bent over and was sick again.

"*Shhh,*" Quayle said.

"He'll be all right." Nitralexis was chuckling in his beard.

They helped Deus as they started the climb up the slope. It was difficult, and Deus was being sick all the time. He had thrown his peasant cape away and Quayle was thinking of doing the same with his Irvin jacket, which was sodden with water. But he was reluctant and pushed on with it unzipped. They had been climbing for an hour when Deus said, "This is high enough."

"All right, God. Just keep your insides inside," Nitralexis said.

"*Horkai,*" Deus said, then collapsed.

Quayle bent over him and shook him. Deus didn't stiffen. He was completely unconscious. Quayle rolled him on his stomach and applied artificial respiration again.

145

"It is not water," Nitralexis said.

"Well, we can't move without him."

"He said to follow the road."

"And after that, what do we do then?"

Nitralexis shrugged. He bent over Deus and slapped his hands and face. "You have water?"

Quayle gave him the canteen.

Nitralexis poured a few drops on Deus' head. Quayle was sarcastic. "He's had enough water. He's just gone to sleep."

"Well, we sleep then." Nitralexis sat down.

Quayle turned Deus on his back and straightened his legs.

"I hope to Christ he wakes up soon. We haven't got much time before morning."

While they waited for Deus to wake up, Quayle and Nitralexis listened to the persistent artillery. It was to the south and east.

"There is some battle," Nitralexis said.

"Yes, and we'll be in it," Quayle said.

"Well, I wish I had my Bréguet."

"I think I'd sooner be here than in that," Quayle said.

"What difference is there?"

It was dawn before Deus woke up. He was sick immediately. Quayle and Nitralexis were both awake. Quayle was very hungry and he wished he hadn't dropped the kit bag in the stream.

"How do you feel?" Nitralexis asked Deus.

"I am filled with greenness. I left my good feelings in the river."

"Well — can you walk?"

"Yes — but it is day — we cannot move in day."

"Why? Come on, let's go."

"It is dangerous. We are within the middle of the Italian's stomach."

"Well — we've got to move."

Deus shook his head.

"He won't move in day," Nitralexis explained to Quayle.

"Tell him we'll go on without him."

"That's no good." Nitralexis turned to Deus. "The *Inglisi* says he has saved you. Now he would like to ask of you his life. He wants us to go on."

Deus shook his head and lay back. Then he sat up and was sick. He looked at Quayle, and Quayle noticed his cheeks were still red, but had greyness in them because he was so sick. Quayle nodded to him.

"*Horkai,*" Deus said. He stood up.

"Come on, *Inglisi,*" he said to Quayle in Greek.

As they walked along the rough edge of the slope they could see the road winding around the valley following the river. The artillery was getting louder. It was hard to tell whether it was behind or before them now, it was so close. Then Quayle saw it bursting to the right, down near the road.

"That's yours, I should say," he said to Nitralexis.

"It is Greek, it is good. Look."

A string of shells burst along the side of the road. It was good shooting, but Quayle could not see anything worth shooting at, not from this distance. Suddenly there was the quick whine and a white puff came through the red earth above them. They all fell flat.

"We're right in the middle of it," Quayle said.

There was a deep sound from above them.

"Italians — that is their cannon," Nitralexis said. "Come on."

The three of them crouched and loped along in the timber, falling flat when they heard the shells bursting above them. Then a quiet quick unpleasant rap of a light machine-gun. It was somewhere below and ahead of them. Quayle looked in the direction of the sound but couldn't see anything. They fell flat when they heard another shell burst above them on the slope. This one was nearer.

"They must be shooting at us. They must see us."

"The stupid bastards — Come on." Quayle was helping Deus along as they ran.

"There's the Greeks." Nitralexis pointed to the white puff of a shell bursting on the side of the mountain facing them. "That must be."

They were running and loping, and there were more shells bursting above them so that the loose rock on the slope rolled down behind them. The white bursts were still throwing up along the road. Then the machine-guns opened up again.

They kept running and crouching until Deus stopped and said to Nitralexis: —

"We are near — We must get into the valley. The Greek is there. He must have retreated to there. He should be where we are now."

"We should go up into the timber," Nitralexis said.

"No, straight on. They will see you running upwards."

"It's nearer," Nitralexis said.

"No — straight ahead." Deus pulled at Quayle and pointed ahead. Quayle nodded. They got up, but the machine-gun started again. Then Quayle saw Nitralexis running up the slope in the clearing, up towards the timber.

"Get down," he shouted. Nitralexis kept running. Then the machine-gun came loud again and Quayle didn't hear the bullets, but saw Nitralexis loosen his feet on the earth and fall as he ran staggering sideways, and slip to earth; and Quayle knew he had been hit more than once. Deus pulled at him and Quayle crouched after Deus as he ran ahead into the timber, and heard the soft bullets over his head but didn't drop, but kept on until he got to the timber. Deus had crouched flat into a rock cleft. Quayle looked behind. Nitralexis was lying on his side in the open. He was awkward-looking and looked ended, because he was without any support from his body but loose against the earth; and Quayle knew he was dead.

They heard the Italians shouting below them. Deus was pulling Quayle's arm. He had the pistol. He was pointing to the empty chambers. He wanted the ammunition. Quayle quickly wondered when Deus had taken the pistol from Nitralexis, and what he would do with it if he gave him the ammunition. He looked at Deus, then opened the square pouch on his canvas pouch and pulled out the small box. He spilled some of the squat bullets into his outstretched hand and gave him the box. Deus rammed the bullets into the chambers and clicked the barrel shut and Quayle wondered how he had known what to do with the gun.

As the Italians came up the slope, Deus pointed ahead and they ran again, crouching into the timber and falling when the machine-gun fired. They came to the beginning of the valley and could hear the movement of feet somewhere behind and below them. They crouched forward and slipped down the valley. Deus waited for Quayle, then pointed ahead and pushed Quayle — motioning him to run across the shallow-dipping earth. The machine-gun opened up again.

"*Horkai. Horkai.*" Deus nodded vigorously and pointed ahead.

"O. K.," Quayle said through his quick-drawing breath.

Deus pushed him forward as they heard movement behind them.

"*Horkai, Inglisi,*" he said with quick breath again. He pointed ahead.

He took Quayle's hand, then released it and turned around and ran back up the slope. Quayle drew breath, then ran across the wide slope in the opposite direction and could hear the machine-guns firing at him. Then he heard the quick sharp explosion of the pistol — then again — and he ran wide and fast across the rock until he stumbled and fell. He lay there panting. He heard the pistol again, and again. The machine-gun vibrated and Quayle looked behind. He saw Deus running flat up the slope and firing the pistol behind him. He heard the machine-gun, and saw Deus stagger — then get up again — and the machine-gun vibrated again. Quayle saw him limping in a flat crouch up the slope. He could see the pistol in Deus' hand. He saw him lie flat suddenly, and lift the pistol and fire. There was the puff of smoke and the delay in the sound reaching Quayle. Then he saw Deus standing up and empty-ing the pistol into the timber until he had no ammunition left. Quayle saw the Italian running up with the sub-machine-gun. He was waiting for Deus to hurl the pistol at him, but he hung onto it, turned, and started to run up the slope. The sub-machine-gun vibrated quickly, and with malice. Deus fell, and the pistol went high in the air and fell into the timber. Quayle could see him lying with the earth, grotesquely and with death as Nitralexis had.

Quayle drew a quick breath and ran again. He kept running until he could hear the machine-gun near him at the right. He staggered and could feel his head bursting and the blood running out of his face. And then he saw the dung-coloured uniform. He saw the gun and put his hands wide, and shouted *"Inglisi, Inglisi"* as loud as he could. He saw the gun come up. *"Inglisi. Inglisi,"* he shouted again. He knew he was crying and it was his life that was crying.

"Inglisi, Inglisi," he said, and his hands were in the air as he stumbled forward and he saw the Greek run to him. He felt the arms grip him and felt the pain and staggered along with the Greek.

"Inglisi," he said. "I'm *Inglisi,"* he was muttering from his head that was bursting.

And he fell limp in the Greek's hands.

Chapter 18

There was silence. He had never heard such silence. There was no sound. Not a sound . . . Silence always had some sound. But this was wrong. There was completely none, thoroughly and utterly no sound. There were objects without silence being silent. It was aggressive and it was directed at him. Such silence . . . Such silence . . . Where is the rushing sound? There is no such stillness. Such silence . . . such silence . . . Come on now — be normal silence, with stillness but with the rushing noise and the detail. Such silence . . .

There was the rushing noise he asked for. Then he opened his eyes. He could see himself running to the Greek and he could hear the artillery, no it was machine-guns, not artillery. He had forgotten when he was running about the artillery. He could hear only the machine-guns, but there was artillery there. Ah — my word yes — you can't kid me — I know there was. And he saw the bread. There was a pile of bread. It was brown with bursting edges like a split sausage, and he didn't believe it. He sat up.

"Where . . . ?" he said, and he was surprised at his voice.

Someone came in. He heard the artillery. "What is it?" Quayle said.

"*Inglisi,*" he heard the voice. He expected Nitralexis. It was a little Greek with the dung-coloured uniform which was a contrast to Nitralexis', who always wore blue. Yes, it was a copy of the British blue.

Someone else came in. He had a big overcoat and a peaked cap.

"Huh. You are awake." He heard the clipped English.

"Yes," he said. "What is it?"

"You're all right," he heard the Greek. It was the one with the peaked cap.

"Yes. I know. I'm sorry. I know that. I'm very sorry."

"That's all right. Here — here's some cognac."

He gave Quayle the enamel mug, and Quayle drank the cognac, and he felt the pain of its taste. He shook his head and felt its warmth. He looked up and saw the Greek in the peaked cap.

"Thanks," he said with the first coherence.

"You're all right," the Greek said.

"Yes. Where is this?"

"This is our hut. You're all right, you were lucky."

"I know."

Quayle got off the bunk and stood up. He felt the circular motion of the earth move to his head, but he was all right. He could hear the artillery, so he was all right.

"I want to get to Janina," he said. "Are the Germans there yet?"

"With Christ . . . No . . . no . . ."

"I've got to get going. How can I get there? Where's the road?" The Greek smiled.

"It's all right. The Germans aren't there yet."

"How near are they?"

"I don't know. We don't know anything up here. Everything's gone wrong. They've bombed Janina a lot. We lost contact with the General there for yesterday. He says it is bad there. We are retreating everywhere."

"What about the Australians, the British?" Quayle said. He was looking at the bread and he felt hungry. "Can I have some of that?" He pointed to the bread.

"Sure," the Greek said. "The *Inglisi* are on the other side of the Pindus. We do not know about them. . . . There are Germans coming down from Koritza."

"Can I get back to Janina before them?"

"Yes — you will be all right. Don't worry . . ."

"I'm not worrying, but I've got to get back to Janina. Will you show me how to get to the road?"

"That's all right." Quayle was breaking the bread and putting it in his tunic pocket. The Greek watched him. The little Greek

152

gave him another mug of cognac. Quayle drank it in a gulp, filling his mouth, then swallowing it. "Will you show me?" he said. He walked to the door.

"Can you travel?"

"Yes — if I can get to the road." Quayle opened the door and the white sunlight astonished him. He shaded his eyes. He could hear the artillery very distinctly now.

"If you wait for a minute he will go with you." The Greek in the peaked cap indicated with his head the small Greek. He said something to the small Greek and he went away.

"He's gone to get his things."

"I don't want to put you to any bother. Can you spare him?"

"What difference does it make? One man won't make any difference now."

"Thank you," Quayle said. He was thinking of Nitralexis, but the time with Nitralexis was so separate from what was happening now that he could not feel what there was to be felt about both of them being killed. He felt nothing. Absolutely completely nothing.

The little Greek came back with a rolled blanket over his shoulder. He had another one. He smiled and showed yellow teeth. He gave the extra rolled blanket to Quayle. The Greek in the peaked cap told him what to do.

"Get him to Janina," he told the small one. "Get him on the trucks going back and get him to Janina. Then come back here. It's all clear."

"I understand," the small one said. He took the order the Greek had written out for him. He nodded to Quayle and Quayle stepped out of the stone hut. He walked a few steps in the mud. As if as an afterthought he turned.

"Good-bye. And thank you. Thank you for everything."

"That's all right," the Greek with the peaked cap said. "I wish I were going with you." Quayle looked at his quiet face and saw that he meant it.

He walked with the little Greek along the mud-deep path. It was

153

fine to walk not expecting Italians to spring from nowhere. He could see the road and the trucks passing by, beneath them. Just as long as the Germans were not in Janina, he would find Helen there and he could get back to Athens. He was not surprised at the acceptance of a German victory. It was just a matter of mathematics. The way we are it's going to be physically impossible, almost, to beat the Germans on land, he was thinking. We haven't got a chance as we are. There's something so wrong with the army — there must be. There's got to be such a new idea in the army, from the bottom up. No — you're all wet — it's a matter of quantity. We just haven't got the stuff — no materials, no airplanes. It's just that. Look for yourself what would happen if you had an equal number of planes up against the Italians — even the Germans. It must be the same on land. But it's not that simple. You've got to know what to do with the stuff — particularly the army. There it is — you can't get away from it. There it is.

"*Airoplanos,*" he heard the little Greek say.

Quayle listened. He could hear the multiple engines. The little Greek was crouching in the timber at the side of the track.

"Come out of it," Quayle said, "they're miles away." He walked on down the path. The little Greek followed him, looking up all the time.

When they got to the road, the trucks that had just pulled out of a parking space were stopped, jammed up close together. The drivers were standing around up the slope away from the road. They were all peering at the bombers disappearing.

"What is wrong? Do you think they can hit you from there?" the little Greek said to them as he caught up with Quayle. The other Greeks looked at the two of them.

"Who is that? Who is it, you with the stomach in his mouth?"

"*Inglisi.* It's an *Inglisi.* An aviator who was shot down. He walked from Valona. He was up bombing there."

"You talk too much," a big Greek driver said.

"Maybe. But he's got to get to Janina. We will ride in your truck."

"I only go to Argyrokastro."

"Well, we go that far."

There was only memory of sleeping and waking as the others ran into the ditch at the side of the road because there was the sound of airplanes. Quayle slept with his head on his arms across the broad engine-cover in the cabin of the Diesel. Sometimes when he was awake he would see the high uneven mountains around him and the deep valleys below. He would hear the engine of the Diesel struggling, and could see the big Greek changing the gears and pulling the big wheel around. He was too tired to feel the danger and the confusion of what was going on.

At Argyrokastro, where it was night, the little Greek shook him and woke him up. Quayle could see the white buildings and smell the acrid bomb odour as he got down. He followed the little Greek, still half asleep. He could feel the wetness on his face as a light rain came down. There were Greeks everywhere around as they walked through the bombed ruins of the town that was clutching the side of the large white mountain.

"Where are we going?" Quayle said to the little Greek.

The little Greek shook his head and pointed ahead.

They had been walking for more than an hour, and Quayle was beginning to feel his head filling with blood again. He sat down on the wet earth of the road and didn't feel its dampness. He wanted to sleep. The little Greek pulled him up and kept his wide hard hand under Quayle's right arm. And they came to the bridge, where there were trucks coming back onto the road.

"Detour," the little Greek said, and Quayle couldn't see him smiling in the dark.

As a truck loaded with soldiers came up the steep bank from the bridge, the little Greek shouted to the driver: —

"I have an urgent *Inglisi*. I have orders to stop you and get him to Janina."

Quayle could barely hear them talking, he was so tired. He heard the little Greek shouting again, and then felt the pressure under his armpit and walked and stumbled into the back of the truck and felt the hard jerk on his head as he dropped on the floor. He went to sleep immediately though he tried to anchor his crazy thoughts. He kept putting airplane engines piece by piece together until he was about to take off in the engine alone and could hear Tap laughing at the idea of an engine flying.

He was only half conscious of the stopping and the shouting and the confusion that was going on.

"How far?" Quayle said. He could think of no Greek because of his head. The little Greek only smiled.

"How far to Janina? How far . . . ?"

The little Greek nodded and smiled again.

"Oh for Christ sake . . . Can't you see I'm asking how far . . . Janina . . . When . . . ?"

The little Greek nodded, then smiled and held up three fingers.

"Three hours?" Quayle said. He had to shout above the roar of the Diesel. The little Greek nodded.

There was haste along the road. The Greek soldiers, who had been tired before the war started, were too tired to hurry even in retreat. They passed with the Diesel and Quayle saw their faces as the truck passed them. They would look up and shout something, and run sometimes, but they could never catch up with the truck, and they would slow down and go on walking as they were before.

There were the climbing villages that were uncertain because they were empty and bombed to half-destruction. All along the road there were bomb craters. And the planes came almost with daylight. Every time they passed over, the Greeks ran into the brush. Quayle could see why, because he remembered the strafing and they passed big trucks still smoking from the strafing the day before.

He lay on the back of the truck. And if it stopped and the little Greek ran into the bushes because of the planes, Quayle would sing at the top of his voice. And it was all his school days when they wore the white surplices and would sing at the top of their voices for the joy of it, and he sang the same songs that they had sung when they weren't singing church tunes. He was repeating the one about

"I care for nobody, no not I, if nobody cares for me." He couldn't think of it correctly or of the name of it, but he sang *dah-dah's* where he forgot the words.

Then the little Greek would come back and smile unhappily when he saw Quayle swinging his legs and singing he didn't care for anybody. But the little Greek didn't understand the relative quality of danger, and the relative feeling for danger, and what Quayle was doing now was too close in time to the machine-gunning. That was the criterion for danger and though he was always afraid when the bombers went over, he accepted the machine-gunning as a greater danger — and he had lived through that, even if Deus and Nitralexis hadn't — so he would live through any bombing. So he sang and then he got onto the one about "Some folks like to sigh, some folks do, some folks do; some folks like to die — " And then he would sing very loudly: "But that's not me nor you." "Then long live the merry, merry heart — " And he would go on and repeat it. He was not happy. But he was not unhappy either. It was physical impulse that made him sing. He was quite aware of the significance of what was going on around him. It was something-or-other in history. This made it all the more relaxed for him, because he knew it was drawing to a close, and he would get to Janina and get Helen and then he would go back and everything would be over. . . .

When the Greeks stayed out in the timber too long Quayle would get impatient.

"Come on back, you silly bastards," he would shout. "They're miles away." The Greeks would take no notice of him, so he would go on singing.

The Diesel stopped when it got to the crossroads near Doliana. There were large groups of Greek soldiers standing around at the roads and a mile of vehicles. It was confusion. There were no officers around and nobody seemed to be doing anything about straightening the mess out. The little Greek went up to see what was causing the blockage. He was gone for a long time. Quayle got out of the truck, went into the timber and relieved himself. When he came back the little Greek was looking excitedly for him.

157

"*Inglisi — Inglisi — Allemands Janina — Allemands Janina*," he said.

"What the hell? Jesus if I don't hear some English soon . . . ! I'm getting fed up."

"*Allemands, Janina*," the little Greek repeated. The little Greek went away and Quayle looked around at the confusion wondering what to do. Then the little Greek came back. He had a tall bearded Greek with him, who looked like Jesus Christ, and had yellow corporal stripes on his arm.

"*Entschuldigen Sie,*" he said in German.

"Yes. You speak German?" Quayle said in German.

"Yes. This one here says you wish to go to Janina."

"That's right," Quayle said. "What's this about the Germans' being there?"

"It is true, they say here. No one will move because they say the Germans are in Janina."

"How do they know?"

"They do not know. They *say* they know."

"How could the Germans get there?"

"I do not know. I only know what they say."

"How far is it?" Quayle asked him.

"Some hours."

"Thank you. I'll walk. Ask the midget here if he's coming."

The tall bearded one asked the little Greek if he would walk to Janina with the *Inglisi*. The little Greek asked about the Germans. The tall Greek said he didn't believe it. He would walk to Janina with the *Inglisi*.

"All right," the little Greek said. "I go."

And they walked past the long jammed column of trucks, guns, motor cycles, mule-carts, limbers, soldiers who were not alive though they breathed and went ahead on the empty road towards Janina.

Quayle expected some transport to be on the road, even if the Germans were in Janina; but they walked along between the valleys and they did not see a truck. They saw no soldiers and no mules. Quayle was beginning to think the Germans must have taken Janina. He was saner than he had been since he had run through the machine-guns. His head was still bursting and it shook and beat him between the eyes from within when his boots jarred. His pants were torn at the bottom and he was too unconcerned to tuck them into his boots. His Irvin jacket was thick and heavy and made him hot as he walked. But he would not throw it away. The hunger was the worst thing. He kept chewing on the bread that he had put in his pocket, but it was not satisfying and he had pains deep in his stomach.

"How far away is this place?" he kept asking the tall Greek.

"No far — it's kilometre seven."

They passed *Kilometre* 22 marked on a rough post. The little Greek was dragging behind, and he kept talking to the tall Greek.

"We will walk into the German arms," he said. His small un-shaven face was a mockery to Quayle every time he looked at him.

"Too bad," the other Greek said. "What difference anyway?"

"Why go on?" the little Greek said.

"I want to get as near home as possible. What about your *Inglisi?*"

"He's crazy. He walked from Valona — Fancy that! It would be simpler to be killed."

"Why don't you get killed then?"

"I go with the *Inglisi,*" the little Greek said. Quayle did not under-stand what they were saying but he liked the little Greek for his arguing. When the road climbed higher and got into the cold wind that came around the mountain edge, Quayle, who was walking ahead, saw the lake of Janina.

"That's the lake," he said in German to the Jesus Christ Greek.

"Yes. We are near."

"What about the Germans? Can you see any signs of them?" the little Greek asked the other.

"Not from here. There's the lake though. Yes. There's the lake!"

It seemed slower walking now because they were so near. Quayle was not thinking so much about the Germans as about Helen now. It was so near that he was not able to think too much about the possibilities of what Helen had done. When the thought threat-ened that she might have gone back in the Bombay on the day he was shot down he blocked it out and looked at the red road ahead of him.

And then he saw the first Greeks.

"Well — the Germans haven't got it. There's some Greeks!" The little Greek beamed and pointed to the mule-cart that was coming towards them from the town, which was roughly indicated in shape along the lake.

Quayle did not look closely at the Greeks in the mule-cart when he passed. They could have been Germans in disguise, but he would not notice that now. He was walking with steady plodding as if he were walking in snow. He passed the road junction, then the trees at the outskirts, then the small houses — then the big tree that over-hung the road where the vehicles had been checked going out. But there was nobody there now.

When he came around through the village outskirts he saw the bomb damage. There was no real shape to any of the indefinite crude houses that had made the village. The streets were tangled with the splintered wood, the confusion of bricks, mud, large holes, twisted wires, burning wood, and there was terrific silence.

He got into the ruins of the main street and then he saw the few soldiers walking around, and the complete deserted feeling of the place was not satisfactory. He wondered quickly about the hospital. This town was dead — and destroyed. And the hospital . . . He walked across the mud square that was nothing but bomb craters filled with water, and he saw the smashed hotel where they had lived. Quayle walked steadily on and he had ceased to be conscious of the little Greek and the Jesus Christ Greek, who were way behind.

Then he saw the hospital. He saw the Greeks around the edge of it and the buses, and smiled because there was life. But the hos-pital building was torn down at one end and the whole of the side was holed with small shrapnel marks and he could smell it. He didn't quite know what it was, but it was mixed with the smell of the destroyed town around his back and the quietness that was superb. Absolutely superb, he thought — those words, too.

He was breathing quickly and he was uncertain about himself

when he walked through the Greeks to the smashed hospital doors. He pulled one of them open and walked into the thick smell of death and things that kept life. He looked for the girl at the desk. She wasn't there. There were women and untidy men walking through the passage in a hurry. He looked around, then went to the Matron's room. No one paid any attention to him.

He opened the door of the Matron's room and walked in. There was a small woman seated at the Matron's desk. She looked up and had wonderment in her face.

"Excuse me," Quayle said. He felt the pain in his head with each word. "I was looking for the Matron."

"*Inglisi*," the woman said.

"Yes," Quayle nodded.

"Hurt." The woman touched her face and nodded to Quayle's face.

"Yes, but that's not it. I'm looking for Helen Stangou."

The woman did not understand; he could see that.

"Helen Stangou," he repeated — but the woman did not understand.

He walked out and went to the Common Room. There were wounded Greeks lying on the floor. They were lying on the floor of the passage and he could see the women there bending over some of them, and some of the women walking around. They paid no attention to him when he walked by.

She was not here. All the people were different.

Quayle walked along the passage and through a long ward of wounded who were thick with the smell. He opened a door. There was a Greek in a white coat. The Greek came to him and touched the bandages on his face. He said something to a nurse. The nurse gave him scissors and he started to cut the bandage. Quayle stepped away.

"No — I'm looking for someone," he said viciously.

"What is it?" the nurse said in English.

"I'm looking for one of — for Helen Stangou. I'm looking for her."

"I do not know . . ." the girl said without confidence.

He felt that it was finished. He walked back through the ward and into a small room next to the Matron's room. There were the girls, rolling bandages and doing something with bottles.

She was leaning over a sink washing her hands. . . .

"Helen," he said.

She turned around.

"It's me," he said. "It's me."

He could see Helen become yellow, then the wide eyes and the face get tangled up and she moved quickly to him, talking incoherently. He gripped her two arms that came to touch his face and he felt her crying, then felt himself crying because he couldn't feel that he was here and heard her.

"Oh. It is you. Are you hurt? Your face . . ."

Then he could feel her because his arms were around her back and she was crying, enormous crying, great crying, and everything was loose inside him and he was part of her crying and the soft smell, and his arms moved with her crying, and his body was warm with it and his hands were with it as her body moved, and his head thick. . . . Because this was everything. This was the plane crashing, and falling into the Greek's hands, and *Inglisi* and Nitralexis and Deus and crashes and lust and warmth and cold and everything.

Then she looked up. He saw her normally and felt it all and only needed her face to tell him.

"Your face . . ." she said. She put her hand up and touched the bandages.

"I'm sorry," he said uncertainly. "I'm very dirty."

"Come quickly — your face. Oh, John." And she cried without him.

"It's all right," he said. "It's all right, Helen. It is."

"They said they saw you be smashed. That's what they told me."

"I know. But I got out. I'm all right."

She was looking at him without blinking and releasing her eyes, and she led him along the passage back to the surgery; and she was crying as she walked and looking at the black bandages on his face and he wondered . . . and felt her warmth and did not want to go with her to the surgery. . . . He suddenly felt the chaos and the haste and confusion of the hospital, and the helplessness and haste of everybody, and the uncertainty and utter hopelessness, and he wanted to get out of it. . . .

"I'm all right. It's all right," he said as they went in.

The doctor was there, and he immediately got the scissors again. As he leant over the table, Quayle saw his own face reflected in the smooth steel medical dish — and was astonished at the black filth of the bandage that covered almost all his face and the hair wild through the bandage space, and the swollen lip and the wild mad look, and the bruise-black of the skin unbandaged, and its dirty confusion and filth over his face. And he was suddenly conscious that he was torn to pieces in his face and his body and his clothes and was mad- and wild-looking. The doctor clipped the bandage and it wouldn't come off because of the hard blood. The nurse brought a basin of water and held his face in it to soften the blood. He felt the pain of its coldness internally and on the wound and he shivered and he felt Helen's hand on the back of his head like a light snowfall. He could hear Helen telling them about himself as her fingers circled the back of his head like a thistletop on your hand . . . And he didn't want to move; but the nurse pulled him up and he could feel the hard parachute silk coming from his face and felt the solidness and the misshapen outline of his cheeks and forehead.

"How did you get back? What happened? They said they saw you smash, and it was in the Italians."

"I was lucky. The timber stopped the plane and I wasn't hurt — except for my face. Do you remember Nitralexis — with the beard — the Greek?"

"The aviator. Yes, I do. Him too?"

"No — he found me. He had a peasant with him and we walked back to Klisura. They got killed when we were trying to get through the Italian lines. I don't know if it was the Greeks or the Italians who shot us up. I just got on a couple of trucks and got down here."

"It is so simple," Helen said. She had never looked so soft and without personal strength to him. "It is just like that." She was gently mocking him and he liked it. He could see the nurse looking at him as she dabbed his face and knew what he was thinking about Helen. She smiled at him and pulled his head down again. He felt the nurse's fingers exploring the gash on top of his head — then the scissors snipping away the hair around the gash, and the razor cleaning it.

"What are they doing to me?" he said to Helen.

She said, "He is a good doctor." Then she spoke in Greek. The doctor explained to her about Quayle.

"He says you are fine," Helen told Quayle. "He says you have had the sun and your face is all right because of that. He says you are very healthy, though you need some rest. He says your face will be a little marked for some months, but it is all right. The cut under the ear will leave a scar."

Helen spoke to the doctor again.

"They will have to stitch the top of your head. But you must bathe."

"Hell . . . just for a bath . . . Can I shave?" He went to touch his face but the nurse stopped him. She held up a small mirror so he would see. He accepted what he saw — the uncertain shape because of the swellings and the black colour of the bruise; the long cut from his right eye down to his jaw and the small cuts along his forehead and over his left eye. His neck had been grazed deeply when the mask had slipped off his face, and he could see the black spread of blood. It was all very unsightly. He could see Helen seeing its unsightliness by the pain of her face that was screwed-up.

"Pretty, isn't it?" Quayle said, and he could see the beard growth through the bruises and the wounds. "No shave, huh?" he asked the nurse.

"No — no shave," she smiled at him. "Bath."

"All right, where is it? Have you got any clothes around here, Helen?"

Helen nodded and went away after looking at him closely. The nurse led him to a small bathroom which was obviously for the hospital staff but had been well used for other purposes by the smell of it.

When he had taken off his clothes, and stood with a white sheet around him as the nurse brought in hot water in a large bucket, he began to feel the excitement of the place. The initial slowness of his arrival and the real feeling of what was going on, which his arrival had dulled, began to come back, and he was anxious again. He felt the urgency.

He felt the urgency again when he had the cleanliness given by the bath. When the doctor came in quickly and sat him down and he felt the physical pain of the stitches being put in his head, because they had no anæsthetic. He did not like the security of the clean bandages they put around his head and the coldness of the water-proof silk that smoothed itself on his hair. He knew of the imminent end of the place by their actions. Nothing was precise. Everything was careless and without thought and with speed.

Because Helen had not come back, he knew there was so much to be done that even she could not get away from the urgency of this place. It had the air of imminent end to it. He could smell it, and feel it, and was afraid of it. He would have to get out of it before he got caught in it.

"I want some clothes," he said to the nurse when the stitching was over.

"We have none. Perhaps Greek."

"Anything," Quayle said. "I want my coat back — the two of them."

"They will dirty."

"I want them back though. I'd like them, please," he said with quiet immediateness.

"It is not good, but I will," the nurse said, and she went to get his clothes.

She came back with his blue coat and the Irvin jacket. She had a thick khaki shirt and a pair of khaki trousers. He didn't ask her where she got the trousers because he knew it was better not to know. She stood there while he got dressed, and he again felt the urgency because he could see the look in her eye about him. He would like to do something about it but he knew it was dangerous — and there was Helen.

"Where is Helen Stangou?" he asked her.

"She will come," the nurse said.

Quayle pulled on the dry khaki pants and his own coat. He felt for the papers in the inside pocket. Then he pulled on the Irvin jacket. Helen came in.

"Come with me," she said.

"Where?"

"Come. I will show you something."

"I've got to get up to Headquarters," he said.

"This will take one minute," she said. He followed her up a flight of stairs to a small ward room with four beds in it. He could see the bulk of men's shapes in the beds.

"Look," Helen said. She was pointing to a sleeping figure in the far bed. It was Tap.

"Tap," he said. He walked to the bed and Helen shook Tap's head. He awoke. He looked wide and puzzled with heavy eyes for a moment, then he saw the outline of Quayle and he smiled widely — and his handsome face was without shape.

"Johnny," Tap said. "You son of a bitch. You bastard. Look at you standing there. Well, Christ, we thought you were dead."

"What are you doing here?" Quayle said to him.

"I got plugged in the shoulder. I got back though."

Quayle looked up and saw Helen smiling widely at Tap. He was suddenly conscious of something within himself that didn't like this.

"How are you feeling now?" Quayle asked slowly without thinking. He was looking at Helen.

"Fine," Tap said. "Just fine. I'm waiting for them to send a Blenheim or something up to get me."

"You'll wait forever, then," Quayle said.

"They said they would. You can come down with me."

"To hell with that. They can't waste a Blenheim for us."

"Have you told Headquarters you're here?" Tap said.

"Not — not yet. I'm just going up there."

"What do you say about this?" Tap said to Helen. He smiled broadly at her.

Helen put her arm through Quayle's.

"She thought you'd got it, John."

"What have you two been up to while I was away?" Quayle said with half humour that he knew was a serious demand.

"You'd be surprised," Tap said and laughed within him. Helen said nothing. He looked at both of them, and again he was conscious of something that he didn't like.

"She was knocked pretty bad." Tap was repeating himself.

"Just as well you were here then," he said to Tap, but he smiled when he said it.

"Yes. Don't you think so, Helen?"

"Yes," she said without any implications. "Tap was very bad when he came in too." Quayle did not like to hear her use Tap's first name.

"Were all the others O. K.?" Quayle asked him.

"Yes. You should have seen the drunk Hickey went on the night you got it. Christ almighty, I didn't see it, but the others told me and he was just pouring the stuff down."

"They didn't leave a Gladiator behind by any chance, did they?"

"No — Christ, no. I would have flown it out ages ago if they had," Tap said.

"Well, I might as well go and see about getting out of here."

"Where are you going?" Helen asked him.

"I'm going up to Headquarters. I'll be back, don't worry."

He turned away. Helen stayed with Tap. Quayle walked down the steps and went outside. There was the confusion outside the hospital.

He walked through it. There was the mud and the wreckage all the way through the town, and the uneven bomb craters that made the whole place a deserted garden.

He walked through it.

*　　*　　*

167

Where the road swung around the cliff to the Headquarters cave, there were high wooden coffins stacked against the wall and some had been smashed in by a bomb that had left its shallow crater in the rock road.

Quayle walked up the steps into the Headquarters, showed his papers to the guard, who saluted. It was the same but with more confusion. He walked to the small ante-cave where the English speaker was. He looked around but couldn't find him. Then another Greek came up, and said: —

"You wish what?"

"I wish to see somebody about calling Athens," Quayle said, looking around at the tired Greeks working in the confusion.

"You are what?"

"I'm a flyer. I was shot down behind the Italian lines a couple of weeks ago, and I want to call my C.O. in Athens. Where can I do that?"

"Excuse. I will get the Colonel."

He went away and came back with a tall man with a clipped moustache showing through unshaven features. He had a wide-collared coat that was almost down to his ankles, and a rakish cap.

"Alex Mellass," Quayle said. He was remembering the first time Mellass had met the squadron when it arrived at Janina.

"Ha — *Inglisi!* The one with the straight nose. You are in a fine mess. Where have you been? What are you doing here?"

Quayle explained to Mellass about the crash and getting to Janina.

"I want to get in touch with my C.O. at Athens. Can you help me out?" Quayle said.

"You come too late. We have no touch with Athens."

"What's wrong now?"

"Perhaps the Germans have reached Trikkala. Perhaps parachute men have cut the wires. *We* do not know. We know nothing here."

"I'll have to get back to Athens. Can you get me a car?"

"Ha. Listen to the *Inglisi*. Can I get an airplane? It is the same."

"Is it that bad?"

"You are gloriously ignorant. Come — we will walk and I will tell you things."

168

"You're busy." Quayle did not want to waste time.

"It is too late to be busy."

"Well, I've got to get out of here quick then."

"Come, I will walk with you."

They went down the steps and the tired guard saluted briskly when Mellass walked by him. Mellass nodded and smiled to him and the guard smiled back almost with confidence. They walked through the smashed town. There were still the casual soldiers wandering without direction.

"You see these?" Mellass pointed to the group of casual soldiers.

"Sure. What about them?"

"They are lost. We have had wonderful Generals."

"What about them?"

"The Generals told them to disband. See, they have no rifles. They were told to hand in their arms and disband and go home. The Generals are our tragedy. When the Italians start into Greece, it is the Generals who do not want to fight. The officers say to the men, 'Do not fight. Metaxas will fix this. He will fix the Italians; do not fight.' They have the guns and the bare hands so they fight the Italians. They come back in retreat because they have no ammunition. I was Colonel then but I say the officers and the Generals are bad, so they make me lower, to Captain, and say all I do is look after the *Inglisi* aviators. We have the staff eating fine in Athinai, but doing no work. The soldiers have no ammunition so they take it with bare hands from the Italians. Ha . . . All the time the officers here are making bad mistakes. Except — you remember — remember, with the whiskers? He is very fine. The others are afraid of him. Even Metaxas. He was very afraid of that General. And when the Germans come he is for fighting. But the other officers are all for the Germans because they are for the King and for Metaxas and Meniadakas. But they had told the men to go home because the British had been defeated by the Germans and it was peace. And the men didn't know. That is when they are afraid in Athens. So they make me a Colonel again. But it is too late, we are defeated. We are like that. It is the Generals. They are the great mistake we make."

Mellass was silent. They had walked through the town out along the road at the side of the lake. Quayle was surprised that he was walking along here when he should have been on his way to Athens. But he could see that Mellass had been wanting to say all this to someone. He was careful with Mellass.

"Where are the Germans now? What about the Australians?"

"It is too hard. The Germans were too many. They come down. First the Australians make the line at Princepe. Then the Germans come with masses of airplanes. What chance have the Australians? Then there is the second line at Metalene and that is where the Germans fight now. The Australians retreat. We heard yesterday, when we spoke to Athens. Soon the Germans will be in Trikkala, and that is between Janina and Athens. Then we have the Germans behind us and the Italians before us. When they take Trikkala we cannot retreat to Athens. And they are nearly there now."

This was something that Quayle could feel.

"What will you do when the Germans get to Trikkala?"

"Nothing. If they come we will fight. We will always fight. We will go into the mountains. They can never find us there."

They turned around and walked back. It was night now and Quayle thought he could hear the artillery in the distance.

"Well, I've got to get back to Athens," he said after the silence.

"You must go to the coast. It is the only way."

"Isn't it quicker through Trikkala over Metsovo Pass?" Quayle said.

"Yes, but the Germans are soon there. And you have no way of getting there."

"Isn't there any way of getting a car?" Quayle said quietly.

"No. There is the broken one and nobody to fix it. You could not take it."

"Where is it? I can fix it."

"They would not let you take it."

"Look," Quayle said. "You show it to me. Let me worry about taking it."

"They will shoot you if they catch you."

"Just let me try it. Where is it?"

"It is foolish. But if it is that way, I show you."

Mellass took him back to the Headquarters cave. They walked past it into the narrow opening in the cliff. It led up the steps into a porch that opened in a courtyard. Quayle could see the outline of cars parked there. Mellass walked to one corner and in the darkness Quayle could see the car.

"Are they all smashed?" Quayle asked, looking at the others.

"They have been used to have spare parts for others. Only this one is whole."

"What's wrong with it?"

"I do not know. It is the gear. The clutch does not work, I think."

Quayle got in the car and started the engine. He pushed the clutch and pulled the gear into first. When he let the clutch out nothing happened.

"Hell. Transmission," he said. "This is going to be tough."

Somebody called in Greek. Mellass paused a moment, then answered.

"It is the guard. Be quiet and stay under the car."

Quayle got under the car. He heard Mellass talking quickly with the guard and the guard went away.

"I told him you fix it for the General. He has gone to get a light."

When the guard came back he had a storm lantern that had been painted blue. He took it with a grunt. He could see better when he scraped some of the blue paint off the globe. He could see the dent in the gear-box. When he worked the clutch he could see that it did not go in and completely engage the gears. It had obviously hit something and the clutch arm was bent. If he straightened the clutch arm it would go right in. He crawled out and told Mellass about it.

"Can you do it?" Mellass said.

"It'll take me a while. What about some petrol?"

"I do not know. There would be some where you landed your planes."

"That's a hell of a way."

"You will only get away if you finish before morning. They would see you here in the day. You must finish before morning."

"Can you keep the guard away?"

"I must go," Mellass said. "But I will tell the guard not to interrupt you. You will be all right, you think?"

"Sure."

"I will come back," Mellass said as he walked away.

Quayle got the few tools from under the front seat and a giant tire lever. He got under the car just as the planes came over. The first he knew about it was the bombing. He could hear the string dropping down the lake road. He lay flat because the noise was big. Then another string dropped across the town and he could see the parachute flare from the bombers driving close. He was still under the car and he decided to stay there. He lay on his back and started unscrewing the pin that held the foot clutch onto the lever.

He swore viciously and with filth as the bombs shook their way across the town. He was afraid one might fall in the courtyard and because it was solid rock burst flat and blow him to pieces. He got the clutch arm off and started to lever it straight, but he had nothing to grip it with. He was not conscious of the quiet until he crawled out to find something to bend the lever with. Then he saw the flames and the red in the black sky as some part of the smashed village burned.

"Oh Christ. Why does this always happen?" he said aloud.

He was vacantly looking for something to bend the lever with. By the red light of the village ruins burning he could see the heavy flat piece of iron. He lay the lever on it and belted it with the large wrench. Slowly he could see the lever flattening out. He smashed his hand once and he sucked the sweet blood, cursing high into the red air. He fell flat when the bombers came back and he could see the bombs dropping over near the hospital and he thought about Helen. She was probably wondering what the hell had happened to him. And he was wondering about Tap. But he didn't have time to think that out now. Just so long as she stayed there until he got this goddam thing fixed.

He got up and belted the lever harder and felt his smashed hand shivering. He finally straightened the lever and he crawled on his belly listening to the bombs, and got back under the car. He could not get the lever arm in place. It slipped because his smashed hand was not strong enough to hold it. By pulling the lever back with one hand he managed to slip it into position. Quickly he pushed in the pin and screwed it tight. He blew out the lantern and noticed the quiet again because the bombers had gone away. He started the engine and pulled it in gear. Slowly he let out the clutch, and it took. The car moved forward easily.

"Thank Christ for that," he said. He took the lantern and went back to the Headquarters cave to find Mellass. He found him yelling into a telephone. He nodded to Mellass.

"O. K.," Quayle said. "I fixed it. I'm going up to the hospital to tell Helen."

"What?"

"I'm taking her with me. I was going to marry her."

"The girl with the hair? What about the other *Inglisi?*"

"Yes. Will it be all right if I drive the car straight out?"

"You will have to chance. Did you get the fuel?"

"Hell no. I'll get that later. I'll come back."

Quayle walked through the burning wreckage of the village. He could smell all the world burning and he was glad when it was taken away in the wind. When he got to the hospital steps he saw the confusion and the large buses that had just come in. There were new wounded that cried as they were carried in. There was great noise and arguing and smells and there was pain mixed with the whole. Then he saw the little Greek and the tall bearded one. He had forgotten all about them.

"*Inglisi,*" the little Greek said. He looked frantic.

"We have waited for you," the other Greek said solemnly.

"*Shh.* Don't speak German here," Quayle said. "Wait. I'll be back."

He walked into the hospital. There was more chaos than before. Wounded, dying Greeks were strewn around the passage and there was the overflowing of death through the place. He could see it and smell it and feel it. He watched the Greek doctors and the nurses walking in the mess and screwed up his face when he heard the shouts of the ones who were not wounded enough to die. He walked by and went to the room where Helen was. He found her stacking bandages that were twisted and dirty with blood and mud into a refuse basket.

"John — what did you do?" She looked at his dirty face. "Are you hurt again?"

"No. *Shh*. I've been fixing a car. We're getting out of here."

"I've been frantic for you."

"Look," he said. "I want to see Tap again. Can I go up there?"

"What for?"

"We're leaving to-night. You too," he said.

"I can't. Can't you see this place? I would not be allowed."

"For Christ's sake don't argue. If we don't get out of here by morning, we'll never get out of here. Take me up to Tap's room."

She walked out and Quayle followed her through the confusion of the hospital again. He walked up the stairs. Tap's room was in darkness. Helen found her way to the bed.

"It's me. Listen," Quayle said to him. "We're getting out of here to-night. Do you feel good enough?"

"How are you going?"

"I'm getting a car," he said quietly.

"Sure," Tap said. "When? I'll have to get some clothes."

"Not so loud," Quayle said to him. "It will be a couple of hours. I've got to get some fuel. I've got to go out to the airdrome."

"That won't take a couple of hours."

"I've got to walk, you bloody fool," Quayle said.

"O. K., O. K., John. Don't get mad. Is Helen coming?"

"Of course, you son of a bitch. What did you think?"

"All right," Tap said. "All right. Swell. I'll be ready, won't we, Helen?"

Quayle turned angrily and went out.

Chapter 19

The little Greek and the big Greek with the beard were waiting for him at the hospital steps. When he came out they followed him out of the confusion of the ambulances and the blood-strewn stretchers that were stacked against the long column.

"Listen," he said to the big Greek when they were away from it, "do you want to get to Athens?"

The big Greek was silent for a moment. Quayle could see he was working it out. He wondered about this definite-looking man who was younger than he looked.

"Yes," the Greek finally said. "It will be all right."

"You might get caught. Wouldn't you be shot for deserting?" Quayle said, to try him.

"I'm not deserting. We were disbanded by our officers. We wanted to go on fighting. I've still got my rifle. I would not give that in. I'm not deserting." Quayle could feel he was definite about it.

"What about the midget here?"

"He wants to go anywhere you go. He wants to get to Athens," the big Greek said.

"Well, ask him anyway."

He asked the midget, who got excited and Quayle said, "*Shh.* For Christ's sake, not so much noise. What does he say?"

"He says he will go. He has his wife in Athens. He has two children and he says the officer doesn't expect him back anyway."

"Yes he does. I'm responsible for him."

The big Greek told the midget that Quayle said he was to go back. He got excited again.

"He wants to come," he said.

"Well, that's desertion," Quayle said. "Don't tell me it isn't."

"Perhaps. I think he had better come."

"You are afraid he will tell about us?" Quayle said.

"Yes. It will matter for you."

"It'll be too bad if you both get caught," Quayle said.

"I do not desert. I am no deserter," the other said quietly and with fierceness.

"I'm sorry," Quayle said. The big Greek smiled carefully at him.

"I understand," he said. "We will go with you."

"Tell him I'll kill him if he says anything," Quayle said.

"It will not be necessary. I will be with him."

"Tell him anyway. Tell him . . ."

"He says he will be with you whatever you do," the Greek said.

"O. K." Quayle could see the little Greek was nearly crying and he did not like that.

"I've got to get some petrol. It's at an air field about five miles out of town."

"What do you want us for?"

"To carry it."

"All right. But how can you get to Athens?"

"Do either of you know the route over the Metsovo Pass?"

They talked in Greek again.

"Yes. We know it. But the Germans are in Trikkala."

"The Germans were in Janina. Do you want to come?"

"Yes. But how will you get there?"

"Never mind that now. We've got to get some fuel from the air field."

Quayle knew he could not risk driving the car out there because he would have to come back through Janina to get on the road. Any car would be stopped. They would have to walk out and carry the fuel in. It would take them till morning.

"We've got to walk out to the air field. Come on. We've got to hurry."

There was another bombing raid as they passed through the town.

Quayle yelled at the two of them and they ran with him until they were past the Headquarters cave. They kept running and heard the bombs stringing across the burning town again. Then all three of them settled into a steady walk.

It was an hour before they got to the turn-off into the airdrome. Quayle could see the large bomb craters in the dimness of quiet darkness. He walked straight to the small timber clump where the Greeks had kept the fuel. There was a square mounting of four-gallon tins. He said "Thank Christ" aloud. He knew they could not carry the tins by hand. He pulled at the limb of one of the small plane trees. It bent, but it would be strong enough to hold four tins. He bent it backwards and forward until it broke at the roots. He pulled out four tins. The big Greek saw what he was doing and pushed the limb through the handle at the top of the tins, bending them until the limb could fit through. He lifted one end and Quayle the other. The limb bent, but held.

"I'll take another one in case this breaks," he said, and pulled at the tree again. He gave the limb to the little Greek and told him to carry it. The little Greek didn't understand what he said, but could see for himself. They slung the weight on their shoulders and got back onto the road.

It took them an hour and a half to get to the edge of the town, which was being bombed again. Quayle did not want to take the petrol into the courtyard. He would have to chance leaving it near the hospital with the two Greeks. The car had enough petrol in it to get him to the hospital and maybe out of town. So he skirted across the fields behind the village and they fell and stumbled carrying the weight over the uneven ground. When he got behind the hospital Quayle said: "I've got to get the car. Don't move from here."

"Where is the car?"

"At Headquarters. There'll be a nurse too and another *Inglisi*."

Quayle ran back to the Headquarters cave. By now his shoulders were completely numb from carrying the petrol. He walked quickly past the guard at the steps and found Mellass. He was talking to somebody who looked like a General. Quayle waited for him to finish. Mellass saluted the General and walked past Quayle.

"Come with me," he said as he passed Quayle. When he was outside Quayle said to him, "It's O. K. I got the petrol. I'm going now."

"How did you get it?"

"Walked out there. I'm taking a couple of Greeks with me."

"Have they orders?"

"No. But don't stop them. They're some of the lost ones you were talking about."

"I'll go with you to the car. Where's the girl and the other *Inglisi?*"

"They're waiting for me at the hospital."

"Once you start, don't stop. I'll get you to the hospital."

"Will that get you in trouble?"

"Perhaps," Mellass said with sadness, "but what matter?"

They got to the car without the guard's seeing them. Quayle started the engine quietly and Mellass got in the other side.

"How do you get out?" Quayle asked him.

"Down there." Mellass pointed straight ahead. Quayle could see the dim outline against the burning red of a great arched gateway. There was a guard there too.

"Drive fast through it," Mellass said. "Don't stop if the guard says anything. Don't stop at all."

Quayle let out the clutch and revved the engine. It was some time since he had driven a car. It lurched and then he put his foot down solidly. He felt the closeness of the gate as they swiftly went through it.

Chapter 20

At the hospital the confusion was increasing. Because there was the hopelessness, there was the added confusion. When Quayle had left angrily Helen Stangou wondered about him. Whatever there was within them both dominated her, and she knew it now. She knew it only because he had come back, and because of the hopelessness.

She pulled the long strings of bandages from the small tins and threw them in the large basket and knew of the hopelessness. Their filth and dry blood did not physically shock her any more. She had been repelled at first by many things about closeness to living and being alive and becoming dead. She had come to the conclusion that no death is clean or without smell or desirable. She was almost afraid of death, because of its straight and immediate effect of the body. Nothing was so abrupt — not even the end of a cliff or the heat and cold, nothing was so abrupt as the change from life to death.

In a purely biological way she was more afraid than horrified. There was no horror left in it after seeing so much. Except then it was attached to so much biological ugliness. Like the boy whose nose and eye had been blown away. Though that was not so bad as the other one who was very old and had his arm and leg on one side blown away . . . the right side . . . No, the left. Which way was he lying? On his stomach. Then it would be the left. He was bad, that was the ugliest of those things. It was all black limbs and yellow face immediately the limbs died, though medically speaking they did not die. And now she would have to leave this. He was angry with her but it was not heroics that had made her say that about not leaving. . . . She could prove that to herself.

"I'll be back in a minute," she said to the stout girl helping her.

She went down the passage and picked her way through the new wounded who had just come in. The nurses and the other girls were rushing everywhere between them. Someone called her as she passed a small group of nurses and doctors. She went to them.

"Hold this," one of the doctors said. She found herself holding a kidney dish, and she could see the doctor hacking with blunt scalpel into the crab-soft flesh of an old Greek who was staring with open eyes that could not blink even with physical reaction. She was thinking about what it would do to her if she left now. She could see the haste around her. She could see that helping this man meant that somebody else couldn't get help and that he would die or have pain. It was all like that. . . . Everywhere here . . . All around her. The doctor said, "That's all." And the nurses and the other doctor got up and went to the next one.

She was dispassionate about it. She moved away before they could make her work with them again. She moved quickly along the long passage with the wounded on the floor, then into the long ward with the dying in the beds. She felt herself detached from this. She only felt attached to it when she could see John in it. With him here, the hopelessness of the impending end had gone. He was movement, and without hopelessness. This was mercy here now without direction. John rejected the mercy, she could see that, because it was tangled up with hopelessness and waiting for the Germans. She would not wait for them. It would be physical defeat, and she had waited so long for John — though she had always thought he was certainly dead. But she had waited so long for him that when he came it was physical victory. If she did not go with him it would be physical defeat. She would be tangled up with this hopelessness, though she might be of some help. Some help, some help, some help.

When she thought of John she could see the lack of hopelessness in him. She could see the straight nose and the straight face. His slight cynicism was real. That's not hopeless though, she thought.

He was very sure of himself and he did not make mistakes. He would not be shot down in an airplane by accident, she was thinking. Not by a mistake, oh not at all, not John Quayle. The quick, certain movement of his body, slight clipped speech . . . She could tell it when he was trying to learn Greek. He was too sure of himself to loosen enough into Greek words.

It was different with Tap. He was young at all ages and without solidness and he had been something to understand with, when Quayle had been missing and they had seen him crash. . . . She walked along the passage which was in darkness and sometimes felt the body of one of the wounded soft against her toe. She would see Tap about getting ready to go away.

She wondered about asking permission to leave. She knew it would not be given. Permissions, orders, putting the bandages into the basket — that was the end of all things. The confusion she saw in walking was the decision. There would be trouble, but there was John and there was the thing bigger than the trouble and the confusion and the feeling of imminent hopelessness.

She went to Tap's bed carefully when she got into Tap's room.

"Did you get your clothes?" she said quietly.

"Yes," he said. "But you'll have to help me get them on. My arm's useless." He had his left arm strapped across his chest and bound tight.

"Can you get your trousers on?" she said.

"No. . . . Look, I'll sit on the bed and you help me."

He swung his legs off the bed. He handed her the long blue trousers that were clean because she had washed them herself.

"Leave your pyjamas on," she said. "It will get cold."

She put his feet in the top of the trousers and pulled them on slowly. She knew he was not so helpless as he made out, but it was no use arguing with him.

"Stand up," she said to him abruptly. He stood up and swayed and sat down again.

"I can't — Jesus — This is going to be tough."

"Come on," she said impatiently. She pulled at the tops of the trousers and he stood up again. With a wrench she pulled the legs tight into his crotch.

"Hey," he said. "That hurts."

"I am sorry. But I have not done this before."

"You're doing all right," he said.

"Do not play games now. We must get out." He was buttoning his trousers down the front.

She pushed his right arm through the sleeve of his coat and put it round over his left shoulder.

"I will wait for you outside. You must go down yourself," she said.

"How do I get there?"

"Walk straight down the passage. Be careful of the men on the floor."

"All right. Don't be long," he said.

She went out as Tap pulled on his flying boots.

She went to the small room where she slept with the two of the other First Aid girls. She put on a heavy coat with letters over a pocket and filled the pocket with handkerchiefs and a woolen jumper and gloves and some letters from her parents. She turned out the dim blue light and went out.

Through the tangle of bodies and movement and noise and pain along the floor, nobody took any notice of her. She pulled open the large doors and in the air she suddenly realized that it was nearly morning. She felt no tiredness, but only the discomfort of having ignored time. To have worked so long and for others, to have done it collectively without individual consciousness of time, was drunkenness.

"Is that you?" she heard Tap say.

"Yes. Are you all right?"

"I fell over a couple of dead men, but I got here."

She could see him sitting at the foot of the steps.

"We can't wait here," she said. "Come to the road farther."

She helped him along as he walked uncertainly. They stopped at the split-off trunk of a tree that had a large bomb crater beside it.

She helped him sit down on the broken tree. She expected Quayle any minute.

They had been waiting for nearly an hour. They did not see Quayle and the two Greeks leave the gasoline just below them. They only saw the car later that came bumping towards them without lights. She could see the two figures coming up from below them.

"Look," she said to Tap.

"I hope to Christ they're not guards or something," he said.

They saw the car stop and the figure get out of the driver's seat and one from the other side. They went to the car.

"John," she said quietly.

"Yes," he said. "Get Tap in the back seat. We've got to get some gas."

"Where is it?" Tap said.

"Just sit there. It's down here. I got a couple of Greeks."

He went with the two figures and the third figure, which was Mellass, followed them. They saw the four of them coming back carrying the cans of petrol.

"We've got no time to put it in now," she heard Quayle say. "Get in."

The two Greeks understood, though he said it in English. They opened the back door and got in. Tap made a sound as they sat down.

"Be careful," Helen said in Greek to them. "He's hurt."

"Who are these bastards?" Tap said to Quayle.

"They're Greeks. They're coming with us," Quayle said.

"For Christ sake what for? We don't want them. Leave them, John."

"Shut up, Tap. They're coming." Quayle pulled the gear and the car jerked and speeded in a great turn and Helen thought they were going into the bomb craters. She could see the urgency and the haste of things with them. She suddenly recognized Mellass as he got onto the running board of the car.

"Down there," Mellass said, pointing to the left.

183

They speeded around the mud path and through the smashed village. Sometimes they climbed over the wreckage, noisily bumping through the mess of twisted wires and wood and bricks. Quayle kept looking behind.

"There's nobody following you," Mellass said.

"Where's this road guard?" Quayle asked him.

"Just ahead. Let me off here," Mellass said.

Helen wondered what Mellass was doing. He would get into trouble for this. They would shoot him if they found out about it. It must have been he who got the car for John Quayle, she was thinking. Quayle stopped the car.

"Well. Thanks for everything, Colonel. Sure you won't come?"

"No, *Inglisi*. I will stay here."

"Jesus, is that you, Alex?" Tap said.

"*Shh,* for Christ sake, Tap."

"What's wrong?"

"Shut up," Quayle said.

"Say nothing about this," Mellass said to Helen in Greek, but quietly so the others could not hear. "Tell the others not to say anything about me. When you get to Athens, tell my wife. We're going into the mountains. Tell her not to worry. We'll be in the mountains. Tell her that. Look for the *Inglisi*. He must hurry to get through Trikkala before the Germans. He must hurry. Tell my wife."

She could hear the finish of all things in what he said.

"Yes," she said to him. "I'll tell her. I will. Adieu. My life with you."

"My life with you," Mellass said to her.

"Come on, John. Let's get moving," Tap said.

"I hope I can do the same for you some day," Quayle said to Mellass.

"You win the war for us, *Inglisi*. That will be enough."

"O. K. Good-bye."

"Adieu," the Colonel said as the car speeded forward. Quayle had it in second gear and was moving it very fast when he passed the guard at the road. He could see the fellow stand up and shout, waving his hands. Quayle pulled the gear into top and pushed his foot down.

Helen turned quickly and saw the dim figure of Mellass and the guard in front of him. She could see all the blood in the burning and the fire in the background and the bombings and the wounded pouring into the hospital and the confusion, the hopelessness and men in the hills and death there, with yellow limbs decaying.

She saw the guard raise his rifle and the white puff of bad powder when he fired at them.

"Look out. He fires," she said. She put her head down.

And all she could feel and think was the bumping of the car and there was nothing behind her and nothing in front of her. There was only Mellass and the bumping of the car and the guard firing at them and Tap saying "What the hell" and Quayle driving without acknowledging anything but himself.

Then she looked up again. It was morning.

Chapter 21

The good road lasted from the lake to the beginning of the steep climb. Quayle stopped when they were well up the slope. He got out and opened the back door.

"How're you feeling, Tap?" he said.

"Fine," Tap said. He had wrapped two blankets around his legs resting on the cans of petrol. "You're a reckless bastard."

"Helen, tell these two to get the petrol out, will you?"

Helen told the two of them what Quayle wanted. He was looking in the boot of the car for something to punch a hole in the tins with.

"Does the *Inglisi* know the guard shot at us?" the little Greek said to Helen. Helen did not look at him.

"Yes," she said.

"They will follow us," the little Greek said.

"Do you want me to tell the *Inglisi* you are afraid and want to go back?"

"Do not worry the *Inglisi*," the other said. He was laying his rifle on the running board of the car and pulling out the petrol tins. "The *Inglisi* has enough worry."

Helen looked at him and nodded.

"What's all the jabbering about?" Tap said. "You Greeks can't do a thing without talking all day about it."

"Shut up," Quayle said to Tap as he pulled a tin out. Helen watched him punch the holes in the can and pour the petrol into the tank. She noticed Quayle's torn hand.

"Your hand, John," she said to him. "Look at it."

"I know," he said. "I did that fixing the car. It's all right."

"Say, Helen. Can you loosen this bandage?" Tap said.

"Now?"

"Yes. It's cutting my arm off."

"We've got no time now," Quayle said. "Put those tins in the back seat," he said to the Greeks. "The tank is full. That's the first lucky break we've had. We'll keep the empty ones."

They got back in the car and started out again. Helen looked at Quayle's torn face that showed through the bandages on his head. She worried about the stitches and dirt already on the bandage. It was grease from the car. But she could see he was without sleep and with complication in his mind so she sat still and watched the road.

Then Tap said to Quayle: —

"How did you get out of that crash, John?"

Quayle did not answer for a moment because there was a sharp turn and a straight climb.

"I hit the trees. They broke the speed down."

"Yes, but I mean how did you get back? That was way back."

"Walked. You remember Nitralexis? He found me. We picked up a peasant and he showed us the way back."

"The Greek too? Where's he now?"

"They got shot. We were getting through the Italian lines."

"Well, I hope the squadron's still at Athens," Tap said.

"They will be, I think."

"Hickey was talking about going back to Egypt. Jesus, that would do me. That would be better than Athens. I'm sick of this goddam country."

"That's very unfortunate," Helen said with quiet anger.

"I'm sorry, Helen. I don't really mean it," Tap said.

Helen did not reply. She was sleepy and not conscious enough to think things out about Tap. She watched the road coming up at them as they climbed in great curves. Sometimes she could see the high range of Metsovo in the white cloud ahead and wondered whether they would get over it in time. The high roar of the car, straining in climb, made her close quietly into an uncomfortable sleep and she could dream only of the smell of hospital on herself and John and Tap making the stuff that made the smell. She was startled when Quayle said, "This car's dead. We'll never get over these hills."

He was speaking to himself and she shut her eyes again and tried to think of Athens and their being married and where she would go with him and what the war would do, and after the war with Quayle and what he would be, and then coming home to see her parents; and the sudden fact that she did not know what John Quayle did beside fly airplanes—but was not worried; but was worried when she thought of the time element and that it was not simply a matter of marrying him. He was still in the war and he would go on in the war, and perhaps she would be in Greece or in England or wherever he was, but he would not be very near any place she could be, even as his wife. She opened her eyes to have reality change the complicated uncomfortable thinking. She looked below through the glass wind screen and suddenly saw Janina. She saw the whiteness over the odd shape that was definite from this height, and did not show the internal wounds it had because the outline was clear. When they passed the great wide turn in the road she saw the town gradually being screened by the side of the mountain until it was completely gone.

She looked around. Tap had his eyes closed and was trying to sleep. The little Greek had wide eyes and looked at her without registering anything. The big Greek was gripping his rifle with both hands and leaning his head on the barrel. He looked at her when she turned around and his eyes accepted her look. Suddenly the car stopped. Quayle got out quickly. She stepped out too. Quayle sat down on the running board.

"My eyes are not so good," he said to her. He had his face in his folded arms.

"Lift your face and let me look," she said.

He was silent and kept his face down. Then he walked quickly to the edge of the high road in front of them. He stopped suddenly and was sick. She was about to go to him when she heard Tap say, "Leave him alone. Just leave him."

"But he's sick."

"Just leave him. He won't want you around," Tap said quietly.

The two Greeks got out and Tap followed them. Helen looked at John. He had sat down on the edge of the road with his knees up. He had rested his arms on his knees and his face hung between them. She did not want to let him be there alone but she knew that Tap was right.

"Will you loosen that bandage for me?" Tap said, coming up to her.

She turned without thinking and helped him get his coat off. She saw the two Greeks breaking bread and cutting cheese that they had in their haversacks.

"Keep some for the *Inglisi*," she said.

"I am doing that," the big Greek said.

Helen did not notice the reproach. She undid the pin that held Tap's bandage tight and began unwinding it from his chest and arm. She loosened it by straining on the remainder of the bandaging and then wound the bandage up again. She kept looking over her shoulder at Quayle.

"He'll be all right," Tap said to her.

"But he seems very sick."

"He's all right," Tap said to her. He walked over to Quayle.

"How're you feeling, John?" he said. Quayle did not answer him. Tap put his hand on Quayle's shoulder.

"Why don't you spread out?"

"It's all right," John said to him. "It's all right."

"O. K., John," Tap said and walked back to the car.

"He'll be all right in a minute," Tap said to Helen.

"What is the matter with the *Inglisi*?" the big Greek asked her.

"He's ill for something. He has been moving too much."

"He is mad, the *Inglisi*," the little Greek said. "He walks from Italy. He walks through the Italian lines right into our lines. He walks from the valley to Janina. He walks out to the airport to get the gasoline. He is mad. All the *Inglisi* are mad."

"The *Inglisi* knows what he's doing," the other said.

189

Quayle had stood up and was walking towards the car. Helen walked to him. She could see the greyness under the bruised face.

"Are you all right?" she said.

"Yes. My eyes are not so good," he said.

"You look pretty bad, John. Take it easy," Tap said to him.

"We've got no time," Quayle said. "Get back in the car."

Tap and Helen were eating some of the bread and cheese. Tap offered Quayle some of it.

Quayle sat down on the running board of the car.

"No, thanks," he said. "We've got to get moving. Come on."

He stood up and walked around to the driving side. He fumbled his way in.

"Can you drive O. K., John?" said Tap.

"Sure. For Christ's sake get in."

He started the car and with more care than before he deliberately let out the clutch. The car moved forward easily. He watched the edges of the road and tried to follow the movement of the road between the spasms in his stomach and in his head. He kept the car in second gear and they slowly wound up the high road towards the white-clouded Metsovo Pass. He watched the road with determination and kept his stomach from being sick again by shutting his mouth tight and swallowing from time to time. He could see the road and the valleys and the sky sometimes and the road and the edges of the road and the mountain in front of them and the road and the road the road the road.

Helen saw him fall forward. His chest hit the horn button and there was the high sound of the horn as the car swung to the left out of control with the wheel locked in Quayle's stomach where he had slumped forward. Quickly it swung to the left and with a quick jerk it hit the soft earth of the built-up side. It jerked them all forward. Helen felt the crush of something into her head. Tap and the Greeks were pulled forward by centrifugal force and the car stalled because it had stopped. Helen pulled herself up and leaned over to Quayle. The horn was still blowing high and with drama. She pulled him from the wheel and he slipped sideways.

"Heip me somebody," she said, unconsciously in Greek.

The big Greek was already out of the car and had opened the door near Quayle. He was easing Quayle out of the seat. Helen got out and nearly knocked Tap over. She ran around to Quayle. The Greek was easing him away from the car jammed against the soft earth to the dry part of the road. Helen pulled Quayle's Irvin jacket zip down and pulled it open. She did not know what to do. She could see the death in his eyes and his limpness.

"John," she said quietly. "Come on."

He did not move. He was completely without thought or feeling or action.

"He looks bad," Tap said. He was bending over Quayle. "Get some water."

"Get some water," Helen said in Greek.

The big Greek came up with a dirty handkerchief soaked in the mud water at the side of the pool. Helen lay it across Quayle's eyes. She could feel his pulse. She was without thought because she did not know what to do. She only knew she badly needed his consciousness. The big Greek was leaning over him now.

"He's very ill. He will not be awake for some time."

"What will we do?" Helen said to him.

"The *Inglisi* was in a hurry. We will have to get on. Can you drive this car?" he asked the little Greek.

"No. I have never driven. Can't you?"

"No. Ask the other *Inglisi* if he is able to drive," he said to Helen.

"He has the smashed arm."

"It doesn't matter. Perhaps he can drive with one arm. Ask him."

Helen asked Tap if he thought he could drive, because the big Greek said they should go on.

"We'll wait for Johnny to come around," Tap said. "I don't think I can drive with this arm."

"He says we must hurry. We must hurry. We can put him in the back. I will look after him. Can you drive?" she said to Tap.

"Not with this arm."

"I will try then," said the big Greek. "Help me put the *Inglisi* in the back," he said to the little Greek. Tap watched them lifting Quayle like a bag of sugar into the back seat.

"What are they going to do?" he asked Helen.

"We are going on. He is going to drive." She pointed to the big Greek.

"Can he drive?"

"No."

"Hell. On these roads. Oh no. I'll do the driving. But we ought to wait for John to get better."

"He was hurrying so much. He was hurrying, we must hurry."

"All right. But I'll drive. I don't feel like risking my neck with that crazy Greek."

Tap got into the driver's seat. Helen got in the back with Quayle. "This is going to be fine," Tap said more or less to himself.

Because there were so many sharp turns that began steep climbs, Tap had to drive all the time in first so he could slow down and take a climb with a slow beginning. He could not swing the car around far enough with one arm. Sometimes he had to stop when the turn was sharp because he could not swing it around quickly enough. He was cursing good and solid every time he came to the steep corners with the sharp climb. He was annoyed by the big man sitting impassively beside him clutching the rifle between his legs.

"How is he?" Tap kept asking Helen.

"I do not know," Helen would say. She was holding John onto the seat by his head. Quayle's legs were across the little Greek's knees. The sun from below them was flicking a pattern across the inside of the hood, and it reflected on Quayle's colourless face.

"Poor *Inglisi*," the little Greek said quietly once.

They were high on the pass before they saw or met with any of the Greeks. First it was the mules with the big two-wheeled carts, then the limbers and the artillery. It was easy at first. Tap could hold the car over on the outside of the road because the Greeks made their track on the inside because it was safer. Then the road started winding again and Tap was not confident any more in what he was

doing. Driving along the road with the straight drop below, he began
to be less sure of what he was doing even when it was slow going.
After passing the first two small convoys, he was struggling to hold
the car.

"I can't do this much longer," he said to Helen.

"What's wrong?"

"These mules and things." Tap stopped and turned around. "I'm
scared I'll drop you all over the brink."

"Can't you go on and make it slowly?"

"No," he said quietly. "I've got to go fast to get up the inclines.
If you're all game, I am. I'll go on if you like."

"You will have to, Tap," she said.

"O. K. How's Johnny?"

"I do not know. He is still almost not breathing. He is very ill,
I think."

"Mostly fatigue. He's had quite a shaky-do."

Tap started the car again and they slowly climbed around the outside of the road, though there were no obstructions. They were getting near the top of the pass. It was already late afternoon and Tap
was wondering what they would do at night. He certainly could
not drive at night. This was impossible enough as it was. They were
hurrying, but he'd drop them all over the edge if he tried driving
at night, he knew that. He could survive the afternoon. He was
thinking he could survive it, when he came to the tail end of the
mess.

Near the top of the pass a truck sprawled across the road in the
thick mud.

"What now?" Tap said and stopped.

As far forward as he could see there were Greek trucks. They
were dilapidated, ancient, broken, muddy, uneven, irregular, and
stopped all the way across the road as far as he could see it winding
the few feet to the top and along and out of sight.

"Look now," he said to Helen. He heard a quiet noise from the
back of the car.

"What is it?" Helen said.

"I've never seen such a mess," Tap said. "They're blocking the road for miles probably."

The big Greek got out and walked to the group standing around the confusion of the rear truck. They did not greet him.

"We have wounded *Inglisi*. They are aviators," the Greek said. His clipped words made them look at him. He was dispassionate in his words, his face, his stance. He was not arguing or appealing. He was just saying.

"Try farther up," the driver of the truck said.

The Greek did not say anything but walked past the truck. He walked right up the winding slope and saw the mess of strewn lorries that would be impossible to shift. We are careless, he was thinking. We have no care with any mechanical thing we do. Why, into the mouths of all the Saints, why did these trucks have to be strewn around the road? We will have to be educated about these things. The Americans can teach us. In the mouths of the Saints, we'll never get past this. I wonder what the *Inglisi* would do if he were conscious. He always knew exactly what he is doing, or he makes believe he knows what he is doing because it is an excellent way to make people do what you want them to do. He is very smart, but we will never get past this.

He walked along the mud at the side of the road and sometimes said "Good day" to some of the soldiers who had gathered in small groups and were sitting around trucks or on the edge of the road waiting for God to signal them on. He had walked into the shadow of the top of the mountain before he came to the end and the head of the confusion. He could see the battered eight-wheeled truck that had once been a construction company's possession. It was jammed against the road-bank, and bogged in the road.

He could see the Greeks bending into its engine and could hear them arguing about some part of it.

"What's wrong?" he said with simplicity when he got there.

The one who was bending into the engine looked up at him.

"Do you know anything about engines?"

"No. I do not. What is broken?"

"That's what I would like to find out and what I'm getting in here for."

"How long will it take?" the big Greek said passively, knowing its provocation.

"From one to four weeks," the other said with sarcasm.

"We have wounded *Inglisi* and a woman. We are trying to get through. Perhaps the *Inglisi* can fix it. I'll get him," the big Greek said and spat deliberately, as he looked at the Greek who showed he didn't think it any use. He walked hurriedly up the road to the top, and noticed it was nearly dark. He hoped the *Inglisi* with the hurt arm would be sensible and not get annoyed.

He could see Tap standing on the running board of the car as he came down the last slope.

"Miss," he called to Helen, "will you ask the *Inglisi* to come with me to see if he can repair the truck that makes the blockage?"

Helen was sitting on the running board of the car on the other side. She stood up and translated for Tap; he got down.

"It's getting dark," Tap said. "Where is this truck? Ask him. You'd better come too. I'll need some translating done, I guess."

Tap looked at Quayle lying on the back seat. "He seems to be just sleeping now," he said.

"I think he will be all right soon," Helen said.

She walked on with Tap.

"If the *Inglisi* wakes, do not let him move. We'll be back soon," Helen called back to the little Greek, as the other ran up after them.

As they walked along the column, Tap's white handsome face and the bandaged arm and Helen caused comment from the scattered Greeks of the column.

"It is a wounded *Inglisi* flyer," they said.

"He has the look of a Greek."

"He seems hurt. Is he walking to Athens?"

"No, they have the car. The woman is his nurse. If we had such women here . . . " they said.

Tap could only see the complete disorder and was thinking that these people would never learn, that when we win the war we'll have to make these people do things properly because it's their stupidity that gets them into messes and we have to come and get them out and they get in our way like now with all this mess stopping and that big Greek walking without saying anything but just looking mad all the time, and that dumb little one, and look at all these little people we're passing now. They'll never learn because they aren't civilized yet.

They came to the truck and the driver was still buried under the bonnet. Helen called him out.

"We have an *Inglisi* here," she said. "Perhaps he can help you."

"He's good if he can."

"Ask him what is wrong," Tap said.

"He says that it will start sometime but it chokes as if it had no fuel, but he says there is plenty of fuel in the tanks."

Tap got up into the high driver's seat, turned the large key and pressed the starter. He pushed the accelerator hard down and fed it plenty of gas. There was a quick splutter, the engine caught, fired for a few minutes, then stopped. He did it twice more and then got down. He leant on his wounded arm and pulled at the carburettor with the other. He finally wrenched the filter top clean off it.

"Tell him to start it," he said to Helen.

The Greek got in the cabin when Helen told him. He pushed the starter, and Tap held the palm of his hand over the top of the open carburettor. The engine stalled as it had before. The Greek started it again and Tap held his hand longer over the space until he could feel the cold sucking choking the engine, then he released it quickly. The engine choked then sprang into cylinder motion and roar. . . . The Greek fed it too much gas and it stopped.

"Try again," Tap shouted in English. "Tell him not to give it too much gas when it starts," he said to Helen.

"What is that mean? I do not understand."

"Tell him not to press the pedal too much when the engine starts going properly."

"Yes," Helen said and told the Greek.

He started it once again. Tap held his hand on the open carburettor until he felt suction again and he released it quickly, then
put his hand back again and released it quickly again and the engine
roared into life and stayed living. The Greek fed the gas into the
cylinders and the engine roared. He put it in reverse and some of
the other drivers from the other trucks came up and pushed as he
roared the engine and inch by inch reversed it out of the mud until
it was straight on the road again and moved forward.

"Thank the *Inglisi*," the Greek said with a great smile to Helen.
"Thank him and tell him we will all pull to the edge of the road
so you can pass by."

"He says they'll pull to the side of the road so we may pass,"
Helen said to Tap.

"Ask him what it was wrong with the car," the Greek asked
Helen.

"He wants to know what was wrong with it."

"Dirty petrol," Tap said, wiping his hand in the dirt. "Sand or
something blocked the pipe. You can blow it sometimes by doing
what I did. Tell him to put the filter back on the carburettor and if
it happens again to do what I did." He started to walk up the hill.

As they walked back there was slow movement in the column
and the big Greek was telling the drivers to pull over to one side
so the wounded *Inglisi* could pass in their car, because the *Inglisi*
with the one arm had fixed the truck that was broken by just putting his hand on the carburettor. It had moved almost around the
curve as a column, by the time they got back to the car. Helen was
walking ahead.

"The *Inglisi* is talking," the little Greek said when he heard Helen
open the door of the car. The little Greek was sitting in the front
seat of the car because it was getting dark and cold. "He was saying
something. I think he is waking."

"John," Helen said to him. "John. Are you all right?"

"Where were you?" Quayle said. He was still lying crookedly on
the back seat and Helen could not see his face in the dimness but
his voice was unsure.

"We were fixing a car. There's a lot of trucks blocking the road."

"How do you feel, John?" Tap said. "You faded out."

"What happened?"

"You went out," Helen said. "The car ran into the earth. You were very sick."

"Where are we now? Who drove?"

"I did," Tap said. "We're on top of the pass. There were a lot of Greek trucks blocking the road. How do you feel, Johnny?"

"Fine," Quayle said. "How the hell do you drive with that arm?"

"We nearly went over a couple of times."

"Can we move now?" Quayle said. He was trying to sit up.

"Yes." Tap looked at Quayle, who was sitting up and coughing, and trying not to be sick — and he was not, because he was bending over to tighten his stomach.

"We're starting now," Tap said. "We've got to get past these trucks."

They were all in the car. Helen was trying to hold Quayle's head down but he would not let her.

"I'm all right," he said and watched Tap pulling the car into gear with one hand. It was so dark now that Tap could hardly see the road. He switched on the lights. Slowly they climbed the curve and caught up with the rear truck in the column. They passed it and John could hear them shouting "*Inglisi*" to them as they passed. They had reached the top and were moving down now, and Tap was driving in low gear so that it would act as a brake. Truck after truck they inched past until they were certain that there was an endless stream of trucks. Then the lights picked out the space between the trees that was clear and they eased past the last truck. Tap stopped as the Greek driver stepped in front of them.

"Tell the *Inglisi* thanks," the Greek said to Helen. "He is a fine person. Tell him that, please. We will all win the war yet. My, he is all right, he has sure knowledge of cars."

"I'll tell him," Helen said. "Good-bye. We hope you get through all right."

"Be careful of the Germans in Trikkala," the weak-knees shouted after them.

"What were they saying?" Tap asked her.

"They were thanking you," she said.

"Is that all? They sounded as if they were giving a speech."

"No. That was all," Helen said.

Tap let out the brake and they started on their way down from the pass.

Chapter 22

There was only the darkness and the clear beam of the white light that made out the road as they came slowly down the high mountain. There was the mud so soft that it splashed across the windshield and twice the melting rain frosted the cold glass. There was the wind that they heard and they could feel its sound against the car because they were going so slow. They were going slow because Tap was exhausted and his arm was so stiff that he could not take any turn now without stopping first. They were taking too long to get off the mountain pass. Quayle had fallen into a natural sleep but he was exhausted also. Helen would not wake him up and sometimes she would sleep. The little Greek sitting next to Quayle was sleeping sometimes. Only the big Greek in front with Tap kept awake. Only he felt the haste.

Twice they stopped because Tap found his arm so stiff that he could hardly move it, and Helen would wake up and get out and rub his arm and he would look for her softness because he needed it now and she would be careful to keep away from him and he was not quite sure about her.

Before morning Quayle woke up. He was not sick, and he felt the cold because he was not fevered any more.

"I'm hungry," he said when he awoke. "Helen, have we got anything to eat?"

Helen was not awake but she woke when he said that.

"He better not eat too much. He will become sick," the big Greek said.

"I'll stop and we can all eat," Tap said.

"Can I take over for a while?" Quayle asked him.

"No. I'm all right."

"Well, can you keep it up? We've got to make time. Can you keep it up?"

"Sure."

"I'll eat something and take over. How're you feeling?"

"All right. My arm's stiff but I'm all right."

Quayle ate the bread and cheese that Helen gave him. He asked for more but she said he would be sick and he did not argue. Then he told Tap to stop the car and he got out. He could feel the weakness in his legs and the bile taste in his mouth.

"I am glad you are better," the big Greek said to him when he got in the front seat.

"Thanks," Quayle said. He let out the clutch and the others were more comfortable because he drove with sureness again and faster down the inclines and did not stop to turn the corners and passed the convoys of Greeks without worry.

He could feel the lightening of the down grade as morning showed it. When he could see, there was the quiet flat winding into a valley and beyond that the plains. He could feel the pleasantness of high earth becoming flat and the sighing of the earth's certainty when it was flat, and he was temporarily happy.

"How far do you think to Trikkala," he asked the bearded Greek.

"We must pass through Kalabaka first. It's perhaps twenty miles altogether."

"Do you think the Germans are in Trikkala?" the little Greek asked Helen.

"I do not know," she said, then to Quayle, "Do you think the Germans are in Trikkala?"

"I don't know," Quayle said. "Maybe. We'll soon see anyway."

"Are you still shivering?" the big Greek asked the little one.

"I am merely cautious. The *Inglisi* is so reckless."

"It is well the *Inglisi* cannot understand you that he would know of your fear."

"I have not fear. I have not, I tell you."

"Leave him alone," Helen said to the big Greek.

"What's he afraid of then?"

"I have no fear," the little Greek said. "I must get back to Athens like you. I have my wife there and children. I must get back like you. I have no fear. But I am cautious."

"Cautious in the bowels of Christ."

"Stop arguing please," Helen said. They ignored her.

"Someone among us should take care. You certainly don't."

"Caution is for women in bed."

"You are a radical."

"At least I have kept my rifle."

"You left your head behind then."

"Why don't you both be sensible?" Helen said.

"He has no sense," the little Greek said.

"How can you talk of sense when you are married and with children?"

"With more sense than you do. Children are more sensible than you."

"I suppose you were the pregnant one in the family."

"What are they jabbering about now?" Tap asked Helen.

"Oh. They only argue. They will be all right," she said.

"What are they arguing about?" Quayle asked her.

"Nothing. It was something about the Germans in Trikkala at first. But now it's personal."

"Tell him if the Germans are there they're there. That's all about it."

"That will not help them. It is much beyond that now," Helen said.

"You come of a very crude family to talk in such a way," the little Greek said.

"You seem to understand it," said the big one.

"I have passed sewer cleaners and heard it."

"Were you in the sewer at the time?"

"If I was, I most certainly would see you there," the little Greek shouted.

"It would only be a sewer for deserters."

"I am no deserter," the little Greek cried aloud. They were both shouting now.

"What are you?"

"If I am a deserter, so is the woman."

"She is nurse to the *Inglisi*. Maybe you are too."

"Just a minute," Helen said. "Can't you be sensible? Neither of you is deserting. Can't you leave it at that?"

"For Christ sake, what's going on?" Tap said in English. "Can't you shut up?" The talk had been rapid and loud and angry until it was vicious.

"They argue only," Helen said.

"Tell them that we'll dump them out if they keep it up," Tap said.

"Don't tell them anything," Quayle said suddenly.

"They're hell's nuisances, John," Tap said.

"Don't be screwy, Tap. They're just getting something out of their systems. Leave them be."

"They are not sure of themselves," Helen said to John. "They are both afraid of being accused of deserting."

"Tell him we do not think he deserts," Quayle said slowly to the big Greek. "We do not think either of you desert. Your war's over, that's that."

"It's just beginning," the Greek said calmly to him.

"Perhaps," Helen said. "But that's a different war. Tell him the *Inglisi* do not think he is a deserter."

"You tell him."

"It will not be the same."

"I cannot. I am sorry, *Inglisi*."

"You're bloody stubborn," Quayle said.

"That's the sign of a good Greek."

"Good Greek or not. You might as well tell him."

"I am sorry, *Inglisi*."

They were all angry now. The conversation was quick and without pause and heated by all of them. There was tenseness now within them all, between them all for each other. There was silence after the big Greek spoke and it was without comfort and sureness.

They drove on with the silence. Quayle could see the flat green country and the warmth and the slight poplars that flanked the road sometimes and the dry ruts into the earth and the plane trees and landscape. It was very quiet and without real movement. There was no war. There was nothing. They were all taking a peaceful drive in the warm country and there was no threat and no hurry and life was good like this without its haste and tenseness.

"I don't like all this," Tap said. It was uneasy breaking the tenseness they had kept for half an hour.

"What?"

"There's nothing on the road. You'd think there would be Greeks or something."

"They've evacuated."

"Yes, but you'd think there would be something around. I don't like it."

"What do you expect then?"

"It's just too quiet. It looks as though the Germans are about ready to come in. It looks as though the place is just waiting for them."

They were uncomfortable all the same, until they found a peasant with his sheep on the road. They stopped and asked him where everybody was, why the roads were empty, and he said the people had gone into the mountains. Yes, into the mountains.

Quayle was following the straight road now and the heat of the engine was warming him thoroughly so that he felt the evenness of his body again and the steady high sound of the engine was like the warmth. The road was uneven in places and sometimes he had to slow down but he kept a good pace most of the way.

"If the Germans were around, they'd be up this road," he said to Tap.

"Maybe. Ask the Greek where this place is," Tap said.

"Where do you think Kalabaka is?" Quayle asked the big Greek.

"Where the rocks rise from the plains. You can see it in the distance now."

Quayle bent low and lifted his foot slightly so they slowed down. He could see the high grey rock on the uneven roundness of plain before them and the road straightening towards it. He leant back and put his foot down hard again. The engine coughed. He lifted his foot slightly. The engine was choking abruptly and stopping then starting.

Finally the car stopped as the engine went dead and Quayle eased in the brake.

"Did you put that extra petrol in?" Quayle asked them.

"No. It's still in the back here," Tap said.

"Pull it out. We've run out."

The little Greek and Tap pulled out the petrol cans from the floor. Quayle unscrewed the tank cap. He got the screwdriver from the pocket in the front and plugged a hole in the top of the can.

"Feel that sun," Tap said. "This is fine."

"Yes. You know these two tins will last us about fifty miles. We may get to Trikkala."

"Maybe we can get some at the next town here."

"I doubt it."

"You know, it's funny, John — " Tap was laughing.

"What?"

"Well, look at us. Like a couple of broken-down ducks. I'll bet Hickey would laugh if he could see us now."

"I wonder where they are."

"I suppose they're in it somewhere. I hope to Christ they've gone back to Egypt."

"I don't think so," Quayle said. "What difference would it make anyway?"

"Hickey must have a whole new crowd on his hands."

"He'll like that." Quayle laughed quietly and lifted the second tin to pour it into the tank.

"Wait till he sees you," Tap said.

"I hope to Christ they've got some planes. Maybe they've got Hurricanes."

"You won't be flying for a while."

"You'd be surprised. There's nothing wrong with me."

"Are you still going to marry her? Helen, I mean."

Quayle looked up suddenly. He tilted the can a little higher.

"What do you think?" He felt the old feeling he got back at the hospital again. There was the strangeness and the feeling about Tap and Helen that he was not sure about. Quayle poured the last of the can into the tank and threw the can away. He looked around and said to Tap, "We ought to get some water for the radiator."

Tap walked to the ditch at the side of the road. He told Quayle there was dirty water here. Quayle threw him the tin and Tap crawled down the incline to get it filled. He came back with the water slopping over him. The tall one took the tin from him and poured it into the radiator. Tap was standing near Quayle as he closed the boot of the car.

"What are you going to do with Helen if we have to leave this place?"

"Leave Greece?"

"Yes."

"Take her with me."

"In a Gladiator?"

"Come off it, Tap. There'll be ways. If there aren't . . . Sure, I'll fly her out in a Gladiator."

"What about in Egypt? No wives allowed. They sent the last lot home."

"We'll see when we get there. Come on, we're wasting time."

Helen had been walking into the timber and she came back again. John looked at her as she walked easily down the road. She swung her head twice to throw her hair back. She had combed it, and washed her face, because it was shining. He smiled at her, and quickly with warmth that was possessive of him; she smiled back and when she reached him put her arm through his and put a warm hand in his.

206

"Your face is not so black now," she said quietly to him and smiled.

"It feels all right."

"You should let me change the bandage on your head. I have some in my pocket."

"Later," he said. "How're you feeling?"

"I am good. One would never believe about war around here," she said.

"Tap thinks it's too quiet," he said.

"Perhaps. I hope it will be all right."

They were in the car again and making their fast way along the dirt road. Quayle pulled the car to a quick stop when he thought he heard planes. He took a quick look out but there were not any. They were nearing the high rocks which were near enough to shadow the white road between the poplars. Then Quayle saw the airplanes. They were flying low and in large formation. He stopped the car and they all got out.

"What are they?" Tap asked him.

"I don't know. Could be Blenheims, but we haven't got that many."

"They're heading south."

"Come on. We'll keep going. They won't come near us. That's the first we've seen all day. I hope this petrol lasts till we can get more. There may be some in this town."

They could see the timbered and stone outline of Kalabaka ahead of them and they could see the form of the monasteries high on the rocks. They got in and started again.

As they came into the village they could see it was smashed like Janina and there was still the white smoke clinging to the wood that smouldered. There was the nakedness of the form of the shells of the buildings. There was black mess of burnt stone strewn across the road, the tree with snapped-off twigs. There was the complete loneliness and the splinters of wood long and jaggered scattered in confusion, and the cold air that was quiet in the warm sun.

"We won't find anything here. It's been bombed too much,"

Quayle said when they stopped because the road was blocked by a small log. Quayle and the big Greek pulled it aside.

"We need some more petrol," Quayle said. "Do you know where we can get any?"

"We might look around here."

"Ask the little Greek."

The big Greek asked the little Greek about the petrol and the little Greek was warm again because he had been spoken to normally and without malice, and he got out of the car and smiled.

"There would be some somewhere here," he said. "We could look."

"Well," Quayle said, "we can spread out and look. It would be in cans, I suppose, and not in drums. Five minutes. We haven't got time for more. We'll just have to take a chance. Will you wait here, Helen? Tell them to wander out and look for drums or tins of petrol."

Helen told the other two and they all walked along the smashed black road and divided into the ruins at the edges of the small village and looked for the cans.

It was death in the village because there was no one there. No one, and the great silence dominated the place. Then the little Greek became quickly surprised when he saw the old man sitting on a heap of ruins, wide-eyed and with puzzlement in his face.

"Hullo, Father," the little Greek said. "Where is everybody?"

The old man was silent, then he looked up blankly.

"They have all gone into the hills," he said flatly.

"And they leave you?"

"I am old," he said.

"Shouldn't you go too?"

"I am old," he said again.

"Do you know where there is any gasoline?" the little Greek said.

"I am old," was the blank reply. The little Greek looked at

the old man for a moment, made a clicking noise with his tongue and walked away.

Quayle was walking through the ruins of a small house to the back, where there were wire chicken-runs, and he could see the mess of domestic utensils strewn out on the earth and the chairs and tables smashed. There was nobody about, and he looked up at the monasteries and wondered whether there was anyone there.

Helen, standing near the car, was wondering about the quiet too. She did not like it so quiet when Quayle was not around. It was not an entirely feminine fear, either. There was uncertainty and hopelessness in the quiet, as there had been back at the hospital in the confusion. It was waiting for something. She could see the quiet in the smashed village as she could still physically see the quiet in the confused hospital. It was all the same. And it was depressing. The very desertedness of the place was depressing. She was feeling the quietness getting into her when Tap came back.

"Nothing here," he said to her. "Not even food."

"How far will the petrol get us?"

"To this next place maybe. This place looks as though everybody just up and left it."

The big Greek came back and he was wiping his hand on his trousers.

"If we were only nearer Germany and could do this to their towns," he said to Helen.

"Did you find any fuel?"

"Nothing. I thought I saw a tin but there was a man very squashed." He wiped his hand again.

"Nothing doing," Quayle said when he came up. Only the little Greek was not back.

"Maybe he's left us," the big Greek said as he got into the car.

"He will not do that," Helen said. "And please let him be. He is old and should not be here anyway. Leave him be."

The little Greek came and Helen watched his small face, and

209

the tight eyes over the creased nose and cheeks that were furrowed like his forehead, and the black stiff hair of his head and beard and the smallness and bentness of his frame. His eyes blinked quietly when he was near her and he said nothing but got into the car. Quayle started the engine and moved off quickly. He did not go fast, but he went just fast enough so that too much of the gasoline was not used. They passed the long shadow caused by the rock with the monasteries, and they were onto the flat road again, passing over the small bridges that were bomb-cratered around; and all along the road now there were the fresh-earthed craters from the fifty-pound and hundred-pound bombs.

Then there was quietness again. The country was flat and the green rolled quietly each side of them. There were numbers of small bridges, and Quayle expected them to be blown up, but none of them was. The long canal that he could see winding at one side had been hit by light bombs, but nothing had been affected. There was quietness between them too. Sometimes they crossed the railroad tracks that had suddenly appeared, and it was more like a returning to inhabited parts because of the long stretch behind them. They passed peasants and their sheep at the side of the road too. Tap wanted to stop and have Helen ask them about the Germans.

"They might know," Tap said.

"I don't think so, Tap," Quayle said. "We haven't time. We'd waste petrol anyway."

"I hope it lasts through this next place," Tap said.

"Maybe the Australians are there."

"I think that was part of the Greek front."

"I suppose this will all end in another Dunkirk," Quayle said quietly.

"It's too bad if it does. What the hell could we do though?"

"I don't know," Quayle said. "There seems to be something wrong."

"Maybe. We just haven't got enough equipment."

"It's more than that."

"We could do with some more men. We haven't got a front either. I get sore every time I think of France caving in like that."

"I don't think it would have made any difference," Quayle said.

"Well," Tap said, "we would have had a front."

"I think we would be bad even if we had the front."

"Why doesn't somebody do something about it?"

"I don't know," Quayle said. "I don't know."

They were crossing the railroad often now and the trees were definite the way they lined the road. They passed through the quiet mud of a bombed village. It was deserted and Quayle saw a broken poplar for the first time as it flicked by the window, and he did not like it. There were definite mountain shapes to the left of them, and more obscure ones to the right, and a river with trees along it.

At high noon Quayle heard the bombers again. He stopped and stood on the running board and looked up. He could see the planes coming straight along the road from the pass towards them. The planes were sure and flying very low.

"Better get out," he said to Helen. "Tell the others."

"Are they to bomb us?" the little Greek asked Helen as the engines were distinct.

"I don't know," she said. "They surely will not. They probably can't see us."

"Walk away from the car," Tap said to her.

They walked through the ditch at the side and into the green wheat field. Quayle was looking at the bombers as he walked. They were obviously following the road. There were about twenty in four groups in V-formation.

"They're following the road all right," Tap said.

"They're pretty sure of themselves too, flying so low," Quayle said.

The little Greek was standing near Quayle, because he was sure of his safety in his nearness to Quayle. He was completely confident of all things, and his safety, when Quayle put his hand on the little Greek's shoulder to steady himself. He looked at the bombers with Quayle.

"*Airoplanos*," he said to Quayle and smiled. "*Inglisi?*" He knew they were not.

"No," Quayle said. He smiled at the little Greek. "*Germanos.*"

The little Greek spat and lifted his face again. They were almost over them now. They were making steady noise that ran flat along the earth.

"Better get down in case they let one go for luck," Quayle said.

They all sat down in the green wheat and watched as the bombers came at about a thousand feet directly above them. The first group passed and they could see the straight cross on the fuselage and the wings and the unquiet menace that was steady.

"That's hellishing good formation," Tap said.

"They're good flyers," Quayle replied to him.

The second group came over. The Greek with the pointed beard was raising his rifle and he sighed and allowed for deflection and fired. Quayle and Tap had been looking at the bombers and had not noticed him, but they heard the shot behind them.

"For Christ's sake," Quayle said. "What do you want to do? Bring them all down on us? Put the bloody thing down." The big Greek looked at him, then put the rifle down.

Quayle was looking tensely at the bombers now. He could see the third group come by and pass over.

"Thank Christ they didn't see that."

"They probably did but have more important things to do. The bloody fool."

"What would they have done?" Helen asked.

"I don't know," Tap said. "Probably dropped a blast."

"A what?"

"A bomb. They don't like being fired at by rifles," Quayle said.

"I am sorry, *Inglisi*," the big Greek said. "I feel bad to let them pass."

"I know," Quayle said to him. "It's just as well they didn't take any notice of it."

They were walking through the waist-high wheat back to the car.

"It is fine wheat," the big fellow said in Greek. The little Greek was feeling equal now and he was benevolent.

"It will never be bread," he said.

"There is plenty of time. It will be some months before it is to be reaped." He was pulling the long green blades as he walked.

"Then the Germans will have it."

"Yes."

"You know about wheat?"

"In my youth I was of a land-owning family. We had wheat like this."

"I have never seen wheat so close before," the little Greek said.

"This is fine wheat. It has been good this season."

The little Greek was happy now and he held out his hand to help the other over the ditch. The big one refused him but the little Greek did not mind and he got into the car.

They were travelling with the monotony of the steady engine-roar again, and it was warm in the car; and there was the haste and the waiting feeling to see if the petrol would last to Trikkala and beyond, because the Germans would almost be there.

They were getting close, and they could all feel it. There was the group of poplars and the plane trees and closeness of timber that was always the rough indication of a village.

"That must be it," Tap said.

"There are the bombers again too." Quayle could see them through the windshield. They all got out again and went to the side of the road. This time it was a different group.

They passed over the village and went on south through Trikkala, which was also abandoned.

"What's the next place?" Tap said.

"Larissa. I don't know how we're going to get there," he said quietly. Tap was in the front seat with him now.

They were crossing one river over a small bridge that was bombed when Quayle thought he could feel the splutter in the engine, but it kept going.

"Can't go much longer," Tap finally said.

"We must be a good thirty miles past that place," Quayle said.

"What are we going to do if it runs out on us?"

"We'll probably be all right if we get to Larissa." Quayle moved his hands around the steering wheel of the car to wipe the sweat that had collected. He half closed his eyes to clear them of the sun making a long shadow before them of the trees on the rise in the ground. They could not be far from Larissa either. If the petrol would last a little longer they would be within reach of it. He refused to think the Germans were there.

The road seemed to wind unnecessarily and it was very empty here. Quayle was almost counting to himself now, from one to ten, then backwards, and making abrupt noises with his mouth. The pastoral land was low and rolling out each side, until they came to narrowing of a sudden rise from the south. They had been following the river all the way and now they climbed a little and crossed the river and kept going on the high level.

"I remember this when I came up. I walked here. This is near Larissa," Helen told Quayle.

The slight incline was keeping them in second gear. There were wide turns and thick mud surfaced the road, so that you could almost hear the gasoline being swallowed by the cylinders. It was on turning one of these wide curves that the engine did splutter, start again and then stop dead.

"That's that," Tap said. Quayle had eased the car to the side of the road.

"What do we do now?" the little Greek asked Helen.

She said she did not know, and waited for Quayle to move. He was sitting with his hands on the wheel looking at the road ahead, trying to remember the map of the Larissa area they used when they were stationed here. They might be able to take a short-cut. It would be too risky, since it might involve walking just off-course and overstepping the road to Athens.

214

"It's certainly empty," Tap said. He had been shaking the car and listening to see if there was the swish in the tank.

"All right," Quayle said. "We might as well get going. We'll walk from here."

The others got out and Quayle looked around to see whether there was anything worth taking with him. There was nothing that would serve a purpose equal to the drag of its bulk.

He stepped out, slammed the car door and started out behind the others, who were already walking along the road. The little Greek was waiting for him and smiled when he caught up and kept in step with him as he took long strides up the incline. Helen looked behind to see whether he was coming and saw the car tucked in the side of the road and thought of it as one of Quayle's deliberately careful acts.

Quayle caught up with her and the three of them walked together. The tall Greek and Tap were about twenty yards ahead of them. Like this, they walked up the incline to the top, keeping steady pace and not talking much. Once Quayle called, "Not too fast, Tap. We've got some ways to go."

"O. K., Johnny," Tap had shouted back and kept going the same pace.

Over the incline there was the flat winding road cut into the slight mountain that had made the incline. They walked unevenly along the earth road and felt the warmth of the sun become heat as their bodies became hot.

"Did we have any food left?" Quayle asked Helen.

"No."

"I'm pretty hungry, too. I could do with a drink," Tap said.

"How's your arm feeling now?" Quayle asked him.

"Stiff as hell. How's your head?"

"All right."

"I should change that bandage," Helen said to him as they walked along a very muddy stretch. Quayle was taking his jacket off.

"Later. Wait until we know how we stand," he said.

"I think I can hear bombing," the big Greek called back to them.

He was walking ahead and Tap was back with Quayle, the midget and Helen.

Quayle lifted one side of his head as he walked. He could hear the deep explosions but they did not have enough *krumph* in them to be bombs, he was thinking. It was too flat a sound and without resonance, and it was separate sounds each time there was the explosion and not the indistinguishable deep running explosions of bombing.

He knew that it was artillery. They were walking atop the incline now and it would soon go down. When they turned the wide corner they could see the stretch of flat leading to Larissa and the outline of the town spreading wide across the river with the timber in clumps around it and within it and the white houses distinguishing themselves.

"Here we are," Tap shouted. He was ahead again.

"I can still hear the bombing," Helen said.

"I said we were near," said the little Greek. He walked ahead to catch up with Tap and the big fellow.

"They don't seem to be bombing it," Tap called back.

"It's artillery," Quayle told him.

"There's a truck on that road." Helen pointed to the north-east. They could see the one truck moving steadily towards Larissa and the white dust it left behind swirling and disappearing in the viscous air.

"What about that artillery? Where's that?"

"Somewhere to the left." That would be north, Quayle was thinking as he said it. That would be in the mountains too, probably; and he remembered from the flying that the nearest mountains to Larissa were the ones they were in now. The nearest to the north were some distance, maybe five miles away.

"I think they're fighting somewhere near here," Quayle said to Tap.

"Come on then."

They walked in a group along the road and they could see the smoke from the town settling low into the sun. They had left

216

the incline, and were now on the flat. It seemed farther away than ever.

When they passed the first house Quayle half expected a German patrol to walk out. But they walked by the scattered houses on the outskirts and there was only the noise of the artillery now. It was long and wide. There was the black smoke too, and that was clearer and they could see the mess of craters along the road. Then Quayle saw the figure at the long bridge they were coming to.

"Do you see what I see?" Tap said to him.

"Yes."

"Well?"

"Well?"

"I hope to Christ it isn't a German."

They walked straight to the bridge. The bearded Greek was walking ahead with Quayle. Tap was unsurely walking on the edge of the road. Helen and the little Greek were behind him. They were all trying to make out the shape at the end of the bridge. Then Tap saw it.

"Look at the hat," he said to Quayle.

They were right at the end of the bridge now. They saw the figure come up to them. He had on the wide-brimmed hat of the Australians.

"What's this?" the Australian said to them. Quayle noticed the M.P. band on his arm.

"Are we lucky!" Tap was laughing happily now.

"I was ready to drop to death," Helen said.

"It's very lucky. My, look at the *Australos*," the big Greek said. The little Greek was quiet.

"What's up?" the Australian said. He was looking at them. He saw Quayle with the dirty bandage on his head and the black face and the ripped torn jacket and the khaki pants that were not part of his blue uniform and the worn grey dirty boots and the ripped Irvin jacket on his arm. He saw the girl, Helen, with sunburnt face and warmth in her wide cheeks smiling, and high breasts and a fawn coat and worn shoes and no stockings, looking straight

217

at him happily. And he saw the tall Greek with the pointed beard and the mist in his eyes and the rifle on his back, and the other little Greek standing behind with the black beard, and the other one, Tap, with the blue uniform buttoned with one arm hanging loose and the other obviously bandaged to his chest and the dirt on his hands from fixing the Greek truck and the collar without a tie though it was open.

"We're certainly glad to see you," Tap said to him.

"We have come from Janina," Quayle said.

The Australian was facing them in the middle of the road. He was being careful.

"We're English," Quayle said to him and pointed to the wings on his pocket.

"What about the others?"

"They're Greek. They're all right. The girl is a nurse who came with us."

"I'll have to see your papers," the Australian said. He was speaking with a broad *a* and the *oi* sound for *i*, and Quayle was thinking it sounded like Cockney and remembered Vain. He took out the papers that were wet and the yellow folding pass that was the British-Forces-in-Greece pass. Tap handed him his. Helen gave him a plain sheet of paper with Greek written on it. The Greeks handed over their soldier's books.

"We're all right," Quayle said. "We were in Janina. We are from Eighty Squadron. I was shot down, and he was in the hospital. We got a car some of the way but we ran out of petrol on the mountain back there. What's it like ahead?"

"I suppose you're all right," the Australian said. He looked at Quayle's black bruised face and was convinced. He gave them back their papers.

"We're just getting the hell out of here," the Australian said.

"Can we get to Athens?"

"There's a signal truck coming through sometime. That's about all that's left."

"How's the war?" Quayle asked him.

218

"Bloody awful. They've been strafing us all day."

"What's been happening? We don't know what's going on."

"It's a bloody mess. You don't know what's been happening at all?"

"No."

"We evacuated Florina. Then we left Elasson. We've been getting hell. They got too much stuff in the air and too many tanks. They've just bombed the hell out of us. We didn't have a chance. We haven't got anything in the air. The boys held them up a lot but they're outnumbered now."

"What's going on now?"

"I suppose we'll hold the next mountain pass. I've got orders to go back to Phersala. The sappers are going to blow this bridge when the signal truck comes through. The Germans are a couple of miles away. You can hear the artillery."

"When will this signal truck be along?"

"Any minute. Say, there's those so-and-so's again," the Australian said.

They could hear the high drum of numerous airplane engines again.

"They've been over all day. You'd better get away from the bridge."

The Australian pulled off his big hat and pulled on a tin hat. Then he looked at Helen and offered the tin hat to her but she smiled at him and shook her head and said "No, thanks" and walked with him in the soft field away from the bridge.

Quayle was behind her. He could see the outline of Larissa just ahead of them. It was fading now because it was getting late and the sun was below the mountain to the west. He could see the line of poplars and the white plane trees with the clear dust pink in the air caught by the sun. He looked up for the planes. They came from due north over the ridge of mountains.

"I hope we get out of here in time," Tap said.

They walked to where Helen and the Greeks and the Australian were sitting down.

"We haven't much time," the Australian said. "The Germans will be coming down the road soon if that signal truck doesn't turn up. That's why they're bombing Larissa, I suppose."

They could see the planes now. They were in four groups flying uneven with a small flying escort above and behind them. As they approached the town, the first group merely inclined itself on Larissa and they could see the sun catching the bombs in clusters as they dropped from the planes. The other planes following did the same, as the first ones climbed and came around for another run-up. There was a second burst of the string of bombs and the black smoke was now straight and widening like a train's smoke, and filtering through the poplars into the redness of the sky in flat quiet and stillness and warmth.

The third group of planes flew over the town and went to the south slightly. Quayle watched them diving individually and then the black smoke climbing high.

"They're after the airdrome," the Australian said. "Looks like they got it too. They had Hurricane fighters there."

"We ought to head for there," Tap said to Quayle.

Quayle nodded and watched the bombers come down again and the smoke grow black and knew it was a plane or oil-dumps on fire. They walked back to the road.

"Look," Quayle said to the Australian. "If we walk on will you tell the signal truck to pick us up? We'll be on the road. We want to get to the airdrome."

"I'll tell them," the Australian said.

"Is the airdrome off this road?"

"Yes. Just keep walking through the town. It goes straight through. When you get to the other side you'll see the turn off the place. You can see the tents. If that truck doesn't come soon, I'll start walking myself. The Germans will be coming down that road any minute."

"Thanks," Tap said.

"It's a bloody mess, isn't it?" the Australian said.

"Certainly is," Tap said again.

"Come on," Quayle told Helen.

"S'long," Tap said to the Australian.

The Australian watched the five of them walking down the road slowly and with no energy. They're certainly a bloody mess too, he was thinking. I'll bet that goddam signal truck got it in the neck. This is certainly like the country around Rose Bay, it's certainly funny being here, I wish to Christ that signal truck would hurry up. I'll wait till they get down a bit and if there's no truck by then I'll take to the hoof, it's certainly a bloody mess, a bloody mess all right.

And he watched them disappear into the redness of the horizon and the black pall of smoke and the poplars; and he was alone right in the middle of this whole world in the warmth and the quietness, and just the wide flat river with the pleasant greenness and the poplars. And absolutely nothing around him — and soon the Germans would be here. This country is certainly like Rose Bay. I think I'll get out of here now.

And he started to walk down the road.

Chapter 23

They could see the Hurricane burning as they walked along the edge of the grass field that had been made an airdrome. They could see the two high trucks at the end of the field and the other two Hurricanes at equal distances from each other. This looks like they're clearing out, Quayle was thinking. We can probably climb on one of their trucks.

They reached the men loading the truck with large boxes.

"Is there an officer around?" Tap said.

"Over there," one of the aircraftsmen said. They were all looking at the five of them. Helen waited while Quayle and Tap walked urgently to the group near the burning plane.

"Are you clearing out?" Quayle said to the Flight Lieutenant, who was looking at the plane.

"Well, where did you spring from?"

"We came from Janina. We'd like a lift on your truck."

"We're from Eighty Squadron," Tap said. "You're Seventy-three, aren't you?"

"Yes," the Flight Lieutenant said. "What have you been doing?"

"This is John Quayle," Tap said to the Flight Lieutenant.

"Well, for Christ's sake! You're certainly good and alive," the Flight Lieutenant said. "They all thought you were dead. You're quite a hero. What happened to you?"

"I crashed. What about the truck?"

"They're leaving now."

"Can you let H.Q. know we're coming down?" Tap said.

"We've no communication now. But I'll tell them. I'm flying back. Those bastards just shot us up. Did you see it?"

"Yes."

"We lost this one. Come on over and I'll tell the Sergeant you can go with him."

They walked back to the truck. The Flight Lieutenant told the Sergeant that the two were coming with him.

"We've got a couple of Greeks and a Greek girl I'm going to marry," Quayle said. He did not like that, but he knew it was better to say it now and save explanations.

"I doubt about the Greeks. We're pretty well loaded down," the Flight Lieutenant said.

"We had better get moving too," the Sergeant said. "Are you taking off now?"

"Yes. Look, take the Greeks, will you, Sergeant? They've brought these officers from Janina. Afraid you'll have to give them a lift. Pitch something off if it's too heavy. All right?"

"Yes, sir."

"Well, the others are waiting for me," the Flight Lieutenant said. "There's a pilot officer in the first truck. That's his Hurricane that's burning. He'll look after you. Give you some food. Look after them, will you, Sergeant?"

"Yes, sir."

"S'long. Glad you're all right, Quayle."

"S'long," Quayle said to him and shook hands. "Thanks for everything."

"I'll tell them when I get to Athens," the Flight Lieutenant said as he walked quickly to his plane.

They stood and watched him climb in. The fitter was there and had already started the engine. The fitter was walking towards them as they watched the Flight Lieutenant taxi with the others to the end of the field to form a rough V. The Hurricanes had just turned around and were in line when Quayle heard the quiet roar. He looked quickly from where he had heard it, and saw the large flight coming from behind the mountains. He saw immediately their square shorn wings and knew they were Messerschmitts. He wanted to run and warn the Hurricanes but they were already taxiing down to lift and take off.

"Look," Tap shouted. He was pointing to the Messerschmitts coming down in a steep dive from the glide.

"Oh Christ," the fitter said as he came. Quayle was silent. He could feel and see and know now what was going to happen.

"Get down," Tap shouted. They were all lying on the grass flat waiting for it to happen.

Only Quayle stood there.

He could see this happening. The Messerschmitts came straight onto the Hurricanes just as their wheels were off the ground, and they were lame with their undercarriages still down. . . .

"You bastards," Quayle shouted as loud as he could.

They came in threes and then there was the burst. He heard the roaring of the Hurricanes and knew they did not know the Messerschmitts were almost on them. There was all roaring and nothing else now. The Hurricanes were nearly above him when the first three Messerschmitts were pulling out of their dive and firing.

There was the quick burst then the long one and the quick one and the roaring. The Messerschmitts pulled up. Quayle saw the kicking of the machine-gun bullets along the field near him. He stood there and looked at death.

The Hurricanes were aware now.

The second three Messerschmitts came on them and there was the burst. The Hurricanes were beating it flat and trying to climb, but there was a burst from each one and a lick of flame and the tracers and the terrific noise, and Quayle standing up shouting, and the Hurricane in the lead bursting into flames and falling in the split fraction of a second, and the white flat *plumph* of it exploding into ten thousand pieces, and the smell already; and still the noise of the flying and the other two Hurricanes still loping flat and climbing, and the third three coming down; and Quayle still standing there shouting and watching the Hurricanes, because they had got more height and were good and climbing now, and were doing the right thing and not waking combat but weaving and climbing; and Quayle knew they would be all right, because the Messerschmitts had used up too much height-value in their initial dive, and were disappearing over the mountain. And there was the smell of the Hurricane burning.

"It was the Flight Loot," he heard the fitter say to the Sergeant. "Proper goner, too. The bastards. The sons of bitches."

"Come on, we'll take a look."

"It's no use," the Sergeant said. "He's a goner." He was quiet.

"The bitches. The frickin' bastards, fancy them doing that."

"What do you expect them to do? Wait for us to ask them?" Tap said. He was angry and standing next to Quayle and watching the high black smoke that added to the smoke in the air from Larissa and from the other Hurricane that had been shot up on the ground.

Helen walked to Quayle and he looked at her slowly when she touched him, and could see that she was crying without sound.

"It is all terrible!"—and she was saying it to the earth and not to the people around her.

"Should we go over and see?" the Sergeant said to Quayle as he looked at the smoke from the Flight Lieutenant's plane.

"Send someone over. There may be something," Quayle said. He did not believe it. The Sergeant told the fitter to go over and take a look. They had not run as they normally would because they could see it was all hopeless. Quayle went with him across the field and Tap was behind. There were the fragments of the plane everywhere, and the burning center of it. There was the high smoke rising from the tangled death of the Hurricane and nothing there, absolutely nothing. Only the blackness and the smoke and absolutely nothing, Quayle was thinking, absolutely nothing.

He turned and walked back, still smelling the blackness of the fuel and detecting the other smell in it, though he was not certain whether it was there or not. But there was absolutely nothing left. Absolutely nothing.

"What a bloody mess," Tap said when he caught up.

Quayle did not say anything.

"I'd sooner be helping to make this than watch it," Tap said, half to himself.

225

Quayle nodded and walked to the truck.

"We'd better get going, Sergeant," he said. He saw the others from the truck now. They had been flat on the earth. There was the young pilot officer who had run towards the Flight Lieutenant's plane when it had crashed. Quayle had not seen him then, but now he did. He watched him walking back and there was quietness between all of them as they climbed into the cabin of the big trucks and on the back and started out.

The fitter who had gone to the plane was driving the truck that Quayle and Helen were in. Tap was in the one ahead with the Flying Officer. The Greeks were in the back of the same truck.

When they got to the road they saw the flat truck with the square front hurrying in its own dust towards them. It stopped to allow the second truck to crumble its way from the low field onto the road. The driver stood up in the open front. He had on the Australian wide hat.

"You'd better get a move on," he said to them.

"Are you the signal truck?" Tap asked them.

"No. We're sappers. We've just blown up the bridge back there. You'd better get a move on. The Germans are a couple of miles down the road."

"Where the hell's the army?" one of the aircraftsmen said.

"Where the hell do you think? They're in those mountains hold-ing the Germans off so you bastards can get away."

"It's a bloody wonder," the Englishman said.

"To hell with you. Where's the air force been? Get a move on," the Australian said.

The fitter pulled the heavy gear and the truck strained forward. The flat truck of the sappers came around them and quickly dis-appeared ahead of them. Slowly the truck gained some speed, but it was slow, and the truck that Tap was in ahead of them was slower.

Quayle noticed the driver continuously looking in the mirror that stuck out one side as if he expected the Germans any minute.

Quayle felt like that himself. . . . This business of feeling the Germans on your tail now is about the same as feeling one on your tail in the air. But this is slow, and it's getting dark. We seem to be the only ones left in the whole area. . . .

"How far are you going back?" he asked the small fitter, who was a Scot.

"To Athens," the Scot said.

"But to-night."

"As far as we get. Everybody seems to be going to Phersala. I think that's Field Headquarters. If these Jerries don't catch up with us . . ."

"Were those three planes the only ones left in the squadron?"

"That's right." The Scot was pulling the heavy truck around the flat corners.

"Who was the Flight Lieutenant?"

"That was Crosby. 'Bing' Crosby. He had the D.F.C."

The Scot was closing his lips tightly when he spoke but he could not keep them closed because his mouth broke into a wide smile. His red hair was sticking in a brush out the side of his overseas cap which was hanging on one ear almost. He was sure of himself when he spoke to Quayle, and did not care if he was a Flight Lieutenant or a Wing Commander, Quayle could tell that, and liked him for it. He watched the dim road coming up and sometimes helped the Scot pull the giant wheel around.

Once Helen laughed when the Scot was changing gears and there was a high groaning noise and the Scot looked at Helen and laughed with great enjoyment, and after that it was fine for them.

"Are you Greek, Miss?" he asked her, smiling without knowing it.

"Yes." Helen could only smile back at him.

"I have a Greek girl in Athens. I'm to marry her when I get back." He was rolling his R's and Helen could barely understand him.

"You will marry a Greek?" she said. She leaned forward to talk to him across Quayle.

"She's some girrl," the Scot said and Quayle smiled at the British in the implication.

"Corporal," Quayle said, "we are to be married." His lips were curled down in a tight smile when he said it. Helen looked quickly at Quayle and smiled.

"Is that so? That's fine," the Scot said. He was laughing now and pushing his cap farther down on one side and they all laughed even though it was quite dark and the truck ahead was barely visible.

"My name's Macpherson." He said it "Macfairsoon."

"From Glasgow?"

"No. Aberdeen."

"What's that one about Aberdeen going round and round?"

"That's Glasgow," the Scot said. Then he sang, 'When I go round to Glasgow, Glasgow goes round and round to me.' That was Will Fyffe. He's a phony."

"What's the rest of it?" Quayle asked him.

He was quiet for a moment concentrating on the road, then he started to sing in the rolling burr that was tuneful and smiling like his face, and sometimes Quayle joined in when he knew the words. When Quayle joined in, Macpherson sang even louder, and together they got tangled-up. Helen laughed contentedly and lifted her arm up to rub the back of Quayle's neck.

"How about some Greek songs?" the Scot said.

"You would not understand."

"Did you understand any of what Macpherson here was saying?"

"Some. But what language is it?" she said seriously.

"That's a version of English called Scotch," Quayle said to her.

"It's just plain Aberdeen," Macpherson said. "What's that song about Mussolini?"

Helen laughed again.

"That's not polite," she said. "The words are not polite."

"Never mind. We don't understand them," Macpherson said. Quayle was thinking that Macpherson's talk was not cheek, and he was not being familiar, and he was surprised at his own feeling.

"No. There is another one."

"No. We'll have Mussolini," Macpherson said.

"All right," Helen said. She was quiet for a moment, then started to hum the song about Mussolini; and when she came to the part that was repetitive about Mussolini, Macpherson joined in, and Quayle laughed at the whole thing as well as at the idea of this Scot with the Germans behind him making Helen sing a risqué song.

They were still laughing when the truck in front stopped and Macpherson stopped behind them.

"What's up now?" he said and got out.

"Mac." It was the pilot officer calling him.

"Yes, sir."

"How about some tea? You have it there, haven't you? Where's the Sergeant?"

"Here," the Sergeant said.

"Well pull out the primus, will you? We'll make some tea."

Tap had gotten down and the half-dozen aircraftsmen on both trucks were stamping their feet. Quayle could not see very well but he saw the pilot officer coming up to him.

"Finley said you were here. I didn't know," he said to Quayle. "We're stopping for something to eat. Finley said you would all be hungry."

"I could certainly do with some tea," Quayle said.

"Mr. Quayle," the Sergeant who was in the back of the truck said to him. "What about these Greeks? They've been arguing to beat the hell all the way."

"I'll see," Quayle said and looked around for the big Greek. He was not around. He did not think about it but saw the little Greek talking in the darkness to Helen near the back of the first truck. He walked to them.

"Tell them to lay off it, will you, Helen?"

"They are both very nervous."

"What of? Tell them we're getting a bit tired of it."

"It won't do much good."

Quayle walked in the dark to where the pilot officer was talking with Tap.

"This is Pete Martin, John," Tap said. "This is John Quayle, Martin."

"We've met," Quayle said. He saw the big Greek beckoning and he walked to him. The other walked away from the trucks down the road so that Quayle would follow him in the dim light.

"*Inglisi*," the Greek said. "I'm sorry. But I leave you. I have gone far enough. I go back."

"What for?"

"It is bad to run away like this. It is good for you because this is not your home. But this is bad for me."

"Don't be crazy. What do you think you're going to do? Fight the whole German Army?"

"It is not that. I will go into the mountains."

"What for?"

"This will soon be over here. We will fight in the mountains."

Quayle was thinking of Mellass. He was silent for a moment and peering into the dimness.

"What's the point in going back now?"

"My home is north of Larissa near Olympus. I will go into the mountains there."

"All right," Quayle said quietly. "I suppose you know what you're doing."

"Thank you. Thank you for bringing me here. You are good *Inglisi*. I am sorry you will have to be beaten here. It is no place for *Inglisi* to fight."

"We're not beaten yet," Quayle said.

"Perhaps. But it will be soon. I will go now. I hope you will be happy with the girl. She is very fine and the other boy too. I will go now."

"Just a minute. Have you got any food?"

"No, I do not need it."

"Wait," Quayle said, "I will get you some. Wait here."

"No, *Inglisi*. I do not need it."

230

"Wait here," Quayle said. He went back to the truck. He found the Sergeant and asked him for whatever food he could spare. He got some bread and tea and walked back to where he had left the Greek. He looked around but he could not see him.

"Are you there?" Quayle said in quiet German. There was no answer. He looked into the darkness. He could not even hear footsteps.

There was only the darkness and the noise of the others behind him.

He closed his hand on the food and turned and went back to the trucks.

Chapter 24

They had started again into the long line of trucks that extended as far as the imagination could picture it in the night. They were not the tail end of it. Other trucks had come in from side tracks behind them. There was slow movement, and long stops in the night that registered something in Quayle's mind between the sleep he took and the pleasantness of the warmth and fullness of his stomach, and the occasional talk he heard between the Australians.

They were all Australians in the other trucks. And there were the flashes of laughter from Macpherson, who sometimes talked to Helen. Also the time when Helen asked him about the big Greek and Quayle had said, "He's gone into the mountains."

And she had said, "They will all go into the mountains."

It went on like that, through the half dullness of sleep and waking, into the red morning.

"This is a nice mess," Macpherson said to him when he was awake.

"How far are we?"

"We seemed to have passed Phersala during the night."

"Are we near Athens?" Helen asked.

"No. We haven't come to Lamia yet. Then we've got those mountains."

"How far forward is the jam?" They were stopped now.

"I don't know," Macpherson said. "It's been like this for the last couple of hours."

"I'll take a look," Quayle said. "Look out, Helen." He crawled over her and jumped down from the high cabin of the truck. It was cold in the morning quietness. The trucks extended as far along as the road was straight. They disappeared around a curve. They were in the middle of the jam of traffic. Some of it was Greek, but most of it Australian. There were two large camouflaged daubed buses ahead that had Greek Red Crosses on them. They were filled with wounded.

As Quayle walked along the edge of the muddy road, he could hear the drivers arguing about the blockage.

"Where's all the road police?" one Australian said.

"That wouldn't do any good. It's these bloody Greeks. They're blocking the road with their refugee trucks."

"Well, the Jerries will be down on us. What a target."

"Did you come from Larissa?"

"No, Elasson. Where's the turn-off for the first field ambulance?"

"Christ. Search me. I'm going back for ammo. There's supposed to be a sign where our dump is, but I'm buggered if I seen the thing."

"This is a proper mess all right. Someone's going to pay for it."

"Where's the line now?"

"Somewhere around Larissa. I dunno."

"They're building defences south of those Thermoplery plains."

"In that bloody mountain pass?"

"Yes. If the Jerries get over that in a hurry they're bloody marvels."

"They got over the last one. Say, have you any oil?"

"Sure. I got a two-gallon. How much do you want?"

"About a quart will get me there."

"Help yourself. What are you anyway?"

"First Field Ambulance. We're South Aussie. Are you the Seventh Division crowd?"

"No, Sixth. What part of South Aussie are you from?"

"South Adelaide."

"How'd you like to be there now?"

"My bloody oath . . . It's funny, we had a lot of Greeks down there."

"There was a lot in Geelong too."

233

"I got to hand it to those bastards. I used to think they were greasy dagoes. They are, too, at home. But I got to hand it to this crowd."

"They did bloody marvellous. Poor bastards. We're up and leaving them, too."

"I wish to hell they'd get a move on."

"I wonder where those frickin' Jerries are."

"They'll have their dive bombers here in a while."

When Quayle passed them he heard the one with the hat say, "Look at that bloke. He's one of the flyers."

"He's done in, all right. I didn't think we had any airplanes."

"You know that's the whole bloody trouble with this. No frickin' airplanes."

"We just haven't got any."

Quayle was out of earshot and he was stepping lightly into the mud. He walked down the road to the bend and turned it. He could see the end of the truck line ahead about a quarter of a mile. He could see the wide solid trucks with their Australian drivers, formed too close to each other. Some of the drivers were out of their trucks talking among themselves, others were hurriedly trying to make tea over primuses in the back. The Greek trucks here and there were hundreds of years old and the people were perched high on the bundles piled on the back and all their belongings. They were silent and the women had shawls pulled tight around their faces. The children sitting quietly and covered by a blanket were suppressed with the whole thing.

When he got to the front of the column Quayle saw the blockage. It was an eight-wheeled heavy R.A.F. truck. The whole section of the back, including the four wheels, had come away from the truck and the structure had collapsed on the road. There was a smaller truck bogged in the mud beside it. There was a motor-cycle M.P. with the white armband. He was telling half a dozen Australians what to do. Quayle did not say anything but watched them trying to push, and under its own power get the small truck past the large one. It was only slipping deeper into the ditch of mud.

234

"What are you trying to do?" he asked the M.P.

"Get this truck past this busted one so we can pull it off the road. It got stuck."

They were pulling it again and the driver was revving the engine high and the thick rubber tires were slipping but suddenly they caught and showered mud over Quayle and the others and lurched forward, scraping and tearing off one of its fenders on the broken truck, but it got past. Quickly the soldiers attached a wire tow rope to the broken truck. A driver got into the broken truck, turned the wheels. The Australians got behind the broken end and gradually they edged and the truck pulled it off the road. Quayle started to walk back to the truck as the column started to move slowly forward. It thinned out with wide spaces at first then gradually it telescoped into groups again and he hadn't walked far before the truck came along. He climbed up. Helen was not there.

"She went down to those Greek ambulances," Macpherson said.

It was then he felt the thumping on the back of the cabin. Macpherson stopped the truck. There was shouting.

"Bombers," Macpherson said and leaped out of the truck. Quayle could see the men from the stopped trucks leaping out all the way along and running into the fields. He looked up as he ran. He could hear the planes and they were coming from the low mountains ahead out of the early morning sun.

"They didn't waste much time," an Australian said to him as they ran.

Quayle was looking around for Helen when the bombers came over. He flattened out as the six of them flew straight along the road from about one thousand feet and dropped the first string of bombs. He felt the earth being sick beneath him and the great sound and the unseparated noise of a string of hundred-pounders falling on the other side of the road — then the climbing roar of the planes disappearing. He looked around for Helen as he stood up. He hoped she hadn't run to the other side of the road.

"Bloody rotten shots," the Australian was saying to him.

The column hadn't been touched. There were shrapnel holes

through some of the canvas truck coverings. Quayle went to the Greek ambulance. He saw Helen in the first one.

"Where were you when that happened?" he said. He was angry at her.

"Here. These ones can't run. Look at them, John."

"What the hell. Don't be heroic. You being here won't save them."

"But they cannot run like the others."

"Too bad."

"Don't be angry," she said.

"I don't want you sitting around here getting bombed."

"That is too bad. There is no doctor. Look at them."

He could see the six stretchers and the dried blood on the floor and could taste the smell of it. There were two looking at him as he looked at them. They were black-faced. One had eyes that were watering down his face. The other's head was bandaged. He could see the limp shapes in the other stretchers and the face of the wan driver turning around and looking at them.

"It doesn't matter," he said. "What the hell can you do?"

"I can fix some of them, their bandages. That one is dead." She nodded to the end one.

"Well, I think you're screwy. I'll be in the other truck behind you," he said.

"Do not be quick with your anger, John."

"I'm not angry. I'll be behind you." He walked away. He knew he was angry with her, it was almost jealousy and he did not know why. He got into the truck with Macpherson, who was whistling under his breath. He smiled at Quayle.

"Did you find her?" he said.

"Yes," Quayle said.

"She's verra pretty." He was smiling.

Quayle looked at him and laughed within himself.

"What are your people going to say when they find out you're marrying a Greek?" Quayle was smiling when he said it.

"Oh. They will probably coot me off w'out a cent. But they ha'nt a cent anyway, so what's the difference?" He laughed again. "Those Jerries are rotten shots, sir." Quayle saw the humour in the "sir."

"Aye," Quayle said. Then he was serious again.

"She'll be all right," Macpherson said to him.

"She doesn't get out when those bombers come over."

Macpherson did not say anything but looked at the climb ahead of them. They had been climbing steadily and now they were passing over a high ridge. Quayle heard the thumping on the cabin again.

"They're at it again," Macpherson said and leaped out as he pulled on the brake. Quayle jumped out the other side and he could see the planes coming as he ran. They swept low. As they came along the road he could see them dip, and the strafing began. He saw the licks of dirt like high splashing drops of water ripping the field between him and the road and heard the high individual, then confused, sound of multiple machine-guns — then the passing roar and the returning echo of the engines as they swept right along the column.

Quayle got up and ran toward the ambulances. He was looking around for Helen as he ran and he could not see her. He could see the car somewhere forward in the column, burning, and the bullets in the side of the second ambulance. He pulled open the big door. Helen was lying on the floor.

"Helen," he said. "For Christ's sake."

She looked up.

"Have they gone?" she said. He looked hard at her. She was staring at him.

"Yes," he said.

She got up slowly.

"You goddam fool," Quayle said to her. "Next time you don't stay here."

"I'm as safe here as anywhere. Look at these. Did they hit anybody outside?"

"Somebody, I guess. Look," he said, "stop being foolish about this."

237

"I think we should take the one at the end out. Could we bury him here?"

"There's no time for that," he said.

"What is the smoke?"

"They hit a truck."

Tap came up with the little Greek then, and pulled open the door.

"Are you two all right?" he said.

"Yes."

"There seems to be somebody hit ahead."

"Tap," she said. "Can you take the one at the end out? He's dead."

"What will I do with him?"

"Bury him. It is bad for the others."

Tap looked at Quayle. Quayle got out and walked past him and went forward to see what was burning. The column was jammed behind a flat-fronted truck that was burning furiously. An Australian was holding his hat in front of his face trying to turn the wheels so it would steer off the road. A tow rope had been attached to it and another truck was ready to pull. When it did, the burning car rolled on its side in the ditch and the water sent up great white smoke. Two Australians were carrying a man from the field to the edge of the road. He was bleeding from the neck.

"He got hit," one of them said to Quayle when he went to help them.

"There's an ambulance down here," Quayle said.

They carried him to the Greek ambulance and lifted him in just as the little Greek and Macpherson lifted out the dead Greek.

"Here's another one for you, Helen," Quayle said.

He went with Tap to see about the dead Greek. Two Australians had taken shovels from the side of their cars and were digging a pit. When it was deep enough they sat the dead Greek in it. Quayle took some papers out of his pockets and looked for the identification disk but there was none.

They covered the Greek with earth and Quayle watched it, black against the yellow staring face. Then he went back to the ambulance.

"Here's his papers," he said to Helen. The driver of the ambulance was helping her clean the dirt from the ambulance floor.

"Thanks," she said to him and put them in her pocket. "I have nothing," she said. "Can you get some clean bandages or something? I have used the ones I had for you. I want some lint too."

"I'll see."

"Tap has gone to look for some," she said.

Quayle, feeling this appeal to Tap, stood where he was and watched her holding the soaked bandage to the Australian's neck. He was a thin-faced boy with lank black hair that she had to keep pushing off his face. His eyes were open and followed her movements; he did not say anything but kept his eyes very wide because he was afraid to close them. Tap came back with some lint and bandages. The flying officer was with him now.

"Maybe I can help," the flying officer said. "I know a little."

"He is bleeding very much," Helen said.

The flying officer crouched at the end of the truck and looked at the Australian. He took the bandage from Helen and let it away from the wound so he could see it. He looked at the Australian and got out of the truck again.

"He won't last long," he said, very quietly, and walked back to his truck.

Slowly the column started again. Quayle told Macpherson he was riding in the ambulance with Helen. He stayed at the back of the ambulance sitting on the floor saying nothing, but looking outside all the time waiting for the planes to come back. The Greek in the nearest stretcher patted him on the shoulder with a bandaged hand and made indications of smoking, and Quayle shook his head. As the truck sloped on the incline the Australian made short noises, then was silent as the truck stopped. Then Quayle heard the shouting and saw everybody going into the fields again — and heard the planes, and shouted to Helen.

"Come on."

She did not move and then the bombs were shaking the earth. He sprawled flat on the bus floor and pulled Helen down and kept her lying flat as the whole earth shook with the bombing and the thin scrapping of the machine-guns again. He could see the bursts through the smeared windows but they were too much across the road to do any damage. Then the planes went away again. Two Australians looked at Quayle as he opened the door.

"How is Flip?" one of them said.

"He's pretty bad," Quayle said.

"Will he be all right?" the other one said. He had a tin hat on.

"I don't know. You better go back. The sooner we get this ambulance going the better." They went away.

As the ambulance moved forward again, Quayle was smelling the atmosphere of the bus. It was staleness and death, and he remembered when he was at school how he used to think and keep thinking some day you'll be dead, and that day must come, you must cease all this, that's the worst part of it, to stop all this walking drinking sleeping and other people being alive, that was the worst part of it because it all passed you by.

"Why don't you go back to the other car?" Helen said. "I'm all right."

"I might as well stay here now," he said.

"You are foolish."

"You're not very consistent," he said. "Why stay here while they're bombing?"

"Why did you stay?"

"I couldn't get out in time," he said.

"Well, neither can I."

"All right," he said very resignedly.

"It only goes to Lamia," she said. "There's a hospital there."

"You'd better not let a hospital see you," he said.

"I will get out before we get there."

"How far are we from this place?"

"The driver said nearly there. He knows my brother."

"Does he?"

"Yes." And Quayle saw the trucks stopping and the drivers running into the fields again. He sprawled on the floor and Helen was beside him. He put her arm around his neck and pulled her around. He kissed her without feeling, without malice, and with certainty; and she was warm and quietly shivering and he pulled her whole body to him. There was the uplifting of earth again by the bombs and he could feel it transmitted through both of them and didn't care about anything, only about being like this, and he could feel Helen giving to him what he was giving to her. They lay like that until the bombing had gone, and she got up slowly and went back to the Australian.

The long column was strafed twice before they got into Lamia. They came down the incline right into the town. It was shambles and still burning. The smoke and fire were flat on the earth.

"You must tell the Australians their friend has gone to the hospital here."

"I hope it's standing."

"It is out of the town. I will go back to the truck." She told the driver she was leaving. She put the thick cotton pad against the Australian's neck and pushed back his lank hair. His eyes were closed now and his face full and white, and she did not know whether he was dead yet. She looked at the others and told them they would soon be in the hospital. They thanked her as she left. She walked back to the truck and got in next to Macpherson. When Quayle came back Macpherson drove quickly through the bombed town, passing the side of the convoy, which made them all shout to him, but he did not care and he caught up with the other truck on the flat, plain, straight road out of the town.

"These are those Thermopylae plains," Macpherson said.

"Yes," Quayle said. He looked at the flat stretch either side. This was fertile land. It was green and tilled, with few rises in it, but ahead were the high towering mountains that dominated the plains and the high Menenditsa peak.

"It will be a wonder if this cold crate gets over yon mountain," Macpherson said. He was leaning low over the wheel and looking at the shadow before him. The road was blocked ahead with the long column in retreat. He shook his head and leaned back. They had reached the foot of the mountain, and the climb began from the flat in a great winding turn upwards. They had not gone far when the planes came back. There was no flat area to run to now, only the gorse bush up the side of the mountain. Quayle and Tap helped Helen upwards.

The string of bombs dropped along the foot of the mountain to the plain. It missed their part of the column, but Quayle, standing up, could see the string bursting like a boy throwing stones into a pool.

It was like that all the way over the high winding pass. They moved a few feet at a time. When they had reached the top of one section Quayle, looking behind, could see the wide stretch of the Thermopylae plains and Lamia and the sea coming in and the wide flat rivers flowing into it. It was afternoon and at times there were flights of sixty and one hundred planes above them, and Quayle could see the retreating units stretching both ways around the mountain pass like a giant caterpillar. It moved slowly and with stops for the heavy strafing and the bombing into late afternoon and early evening. By that time they were nearly over the pass and it was flattening out, approaching the plains of Levadia.

At nightfall the first truck pulled off the road at a shallow turning. Macpherson followed them and pulled away so that they were parked sufficient distance from each other. Quayle got out and helped Helen down. He wondered why they were stopping, walked over to the other truck. Tap and the flying officer were out and looking around. The driver had the bonnet off the engine and was delving into the insides.

"What's wrong?" Quayle said to them.

"We're stopping here," the flying officer said. "There's something wrong with the oil feed in the truck."

"How long will it take?"

"We must wait until daylight to fix it, I think."

Helen had walked away from them and disappeared into the

timber across the field. Quayle watched her go, then went back to the other truck. He did not want to wait around here all night. He was fantastically tired, but he could postpone sleep until he got to Athens. Being so near now, it seemed a waste of time to stop a night here.

"They've got oil lead trouble," he said to Macpherson. "What about going on?"

"Can they do without us?" Macpherson said to him.

"I don't know," Quayle said. "Why don't you see?"

Macpherson walked over to the other truck. Quayle could see the light of the primus near the truck. He could hear the Sergeant shouting for the flat kettle, and the aircraftsmen arguing that it was under all the kit and he couldn't get it out and that a canteen dish would do.

"I think I'd better stay in case they have to be towed," Macpherson said when he came back. "They won't last long on that pipe."

"All right," Quayle said and walked back to the other truck. Helen had come back and was sitting next to Tap on a tarpaulin they had spread out next to the truck. The flying officer was pulling a mug out of his kit.

"Hullo, John," Tap said. "We're giving Helen some tea. Have you got a cup?"

"Count me out," John said. "The Sergeant is making some over there."

They could hear the continuous rumble and see the long shapes passing all the time on the road as the endless column kept moving back.

"We always seem to be stopping for tea," Quayle said. He was annoyed at the delay.

"It's that oil lead," Tap said. "Can't help it."

"Yes. We could pick up another truck."

"One night here won't make any difference. I'm pretty tired. So is Helen."

"Where's the little Greek?" Quayle suddenly asked.

"He's around."

"He has gone away to relieve himself," Helen said and eased over next to where Quayle was standing so that she was sitting near his feet. She pulled at his trouser-leg for him to sit down, but he merely touched her shoulder.

"I wonder if there's anybody left in Athens," Tap said.

"What the hell?" Quayle said to him.

"Well, look at this going on. The whole army's going back," Tap said.

"Probably Athens is full of the army, then," Quayle said.

"I don't mean that. I suppose all the bomber squadron boys are gone."

"If there's any left."

"I wonder where all the Hurricanes are?"

"Still in Egypt," the flying officer said. He was rubbing the blond beard around his chin and leaned back to lie flat out.

"The army has taken a beating all right, hasn't it?" Tap said.

"What did you expect?" Quayle said.

"I don't know. Not a wholesale retreat anyway."

"We will always retreat," Quayle said. "How can you do anything else when you haven't got anything clear-cut like the Germans? Or an army like theirs?"

"Maybe," Tap said. "But I still say we'd beat them if we had equal strength."

"Like hell," Quayle said. "All our methods are ancient. Everything."

"What's got into you?"

"Skip it," Quayle said and walked away back to the truck. "How's the tea coming?" he said to Macpherson, only to break the abruptness of how he felt with himself.

"It's nearly ready," the Sergeant said. "Will the lady eat here?"

"She'll be over there," Quayle said. He didn't know what was forming this solid and continuous anger in him. It was when Helen was around and with Tap that it was there, and when he was talking with Tap about what was happening, and he was not thinking of it too much. It was Macpherson that made him feel normal.

"What do you think of all this retreating?" he suddenly asked Macpherson.

Macpherson was silent for a moment, then he said casually, "Pretty bad. But we expected it."

"What do you think will happen now?"

"Dunkirk. We can always get out of the mess." Macpherson was not talking seriously but Quayle knew he was serious in his meaning.

"Here's the tea." Macpherson handed him a mug of tea. "There's no sugar."

"I don't take it," Quayle said about the sugar.

"I suppose we'll just have to hang on to what we've got until we starve th' Germans out."

"I suppose so," Quayle said, sipping the hot tea.

"We'll do better when we fight on our own place."

"You think they will invade England?"

"I d' na know." He was suddenly broad in his accent. "They ha'nt a chance i' they do."

"I hope you're right," Quayle said.

"So do I," Macpherson said, smiling.

The Sergeant and some of the other aircraftsmen had been listening but not saying anything because they had not been spoken to by Quayle. They could not offer conversation. Quayle felt the quietness from them all for the first time and realized the exception in his talking to Macpherson and that he was no part of this group. He should move away, but he did not want to go back to Tap. He wished Helen were here and he suddenly said to Macpherson:

"Go over and ask the Miss Stangou if she will have some tea over here."

Macpherson got up and went away. Quayle listened to the heavy rumble of the continuous retreat and the voices of the others talking carefully, because he was there and they were restrained, and Macpherson came back with Helen.

"I have had the tea," she said. "But I think about the bandage on your head. How is it?"

"It's all right," he said.

"I got some bandages in there if you want any," Macpherson said.

"It doesn't matter," Quayle said.

"Yes it does. May I have them? I will change it in the morning when I can see."

Quayle was lying down on the broad canvas now and there was mist across the sky and slight dampness in his face. Helen was sitting near his head and she was feeling the bandages and rubbing his head softly at the same time. All the physical tiredness came on him quickly and he fell asleep. He turned over. There was the rumble of the retreating column still going on. Everything else was quiet. He saw the figure on the tarpaulin wrapped in a blanket. He leaned over. It was Helen.

"Helen," he said quietly. She awoke.

"What is it?"

"It's raining," he said.

She covered her head with the blanket. He put out his hand and she took it. Slowly she eased the blanket over him as he lay down and he could feel the wetness under him.

"You will get wet," she said. There was nothing dividing them now and he could feel the warmth of her as he put his arm under her head and lifted it up so that she was in the crook of his arm. He had the other arm over her waist. Her arm was quietly across him. He eased himself towards her and felt the whole warmth of her.

"Be gentle, John. Please be gentle."

"I will," he said very quietly and easily. He was not awkward.

"I love you like this," she said.

"Yes," he said. "Yes. It is everything."

And then there was the silence and the coldness of the damp blanket on his face and the warmth through him and through her. And the silence.

Chapter 25

In the white rain of the morning the aircraftsmen were making tea over the primus and the retreat was still going on. The feeling of threat, which had been lost in the night, was there again. The driver of the other truck was trying to fix the oil lead and Macpherson was helping him. Quayle looked at the traffic on the road and knew that he would have to move on quickly.

"We will go on," he told Helen who was wrapping a clean bandage on his head.

"Yes," she said quietly.

"Look," he said to Tap when he came up. "We're going on. It's no use waiting around for this to be fixed. We're wasting time."

"It won't make that much difference," Tap said, pulling at his bandage.

"Maybe. But Helen and I are going. Do you want to come?"

"No. I'll wait with Martin," Tap said. He was struggling to loosen his bandage.

"All right," Quayle said. He walked to where Macpherson was swilling some of the engine parts in a half-tin of petrol.

"We're going on," Quayle said to him. "Thanks for everything."

"That's all right," Macpherson said. He stood up and smiled at Helen. "I hope you get married all right." His hat had slipped almost off his head.

"You too," Helen said. She was looking at his freckled face intently.

"Where's the little Greek? I haven't seen him at all." Quayle turned around.

"He is near the other truck. I will tell him," Helen said and went away. "Good-bye," she said to Macpherson as she went. "Very good luck to you."

"And to you," Macpherson said, with his hands on his thick trousers.

"Well, I'll see you somewhere," Quayle said to him.

"Yessir. Good-bye." There was no handshake.

"S'long," Quayle said.

"What's the hurry anyway?" Tap said to him as they walked across to where Helen and the little Greek stood.

"I don't know. I don't want to wait around here," Quayle said. He did not know why he was in a hurry. Athens had been the end of the journey to him, and he was anxious to get there because there was no relaxing until he did.

"I'll see you in Athens," Tap said to Helen.

"Yes," she said. It was noncommittal.

"Come on," Quayle said. "S'long."

"S'long then," Tap said. The flying officer half-saluted them.

Quayle walked with Helen and the little Greek to the road. He hailed the first lorry and asked the Australian for a lift to Athens.

"Hop in the front here," the driver said. There was another Australian sitting there.

"We'll go in the back," Quayle said. "Let him stay there."

"It's all right. He doesn't mind." The other one was getting out.

"No. We'll go in the back," Quayle said and the three of them walked around to the high canvas-covered back and climbed up. The truck lurched forward. They watched the two trucks parked in the field disappear as the mist settled low in the distance.

"Why has the other *Inglisi* remained?" the little Greek asked Helen.

"He wishes to remain with the blond *Inglisi* with the truck."

"Has he quarrelled with this one?"

"Not at all," Helen said carefully. "This one is in a hurry."

"That I know. He is always in a hurry," the little Greek said.

Quayle lay on the back of the jolting truck. It was empty except for two rolled kits in one corner. Helen was sitting on them. He smiled at her. He could see the little Greek looking closely at him. He had almost forgotten about the little Greek. His black beard and wild hair were blacker and wilder and his face thinner than before. His forehead was crumpled and his eyes were not receptive to Quayle's look at first, then suddenly they widened and he smiled at Quayle. Quayle smiled and half cocked his head, and the little Greek beamed in return. Everything was all right again.

"Will you mind going to Egypt when this is over?" he said suddenly to Helen.

"I do not understand," she said.

"This will soon be over. I will have to go back to Egypt."

"I would tell you once, you remember, that it was not simple."

"It's simple if the thing is important enough."

"All right then," she said. "If we are to go to Egypt, then it is that way."

"I'm sorry about you, leaving your parents. Perhaps they would go too."

"They would not leave," she said.

"We will see," he said, half turning to look at her. There was quietness and patience in him now and the strange anger had gone.

"My father would think that running away."

"It's going to be unpleasant for him if the Germans come in. His name is in the book, isn't it?"

"I do not think he will leave."

"Do they know about us?"

"I wrote and told them about it when you did not come back."

"What did they say?"

"I never got an answer."

"What do you think they think about it?"

"They may be surprised. They will be pleased."

"I don't know what sort of life there is for you."

"No one can look very far ahead in these times," she said.

"I won't try to say what's going to happen to us."

"I will accept it," she spoke quietly and surely.

Quayle looked at the incline dipping behind them and braced his feet for support against the sides so he would not slip out. The little Greek was clutching the side of the truck and was trying to sleep. Quayle was remembering the time he was lying on the truck floor singing "I care for nobody, no not I, if nobody cares for me," and he whistled it softly now.

"What will your parents say?" she said to him then.

"They will be curious and think it is very hasty and want details."

"Where are they now?"

"In the Isle of Man. That's an island near Scotland and England."

"Is that where you live?"

"Yes," he said. "But not now. I do not want to live there afterwards."

"Have you any brothers and sisters?"

"Two sisters. One is at home. I don't know where the other one is now. Somewhere in London, I think."

"What is it like in the Isle of Men?"

"Like this." He pointed outside. "It's always misty in the hills."

"Do you like it like this?"

"No. I'll take the sun. I like Egypt like that."

"What did you do before the war?"

"Everything," he said. He did not want to talk about it. She was silent then.

The truck had climbed the narrow road caught between the high cuts in the mountain. It wound slowly upwards around the edge of the peak that held the range together. It was like a long slow scenic railway and Quayle was thinking of the railway that went up to Laxey Glen in the Isle of Man.

"What will you do when we get back? You cannot fly like that with your head still with the stitches in it." Helen had taken off her coat and put it under his head.

"I can fly," he said as he lifted his head up. "If there are any planes left to fly."

"Will they allow you?"

"It doesn't seem much use now anyway."

He was suddenly feeling strongly about it all. He did not want to be eliminated in the tail end of this mess. What if I'd been wiped out in Libya, everything would be going on the same. It's a hell of a waste and nobody's getting anywhere. It's not much use like this at all. How the hell can we win anything? What's the use of thinking like that, my boy? That will get you into a fine mess. Either you believe you win or you will be afraid to climb into an airplane again. To hell with that, but I'd like to see this whole business cleaned up. It will have to be done by the army and the army doesn't seem to be able to do anything. We're always behind. We don't seem to have anything set out. What the hell. Even the planes. We get more planes, but so do the others and we're always outnumbered. We could make a hell of a mess of their air force if we had even an equal number. That's right all right. Look at that time when we lost Vain. Another flight of planes in that scrap and it would have been different. They would all be different. It will be a long time coming that way but what's the use in the air if the army's no good, and this proves it's no good, though these Australians seem to be all right, but they're going to get fed up with being pushed around. That's all very fine; but what's the use if you don't have the whole thing reorganized? There will be reorganization. Well, who's going to do it? . . . How do I know? . . . What about the ones at the top? They've got too good a job; boy, when I think of some of those guys the way they hang onto their jobs and they hang onto them at all costs! That's where it starts. Who are you going to put there? I don't know. . . . It's waste for Macpherson to be driving that truck. We're all wet on that, too. We pick the wrong ones for flyers. Tap should never be in the air. He's going to get it one day. He's goddam careless. I wonder how in the hell he ever got out of that Elbasan scrape that day. He flies his plane all right, but he gets into a mess too easy.

"I wonder if there are any Gladiators left?" he said aloud but to himself.

"What?" Helen had been wondering what he was thinking about. "That's the planes we fly. It will be a miracle if there's any left."

"What will you fly? Do you bomb when you have no fighters?"

"No. Maybe they'll give me to the Hurricanes. If there's any Hurricanes."

"I do not want you to bomb," she said and he laughed at her.

The truck stopped then. They were at the flat end of the other side of the pass. Quayle got out as he heard the planes and helped Helen down. The little Greek was already into the wheat field flanking the road. The Australian was running with the other one to the ditch. The long stream of traffic both ways was stopped dead and the planes coming out of the sun were picking the flat stretch.

"We'd better get farther away," he said to Helen.

They ran through the resisting wheat, then fell flat as the first string of bombs hit the road. Quayle could see at least sixty planes in the glance he took upwards. They were flying straight along the road, and above them was a fighter escort of maybe fifty Messerschmitts.

"They must be on a bus route," he shouted to Helen as the next string dropped. He could see bombs coming from the second flight only. By the time they were nearly overhead he pulled Helen's face flat into the earth and pushed himself down as the bombs exploded less than one hundred feet from them and the high shower of mud and the vibration shook him. He clung desperately to the sanity of the wet earth and felt every smash that it took in deep rumbles and screaming noise.

"They were very near," Helen said when he let her up. She was wiping her face.

"You can always tell when they're coming near. You watch them next time," he said.

"I am afraid enough now."

"You're less afraid if you watch what's going on."

"What do you see?"

"You can tell when the bombs come out of the plane if they're

252

going to be anywhere near you. You can see the bombs leave the plane but you lose sight of them as they get close to you. But you've got a rough idea. It is better if you know what's going on."

"I will try next time," she said.

There was an M.P. at the head of the convoy section they were in. He was sitting on his motor-bike shouting to the two Australians when Quayle and Helen and the little Greek came back.

"Keep your truck back until the ones ahead get over this flat stretch," he was shouting, above the roar of his intermittent motor-cycle.

"We'll get the hell bombed out of us," the Australian said back to him.

"Look, if you wait here we can thin this out a bit. This has been bombed all day." Quayle noticed the holes in the earth all around the road and sometimes on the edge of the road where the bombs had hit. There was a straight string of bombs holing the field directly parallel to the road. When the bombers came back, Quayle pulled Helen into the shelter of one of these red-earthed holes and the little Greek, seeing them, made for another and stayed there until the bombers passed over.

The road had been cleared before them by this time and the Australians got back in the truck. They started again and speeded over the flat area that was a mess of bomb-holes. They were then beginning the last climb before Athens.

The nearer to Athens they got, the greater the haste seemed to be and the heavier the threat of the war long behind them. There was always the bombers flying over and the threat of bombing was never away. But they eased down the last winding slope and could see the olive fields and the sea and Athens stretching behind it with the high rock of the Acropolis and the mount where Paul gave his sermon.

With this in sight, the truck made the last stop before Athens. It pulled off the road near a stone house and a medical officer in a long British trench-coat with two pips on his shoulder was drinking tea in front of an open fire on a cement block.

"Could I get some tea around here?" the Australian driver said as he got down.

"Help yourself." The medical officer pointed to a large container near the fire.

When Quayle appeared the medical officer walked over to him.

"What's wrong with your head?" He was looking at it with that downward professional glance.

"Nothing," Quayle said. The little Greek was already holding a mug out for some tea.

"I'm here to pick any of your fellers coming back with wounds," the young medical officer said. He was blond with a white moustache and thin balding hair. He looked at Helen.

"I am a Greek," she said, because she felt his question.

"Can I have a look at your head? Bend over," he said to Quayle.

"It's all right," Quayle said, without bending over.

"He has stitches in it. There is a cut," she said.

"Come on," the young medical officer said to him. Quayle bent over and the bandage came off as Helen automatically undid the pin that held it.

"You can get those stitches taken out now. You better go straight to the hospital when you get into Athens. We still have one at Cephisia."

The Australian handed him a mug of tea, and a china cup that had appeared from somewhere to Helen. He was sipping his out of a canteen lid.

"What's it like farther up?" the medical officer asked them.

"Tangled up," Quayle said, sipping the hot tea.

"Have the Germans got to Lamia yet?"

"I don't know. They weren't there yesterday. Or the day before. I've forgotten."

"Are you a nurse?" the medical officer asked Helen.

"She's a nurse from a hospital at the front. They sent her down with me," Quayle lied.

"Have they started to evacuate yet?" Quayle asked him after the silence.

254

"I don't know. There was some talk of an evacuation from Volos."

"What's it like in Athens?"

"In a mess. Everybody is expecting the fifth columnists to take over."

"Has it been bombed?" Helen asked.

"No. Not Athens. They've been giving all the airdromes and Piraeus a pasting."

"Have you seen any airplanes, ours I mean, around?"

"Not many," the medical officer said. "They were talking about parachutists. Did you see any?"

"No," Quayle said. "Were these planes fighters or bombers?"

"I think they were bombers. Blenheims. They've been dive-bombing a lot."

"Are you ready?" the Australian said as he threw the tea leaves into the fire.

Quayle and Helen went back to the truck. The little Greek was already there and held out his hand to help Helen and then to help Quayle who took it and got up as the truck started. The medical officer had walked over with them.

"Hope you enjoy that warm bath," he said to Quayle, smiling. Quayle felt the dirt all over him and his greasy hands with the large black blood-clot on the back from where he had cut his hand.

"Thanks," Quayle said as the truck slipped forward. "S'long."

"S'long." The medical officer gave a half-salute for the benefit of Helen, and the truck wound on down the now good road through the olive fields to the edge of the sea.

"I'll go straight to Headquarters," he told Helen as he sat back. "Then we'll get in a taxi and take you home."

"You must go to the hospital."

"It can wait a couple of hours," he said. He looked at the little Greek and realized he had hardly said a word since they had left the camp this morning. "Ask him where he wants to go." Helen asked the little Greek, and he looked at Quayle and said to her, "I will be all right if you let me off anywhere in the town."

"You had better be careful the police do not see you," Helen said.

"I will be," he said. He was comparatively happy now and being so near to home was better than actually being there, because the anticipation was better than the result.

"He says we can let him off anywhere," she told Quayle.

Quayle put his head through the canvas door leading to the driver's cabin.

"Are you going right into town?" he asked the Australian.

"Yes. Where do you want to go?"

"We want to let the Greek off. Then to Headquarters."

"Where's your Headquarters? In the same building as ours?"

"It was at a school the last time I saw it."

"I know where it is," the other Australian said. "It's still there, I think."

"O. K.," the driver said and Quayle sat back. They were around the water's edge now and passing through the intermittently bombed streets of Piraeus that looked deserted and strangely unrestful. They climbed the slight hill, saw the Acropolis in the late sun shadows, and the high Church of St. Mary, and the woods with their fists closed and the whiteness of the whole town caught against the black mountains that supported it.

Through the comparatively quiet streets, except for the fast-moving Australian army trucks, they found their way beyond the King George Hotel. There was no one in the square. There were no cars parked in the streets. It seemed like a Sunday, though Quayle knew vaguely that it was not a Sunday. There was the air of something about to happen in the quietness, and the few people were hurrying, and the occasional Australian soldier had his rifle on his shoulder, and the police had short rifles slung across their backs. Only an occasional bus broke the bareness. It was like that all the way up the hill to where the little Greek said to Helen, "I get off here."

Quayle called to the driver to stop when Helen told him the little Greek wanted to get off.

"Tell him to keep out of sight for a while," Quayle said to Helen.

"I did," Helen said. The little Greek had stood up and was holding out his hand to Quayle. Quayle took it and there was quick firmness and regret in the little Greek's handshake.

"Tell the *Inglisi* good-bye," he said to Helen.

"I will. We hope you will be all right," she said to him.

"Tell him that when he wins the war and comes back to come and see me."

"Yes."

"I live in the street near the church." He named a place and a house.

"I will tell him," she said.

"Tell him he's all right," Quayle said.

"Yes," she said.

"Tell him he will always be welcome. And yourself too, Miss." He used the very polite form.

"Thank you."

"You will be married?" he said to her.

"Yes."

"I hope for your happiness and your clear future. Tell him good-bye."

"Thank you. Good-bye," she said.

"*Adieu, Inglisi,*" the Greek said directly to Quayle. He was now on the road looking up at them. Quayle saw the complete puzzlement in the eyes and the forehead, and the struggle in the features and the hunger in the shape. He cocked a hand to him.

"*Adieu,*" Quayle said. The truck moved forward. The little Greek stood there watching it disappear. He lifted his hand. Helen sat down as Quayle — still standing in the jolting truck — looked back at the little Greek now covered by the white dust from the road, standing there alone in the quietness until the truck turned the corner and he was out of sight.

Chapter 26

When the Australians stopped the truck in front of the school where the large blue flag with the circle in the middle of it was flying, and the two blue-clad guards stood outside with sub-machine-guns, Quayle shouted thanks to them. They did not wait to talk but shouted a "S'long" to them and disappeared. The guards were slightly careful of Quayle because of his black wounded face and torn clothes, and Helen. They would not let Helen pass them to walk up the big steps to the building.

"Let her up the steps," Quayle said to them, showing his torn papers.

"Sorry, sir. We've got strict orders."

"Wait here," he said to Helen. "I'll send someone down to get you."

"Please hurry," she said to him quietly. She was conscious of her own appearance, of torn clothes and mud and tangled hair and sunburnt face and worn shoes and no stockings and no hat and dirty hands.

Quayle walked up the steps past the guard. The place had been changed around. He asked his way to the Wing Commander's room and found it in the narrow passage. He walked into the small room first and the clerk there stood up.

"I want to see the Wing Commander," Quayle said.

"He's busy," the clerk said. There were people rushing around and great packing and storing going on through the next room, which Quayle could see.

"I'll go straight in," Quayle said. He walked through the three-ply door into the map-walled room of the Wing Commander. He was talking loudly on a phone. A Squadron Leader Quayle had never seen before was sitting in a chair next to the desk. Quayle automatically looked to see if he had wings, and saw he didn't.

"I'm sorry to butt in," Quayle said to the Wing Commander, who was looking widely at him.

"Quayle!" the Wing Commander shouted. "Well, God almighty!"

"I'm just back," Quayle said.

"Well, Christ. We were certain about you. Hell. I'm glad you're safe." The Wing Commander had got up and was slapping Quayle on the back.

"Could you tell the clerk to let someone waiting for me at the gate in?"

"Sure." The Wing Commander called to the clerk. "Tell him yourself," the Wing Commander said.

"I left my fiancée at the gate. Could you bring her in?"

"I have to have a written order."

"Write it and sign it for me," the Wing Commander said. "Well, how did you get out of it? What's happened to your face? You look in a bad way."

"It just looks bad. I'm all right," Quayle said. "Where's the squadron?"

"What's left of it is out at Glyphada. Will Hickey be mad! I'm sorry, John." And the Wing Commander introduced the Squadron Leader, who was from Intelligence.

"Hickey went on the biggest binge of all time when you copped it," the Wing Commander said. He answered the phone with a few words, then went on: "The Greeks told me that he wanted to go out and find you in the middle of the night and they found him on the airdrome stiff as a poker. What about your face, is it all right?"

"It's all right."

"Well, how did you get out of it?"

Quayle told him. "Tap's on his way too," he ended. "We picked him up at Janina."

"We were going to send up for him but we lost all the Blenheims."

"How's it going? Is the squadron intact?"

"Hickey, young Finn, and Sergeant Crowther are left. He was down here when you were up there. They've been getting hell. We've had to keep them down. They haven't got a chance against Messerschmitts. Too inexperienced anyway."

"What's happening now?"

"Soon be over," the Wing Commander said very quietly. "We were so outnumbered that it was slaughter."

"How many planes has the squadron got left?"

"Four. Three are all right. Finn is too inexperienced. The only others we've got to replace them are Hurricane boys and it's no use putting Hurricane boys in Gladiators."

"What's wrong with Crowther?"

"He's all right. But you can't put two up alone, Quayle."

"Well, I'll be out there now."

"You won't fly with that face."

Then the clerk came in and said the young lady was outside.

"This is Helen Stangou," Quayle said when Helen walked slowly in. She had combed her hair and it was shining and her brown sunburnt face was tight and her eyes clear, and she looked very healthy, but Quayle noticed her torn clothes as being conspicuous for the first time. The two others said "How do you do" to Helen, who smiled at them and said she was fine.

"Can I borrow a car from somewhere to get Helen home?" Quayle said.

"Hickey's in town somewhere. He's got the station wagon. We're pretty short."

"Can you get the clerk to find him?"

"Yes. But you ought to go to a hospital with that head."

"Look," Quayle said. "If any ship goes out with the British women in it, would you fix it up for Helen to go?"

"I'll see what I can do," the Wing Commander said. "If you'd like to wait downstairs I'll find Hickey and he can give you a lift

260

out. But you go to the hospital. Can you make him, Miss Stangou?"

"He does not obey me," Helen said, quietly smiling.

"Well, he ought to go there straight away."

"Thanks anyway. We'll wait downstairs for Hickey. Sorry to have busted in."

"It's a pleasure to see you back," the Wing Commander said. "Good-bye, both of you, and get him to hospital, Miss Stangou."

They waited silently, and Helen self-consciously, in the small office near the steps. Quayle saw the station wagon, much battered now, stop outside. Hickey, looking tired and with his moustache shaven off, walked slowly up the steps. Anderson, the squadron doctor, was with him. He looked tired and fed up too. Both wore heavy blue overcoats and their trousers tucked into their boots. As they came up the steps Quayle walked out the door to meet them. Helen followed him. Hickey walked in, looked up and saw Quayle standing there. "Hello, Hickey," Quayle said. Hickey was silent. He was looking hard. It was Anderson who grabbed Quayle's hand.

"John Quayle," Anderson said. "You son of a bitch."

"Well," Hickey said quietly. "It is you."

"Sure. Didn't the Wing Commander tell you?"

"No." Hickey was shaking Quayle's hand. It was all he said. He was shaking Quayle's hand vigorously.

"How are you?" Helen said to them. She could see the pleasure and great surprise in Hickey and liked him very much just then, though she had always liked him. She could see that he was tired and that now he was suddenly bright and deliberately restrained as Quayle always was. She liked the small scene of surprise and the silence that was now between them.

"Are you hurt still?" Hickey said to Quayle.

"No. I'm fine."

"I'm certainly surprised."

"Yes."

"Well, come on. Where do you want to go? They said something about a hospital."

"I want to take Helen home first," Quayle said. They were

261

walking down the long steps now and past the guards. They got in the station wagon.

"Where do you live, Helen?" Hickey said. He was speaking lightly now and she noticed he used her Christian name.

"At Glyphada. Straight along the road at the bottom of this hill."

"How did you get out?"

Quayle was getting sick of that question. "The trees broke my fall. I walked back with Nitralexis."

"Where is he?"

"He got shot getting through the Italian lines." Quayle went on, and said he'd picked Tap and Helen up in Janina and come along as fast as the retreat would carry them.

"We've been having some shaky-do's," Anderson said to him.

"So I hear," Quayle said. "I'll be with you to-morrow. I've just got to get a few stitches taken out."

"Don't be so bloody tough," the doctor was saying. He had already taken the bandage off Quayle's head as they moved along in the car. He had not asked Quayle anything, but was looking for himself. He lifted the bandage slightly and looked at the wound.

"You're bloody lucky," he said to Quayle.

"I can fly," Quayle said.

"You probably can," Anderson said. "Your face looks pretty."

"How long will it take for that to clear?" Quayle asked him. He could see Hickey looking at the wide blood clots right down his left cheek and the large bumping scrape across his forehead.

"Month or so. You're going to look pretty when those scabs come off."

Helen was winding the bandage on again.

"Can you take the stitches out?" Quayle said.

"Sure, in the hospital," Anderson said. "But don't be so bloody tough. You probably need some rest up and a couple of good meals."

"He fainted once," Helen said quietly.

"He didn't!" Anderson was having fun with Quayle's toughness.

"Yes. I think it was with lack of food or something. He nearly dropped us over a cliff when he was driving the car. He was unconscious for some hours."

"I'll take a look at you. Does your stomach feel all right?"

"Sure. I'm all right," Quayle said. He told Hickey to turn off into the long lane that led to Helen's house.

"Will you come in?" Helen asked them when the car stopped. She was looking at Quayle.

"No," he said. "Look. I'll go and get these stitches out and come back to-night." Anderson laughed when Quayle said that.

"Never mind him," Quayle said. "I'll be back to-night. Are you all right?"

"Yes," she said and smiled.

"Well, s'long until to-night."

"S'long," she said. She smiled, and Quayle looked quickly at her, then got back in the car.

"I'll be around to-night. Tell your family," he said as they drove off.

Chapter 27

They took him to the Glyphada hospital, which was not far away from Helen's home. It was a long building five stories high that had been a summer resort. They took him straight into the room that had been rigged for operations. There were four or five doctors working on people under the high lights. One of the patients was a German, Quayle noticed. An English nurse pulled the bandage off Quayle's face.

"When did you get here?" Quayle asked her.

"Me?"

"English nurses?" Quayle asked.

"A month or so ago. Bend over. Do you want the covering off, Doctor?"

"Leave it on," Anderson said. He had taken off his coat and washed his hands. Hickey was sitting on the long table next to Quayle.

"Scissors," Anderson said to the nurse. He took them from her and pulled off the oil-skin covering and the lint. Quayle felt the coldness of the air against the bared part of his head.

"See how tough you are, Quayle. This will hurt a bit."

"That's what they all say," Quayle said. He felt the snipping of the stitches. The doctor held out his hand and the nurse gave him the pincers. Quayle could feel the light touch of them, then the jerk as one of the stitches was pulled out. He jumped.

"Tough, hell," Anderson said.

"How about changing places?" Quayle said as the next four came out quickly.

264

"O. K.," Anderson said to the nurse. She was plump and round-cheeked and Quayle felt the wholeness of her wide arm around his head putting a lint bandage on it and helping him off with his shirt. Anderson inspected his chest with tappings and felt his stomach and asked him about pain. Quayle said he had none but was stiff around the knee. Anderson bent his leg and felt the knee-cap. He finished up looking at Quayle's hand.

"Give him a bath," he said to the nurse.

"What about it?" Quayle asked him.

"You're all right," Anderson said. "Need a good meal and a couple of days' rest."

"When will I be able to shave?"

"Month or so when those scabs come off, and don't pull them off."

"I can take the bath at the airdrome. Is that where you're living now?"

"You'll take it here," Anderson said.

"Come on," the nurse said to him.

"I'll skip over and get you a uniform," Hickey said. "You can have one of mine. Your own things were sent back to Egypt."

When the nurse took him to the large bathroom and started helping him undress he told her he could bathe himself and undress himself.

"Don't be silly," she said. "Not the way you've got to be bathed. Look at these clothes. Look at the shirt." She held up the dirty shirt.

"I know," he said.

"Get in that bath."

He was embarrassed about it but lay down in the warm water that smelled of some antiseptic. The nurse bent his head forward and put a towel around it to keep the water out of the wound. She washed his neck slowly and his back, then lifted his legs and scrubbed them. Quayle was relaxed now and he felt the physical comfort of relaxing and getting clean.

He dried himself and stood in a white gown Anderson had given him, until Hickey came back with clothes. He pulled on the clean shirt and the uniform, thanked the nurse and went out through the bustle and the confusion in the corridors and the rooms that he had not noticed before. There was a group of walking wounded at the foot of the stairs.

"They're leaving," Anderson explained. "Going to Crete."

"Has there been much evacuation?"

"Yes. Women, and some wounded."

Quayle was thinking about getting Helen off and he had asked Hickey to drive him to Helen's place. It was dark now and he stumbled as he walked up the stone drive of the Stangou house. Hickey and Anderson waited for him in the car. He knocked at the door. The place was in solid darkness and there was no answer. He knocked again and he could see the house had been left. He walked around to the back door but it was barred with a wooden paling. He knew the Stangous would go. He was wondering where she had gone — where the whole family had gone. He was worried about it, because Helen would not know where to get in touch with him. Maybe she went to a relative's place. I can't risk asking anybody around here. Where the hell could she go? The whole family . . . She must have known where the family had gone. She's got sense. She will find me. I'll come back later and look. Maybe Lawson is in town. Maybe he knows where they are. I wonder where the hell she is.

He walked back to the car still wondering about Helen. Hickey drove to the airdrome.

At the airdrome they went into the long mess where the bomber pilots were, and Quayle saw young Finn suddenly jump up and come to him.

"The prodigal returns," Anderson said.

"John," Finn said, shaking his hand. They were all shouting to him.

"Clear a way for the miracle," Anderson said. They gave him

266

a place. Anderson and Hickey sat down each side of him and they were soon eating, and questions were being asked him from both ends of the mess; some of the men he did not know but he recognized some of the Blenheim boys from the desert and a few that had been in Athens before. Quayle was too busy eating to pay much attention to them all.

"They've certainly brought some new talent in," he said to Hickey.

"That's about all it is. There might be two planes to go around this whole crowd." There were at least thirty men with wings over the pockets. "They're mostly leaving to-morrow. Just haven't got any planes. Six Blenheims went out yesterday and none came back. We lost the last two Hurricanes about two days ago. There's one here but it's so shot-up it won't fly for a while. It's some mess, John."

"Yes. I saw some of it coming down. Did you know Crosby?" Quayle was wondering what to do about finding Helen.

"Yes."

"We saw him get it in the neck a couple of days ago."

"That Hurricane out there is the only one left of those three. You must have seen them getting shot up as they were taking off."

"Yes." He was wondering where he could find Helen and was worried about it.

"Say, you'd better write out your report sometime."

"The Wing Commander tells me you're all grounded." He was thinking of going back to the house to see whether Helen had returned.

"Yes. I can't take Finn and Crowther into this mess."

"Look," Quayle said. "I'm all right. I can fly. Anderson said so." Quayle was feeling the way Tap had said it that day that it was better helping to make the mess than watching it from outside. This feeling of being discontented sitting around doing nothing was stronger than the desire not to be eliminated in the tail end of this.

"Maybe," Hickey said to him. "I'll tell Wing about it. There's nothing much we can do."

"If there's going to be an evacuation it will be hot."

Quayle was immediately thinking of Helen again and wondering wildly about her. He didn't know what to do, he didn't know where to look. He was afraid to go to the Red Cross Headquarters, because she would be discovered. He was thinking of Lawson. Maybe he would know where she was. He wondered if Lawson was still here. Helen might go to H.Q. and let somebody know.

The other pilots were getting up from the table together.

"We're all going in to Maxim's to farewell this place," Finn said. "Do you want to come in, John?"

"I've got to go in."

"Are you coming, Hickey?"

"Yes. I'll give you a lift, John. What about Helen?"

"That's why I want to go in. Do you know if Lawson, that American, is still here?"

"He was here a couple of days ago."

"I'll go in with you," Quayle said.

Chapter 28

Athens was filled with Australian trucks coming through to pass to the south. Quayle could see the evacuation had begun. He wondered if there was any evacuation from Athens itself. There was an air-raid warning on as they came through and they could see the searchlights and the anti-aircraft fire over Piraeus and hear the bombing. Quayle got off at the King George Hotel; the others went on to the night club, Maxim's. Quayle asked the porter of the dimly lit hotel about Lawson. He was new and looked curiously at Quayle.

"He has gone to Maxim's for dinner," the porter said.

Quayle thanked him and picked his way out between the large expensive bed rolls and kits. It was the deadwood in the G.H.Q., getting out while the going was good. He groped his way around the streets to the night club. If Lawson didn't know where Helen was he would go back to Stangou's house. This was getting too close to lose her for long now. It was far too close. When he walked down the night-club steps he could hear the high noise and the open door showed the mess of blue uniforms and the khaki and the tangle around the bar of people feeling the hopelessness. He could see the ones from the mess. He looked around for Lawson.

"Hullo, Quayle, you bastard," someone shouted to him. There was over-gaiety in everybody. He cocked a hand. He could not see Lawson anywhere. He saw young Finn and walked over to him. He was sitting at the bar with Hickey drinking Scotch.

"I'm looking for Lawson," he said.

"Have a drink, John." He shook his head. Then Hickey pointed to a table near the edge of the floor. Just then the orchestra started and the wild girl that had been in the Argentina came out and started to do her fanatic dance. Quayle walked around to Lawson, who was in civilian clothes.

"Hullo," he said to Lawson. Lawson looked hard at him, then jumped up.

"Quayle! Thought you were dead. Good God. Sit down."

"Thanks," Quayle said. Lawson mentioned the names of the two women and the army officer at the table. "Do you know where Helen Stangou's family went?" he said quietly to Lawson.

"Stangou?"

"Yes."

"Christ. Well, I know his office. You certainly do things all at once."

"Would anyone be there now?"

"I don't know."

"Well, I've got to get her out of here. Are you going to evacuate?"

"To-morrow," Lawson said quietly and carefully.

"Look," Quayle said. "Maybe you could take her."

"I think we're only going to Crete."

"I just want to get her out of here. Look. She's sensible. She won't bother you."

"It's not that."

"Well, show me this office, can you? I don't want to get you out of this."

"It's a pleasure," Lawson said. He stood up. "I'll be back in a while," he said to the others. They went out into the street together.

"They had shifted from their home," Quayle explained.

"Yes," Lawson said. "He's scared of these fifth columnists. Did you know the Greeks made peace to-day?"

"No."

"Yeah. Fifth columnists are about to take this place over any minute."

"It seems deadly quiet."

"Yes. Everybody is waiting for it. Those young E.O.N. bastards have been going around the street all day pulling down the posters that told the Greeks to fight. They're putting up angels hovering over Greek soldiers."

"Are they all the fifth column?"

"A lot of it. Something is going to happen. You can feel it."

They were walking along a dark silent part of the street. It was as if it were about to rain in a desert. There was the threat in the silence and the absence of people in the streets. There were no police either. Lawson turned into a narrow-staired building. He pushed a button for the lift, but it didn't come, so they walked up the dark wooden stairs. At the top Quayle walked through two small rooms with Lawson, and into a larger one. Stangou was sitting at a desk. He looked up.

"I've brought a friend of yours," Lawson said.

"Mr. Quayle," Stangou said, and got up and shook hands with Quayle. Quayle found himself looking closely at this man as the father of Helen, and being curious about him.

"Is Helen all right?" Quayle asked him.

"Yes. She came. She guessed we had gone to my brother's place."

"I'll leave you," Lawson said.

"Well, thanks," Quayle said. "What about this ship leaving?"

"Tell her to come to me at the King George about twelve o'clock noon."

"Thanks. Good-bye, Lawson."

He went out.

"That's what I wanted to see you about. Can I see Helen?" Quayle said to Stangou. Stangou told him to sit down and he walked around and sat on the desk.

"Helen said about you getting married."

"I don't like to ask this, but I want her to leave here to-morrow with Lawson."

"That will be up to Helen."

"I know. But I know about you. It's not going to be so hot for you."

"Would you like to come home? We are at my brother's."

"Yes," Quayle said. He knew he had not convinced Stangou yet. He also knew that whatever Helen decided would go. But he was doubtful about Helen now. Stangou got his hat and they went out.

They waited long for a bus and got into it. Stangou asked how Quayle had got back and Quayle told him. They deliberately avoided talking about Helen. When they got to a stop near the sea they got out and walked to a small stone house. They went in. Mrs. Stangou and another man and woman were there. She came to Quayle and smiled. "I am pleased about you getting back. I am very happy," she said. She was suppressed.

"Thank you," Quayle said. "I am happy also."

Helen came in and she had cleaned herself and had put on a blouse and blue skirt and low-heeled shoes and combed her hair, and had slight lipstick on, which he noticed immediately — and the brightness of her face and its tightness.

"Hullo," she said to him and took his outstretched hand.

"Have you had dinner?" Mrs. Stangou asked. She introduced the other two.

"Yes, thank you," Quayle said.

They all sat down in front of a round iron stove and a large cat jumped up on Helen's lap; and they all laughed when she said something in Greek to it. Quayle looked around and was less sure of himself in the warmth, and wondered at himself sitting here on the floor of this house while the universe was thundering outside. He knew he would have to say it sooner or later so he said it then.

"I was wondering, Helen . . ." he said.

"Yes?"

"Lawson is going out to-morrow. The evacuation is on. I was wondering if you would go. He said if you were at his hotel to-morrow at twelve you could go with him. I know about your mother and father. Maybe they will say something about it." It was long for him, but he wanted it all said at one time.

There was the silence.

"Will we go outside?" Helen said. She stood up.

He followed her outside into the darkness. He felt that he had been clumsy.

"I'm sorry," he said to her as they walked.

"Do not be," she said.

"Will you go? I think it's about the only chance."

"Is it?"

"Yes. I think so."

"I don't think I can go," she said very slowly, then quickly at the end.

"Oh Christ."

"Don't be with anger."

"I'm not. I was wondering what the hell it's all about. Everything, I mean."

"It's very difficult to leave. You can see that."

"Yes, I can. There's not much brightness ahead either way."

"That I know." Helen had fallen back into the strange formal English that she had used when she first met him.

"I know you don't want to leave your mother. I suppose your father will find it tough. But I don't think that's your future."

"Astaries was killed at the front," she said suddenly.

"I'm very sorry," he said. "God, everything happens."

"Yes. You see it would also be running away to go now."

"This war doesn't end in Greece, if that's what you mean," he said.

"Perhaps not. But I live here. I've never been anywhere else."

"That is just a matter of adjusting yourself."

"And I can't leave my mother. What if something happens to my father?"

"That's what I can't argue about with you. That's up to you."

"I know. I just can't leave," she said.

They had walked down towards the sea and Quayle had taken her arm. He pulled her around as he had done before and kissed

273

her with firmness on the mouth and pushed his body close to her and felt her breasts tight and strained through the blouse.

"I don't care about anything," he said. "I can't leave you. That's all I know."

"I don't want to stay like that either. I want to go with you."

"I'm sorry, but it's the only chance we've got. I think you should."

"I can't."

He was silent. He knew there was no use arguing. He would have to let the thing work itself out.

"We'd better go back," she said.

They walked in silence back to the house.

It was obvious when they went in that there had been discussion between the four people about Helen's going away. Quayle sat down and there was silence.

"We will not put anything before you," Stangou said into the silence.

"Do not talk about it," Helen said in English.

"We know you stay because of us. That is foolish."

"If I go away there is the Germans in here. I am on the other side and the war will go on. It will keep war for a long time."

"We are better off than most people."

Quayle could see they wanted to talk about it all in Greek, when they could use words easily. He stood up.

"I will go," he said. He looked at Mrs. Stangou and saw her wide eyes, and the suppressed smile in her eyes that didn't have enough to prompt them to smile, and the white hair and smooth skin and crumpled forehead.

"I am very sorry about everything," he said.

She only smiled at him.

"Good-bye," he said to the others.

Stangou walked to the door with Quayle and Helen. "Do not worry, we will work it out," he said to Quayle. "Good night," Quayle said.

Helen walked with him to the bus stop.

"Let me think it out. I can't just leave coldly," she said.

"Your mother could go too probably. You could all go."

"I asked them. My father will not leave, so my mother will not."

"I can see everything. But I can't leave you here."

"I know. I know. In all the Saints I know."

"I will come around to the hotel to-morrow. You've got to be there."

"Let me be, John. Let me be."

The bus came. "Good-bye," he said to her. He held her closely and softly and felt the weight within her and within himself and accepted it slowly. She kissed him carefully on the lips, avoiding his hurt face, and he got into the bus. In the darkness he could see her standing there as he walked back to sit down. Then there was too much darkness and he sat down.

Chapter 29

When the bus stopped in the large square Quayle got out. He wanted to see Lawson again because of Helen. The driver pushed open the door for him. Quayle had been the only person in the wide khaki ramshackle bus and the driver touched him lightly on the back as he went and said, *"Inglisi?"*

"Yes," Quayle said.

"I am sorry, lose. We did?"

"I'm sorry too," Quayle said.

"There comes again," he said.

"What?"

"We will come again," he said, and Quayle understood him.

"Yes," he said. "Good night."

"Adieu, Inglisi," the bus driver said as he closed the door.

At the night club, Maxim's, there was noise now, and the bombing of Piraeus was lighter and louder than before. It had just started. The siren went as Quayle crossed the square to go into the large cabaret. It was confusion now and only lights around the edge of the floor lit the place. There was a tall lad with wings over his pocket playing the piano with great flourish. He had pulled his hair down over one eye and was burlesquing his movement, but he knew what he was doing and his fingers were uncautiously finding the keys, but finding them perfectly, because he was too drunk to be cautious and hesitant. This was the high sound right through the place and nobody was taking any notice of him, and everybody was shouting and some of the boys Quayle had seen out at the mess were scrimmaging in a mock Rugger game on the floor and there were two lying carefully at the edge and the girls who were in the cabaret show were around the edge shouting to them all as they scrimmaged.

"Quayle," one of them shouted to him as he came in. "Come on. Get in this."

"No, thanks," Quayle said and walked around to find Lawson. He saw Hickey sitting at the bar.

"Did you find her?" Hickey said.

"Yes," Quayle said. He could see the relaxed look in Hickey's face because there was ease of drug-alcohol unstiffening him into rest.

"How're you getting her out?"

"She doesn't want to go."

"You know, every time I look at her, John, she doesn't look like anybody at all because her face is so different. You know."

"Yes," Quayle said. Hickey asked him what he wanted to drink and Quayle said he had to find Lawson, and Hickey replied that Lawson had gone out about a story or something and would be back later; so Quayle said he would have beer, but Hickey ordered him Scotch and made him drink it with persistent encouragement.

"Look at all these young bloods going mad," Hickey said tiredly.

"They're hitting it up a bit too much."

"What the hell," Hickey said. "You try to be too tough, John. These kids are all right. They've been sitting around for so long. No bloody planes. Not a plane to go, among all these."

"You're getting soft," Quayle said.

"Soft hell. You've been missing things while you were away."

"I suppose so." Quayle was making allowances for Hickey's being tired and like this.

"Yes, you have. Christ, you should have seen the do we lost Constance on. That day you went, we came straight back here the next day. Well, a couple of days after that the Germans started in and there were only four of us. We ran into about a hundred Messerschmitts, you know. You should have seen them. We diced it with the bastards. We actually got four of them, with Gladiators.

277

Old Constance got about half a dozen on his tail. He was taking evasive action but they were all around him. They were all around all of us, and every time I went out to help him they blocked me. It was just like a cat-and-mouse and then old Constance just flipped over and broke up."

"What about Singleton and Money?" They were the remaining two that had been in Athens beside Crowther.

"In one do. We went along with Hurricanes on a convoy. We got all mixed up. I don't even know what happened to them. I didn't see them. One of the Hurricane boys put in a report that he had seen them both go down in flames. That was the day we lost all the Blenheims. Just went up and didn't come back. Do you remember Davies of Two-Eleven?"

"Sure."

"He was Squadron Leader then. What's-his-name got wiped out. They just went off like flies around that time."

The noise had died as the flyers left the floor because they had got tired and they sat around the crowded tables in the dimness and Quayle noticed the lack of khaki now and the girls being very free with the flyers because they knew how they felt. Hickey was looking around too and he turned to Quayle and lifted his glass and said, "Here's to prostitutes. Look at them all. You know, John, they know how a man feels better than any woman. They certainly do and they're pretty generous with condolences. They mean it too. Look at them."

Hickey had ordered Quayle another drink, and Quayle was drinking it because he was feeling the weight because Hickey was feeling it. He had not thought Hickey would feel it so much, and knew he would be sorry when he realized that he was showing it, even if it was only to Quayle. He could hear the piano very clearly now and the half-lighting of the place was still enough to make the notes sight as well as sound. The boy was too busy playing to do much burlesquing now and Quayle looked at the quiet stoop and the ease of the boy and heard the high murmur around as the others were trying to get drinks.

Once a small man came out and shouted that the place had been closed and that the orchestra had gone, and the police said he had to close and the lights would be turned out. Someone got up and shouted to him that if he turned the lights out they would wreck the place, and it was not vandalistic because they knew they had the right to this just now, and the small man went away and the boy at the piano — who hadn't stopped and was surrounded by the empty chairs and small instrument stands of the band — went right on playing, and nobody knew at all what he was playing but it was the background for all the noise.

Lawson came in. Quayle had to buy a drink in return for Hickey and the three of them sat at the bar.

"What was the story? Do you just go out like that when a story happens? How do you know anyway?" Hickey said.

"Pimps," Lawson said. He was drunk too. "No. These fifth columnists are going to take over the place. You can feel them. I know some of them but they're keeping well hidden."

"Say. About to-morrow . . ." Quayle said to him.

"Did you find her?"

"Yes."

"What did she say?"

"I don't know. Look, if she comes she'll be around at your hotel at noon."

"Fine," Lawson said, drinking. "I'll look after her."

"I'm not sure she's going," Quayle said. "Her brother was killed at the front."

"I know. Who told you?"

"She did," Quayle said.

"Her father didn't tell them. He thinks the Fascists had him shot."

"Christ." Quayle could see the firing squad that day at Janina and the rain, and could see the face of Astaries in the one who was young but did not look like Astaries; but he could see that happening, and it was the whole piling down on him of all feelings for all things.

279

"Jesus. What a mess," he said slowly. "What a mess."

"Have another drink," Lawson said to him.

"No." Quayle shook his head. "Let's get out of here, Hickey."

"Sure. It's my bedtime. I suppose they'll paste the airdrome again to-night."

Quayle was still seeing Astaries Stangou being shot by the firing squad and he knew it was all something to do with the high noise and it was weighing on him.

"Listen," Quayle said to Lawson. "I'll be at your hotel at noon to-morrow."

"Are you coming too?"

"No. I want to see about Helen."

"All right," Lawson said. "S'long."

"S'long," they both said and walked along the side of the cabaret floor and heard the last of the shouting, and as they pushed up the steps through the swinging doors Quayle could hear the piano and the careless way the boy was playing it and the smoothness though he did not know what it was.

It was dead when the swinging doors cut it off. Instead, there was the noise of the bombing of Piraeus still going on and taking its place. Quayle felt the reality of the bombs, and felt less weighted. They walked to the car and drove to the airdrome.

Chapter 30

The airdrome was bombed all night and they were in the slit trenches most of the time. Twice fires were started and they were all putting them out. In the lateness of the early morning there was the spell from the bombing. They were all eating breakfast in the long mess and some of them got up to roll up their kits. Then the trucks came and they got into them with their kits and one by one they drove off to be evacuated and Quayle could feel envy of them and the warmth of Egypt and the no-war and no-struggle atmosphere in Cairo. He had the same feeling about Cairo that he had about Athens. That once you got there it was fine.

At noon Hickey took him into Athens which was very quiet now and there was the imminent air in it. The dim sky made it worse than yesterday when there had been sun. They both went into the King George Hotel and there was the confusion of people there and a large group of war correspondents with uniforms and small kits and typewriters and women who sat in the wide chairs and were strained because they were waiting. Helen was not there. Neither was Lawson.

Quayle stood on the steps of the hotel with Hickey and looked at the square. The wind was catching the dirt in the streets and the leaves because no one was bothering to sweep the streets. The wind caught them in little swirls against the corners of the buildings and they collected dismally as they settled down.

Hickey said he had to go up to Headquarters and he left Quayle standing there in the dust of the dull day on the steps. Then Lawson came out.

"Is she here?" he asked Quayle.

"No. What time is it?"

"About half-past twelve."

"She might turn up," Quayle said.

"Sure." Quayle noticed the rolling of the "r's" and the quiet certainty of this American.

"What time do you go to the boat?" Quayle asked him.

"God only knows. This is a British Embassy affair. It's a Greek boat, I think, but you never know. They sent one out last night and it got the hell bombed out of it."

"Where does it leave from?"

"Somewhere at Piraeus. It'll be the only boat around."

"Is there anything left of Piraeus?"

"Not much. That place is sure going to suffer. It won't be long before you guys will be bombing it."

"I suppose so," Quayle nodded, then asked Lawson what he thought of all this.

"What do you think of it?" Lawson repeated, and Quayle knew that was Lawson's answer.

"What's the answer to stopping it all?"

"You're asking me?" Lawson said. "Is this the Great Awakening?"

"Maybe."

"It's got to be much worse than this before you get any change."

"Who's going to make it?"

"The trouble with British officers is that they're too segregated from the men. It might come from them," Lawson said.

"Who? The officers?"

"No," Lawson said angrily, "the men."

"How?" Quayle was not being naïve. He wanted to hear what Lawson thought about it.

"I wish I knew," Lawson said. "It certainly won't come out in the Middle East. There's no political pressure. There's no sympathy between the British and the local populations. Maybe in England. Maybe," he said.

"Maybe," Quayle echoed.

"You were asking me," Lawson said.

Quayle was thinking of Macpherson and Astaries Stangou and he did not know why. he was tying them together. He could see Macpherson facing the Greek firing squad and himself running to stop them shooting Macpherson and suddenly Macpherson turning out to be the Greeks and not Macpherson. He was apologizing to the Greek firing squad for stopping them. He was standing by watching the Greek firing squad shoot the Greeks, and they fell, all except the one who stood there, the single shot killing him, and him falling straight down with the hessian bandage coming off, and Quayle looking closely at him and the Greek turning out to be Macpherson after all, and Quayle turning around and shooting the firing squad with a pistol that was suddenly in his hand and Macpherson suddenly getting up and walking along the path with him to see Helen and saying to Quayle "You see what I mean" but in Helen's voice.

"It's all very complicated," he said to Lawson.

When Hickey came back it was after one o'clock. Nobody had gone down to the boat, and Helen had not come. Hickey asked him why he didn't go out to Stangou's and see about it. Quayle didn't tell him why, but knew he would go out soon. He had to try again.

"Can I borrow the car?" he asked Hickey.

"I'll drive you out there. Maybe we can bring her back with us."

"All right, thanks," Quayle said and they left Lawson and drove out along the bus route.

Helen came to the door when they found the place. Hickey waited in the car. She looked at John as if he were a stranger and, using the polite form, asked him in. There were two small fibre cases in the hall. Quayle looked at them, then he looked quickly at Helen. She was stiff and without feeling, and being too sure and stiff with herself.

"I was just coming," she said. Her mother came in with Stangou.

"Good morning," Quayle said to them politely.

283

"Good morning, John," Mrs. Stangou said and he noticed the familiar form. It was the acceptance that he knew meant Helen was coming with him. He felt the weight of the thing again. He could only look at the three of them standing there and could not say anything. Helen was pulling on a round-brimmed hat and she was standing there waiting.

"I am very sorry to do this to you," he said to them.

"We know how it is," Stangou said.

"We will come back the moment it's all over," he said.

"Yes. We are sure you will. We are glad for you both."

"I will wait in the car," he said. Mrs. Stangou was standing there, without expression and looking closely at him as he had found himself looking at Stangou yesterday in the office. Quayle suddenly stepped forward and kissed her quickly. He felt the warmth of suppressed crying. He shook hands with Stangou, who held his hand warmly then released it quickly. He could feel this whole thing and the suppression within them, that they did not break down before him or before themselves. The extreme quiet feeling of Helen standing there with her hat on, and the tight lips and clear eyes without movement. The three of them, about to break up.

"Good-bye," he said to them at the door. "And thank you. I'm sorry for everything."

"Good-bye, John," they both said to him, and he had never felt the use of his Christian name like that before.

He walked out and down the path. He was crying within himself for the first time since he had left off being young. It was all too quick. These people are strangers. I've seen them only two or three times and look at all this. He was not sure of himself any more. He was thinking of Astaries and Macpherson together again. He wanted to talk about it all but knew he would not, even to Helen, and there was Helen back there and this thing breaking them all up.

She came out almost immediately with the two cases that Quayle had not thought of picking up. Hickey was silent as she got in the car, and Quayle helped her in. She sat in the back alone and Quayle could see that the stiffness and restraint had been so that they would not break when she had said good-bye to them. He could see the quietness now of these three people breaking up, because he had broken them up. The stiffness of strength in them, and still in Helen. Because it was only starting for her and the stiffness would have gone out of the two back there now. It was all over. The suppression in her mother would be breaking now. The quiet depression of her father who would accept this and the weight of all things. And Quayle felt the whole thing as his own.

When they got to the hotel Quayle saw the others had gone and the lobby of the hotel was dead empty and there was the same imminent quiet there now as there was in the streets.

"We'll go down to Piraeus," he said to Hickey. And Hickey drove through the silent streets and Helen could feel only the high whirling of all things in her head. She did not notice the physical exterior of things influencing individual feeling behind the exterior.

There was the same feeling for Quayle and Hickey in these bombed streets as there was in Athens; in the rough low stone houses, white in the dimness of clouded sky. Hickey did not like being around the dead place with living people caught inside it. He speeded through the streets to the dock front. They could see the one upright ship in the mess of sunken ships and broken docks and black scorch of bombs. Hickey finally found the dirt road, littered with bomb holes and debris, leading to the smashed end of the docks where the green ship rested. There was a confusion of black-clad people and uniforms and some broad Australian hats around the boat which was only about three thousand tons and was flying the Greek flag.

"This is it," Hickey said.

"It's small," Quayle said and that was all he knew he could say.

"What will I do when I get to Crete?" Helen said. It was strange to Quayle to hear her speak.

"You'll either go on to Egypt straight away or wait there. I'll probably turn up there in a couple of days. I'll find you. Lawson will look after you."

They walked aboard the flat plank. The Australian guard at the boat (where there was coal being loaded into the bunkers among the mess of people and confusion) did not stop them, because the dimness of day was fading into early evening. He could not see everything.

Lawson was rolling out kit on one of the forward decks when they found him.

"You finally came," he said to Helen.

"Yes."

"Where's this boat going to?" Quayle asked him.

"Crete. Suda Bay, I think. Then Alexandria."

"Will you stop her getting lost?"

"She'll be all right," Lawson said. Then to Helen, "It's better up on deck here. Leave your things with ours."

The war correspondents were grouped together and an Australian Sergeant with them had rigged up a Bren gun. Some of them had green tabs with *British War Correspondent* written on them and others had the same as Lawson — *Foreign War Correspondent*. They were all treating the affair as a bright game and continuously looking into the air for bombers. Lawson introduced some of them casually and they nodded to Quayle and looked curiously at his face. Some of them knew Lawson. One American took Helen's cases and put them next to his bed-roll.

"You can have this," he said. "I've got another one."

She thanked him quietly and he could see the restraint in her and the quietness of her and let her walk back to Quayle without talking any further. It was early darkness now and Quayle could feel the bump of the ancient engines beneath the deck. He was reluctant to think of leaving, but he knew the confusion would not allow any warning of the boat clearing off. There was the noise of all the people packed along the deck, and the soldiers shouting down the hold. Quayle suddenly heard them talking about prisoners.

"What's that about prisoners?" he said to one of the war correspondents.

"The hold's full of German prisoners," he said.

It was then he heard the talking from the other side. It was the high laugh and the shout.

"That's Tap," Hickey said. He was sitting talking to Lawson.

"Yes." Quayle heard him.

"Hey, Tap," Hickey shouted. They could not see him.

"Hickey. Where the hell are you?" Tap came towards them. "You son of a bitch." Tap was laughing very happily. "And Johnny!"

"Where did you come from?" Hickey said. They were shaking hands.

"Are you on this trip too?" Tap shouted.

"No."

"Say, what's the idea? Were you going to leave me up in Janina?" he said to Hickey.

"Christ only knows. Are you going out on this?"

"I went up to H.Q. and they sent me down to get on this thing."

"Well, how are you?" Hickey said.

"I'm fine. What are you doing here?"

"We brought Quayle's girl down."

"Helen?" Tap said. "Is she here?"

Helen had stood up and she said "Hullo" quietly to him.

"This is fine." Tap was very happy. He put down a small kit bag he had gotten from somewhere.

Quayle heard a shouting of Greek and the bell going.

"They are saying to take away the ropes," Helen said quickly.

"I'd better go," Quayle said.

They walked to the gang-plank. The ropes had been thrown off by now and the engine was struggling.

"Are you going to fly again?" she asked him.

"I don't know," he said. He had brought himself close to her. He kissed her carefully and with little deliberate warmth. He could feel her hands against his back and the quiet shaking inside her and knew that she had come closest to breaking but had not, except inside. She felt the great tenderness of him and felt for him because he was feeling how she felt about it all. She wondered about

287

all that was in him, and if it had caught up as it had in her and not broken. She could not tell about him.

"I'll see you in a while," he said. The others had come up by now and Hickey was saying good-bye to her.

Quayle was suddenly glad about Tap being there and his laugh was good for them all now. He felt the warmth of Helen's hand as he slipped his from it into the contrasted cold air. He walked off the gang-plank.

"S'long, Tap," he said stiffly.

"S'long, John," he said. "We'll look after Helen."

"Thanks."

"S'long, Hickey."

"S'long," Hickey said. The boat had pulled out with the engines vibrating and it was so dark they could not distinguish the shapes of their figures as it reversed out of the dock, but they could hear the voices.

Tap shouting . . .

Lawson laughing, then calling a mock "Cheerio" to them . . .

Helen saying with carefulness, "Good-bye."

"Good-bye," he shouted — and turned with Hickey to go away.

They watched it for a moment, then got in the car and drove along the dirt road. The searchlights were hitting the clear sky and they heard the air-raid siren.

"Step on it," Quayle said. He heard the first bomb explode almost at the same time, to the left along the section of destroyed water-front. Hickey stopped the car and they leapt out into the slight dip in the road and felt the earth taking the bombs and the debris flying over them and the cold whistle of the bomb fragments and the bombs stringing along the dirt road to the boat pulling out.

"Come on!" Hickey shouted. "We'll get out of this." They ran to the car and they could hear the long deep threatening roar of multiple engines as they sped through the torn gates of the dock and along the road. They could see the bursts to the left of them, then suddenly the flame; and they could feel the jolt of the blast of the car as the bomb exploded behind them; and the black earth was red like the black sky and the searchlights groped. The car leapt through the white streets in the dark shadow with the ashes all around them. Hickey turned the lights full on, so he would find his way out, and they careered through the bombing up to the hill where it was comparatively safe.

"Stop," Quayle shouted to Hickey. And he stopped.

Quayle got out and looked at the bombing of the harbour. He could see the flames and the bombs stringing the water where the ship had been and near it. They could not see the ship, but only the bombs near the dock.

"I think it got away," Hickey shouted above the noise of the anti-aircraft pulling at the sky and the high tracers licking at the small planes that caught their wings in the lights.

He got into the car and they drove off.

Chapter 31

There was nothing but bombing and the feeling of disaster in all the place now. The wounded were coming into the hospitals fast and Doc Anderson was living at the hospital. The only movement in town was the occasional movement of wounded and the confusion started again as the large evacuation began again. Some of the troops came through at night. For a while the threat of the fifth columnists and the parachutists was not there because there were so many of the Australians and New Zealanders in town. Then they evacuated from the south and there was quietness and fear again.

The Blenheims arrived to cover the evacuation from the south, and the airdrome was moving again after the dead quiet. Then the Blenheims shifted to another airdrome and some went back to Crete. Quayle and Finn, Hickey and Sergeant Crowther were the only pilots left at the airdrome. Hickey tried persuading Quayle to go south with some of the ground crews to evacuate, but he stayed. He knew they were holding the Gladiators for something, and he wanted to be making the mess rather than be in it.

It came on the day when they had had the rain at night and had gotten some sleep, and the aircraftsmen who were left were making the breakfast. In the loneliness and the desertedness it was good to hear. Hickey got the order that they were to cover a section of the evacuation south at Argos. They were to patrol at five thousand over the area and break up any enemy formations.

"I'm going on this," Quayle told Hickey. Hickey knew Quayle had been waiting because of this. He would not argue. He would sooner have Quayle than anybody, and he was glad about it. Finn was too inexperienced.

"Just as you say," Hickey said.

"What sort of condition is your plane in?" Quayle asked Finn.

"It's all right," Finn said.

"You'd better go south with the next crew going," Hickey said to Finn.

"Don't you think I ought to hang around?"

"No. You won't be needed. I'll give you a movement order."

"O. K."

"Get Crowther, will you?" he said to Finn. Quayle had not seen Crowther since he had come back, because he was living with the other Sergeants; and he had missed seeing him.

"When do we go?"

"Eleven hours. That's about an hour."

"I'll have to borrow Finn's flying kit."

Finn came back with Sergeant Crowther, who was small and had thin balding hair and spoke Scotch dialect somewhat similar to Macpherson.

"Hullo," he said abruptly to Quayle. He was always stiff in his manner.

"Hullo, Crowther."

"Glad you got back."

"Thanks."

"We're going on a how. Eleven hours," Hickey said. Quayle was asking Finn for his flying kit, and Finn went out to get it.

"We're covering an evacuation," Hickey said. "It ought to be pretty warm."

Crowther was standing, because he could not sit unless Hickey told him and Hickey was not thinking so Quayle pushed a chair under him and he sat down. He was dressed in the heavier wool of the ground crews that Sergeant Pilots had to wear.

"Are you coming?" he asked Quayle.

"Yes."

"How does your face feel?"

"There is nothing wrong with it," Quayle said. He was looking differently at this little Scotchman who had clean red lips and teeth and a blond moustache. He was clean-featured, with a definite line along the top of his nose, and his manner was slightly resentful. He was deliberate in his speech so that he wouldn't loosen. Quayle knew it was because he was a Sergeant Pilot and felt the difference. He knew he would act the same, and wondered why they had not given him a commission. He remembered Crowther doing aerobatics over the air field near Fuka one day to test his plane. He was always doing something to it, because he had worked through from a boy in the air force. He was once making Gladiators and he knew more about them than the fitters, who were always asking him, and he naturally felt bad about that too.

"I'm flying Finn's plane," Quayle said. He did not want to ask Crowther to look at it because he knew that would be presuming, and he did not want to hurt Crowther that way. I must be getting sensitive, he thought to himself.

"Yes. Do you want me to look it over for you?" Crowther said, standing up.

"Thanks," Quayle said.

"I'll get my kit," Crowther said. Quayle was very glad that Crowther did not resent him and would do this for him.

They walked over to the plane that was at one end of the airdrome. Crowther had a small tool kit in a grease-covered dark brown roll of cloth. They felt the warmth as they walked, and Quayle was looking at the high cloud in patches.

"You were pretty lucky to walk away from that mess," Crowther said as they walked. "It was bad from the description I heard of it."

"You're right. It was the trees that saved me."

"Give me a Gladiator every time."

"For me too," Quayle said.

Crowther got out and pulled the panel from the fuselage and unrolled his tool kit. He chose a small spanner and worked on the wire of the controls, loosening one and tightening another. He did the same on the wings, and the fitters watched him as did Quayle as he tested them again and readjusted them. He tightened the wire struts with another flat key-shaped instrument, then put his weight on one of the ailerons and watched the others move, then adjusted one on the other side.

· "I think that covers it," he said to Quayle.

"Thanks."

"It's a pleasure," Crowther said. He was burring his *r*'s like Macpherson and the work seemed to have loosened him up. They walked back towards the airdrome buildings, past the burnt section.

"Would you sooner be building them than flying them?" That was almost a too simple question, Quayle knew.

"I'd sooner be building them." That was more honesty than Quayle had known before, because you weren't supposed to say you would sooner be on the ground than in the air.

"Maybe you're right," Quayle said.

"For me, yes. It's a pity we didn't get together before. I adjusted your old Gladiator for you a few times."

"I didn't know it."

"I know. It's a pity. We would have been good. I know how to make them fly. You know how to fly them better than anybody."

"You fly all right yourself."

"Purely mechanical," he said. Quayle was astonished at the sureness of his speech and its sense. It was like talking with Macpherson.

"That's why Hickey's good," Quayle said.

"Yes. But not me. Did you know that it was Hickey who taught me to fly?"

"No. I didn't."

"Yes. He was training then. He used to cover the cockpit with the hood and make me go through aerobatics by movement of the stick and the rudder. He used to make us do aerobatics by calculation and not by feeling where we were going. That's why he thinks you're a good flyer," Crowther said to Quayle.

"That's why he's good himself," Quayle said.

"You two must be the last of the aerobatic experts. When Gladiators go out there's not going to be any more real dogfights. It's all formations with Hurricanes and Spitfires. It's a pity."

"Yes. I suppose we become a Hurricane squadron after this is over."

"That's where I drop out," Crowther said. "I can fly these things because I know all about them. I don't know enough about Hurricanes."

"I think it's like that with me," Quayle said, and he meant it. They had reached the mess buildings and Crowther went on to put on his flying kit.

"Thanks a lot," Quayle said after him.

"It's all right. Any time," Crowther said.

A few minutes before eleven o'clock, they were lined up at one end of the field. The five fitters and riggers and Finn were standing at the other end of the field. The three planes had taxied down across wind and they were giving rev bursts with their throttles as they turned. Hickey was slightly ahead, Quayle was on the right and Crowther on the left. Quayle buckled his seat harness and used the back of his silk glove to wipe the moisture from the glass covering some of the instruments. He pulled on the leather glove, heard Hickey in the ear-phones.

"Let's go."

"O. K.," Crowther said.

"O. K.," Quayle said. He pushed the throttle forward as Hickey moved slowly; then gave it more as the speed quickened. He could see Crowther on his left and he lifted a hand and waved as they became airborne, and Crowther waved back to him.

They climbed and headed directly south-west, passing over the edge of Athens and over the islands in the bay. They could see the cloud shadows on the moving water and the whiteness and movement that gradually stilled as they got higher until the sea looked placid because they were too high to see the movement.

"What time have we got to be over the target, Hickey?" Quayle asked him through the phones.

"Eleven thirty-five."

They had discussed the map before they took off, and Quayle was looking at the one-to-one-million coloured War Office map on his knee. They would pass over the range north of Argos and fly along the railway and the road, both of which ran together to Argos.

"Keep your eyes behind you, John," he heard Hickey say. It was his humour.

"Am I a novice at this game?" Quayle said back to him.

"Yes, you old bastard. How long is it since you've flown a plane?"

"Christ only knows."

"I hope you haven't forgotten. This is sure to be nice and warm."

"I feel cold anyway."

"I'll watch for you in the middle of it," Hickey said and switched off.

The Intelligence report had said there would probably be bomber opposition and fighter escort. The movement around Argos had been collecting in the last few days and the evacuation was going on from Argos itself and the beaches stretching south and southeast. When they passed over the mountain they came to the section where the road wound through the pass. Quayle could see the tangle of traffic on it, and the spreading-out as they came to the plains of Argos. But along the beaches there was great movement. There were small ships in the bay, and small craft on the beaches. Quayle could see the craft moving from the beaches to the ships. Around the town of Argos itself, which was in flames, Quayle could see ships at the wharf, and there was bombing going on there as they approached it.

"Look what's below us," Crowther said into his phone.

"Stukas," Hickey said.

"Hundreds of them."

"I can hear them in my goddam earphones talking," Quayle said.

"We'll go down in formation," Hickey shouted. Quayle was pushing the safe from the gun button on to FIRE and watching

Hickey's wings. There was an unbroken formation of twin-engine bombers making a run from almost due west.

"We'll go into their formation group," Hickey said.

"Look behind them," Crowther was saying. There was the gaiety of extreme danger in everything they said. Quayle felt the stomach-sickness that had nothing to do with the high bumping of the Gladiator but with the tenseness of straining to keep alert and of looking behind all the time. He tried to relax, but immediately the loose grip on the stick loosened the control and he felt the swagger in the plane.

"Here we go," Hickey said. He pulled over, slipping his wings on one side. They were almost five thousand feet above the square-ended German Heinkels, and Quayle knew he would black-out at the end of this dive. They were going to approach the Heinkels head on and underneath. He was straining to stop himself black-ing-out because he did not want to crash into one. He could feel the warmth in his head and his cheeks puffing out as they took the dive and the three of them were still holding formation as they screamed like a dying man until they had flashed directly in front of the Heinkels.

Hickey's judgment was perfect; and as they pulled up and out of the dive Quayle was thinking that Hickey had allowed for everything, then he blacked-out suddenly, and came-to with the climb still going on and the bellies of the Heinkels in front of him. He could see Crowther fire as he banked off to the left.. He could see Hickey way ahead of him, climbing almost straight up into a Heinkel.

Quayle got the white-engine stubs of one Heinkel in his sights and he pushed the gun button. It was so long since he had felt the shake of the guns that he jumped when it started. He kept the Heinkel in his sights and pulled away as he lifted his finger off the button.

Quayle looked around for Hickey and Crowther as he climbed to get height over the bombers. He could only see the Heinkel going down in flames and the ragged formation of the remainder; and then he saw the flock of square-tipped single engines coming on him.

"Christ. Messerschmitts," he shouted aloud.

He could see Hickey in that flash too. He pulled over to get near him as he climbed. It seemed slow and the Messerschmitts came down on them in groups of six in straight-line formation. Quayle saw Hickey slip off on one wing and straight-loop miraculously with no speed and no dive and he himself pulled off to the other side and came around in a wide circle as three Messerschmitts came down underneath him. He fell off one side as Crowther had done and then saw the other Messerschmitts coming in from the other side. All he could see was black Messerschmitts, square wings, fire from leading edge of wings, no undercarriage, the down-pointed nose and crosses on the white underneath of the wings, the black head of the pilot in the glass cover of the cockpit, the wireless mast behind him, the gleam of the air screws in the sun.

He looked above him and saw the three in a straight dive and saw the tracers come up underneath him and he climbed in a straight heap. He flipped in a tight turn as two more came at him in the dive and then two came at him head on. Nothing but Messerschmitts. This is it. This is it. Here it is, any minute, wonder what it will be. Here it is, any minute. And then he saw Crowther with the five or six converging on him from abeam, and the mess of their tracers tearing into him and the great pieces flying from Crowther's plane and the black smoke pouring from the flame and sudden disintegration of the plane in mid-air, and no parachute bursting white. No parachute bursting white . . .

He saw the black burning streak of a Messerschmitt come close past him as he looped again from a dive and got three away from his tail. He saw Hickey, and he was hemmed in too, and was pulling around in a defensive circle.

"Get out of it, Hickey," he shouted into the microphone, and all he could see all around him was the black mess of square-tipped planes and tracer bullets, and twice he felt the jolt on the fuselage and knew that he had been hit. He was weaving and looping frantically. He couldn't hit out in a given direction. He was doing everything he knew and his head was thick and he was blacking-out at every zoom. His compass was spinning madly and sometimes that was all he could see, and he wanted to laugh at it; and then the tracers would come all around him again.

He didn't see Hickey get it. He only saw the smashed sections of the Gladiator tearing apart as the Messerschmitts tore around it and ripped it to pieces and the white yellow tracers burning it all up in the the high air and he knew that Hickey was gone like that with the smoke and the yellow tracers in him.

Quayle climbed frantically when he saw a space with no black planes in it — and nearly collided with the German, who came up underneath in a faster climb; and he could see the German's face with no goggles covering his eyes, and the quick look sideways from the cockpit and the return of his own look to the German in the second it flashed past. There was his own pressure on the gun button as it went past, and himself pulling the plane over in such a strain that he did not think the plane would hold together.

He was falling straighter and deeper than he had ever done before. His cheeks puffed out his eyes, and his nose was thick with blood and his mouth tasting of it and the bile of his stomach. He was not looking around for anything because he was going too fast. He was slightly crazy and did not care what happened, and he strained out at two thousand feet and felt the whole plane bend, and stagger head up, and he pulled it over in a loop and blacked-out.

There were still Messerschmitts on both sides and behind him, and he headed for the deep valley. He knew only roughly where he was going, and he could see the Messerschmitts converging in on him again, and he pushed the nose down again, though the mountain to the right of him was higher than he was. He fell straight down into the valley. He banked and flew sideways along the edge of the mountain, and curved right around it until he was nearly right on the earth. The Messerschmitts came right above him. He kept flying flat along the valley and turning around it, and tried to climb the round cone of a peak to head north after he took a quick look at his compass. He looked quickly behind, and there were the six Messerschmitts still directly behind him and three above him, slightly to the left. They were scared to bring Messerschmitts as low as he was holding the Gladiator. Another one was on the other side, trying to come down low and turn and get a broadside attack on him.

The blood was trickling down his neck, and he felt its coldness against his tight neck bulging into his tight collar. He could feel the coldness of his stiff hands. He pushed the nose down farther as the green valley of timber dipped. He followed the slight humps around, flying on one wing around each one and with full throttle so that he rocked from side to side and his engine screamed at the strain and the struts screamed above the engine.

He looked desperately around. The Messerschmitts were closing tighter and closer and they had throttled back so they would not pass him, because they were so much faster. They were afraid to come low enough to give him a burst. He took a quick look below and above, and taking a death chance on whether the plane could take it or not he kept the throttle full open and he pulled viciously on the stick and did a straight tight loop.

The Germans saw the sudden whisk of a Gladiator come up from the earth and bend over backwards in a fantastically speeded and tight loop that they did not believe; then the Gladiator fell off upside-down on one wing, and they thought it would hit the cone of the mountain, and they came around in a wide turn.

Quayle pulled the stick over to the right and kicked on the rudder as he saw the tangle of earth coming at him. The vicious speed of the plane whipped it too far over and Quayle pulled the other way to counteract it. He looked behind him. The Messerschmitts had lost a thousand yards on him because they were coming around in a wide climbing turn. He had changed his course 180 degrees with the loop, and he bore through the valley to the north-east and went lower and then side-slipped down a shallower valley. Then he did a complete turn around a wide series of low hills, so that he was now flying a few feet from uneven earth. Every time he saw the deepness in the colour he pulled up slightly. He could feel the sensation of speed as he never felt it before. He was flat out, and a few feet from the ground, and the earth was tearing by him. He looked up and behind him. He could see only three Messerschmitts, to the left and way above him. They had obviously climbed to look for him. He put a slight mountain between himself and the Messerschmitts and then set the course roughly north-east though he did not know where he was.

By the time he saw the sea again he could not see the Messerschmitts. He was feeling drunk and crazy and he could not think of everything. He started to count the instruments then sang loudly about I care for nobody, no not I. He pulled back the cockpit cover and felt the blast of air and its coldness. There was complete looseness in him for all things and he refused to think about Hickey and Crowther and he wanted to stand up on the cockpit and dance and he bet the air it couldn't pull him off and he bet the plane he could pull it out of anything it could start. He would let it have the controls to prove it and he let them go. The plane pulled on one side and went into a spiral spin. He was at six thousand and he felt the flat movement of the plane gaining speed and the shaking behind him. He thought about the times he had been hit and knew that the tail unit was loose somewhere and he shouted out aloud, "Go on. Come apart. See if I care. Go on."

Then he took the controls again and pulled it out of the spin in a straight climb. He was simmering down and he could feel the coldness in his head again. Later he saw the clear line of the coast and Athens ahead. He wanted the plane to be steady now and he kept his eye on the coast and closed his mouth tight. He felt the swaying of the plane as his arms were not sure of the control of his fingers, and the plane rocked. He fixed his eye on the coast and the whiteness of Athens forming and then suddenly he coughed and wanted to be sick and couldn't, and he coughed so that his stomach hurt and his eyes were thick with clear tears of sickness. He bent his head down and coughed viciously and was suddenly sick.

The plane had lost height and he was feeling the emptiness and death inside him as he groped around and pulled the cockpit cover over because he was deadly cold, and he looked around for the airport and he saw the Glyphada road. He kept the plane up because he was afraid of losing height now. He climbed over the Parnes and turned around. He saw the airdrome and he put the nose suddenly down and straightened out too late and had to go over the airdrome. He did a wide turn back and put the flaps down and came in very low over the trees and not too fast. He felt the bump of the wheels on the earth with great surprise and he let the plane roll and automatically let the flaps up and put the brakes on. He pulled the engine switch and it cut out. He sat there with his hands on the stick and he was too sick and too hazy to move.

The fitters came over and lifted him awkwardly out. He was not completely unconscious and every time he tried to help himself he got tangled. They avoided the sickness all over him and laid him on the ground and he sat up.

"Sorry," he said. "There's a mess. Sorry."

They tried to lift him but he pushed them away. Two of them lifted him up by the arms and he walked uncertainly between them with the coldness and heat coming in rapid changes in him again until it was too rapid and he suddenly pushed them away and was sick in great bends.

Then he quietly fell on his face, unconscious.

Chapter 32

As he left Athens behind he took a deliberate last look at the white city in the clear haze. It was very well formed and the Acropolis was clear, jutting in the middle of it. The Lycabettus dominated the whole city, and the Parnes was like a stage backdrop to the whole white section of the buildings. It did not fade. He took a deliberate look and turned around and did not look at it again.

He remembered vaguely the day's events and yesterday's patrol, his lassitude from that experience, his failure to feel anything, not even the immediacy of the fact that the Germans had broken the last of the defense lines and weren't far from Athens. Only the urgentness of the warm sun, and a loneliness as he waited for orders, had seemed real. He had said good-bye to Finn and to Rutger, one of the fitters. And then he remembered the voice on the phone — "That you, Quayle? You're to take it to the Canea airport on Crete. Report there."

Soon there was nothing but sea below and sky above. There were only the movement of the bumping plane sometimes and the continuous check his eye kept on the instruments that hinted to Quayle that he was moving. He was not looking around for enemy planes. He had ceased to consider them. There was only the lethargy as if he had been sleeping in the sun for a long time. Or as if he had been sick for a long time and the flat placidness of anæmia had caught him.

He found Canea, saw that it was a little white town spread around the sea and at the side of a mountain and a plain. It was a dangerous approach but he did not think of it and came in across wind almost forgetting to put down his flaps. He landed carelessly and he noticed the Blenheims around the edge of the field. He found a small hollow and turned around in it and cut off his engine. He left his parachute in the cockpit, pulled the hood over it, and walked to the building where he could see the blue-uniformed men leaning against it in the sun. He found the officer he wanted in a small room with a heavy wooden table that had once been used for domestic purposes. He reported himself and handed over the operations book that he had carried with him.

"Pretty risky carrying this," the Squadron Leader without wings said to him. He was a short balding man with an exaggerated accent.

"Maybe," Quayle said without feeling. "It's pretty confused over there. I didn't want to leave it there."

"The Corporal will show you to the quarters."

"Am I to stay here?"

"Yes. Until something comes in from Cairo."

Quayle followed the orderly, unbuttoning his harness as he went. He felt the warmth of the sun as he crossed the short grass stretch to the other building. The orderly pointed out a bed to him and he threw his Irvin jacket on it and the trousers. It was warmer here than in Greece. There was a confusion of kits all around the small room with the four beds in it; three flyers walked in as he put his jacket down.

"Are you Quayle?" one of them asked.

"I'm Quayle," he said.

"Tap Finley mentioned you. I'm Warren. This is Ansen and Black."

"How're you?" he said placidly. "Is Tap here?"

"Yes. Have you had anything to eat? How about some tea?"

"Thanks, I will."

"Tap's gone over to get his kit. He'll be back any minute."

Quayle followed them to the square tent that had a deal table in the center with thick cups and enamel teapots on it. Half a dozen flyers were sitting around eating bread and butter and sipping tea.

"This is Quayle," Ansen said and introduced him. They were mostly Blenheim pilots and observers. Some he remembered seeing in the Maxim night club the night he had been there. They remembered him and asked after Hickey. He told them he got it yesterday and sat down and drank the tea before him not looking around and not showing any interest in the conversation. It was all too quiet and the quietness and lack of upright tenseness was too quiet also. Then Tap came. He was smiling all around his face and he had a clean bandage on his arm and a clean shirt on.

"When did you get in?" he said to Quayle as he came up and hit him on the back and Quayle put down the tea as it shook and spilled.

"Just now. Where's Helen?"

"She's all right. She's over at Suda Bay. Where are the others, Hickey and Finn?"

Quayle shook his head. "Hickey and Scotty Crowther got it in the neck yesterday. Went over to cover some evacuation and ran into a swarm of Messerschmitts. Finn's somewhere on the way."

"Hell. That's bloody awful. Hickey?"

Quayle nodded and held the cup of tea in both hands, blowing absently into the brown liquid and forming circles and half closing his eyes. "It was pretty hot," he said.

"What did you say about Finn?" Tap asked.

"He's evacuated somewhere. He left this morning."

"Poor old Hickey. How did you get out of it?"

"Crawled along the ground. Got lower than they could and dodged around valleys."

"Poor old Hickey," Tap said again.

Quayle nodded.

"Is it all over now?"

Quayle nodded again.

"Jesus, fancy Hickey getting it. Just the luck to run into Messerschmitts."

"Has Helen got some place to sleep?" he asked Tap slowly, deliberately.

"Yes. They've rigged up quite a colony for British women evacuated over there. Lawson and I made them take her though they didn't want to at first."

"How did you get over there?"

"I'll take you over — In the truck. She was pretty quiet all the time."

"Did you get bombed?"

"Once. Nothing much though. One Stuka. What happened when you met them?"

"The Messerschmitts?"

"Yes."

"Nothing. I hardly got a shot in. I was just dodging. Crowther was flying like Hickey. He got a Messerschmitt, then they came at him from all sides and he just blew up. It was the same with Hickey. They were everywhere. I nearly tore the Gladiator to pieces getting out of the way."

"What luck. Fancy running into Messerschmitts."

They had walked from the tent to the fence-sided truck and they got in the front seat. Tap told the driver to take them to Suda Bay and to step on it. They hummed over the quiet dust roads around the edge of Canea village, less white so close up. Then across the rise to the sharply hooked U bay with the cement docks and boats in the harbour and soldiers around the water-front and quiet busy movement in the warmth.

"It's a sort of camp," Tap said as the truck turned off the asphalt road along a dirt road cut into an olive grove in the red soil. The truck stopped at a rough stake pegged into the ground. There was a guard and they showed their papers.

"We'll walk from here," Tap said. "This is the boundary for traffic. They're scared of bombing."

"What did they say when they didn't want her to come to this camp?"

"They just said she wasn't British," Tap said.

"What happened to the other Greeks?"

"They went into another camp. It was an old barn or something."

"We're pretty good at that," Quayle said quietly.

"What?"

"Nothing."

They had come to the edge of the rough red soil of the olive grove. The fine leaves were shading the soil in wire-netting patches and it moved in colour as the wind took an occasional breath from the trees. The square tents of the camp suddenly began to show themselves through the thickness of the shadow. There were tents at irregular intervals under the highest olive trees spread right through the grove. Women walked to and from tents around. Some were sitting on blankets in the sun patches. Tap led Quayle through this and they could hear children laughing somewhere as they walked to the red-coated tent.

"This is it," Tap said. "Are you there, Helen?" he called.

"Is that you, Tap?"

"Yes."

"I will be a minute."

"Hurry it up."

There was silence, and Helen suddenly came out of the tent and, as she bent down to get under the flap, her hair fell in the sun over her face. She stood up throwing it glistening back.

"Look," Tap said. He was pointing to Quayle, but she had already seen him.

"Hullo," he said to her.

She kissed him easily on the lips and he felt the warmth of her hand on his neck again.

"When did you get here?" she said.

"A couple of hours ago."

"How did you come?"

"Flew over."

"Look," Tap said. "I'll leave you. I've got to go up and get this bandage changed. You can pick up any truck along the road going back, John."

"I'll be all right," Quayle said.

Tap bowed with alacrity to Helen and walked away, whistling the song about Mussolini that Helen had sung that day in the truck. Macpherson was there again in Quayle's mind and he wondered if he had been evacuated to Crete. He would ask the stragglers officer about him. He had been watching Tap walk away and he turned to Helen.

"I'm glad you're all right," he said.

She smiled at him, and he felt it physically as he felt the sun.

"This is very peaceful here."

"Yes. Do you have all that tent to yourself?"

She was smiling at his new awkwardness, but she could see the tiredness in his eyes and the crumpled forehead. She looked slowly at the blackness of his face and wondered if it was hurting him because she could see the skin puckering up around the edges of the hard blood.

"No. There is an Englishwoman too."

"What's wrong with my face?" He saw her looking at it.

"Nothing. Does it hurt?"

"No. Why?"

"I think the blood will come off soon. It looks like that."

He lifted his hand to his face and she put her hand up and pulled his hand gently away.

"Can you stay?" she said.

"Yes." He put his other hand to his face and felt the hard blood. She took that away too.

"Your hands are dirty. Leave it."

"It's something of a mess, isn't it?"

"Are you beginning to worry about it now?"

He smiled at her, and she saw the tiredness again.

"Wait a minute. I will get the cover and we can sit in the sun."

She went in the tent and came out with a blanket. She spread it out.

"Is it all over?" she said slowly as they sat down.

"In Greece?"

"Yes."

"I suppose so by now. The evacuation is probably still going on."

"Will they get them all out?"

"I don't know. I doubt it."

"What will happen now?"

"Nothing much here. Maybe they will invade England. Maybe."

"Do you think they can take England?"

"No."

Quayle was lying down on the blanket. He suddenly got up because the sun was getting too low and the shadow was moving quickly across them.

"Shall we walk?" he said.

She stood up and they walked unevenly across the red soil through the comfortable shadows. When they got to the road he helped her over the ditch and they walked along in the late afternoon sun.

"Do you have to go to Egypt soon?" she said to him.

"I don't know. I'm waiting for orders," he said. He was looking down the long road. "This is a warm place," he said. "I landed at the other end the last time. It was colder there."

"When were you there?" she asked him.

"When we came over. Just before I met you."

"Will those small planes fly from here to Egypt?"

"Yes."

"You will fly back then."

"I suppose so. They might as well leave it here though."

"What?"

"My Gladiator. It's the last."

"Where are the others?"

"They got shot down yesterday."

"Mr. Hickey and the other one?"

"You didn't know the other one. Yes, Hickey."

"I did not know. I am sorry."

"It's all right."

"Were you fighting too?"

"Yes."

"I am sorry about Mr. Hickey."

"Yes," he said. "Hickey was all right."

"Did you know him for long? He was older than the others."

"He was a Flight Lieutenant when I joined the squadron. I knew him since then."

There was easy silence as they walked up the hard rock of the gradual slope that grew into a mountain. He helped her over a cracked rock.

"He was pretty wild then," Quayle said as he eased himself down and undid his coat.

"He seemed very quiet." Helen had sat against the cracked rock.

"He seemed that way. Look at the birds fighting." He pointed to the gulls wheeling along the mountainside and at the quick dodging as one chased the other one.

"It is very good here," she said, and sat next to him. He was lying back.

"It's warm," he said. "That's why."

"I always thought the English like the cold."

"I suppose some do," he said. "I'll take the sun."

She knew they were like this because he was still wondering about what was going on. It was the same reason that gave him the tiredness and the crumpled forehead. She could see him being careful with himself about what had happened. She did not touch him, though she wanted his warmth, because she was also being careful with herself. It was complicated. What was going on and what was happening. She knew she was clearer about it than he was, but she did not press him about it.

"There goes the sun," he said. It had drifted behind and sideways across the sea and the small mountain range to the west. "We had better go back," he said. They stood up and moved with easy motion down the slope.

"It certainly is different here," he said as they walked along the road.

"Was it very bad in Athens?"

"It was more or less the same as before. They were waiting for the Germans."

"Did the Fascisti do anything inside?"

"I think that was bunk. I don't think any real trouble would have started. They would have been stopped."

"We thought that once before. That is why we had Metaxas."

"That was different," he said.

"That's what my father had said." She deliberately told the lie.

"Come on," Quayle said to her and they walked down the road back to the camp.

Chapter 33

He did not return to the camp until afternoon of the following day.

"I'm sorry I'm so late," he said when he came.

She asked him what happened.

"I was seeing about what was happening."

She spread a blanket in the sun and he sat down on it.

"They don't seem to be in any hurry to get rid of me," he said.

"Will you be flying?"

"Maybe. Token patrols. Can you come over to the other side of the town this afternoon? I found a Padre. Will it be all right?"

"What?"

"The Padre. I know how you feel."

"This is very fine," she said and laughed high. "What difference does it make? Do you care?"

"No. Maybe I would otherwise, but this isn't any time to worry about it."

"You are very sure?" She was smiling at him.

"What the devil. Are you pulling my leg?"

"No," she laughed again. "It is fine. It is very fine."

"Can you come now?"

"Yes." She leaned over in a purely feminine movement and kissed him with deliberate relish and humour on the mouth and rubbed her nose against his forehead where there was no blood.

"What's that for?" he said.

"Must it be for anything?"

"Things like that usually are."

"How do you feel?"

"Fine." He was wondering.

"Well, it's because you feel fine."

"Shall we go?" he said, sitting up beside her, moving his legs out along the blanket in the warmth.

"I will get a hat," she said. She had a print dress on and a white jumper over the top of it. She stood up to go in the tent.

"You don't need a hat. Come on," he said as he stood up.

"Do not the English wear hats in church?"

"We're not getting married in a church. Come on."

"All right," she said and they walked over the rubble of the chrome earth in the olive shadow to the road. The truck was waiting there for them and they got in. They went through Suda Bay town along the water-front between the bombed houses and up the slight side of the mountain. They came to the army camp and there was a guard standing near the oil barrels that made a block across the road near the barbed wire. Quayle showed the guard his papers and the guard asked about Helen.

"We're going to see Padre Nixon," Quayle said.

"What about?"

"Getting married," Quayle said.

"You seem to be all right."

"Do you want me to go in and get the Padre and bring him out?"

"No. It's all right. You can go in."

"Thanks," Quayle said, and they drove in.

Quayle directed the driver to stop in front of the weatherboard house. He helped Helen down and noticed her brown legs as she jumped from the car. "No stockings either," he said to her, and smiled.

"It is your fault," she said.

"I hope the Padre doesn't mind."

"Will we have to know anything to say?"

"No. You'll be all right."

They walked into the hut and she had put her arm through his. There was a small table with a typewriter on it. A small man with white hair and rimless glasses and a sunburnt nose came out with some papers in his hand.

"Good afternoon," he said to them.

"Can you go ahead and do it now?" Quayle asked him.

"You want to get married now?"

"Yes. Were the papers all right?"

"Yes. Have you anybody with you?"

"No," Quayle said. "Is that necessary? This is Miss Helen Stangou. This is Mr. Nixon."

She shook hands and the Padre put down the papers. He had on a khaki shirt and shorts. She could see the red V on his neck where the sun had burnt it.

"You should have someone," the Padre said.

"The driver," Quayle said. He shouted out the door to the driver and asked him to come in. The large-boned Yorkshireman stepped carefully out of the truck where he had been dozing in the sun. Quayle asked him if he minded being around while this went on. He smiled and said he was very glad to. The Padre had put on a light khaki drill coat and he got a prayer-book from the next room.

They stood together and, as the Padre read from the prayer-book, Quayle looked at the dust from Egypt ingrained in the rough outside of the surface, and the gold edges browned with the heat. He did not hear what the Padre was saying and was not directly thinking of Helen but indirectly about all things around them and he was wishing that Hickey were here, and Macpherson and Nitralexis. This would be the time for Nitralexis to be deliberately happy. He could see Nitralexis laughing at the idea, and he was wondering if Nitralexis would have left Greece if he had lived; and he didn't think so, because he would have stayed with Mellass probably, when Mellass went into the mountains. Mellass would think this good, too. That would be fine: Hickey, Nitralexis, Macpherson and Mellass. That would be all, and it would be simple like this.

He could see the dust on the white paper near the typewriter and outside the white tents and the movement of the troops. He could see the bleached eyebrows of the white-haired Padre, and wondered how old he was; and he could feel Helen's hand warm in his as

the Padre was saying something. Now that he was deliberately trying not to listen he had to listen and hear it all.

Then the Padre closed the book as though one whole section were
over, and he told them to put out their hands.

"Have you got a ring?" he said to Quayle.

Quayle put his hand in his coat pocket and took out an edged
silver ring. He could see the brown on Helen's arm where the few
days here had browned her; and the largeness of his own hand and
the squareness of it, and Helen's long fingers. Then the Padre was
saying something about holy wedlock, and Quayle was trying to
remember what he was saying but couldn't, and the Padre said
their names quite unexpectedly, and then "I pronounce you man
and wife" and told him to put the ring on Helen's finger. She held
out her right hand.

"The other one," Quayle said to her. She looked surprised and
held it out. Quayle pushed the ring on it, and it was too big; she
bent her finger so that it would not fall off.

"That's all," the Padre said as they stood there. "I'll have to send
the form to you." He was smiling at them.

Helen could feel nothing. Neither could Quayle, except that this
was like the feeling of doing something for the first time — like the
first time he had flown, because it was the beginning of something
he was going to do for a long time, and do with a definite purpose
and with indefinite developments.

"Thanks," Quayle said to him as the Padre shook hands.

"I cut it down a lot for you," the Padre said. He was looking
keenly at Quayle.

"You did?"

Helen did not say anything but shook the Padre's hand and smiled
at him, and the big-boned driver shook hands with both of them
and said it was pretty good, yes, pretty good, because it was the first
wedding he had been to.

"Well, let's go," Quayle said. "S'long, and thanks," he said to the
Padre.

"Good-bye. I hope you will be all right." He nodded his head when
he said that.

"Thanks," Quayle said again as they got in the truck.

"Good-bye," Helen said to him. The Padre looked at her and he knew a lot of things. He was undoing the top button of his shirt as the truck turned around. He smiled and lifted his hand.

"Good-bye, Mrs. Quayle," he said to her. She only looked at him and was surprised.

As they bumped over the dirt road she looked ahead of them. At the guard post the guard asked them if they had got married and the driver said "They certainly did" and drove on. She felt the weight of the silver ring on her finger. She had put the tip of that finger in the palm of her hand because she was afraid of the ring falling off. She could hear the driver suddenly whistling the Wedding March from "Lohengrin," and Quayle looked at her and smiled.

"Can't you be a bit more original?" she heard him say to the driver.

"What?"

"Nothing," and Quayle's quick laugh.

"Where did you get the ring?" she asked him and held it up.

"I spent half the morning looking for it. I got it in Canea."

"I will have to grow my finger more."

"Won't it stay on?"

"I don't think so."

"Try it; unbend your finger."

"It might fall off."

"Put your hand under it." She could see he was laughing. She looked at him and then at her hand and shook her head.

"Here," the driver said. "Wrap this around it." He gave Helen a piece of string.

"You will tie it to my finger?"

"No. Wrap it around the ring."

Quayle had taken the string. He was pushing it between Helen's finger and the ring because she would not unbend her hand to take it off. He wrapped the string around the ring until it was tight on her finger. He tied the ends and she saw him laugh and turn the part with string on it underneath.

"There you are," Quayle said.

"That's very fine."

"I wish Hickey could see this," he said and laughed quietly.

She was not surprised and he was not being serious suddenly but still laughing and there was no depression in the statement. And because he mentioned Hickey, which was not usual, she asked him about Hickey.

"What would he have thought?" she said.

"He would have enjoyed this," Quayle said with certainty.

"Where was Tap?" she asked him.

"I don't know. He's going to be surprised. He thought we were fooling."

"Did Hickey?" she asked. That was important.

"No." Quayle was quiet. "He knew."

She was silent then, and was watching the dust from the front wheels of the high truck billow out and catch in the edges of the small scrub trees that grew along the edge of the road. She saw the men running from another truck in front up the slope they had just come down.

"Air raid," the driver said and stopped the truck.

She got out after him and waited for Quayle and they hurried up the slope over the rocks where the scrub was. They could see Suda Bay bending just before them and the shadow of the cloud hanging over one end of it and moving as the cloud moved.

She heard the planes suddenly because they had been hiding in the cloud. She saw the black thing with legs, coming in a straight dive, and heard Quayle say "Stuka." She crouched behind the rock because the driver did. She saw Quayle standing up and heard the blast of the string of bombs.

"Come down," she said to him.

"It's all right. We're too far away."

She straightened up. She saw the first Stuka flattening out and the second one coming down and saw the sun glint on the large bomb coming from it.

"They're after the *York*," he said.

"What is it?"

"The battleship. She's half sunk in the bay. That's where that anti-aircraft is coming from."

Helen could see the white puffs following the two planes as the third one came down and she heard the machine-gunning.

"Look out," Quayle said to her and crouched down.

"What is it?" she said above the roar.

"They're strafing." The noise was moving the rock as the string of bombs went off. Then they stood up and could see the planes in the white puffs disappearing, and the echo of the explosions from the hills. She waited for Quayle to move back to the truck. He stood there. The driver had gone back. Then Quayle moved back and helped her down the rocks, though she didn't need it. She got into the truck and they drove off.

Through the town there was still the smell of the explosions and the hurrying of soldiers, and some Australian nurses in grey uniforms through the streets, and Helen wondered who they were. He told the driver to let them off at the road junction and asked him to come back in a couple of hours.

They walked up the slope beyond the olive grove. They came to the flat stretch between the red earth that was tilled and the hard rock. It was soft. Quayle sat down and pulled his coat off. Helen was sitting near him. There was a nettle that she had not seen, and her arm slipped over it. She said "Ouch" and drew her arm away. Quayle looked at her for a minute then laughed. He leaned over and put his hand on her shoulder. It was slightly clumsy but she did not seem to mind. He pulled her down to the soft earth and she was laughing too. He kissed her with the assured right that comes of marriage.

"This is fine," he said.

"That hurts," she said.

"This is fine," he said again. Then: "But I've got to see about getting you to Egypt."

"Not so soon."

"It's no place to be, around here. You saw that raid to-day."

"That is only in the town."

317

"Yes, but anything can happen."

"But not yet," she said.

"It's not going to be healthy around here."

"Why?"

"Anything can happen. I'll be shifted back to Egypt anyway."

"When?"

"It could be any time."

"Let me remain some short time."

"Maybe," he said. "What happened to Lawson, by the way?"

"He went to some other part of the island. Hold still a minute." Helen could see the blood leaving the top of his left cheek near his eye. She took her handkerchief and wiped away the hard section and there was an inch of red skin showing.

"Your face is coming to pieces," she said.

He went to put his hand up and she kept it down. She could see his eyes blinking and the straight nose running into them. She ran her hand through his fine hair and it bristled warmly against her skin, but with fineness. He sat up and took his shirt off, then lay back resting on it. Helen pulled off the white jumper and he could see the brown of her neck.

"You like the sun," she said.

"It's pretty good," he said.

"Don't you have it like this in England?"

"Not where I come from."

"What do you do in your island?"

"They farm mostly. There's practically no living to be had there now."

"I mean you."

"I only went to school there. I went down to London."

"What for?" She had half spread out beside him, but still crooked her legs up.

"University," he said.

"What were you in study of?"

"Building bridges, an engineer."

"Why did you stop?"

"I didn't. I got into this while I was there. I knew I'd have to fly sooner or later so I joined the University Air Squadron. They turned it into a bomber squadron when war broke out so I switched to Eighty Squadron."

"What about the bridges?"

"I don't know," he said. "A lot of things are going to happen. It will be a long time before I can get back to thinking about that. . . . This sun's going to go behind that mountain pretty soon. Shall we go up higher?"

She stood up and he gave her his coat as he pulled his shirt on.

"Leave it off," she said.

He shrugged and took it off again. They walked up the slope and she was still carrying his coat as he climbed over the rocks. He did not help her because she was moving as nimbly as he was. The earth was grey here and covered with fine soft grass over the rocks. They lay down and Quayle took the coat from her and spread it out for her. She lay down and allowed her print frock to slide so that her legs were bared to the sun. She pushed off the sandals.

"It will seem funny to be without sun," she said.

He was silent.

"Doesn't the sun ever come there?" She was repeating the question. She wanted him to talk about it.

"Where?"

"At your home."

"Sometimes. Not this warm."

"Will they mind about me being Greek? The English are funny."

"Maybe. We're not there yet. It's too far away to worry about it."

She put her hands under her head and let the sun warm her face.

"Could you go back to the school after the war?" she asked him. She wanted to know more. She wanted to start the intimateness that should be between them.

"I don't know." His eyes were open now. He was silent for a moment, because he was thinking. He was thinking: I would like to tell Helen this whole complicated thing that is in me. And I cannot talk easily because I have no means of talking and it would be too quick and too softening. I would like to tell her and find out from her but she is reluctant for the same reason. "I would like to go back," he said in the attempt, "but I would want it differently. I would want it, yes . . . differently."

He paused before saying the word because he wanted to go on and explain about the feeling that he had for the sheer physical act of doing something that was real and not unreal like this. But he could not say it.

"I know," she said.

But she knew she only slightly grasped his feeling, and wanted to know more.

"Something that has no emptiness," she said.

"Maybe," he said. Then, "It might be different if — " he paused, went on very carefully — "when you were around."

She nodded to him. She knew he wanted to say more.

She wanted to say more herself. She knew she couldn't, because he would have to set the pace. She wanted to talk about the whole idea of their feeling for all things. But his reluctance to talk in usual terms barred her. He would not accept the normal phrases because he was afraid and suspicious of them, and they were the only ones she knew in English. She was finding that out. To discuss even events more pointedly she would have to be circumlocutory and not use the clichés that he was suspicious of. Yet she wanted to tell more now, and know more now about them both.

"We do not argue enough," she said very quickly.

He laughed and knew what she wanted to say and what she was feeling. He tried to react and express his own feeling to her.

"It will take time," he said. "Things will happen."

What he wanted to say was that as they got into situations they would agree and disagree, and gradually they would become more intimate. He wanted to say that he had never been intimate with anybody and never allowed it. And to ask her to be patient, because he could not suddenly tell her whatever there was to tell. But he wanted it desperately. He wanted the security that intimacy of thought would bring; and the sureness between them it would bring; and the physical warmth he had never known because his had not been a demonstrative family with affections.

"And it is not normal times," she said.

And what Helen wanted to say was that it was because he was in danger continuously, and she did not want to talk it all out unless he did. She would wait. Yes, she would wait for him to start. She wanted to give him the security of her complete affection; not of the immediate feeling between them, but of the long affection of intimacy. She wanted to give that to him and have it herself from him. But she disliked the words also, and she could not say it. . . . We will have to wait, she was thinking.

"I'm sorry I'm not more argumentative," he said with deliberate lightness.

He meant that he was sorry that he did not loosen up more so that they could argue and talk about real things, events, war, people, death, revolution, the development; and what he wanted to find out and do within this. And he was afraid to use the words for it all.

"I'm not so good myself," she said.

She was thinking the same thing, almost in the same order, except that she wanted to tell him what her father and her brother had done; and what they thought and what she thought was the most vital thing in life, developments, history.

She knew then that they had both tried to break into each other's mind, and they had failed. Desperately and miserably.

She remained silent after that.

Quayle lay back again, still thinking about it.

When the sun went down behind the mountain they climbed down the slope and walked along the asphalt road. Quayle put his coat on as the cool wind from the sea found its way down the olive groves. They were silent as they walked.

"I'll see what's going out of here in the next few days," he said to her.

Helen did not argue with him, but she knew that she did not want to go unless he went too. She knew vaguely that in Egypt would be the extreme urgency of war again. Here, there was sufficient temporary lull to make easy living acceptable and not unnerving. The longer she could stay here the better it would be for them. She did not want to be suddenly in Egypt without knowing what was going on with him, because *now* was important. She knew it would be difficult, but she would not argue about it with him.

"Do you have to go back to Canea now?" she said.

"Yes. I have to report."

"Will you be back to-night?"

"Maybe. How do you get on with the Englishwoman?"

"I never see her."

"Yes. Tap found her. That's why."

"Yes. He was making jokes with her the first day."

They had reached the dip where the road became dirt. The truck was there. Quayle told the driver he would be back in a minute and walked through the now deep-shadowed olive grove to the tent.

"I'll try and get back," he said.

"Yes."

"S'long," he said and kissed her warmly. He looked at her carefully for a minute. Helen could see he wanted to say something. But he only touched her face lightly and walked away. Helen watched him go, then walked into the tent.

The tent had the complete air of temporary life. There was depression in the billowing of the canvas and the mild attempt to make the place warm and the clothes hanging on the tent pole. It would be better to be in the open. She remembered the small house with the well and the cumquat orchard around it at the other end of the olive grove. There was a woman there when she passed it before. She would try it anyway. She pulled her jumper over her head and walked out.

It was creeping with evening as she found her way along the grove and through the barbed-wire fence and over the small water channel to the house. It was made of the mud that most villages were made of but had been painted pink with rough pigment of the island. It was low and there was a worn track to the well which was shadowed by a large cumquat tree. She walked past this to the door.

She knocked, then called in Greek to ask if anybody was there. A woman came out.

"Good evening." Helen was polite.

"Good evening."

"Is this your house?"

"I live here with my husband. Yes."

"Could I talk to you about it?"

"About what?" The woman was small and tired with greying hair but smiling corners to her eyes and an upward curve creased where her mouth ended.

"I was wondering if you have a room that you would permit me to live in."

"Would you come in?"

"Thank you," she said. She went in the low doorway to the wooden-pillared room with a long wood-burning stove across one end. There was a man rocking on a chair under a lamp. He stood up and bowed to Helen, then sat down again. He was in the smooth but dirty tunic of a Greek officer.

"She would ask of a room from us," the woman said to him. "This is my husband," she said to Helen.

"I am happy to be allowed within your house," Helen said politely.

He did not ask her to sit down. He looked up at her.

"Have you come from Athens?" he asked her.

"Yes."

"What is going on there now?"

"I left some time ago," she said to avoid discussion of it.

"You could have a small room that had been of my son," the woman said.

"How long would you remain?" the man asked her.

"Perhaps some weeks. I do not know. My husband is leaving soon," Helen said.

"You would have your husband here too?" the man said.

"Yes."

"You can pay?" he asked.

"With certainty," she said. He named a price and she nodded.

"It is all right, I suppose," the man said.

"Thank you," Helen said. "We would like to come to-morrow."

"Yes," the woman said. "That will be all right."

They walked to the door. Helen said "Good night" formally to the man, who stood up again and said "Good night." The woman opened the door for her and nodded when Helen thanked her.

"It is all right," she said. Helen told her it was fine.

"Good night." Helen held out her hand and the tired woman accepted it.

Chapter 34

Quayle had taken a bath in the round tub that they filled with water from one of the wells. He had looked at himself casually in the square mirror. He saw the blackness of his face and the dark beard getting longer. He could see the small red part where the blood had come off that day. It was beginning to itch all over his face and he could feel the dryness of his skin from the sun. He walked away from the mirror wondering about whether he could shave or not. He sat down on the bed to pull on clean socks that Tap had given him the day before. He wished he had a clean shirt and was thinking about having the one he had on washed the next day, when Tap came in.

"Where were you all day?" Tap said to him.

"With Helen."

"How is she?" Tap said and sat down next to him.

"Fine," Quayle said. "We got married."

"Well, hell's bells. Why didn't you tell me?"

"You weren't around."

"I was only up at the hospital. You could have got me."

Quayle shrugged and pulled his boots on.

"How's your arm?" he asked Tap.

"Fine. The doctor up there says I won't be doing any more flying."

"You won't?"

"No. There's something wrong with a bone in my shoulder."

"Will your arm be all right?"

"Sure. Just not good enough for flying."

"That's too bad," Quayle said.

"Is it? Say, I thought you were kidding about marrying Helen."

"You did?"

"Sure. What did they say about her? I mean she's a Greek."

"What about it?"

"What are they going to say at home, then?"

"What difference does that make?"

"I didn't think you meant it," Tap said laughing.

"How did you get on about that boat that was leaving?"

"It was an oil tanker. I don't want to get blown up."

"Are there any more going?"

"I don't know. I don't care, anyway. This is a holiday being around here. Has dinner started?" Tap asked him.

"I think so." Quayle pulled on his tunic and walked out with Tap. They went into the square tent with deal tables and enamel teapots. The Corporal asked them what they wanted. They told him and sat down to wait for the food. Tap poured himself a Scotch with water from bottles at one end of a table and asked Quayle if he wanted it. Quayle was leaning back in a chair half asleep and said he didn't want it. They were more or less silent during the meal and when Quayle had finished he said "Good night" to Tap and went out to bed.

Chapter 35

It was early morning when Quayle got up. He had to do a patrol over Suda Bay. The fitters and riggers had worked on the Gladiator and it was on the field ticking over when he went out into the early sunlight. He pulled on the parachute harness, stepped into the cold cockpit and took off immediately. The operations officer marked him off as he left. Three Blenheims had already taken off. There were two other Blenheims on the edge of the field as Quayle pulled the stick back and lifted the heavy plane over them. He had to bank and go straight into a stiff climb to pull out around the mountains.

The patrol was simple. There were troops coming in at Suda Bay. He was to make patrol around the bay and northwards to protect ships coming in. He could see they were already coming in when he had climbed over the bay. They were tall ships compared with the destroyers bringing them in. The cold sun had made the sea warm with hard light as it lifted from the horizon. He wondered what he would do if there was bomber opposition. It was not expected, they had said. The Blenheims were around anyway. He kept looking behind him for both Blenheims and enemy aircraft. He found the Blenheims and switched in his wireless.

"Hullo there," he said to them and repeated the code lettering.

"That you, Quayle?" one of them said.

"Yes. I'll come in above you."

When he got back they were still eating breakfast in the mess tent. "Here he is," one of them said.

"Did you hear it?" Tap said as Quayle walked in.

"Hear what?"

"You got the D.F.C."

"I did?"

"Yes," one of them said and pointed to Tap. "So did Finley."

"Hickey got a D.S.O. and a bar to his D.F.C.," Tap said.

"That's going to do him a lot of good," Quayle said. He had been feeling good, but not now.

"How do you know about it?" he said to Tap.

"They told me up at Operations."

"I didn't think H.Q. even knew we were here," Quayle said as he sat down. They were all congratulating him and Tap shook his hand and Tap was very happy with this. Tap was laughing as he did when he had been drunk for some time and was trying not to get too sober.

When Tap went out Quayle finished his breakfast in peace. Then he reported and wrote out the short operations report and asked if he was wanted. They said he wasn't so he asked one of the truck drivers to take him over to Suda Bay.

When he got to the water-front he went into the small brick building with sandbags around it and the sentry saluted him. He found the naval officer he wanted and asked him about ships leaving for Egypt. The officer said there was the oil tanker leaving to-day and a convoy of troops to-morrow, probably unescorted. Quayle told him that he had his wife here, and the officer said she would have to go with the other women. There would be a ship sometime for them. Quayle asked the naval officer to let him know at the Canea airdrome. Then he went on to Helen.

Helen was outside the tent brushing her hair when he walked through the olive grove to her. The sun had come up high enough to shorten the olive-tree shadows sufficiently to have sun patches between the trees. Quayle walked deliberately around these to catch the warmth. Helen watched him walking without haste towards her.

"Hullo," he said to her as he came up. He kissed her carefully.

"Hullo." She was looking to see how he was feeling.

There was silence while he sat down. She stopped brushing her hair.

"Go on," he said to her. "Don't stop."

"Were you doing patrol this morning?"

"Yes. Did you know?"

"Yes," she said and sat down next to him. "Tap was here."

"When?"

"Half an hour before. He said something about getting a medal."

"Yes. He got the D.F.C."

"He said you got it too."

"Did he?" Quayle unbuttoned his coat and lay back.

"Yes. Did you get it?"

"Yes."

"And Hickey got something else."

"A D.S.O."

"What does that mean?"

"Distinguished Service Order," Quayle said.

"Is that good?"

"Pretty good. About the best except the V.C."

"You don't seem pleased."

"Why should I be?"

"I don't know. I am glad about it for Hickey."

"It might have been all right if he was around to enjoy it."

"What about yours? What did you get it for?"

"I don't know. I haven't seen the report."

They were silent a minute. Then Helen stood up and told him to come with her.

They found their way along the grove, through the barbed-wire fence and over the small water channel to the house.

"I came here yesterday," she said. "They can give a room to us." Helen knocked on the door.

"What did you do, just ask them?" Quayle looked around.

"Yes, why?"

"Nothing. You Greeks are pretty friendly people."

"They will want us to pay."

Quayle laughed at her. Then the woman came to the door. Helen told the woman in Greek that this was her husband and could they see the room. The woman looked at Quayle and seemed surprised. Quayle bowed his head to her.

"He is an *Inglisi?*" she said to Helen.

"Yes," Helen said as they went in.

"We thought your husband was Greek."

"No. He's an *Inglisi.*" The woman was silent. They looked at the room and Quayle said it was fine. It was small and had a low home-made double bed with a multi-coloured patch quilt over it. There were a wooden chair and two small tables. The low ceiling faded into a small window and the sun cut through the dim light.

"This is fine," he said as they went out.

"Will you be able to come sometimes?" Helen said to him, deliberately casual.

"I think so," he said. "I'll get away somehow."

"I do not know about food," she said. "I think we will get it here if you do not mind it. There is no meat."

Quayle walked over to the well and picked a ripe cumquat from the tree.

"I think I can survive without meat."

He picked some others and as they walked back to the tent he bit the soft stones and chewed their bitterness, then made the taste sweet again with a fresh cumquat.

He was whistling "I care for nobody, no not I," as he carried the two cases from the tent to the house. He kicked a sod of earth from in front of him and smiled at Helen when she looked at him. She knew then that she had done the right thing, and she was happy.

Chapter 36

They lived a smooth life, though it was without complete regularity. On the nights when John could stay at the house they were happy for the intimacy without giving thought to it. The Greek who owned the house was slightly unpleasant when he found out Quayle was English. He had been the manager of the olive orchard, and the war had disturbed his life. He had been called up with the local garrison and his groves were taken over by the English as camp areas. He was quietly resentful of Quayle, and Quayle knew it, though he deliberately went out of his way not to provoke the Greek.

But it was pleasant. On the days when he was not standing-by at the airdrome, he would sit in the sun at the back of the house in the rough chair and eat the cumquats that Helen had picked for him.

They were without need for expression. Their quietness, and Helen reading while he slept sometimes, or Helen trying to teach him Greek, and the sun getting warmer, and shifting around so that they were in it . . . Helen's brown face and the light surface that was glistening on her black hair gave Quayle great happiness in seeing her.

There was no haste and no imminence. At the airdrome there was casualness too. Sometimes Tap went over to the house with Quayle and they would eat bully beef and canned peaches on a blanket. Quayle was always the same and he had been burnt by the sun and lay in it listening to Tap because he could accept it. His face was peeling and the sun had covered the unsightly redness with the dry surface. Tap called him piebald but he was not worried about it.

The evacuation of Greece had been completed. Stragglers appeared every couple of days in from the Peloponnesus. Suda Bay was bombed and Canea was strafed twice and a Blenheim set on fire. The Blenheims had moved to the other end of the island for a while. The trouble in Iraq had started, and one day they heard on the wireless at Canea that Rudolf Hess had landed in England. That day Quayle came from the airdrome after a morning patrol over Suda Bay. Helen had been bathing in the tub that sat in the middle of the yard and she was drying herself in the sun, half-dressed, when Quayle came.

"You look good," he said to her.

"Thank you." She was sitting in the chair he usually used.

"Don't get up."

"You are very polite."

"Yes," he said and sat down on the sand-hard floor in the sun. He leaned up and pulled her black hair quickly, then let it go and lay back taking his coat off.

"I will miss this sun," he said.

"Why?"

"What would you think of going to England?" he said.

"We will go there?"

"How would you feel about it?"

"I feel nothing. It is good. You want to go?"

"I was thinking of applying for transfer."

"I thought you did not like the cold."

"I don't. This has been fine. I just think it's a better war in England."

She knew then what he had been thinking about during those days.

"How is it better?"

"I agree with Lawson. Nothing much can happen out here."

"The war will go on," she said.

"Yes. Battles maybe. Anything real will happen in England."

"Why?"

"That's what I want to see. Would you mind going to England?"

"No. How could I get there?"

"Ship."

"Do you think it's going to happen soon?"

"What?"

"What you were talking about." She was being very careful with him.

"No. Maybe quite a while. I want to see."

"England is very slow sometimes," Helen said.

"That's a generalization, isn't it?" She knew it and nodded.

"Who will make all the changes?"

"I don't know," he said. "Anybody that comes up, I suppose." He was silent as he pushed his flying boots off. "Did you wash those socks for me?" he said as he pulled off the ones he had on.

"They are hanging on the well."

"Thanks."

"When will you be able to get some clothes?"

"In Egypt," he said. Two days before he had stripped to the waist while she washed his only shirt and dried it in the sun and ironed it with the stove flat-iron.

"There is practically nothing left of your socks. Who mended them the last time?"

"Tap, I suppose. They're his socks."

She was silent for a moment, then she said, "What will Tap do now that he can't fly?"

"I don't know. He'll probably go down to Headquarters."

"Does he like that?"

"He says it's the solution to everything. He's had enough."

"He is very complicated," she said.

"Not Tap. He's not complicated enough. Hickey used to say that Tap should have grown up in the twenties when Hickey did, because he would have had a fine time."

"It's always a pity about Hickey," she said quietly.

"Maybe. It settled his problems all the same."

"What problems?"

"He was trying to keep about twenty of his family on his salary."

"Is that all?"

"No. He was too honest for G.H.Q."

"He did not seem worried."

"He worried all right. Do you remember Richardson?"

"The tall one?"

"The one that was shot parachuting."

"I remember," she said.

"Richardson used to worry. He didn't show it either. Hickey found out he was in trouble with some Egyptian girl. He made a trip down to Cairo to persuade a friend of his to perform an abortion."

"Richardson did not seem like that."

"Like what?"

"Careless." Helen said it slowly.

Quayle smiled. "He was about the best of the bunch." He was still smiling. "Even if he was careless."

"It is a pity about them all," Helen said.

Quayle was silent. He had shut his eyes and was dozing into light sleep made of sun. Helen stepped over him and went into the house to put on a dress and shoes. When she came out Quayle had taken the chair and was asleep with his mouth open. She took the socks he had taken off and got some water in a bucket from the well, poured it into the tub and washed them. She hung them on the well in the sun and took the other pair. Then she sat down next to Quayle on the sand-floor and began to darn the holes. She suddenly heard Quayle make a deep sound.

"The epitome of marriage as they would have it," he said. His half-closed eyes were looking at her in amusement.

"What?" she said.

"Darning socks."

"As who would have it, I mean." She looked at him and he turned on his side. He shrugged and sat up.

"I'm hungry," he said.

"I forgot to tell you," she said. "The officer would like us to bring our own food."

"He would? Since when?"

"He told me this morning."

"Why the sudden change?"

"He does not like the English."

"I knew that," Quayle said.

"I heard him tell his wife before that the English have too much food."

"What's wrong with him?"

"He liked Metaxas."

"God. There're all types."

"Can you get food?"

"I can get it from the NAAFI. But what's he got to moan about?"

"He has lost this year's olives."

"You want to tell him about Nitralexis or Mellass some day."

"He would not understand."

"No."

Quayle stood up and put his coat on. He pulled on the clean socks and his boots.

"I'll go down and get some bully beef," he said. "Can we cook anything?"

"The woman said it would be all right."

"I'll be back in about an hour," he said. He kissed her and walked across the grove and down to the road to catch a truck into Suda Bay.

He climbed the stiff path from the road where he got off the truck to the big warehouse that the NAAFI had taken over. An aircraftsman saluted him as he went by and he did not notice immediately. He half-waved his hand when he did, because it was awkward when you did not acknowledge a salute though he disagreed with the whole idea. He walked in the small door to the long room stocked high with canned goods and cases unopened. There were two or three army officers buying stuff. He asked the Palestinian clerk for some bully beef and then he felt the arm on his shoulder.

"When did you get here?" the voice said. He turned around.

"Hullo, Lawson," Quayle said. They shook hands.

"How're you?" Lawson said to him. He was dressed in khaki shorts and was sunburned and his blond hair was wet with perspiration.

"Pretty good," Quayle said. "Thanks for bringing Helen over."

"How is she?"

"Pretty good."

"Is she still here?"

"Yes. I can't get her out yet. Where have you been?"

"Looking around this place," Lawson said.

"Did you see anything?"

"No. There's nothing to see."

"What were you looking for?"

"Defences. It's like hunting for gold."

"Is it that bad? I thought they were building defences."

"They've got a couple of naval guns here and there." Quayle paid for the bully beef and the crackers and peaches he had bought and Lawson took the two bottles of lime juice and Scotch from the counter.

"Do you want to see Helen?" he asked Lawson as they went out.

"Sure."

"Would you come for something to eat?"

"Have you got a house or something?"

"We've got a room."

"That's swell. When did you get married?"

"About two weeks ago."

"That's swell. How're the others?"

"Who?"

"Tap and Hickey and the others."

"Tap's all right. Hickey got eliminated."

Lawson did not say anything and they walked carefully down the slope. They hailed trucks until they found one going out towards the olive grove. It was almost dark, and the long red evening was beginning to shade itself. They got off the truck at the dirt road and walked through the olive grove to the house.

Helen was pleased to see Lawson. She was in the room, and Quayle put the cans on a small table. Helen shipped them to the bed and pulled the table to the center of the room when Quayle told her Lawson was staying. Lawson was following Helen around with his eyes.

"It suits you," he said to her.

"What?"

"Marriage."

"That's the sun," Quayle said. He was looking at Helen too and looking at Lawson following her around, and he saw Helen's beauty as if he were seeing her for the first time.

"I think we ought to have a drink on this," Lawson said. He was opening the tall bottle of Scotch.

"You know, I'm going to be mighty glad when I can get some bourbon," Lawson said. Helen looked at Quayle.

"American whiskey," he explained to her.

"Have you got any glasses?" Helen gave him two glasses.

"Don't you want any?"

"No," she said and began opening the tins of bully beef.

"We've got to have a toast. Come on, a drop." He got a cup from the table and poured out a small amount. He gave it to her.

"Here's to you," he said to them. "Here's to all of us." And they drank. Helen screwed up her face when she put the cup down and Lawson laughed at her. He sat down on the bed.

"When are you going on to Egypt?" Lawson said, sipping the whiskey.

"I don't know. When I can get Helen back."

"I wouldn't wait around too long."

"Why?" Helen asked him.

"If anybody takes a crack at this place it's gone."

Lawson had poured himself out another drink and filled Quayle's glass. "Here's to the sun," he said and drank again. He leaned back on the bed.

337

"Have we got anything here?" Quayle asked him.

Lawson shook his head and swilled the whiskey around in the glass. "No airplanes. No pursuit ships. No anti-aircraft."

"What's it like down the other end?"

"Not a goddam thing."

"It would be pretty hard to take it," Quayle said.

"Maybe. I just hope nobody tries."

"I thought they left most of the stuff they brought out of Greece."

"You were up in the air, Quayle." Lawson stood up and walked around. "They didn't get anything out of Greece," he said.

"How many men got out, then?"

"Maybe thirty thousand. It's pretty good, considering."

"Have you heard anything of what is happening in Athens?" Helen asked him.

"Only on the radio. The Germans are taking all the food."

"There's no food to take," Helen said.

"Maybe. But they're battering the Greeks around looking for it."

"The more they do the harder the Greeks will take it," Helen said.

"The Greeks feel pretty sore with the English at the moment," Lawson said.

"Won't they forget that?" Quayle said.

"Maybe."

"They're pretty sensible people," Quayle said.

"They're getting it in the neck from the Germans. You can't be sensible long when that happens. They'll feel sore for quite a while."

"The food is ready," Helen said. She had spread the bully beef on plates and buttered the black Greek bread. "They will not be quiet for the Germans," she said quietly as they sat down.

"I agree." Quayle drank the last of the whiskey in his glass.

"If they can do what they were doing in Albania, they can be a pretty big handful for the Germans." Lawson was bending the hard bread in two.

"They will never give in," Helen said.

"I wonder what Mellass is doing," Quayle said to her.

"They will all be fighting," she said.

They ate the beef and hard bread and Lawson poured himself some more liquor. Quayle shook his head when Lawson offered the bottle to him. They talked about the olives and the Greek who owned the house and revolt in Iraq and Hess going to England, which they all said was strange and not clear-cut.

When Lawson said he would have to be getting back to Canea, Quayle said he would go with him because he had a patrol the next morning and would have to stay at the airdrome overnight.

"I'll be back about ten to-morrow," he told Helen as they left.

"All right," she said. "Good night."

"Good night," they both said. She went back into the house to clear away the dishes and wash them in the sink.

Chapter 37

Quayle was drinking tea in the long-tent before he went on the patrol. The sun was red below the horizon and the high sky was lit, the low sky was purple with the last of night. The bombing came with the high drone of engines. He felt the first string shake the tent as the planes glided in and opened up as they made the bombing run. He flattened out and the orderly fell near him.

"Air raid," the orderly shouted.

Quayle ran outside as the next two dropped and he flattened out. The others were running from buildings in pyjamas and crouching in the slit trenches. Quayle looked for the Gladiator, saw it on the very edge of the field with the covers off. He wondered if he could make it, but he saw the Stuka coming down as if to pick him out personally and he leapt into the slit trench in the soft earth. The four bombs ripped across the airdrome.

As the lull developed, Quayle looked up and ran a hundred yards towards the Gladiator. He could see a Blenheim toppled over at the other end of the field. He flattened out again as a Stuka climbed and winged over and came down like a thunderbolt and the small string of fifty-pounders punctured the field from one end to the other. He lifted his head to look, and the second Stuka came again.

He ran another fifty yards in the next lull and was near the Gladiator now. He looked around for the crew, who had been working on it. He saw the group behind the boulders. He went over to them in a crouching run as he heard the Stukas coming back again.

"Is that Gladiator all right?" he shouted as he ran.

"It hasn't been hit," one of them said as they ducked.

"Is it ready?" Quayle said.

"No. No ammunition." They ducked again and one small bomb landed between them and the Gladiator, and Quayle looked up quickly, but the Gladiator was still standing there.

"I'm taking off," he said. "Will one of you give me a hand?"

"The belts are still loose in the boxes," the armourer said.

"It doesn't matter. I just want to get it off this field. Come on."

Two of them ran with him and, while he climbed into the cockpit, one of them pulled out the loose ammunition belts and clamped down the panel on the wing, while the other helped him start and turn around. Quayle kept the cockpit cover back and looked straining behind him. He saw the Stuka coming down, and he revved the engine down and crouched as he saw the bombs coming. He felt the whole impact of the blast on the Gladiator; and half standing to see the holes in the field he revved the engine again and taxied straight across the field and lifted the heavy tail in a down-wind take-off. He had to ground-loop almost to avoid the sharp rise at the end of the field, and he found himself directly under the belly of a Junkers 87 B — a Stuka. He could have touched it before he slipped away as its rear gun started after him. He looped on nothing and climbed off the top of the loop. He could see the chain of Stukas coming around in an almost perfect circle. He pulled the nose up to get height.

As he climbed to get protective height he could see the second group of Stukas attacking Suda Bay. There must be fifty around here, he was thinking, as he kept swivelling his head around to see if anything was on his tail. He knew he would be fairly safe if they had not brought fighter escort. He could dodge Stukas, but he would have some time getting out of the middle of fighters, particularly since he had no ammunition. He watched the flat rising bursts of the bombs as he climbed. They were pasting the place seriously this time.

He was suddenly surprised to see a straggled group of twin-engine Heinkels or Messerschmitt 109 F's coming from the east, way below him against the now red sea, almost out of the sun. He guessed they were Heinkels and had been raiding another place on the island.

He didn't like this. Why the sudden interest in Crete? There must be more than one hundred bombers within immediate sight. What the hell could they do? They might try bombing out the airdromes. No. This is what they usually prefixed something else with. Air troops maybe. They might have the whole Italian Navy escorting stuff in.

Quayle watched the Stukas go to the west and he came down and landed. The field was pitted with large and small bomb craters but he picked a strip across-wind and side-slipped in. There was one Blenheim burning and another one toppled over. Quayle taxied to the end of the field where there was a wide ditch. There was a clump of timber and a rise in the ground the other side of this ditch, and it was the only protection on the whole airfield. But the ditch was too wide and deep to cross. He left the Gladiator as near it as possible. Then he ran the length of the field to the mess tent because he was cold. He had not had any flying suit on. The sun was climbing up now and it was warm. The black smoke from the Blenheim was the only cloud. The hangars and the mess tent had not been touched.

"That was pretty slick," one of them said to him as he walked into the mess tent.

"Did anybody get hurt?"

"A fitter. One of the ones that helped you off. Got a scratched hand or something."

Tap was there now too, still in his pyjamas with a tunic over his pyjama coat.

"What do you think, John?"

"I don't know. Something's going to happen. They don't do that for nothing."

"Two Blenheims gone too," Tap said.

"They ought to put a bridge across that ditch. We could shelter planes in that timber," the Blenheim Squadron Leader said.

"We've been trying to persuade the army to come over and do that for about a month." It was the liaison officer. "They didn't have time."

"They'd better," Tap said. "If they start anything, this is the only airdrome. They won't keep planes long if there's no protection."

They were all accepting the bombing raid as being an early morning sweep, that it was over, and that was that, and now let's have some breakfast, and something was going to happen sometime, but let's finish breakfast. But it was not a matter of finishing breakfast, Quayle was considering. He was wondering what was about to happen, when he heard the sharp tooting of motor horns for air-raid alarm and he went out with the others. They went up the bare rock face to the slit trenches as they saw the large formation of bombers coming from the west. Quayle knew it was useless trying to get the plane off. The Blenheims had taken off and were not in sight, but it was too late now and the German group flew straight over the air field. The heavy 3.7 anti-aircraft opened up from somewhere and there were white puffs behind the group. The machine-guns opened up and Quayle could see the tracers falling short of the planes as they made a run in formation over the airdrome. There was the glint of grouped careless bombs, then the fantastic burst of numbers of them and larger numbers until individual sounds were not distinguishable and sight was uncertain as sound.

It went on all day. There was only one break of more than half an hour. Twice, two groups of Messerschmitts strafed the airdrome and one was shot down by efficient cross-fire of machine-gunners who had been dispersed around the airdrome. The Blenheims tried to land once but had almost to exhaust their petrol, then run in and stay in. The bombing did not give them time for refuelling and the stores of fuel were on fire.

At night it settled down a little and they left the slit trenches and managed to get something to eat. Quayle was wondering about the Gladiator; it was still standing at the very end of the field and nothing had touched it yet. They were all anxious now.

"This is the beginning of something," Tap said as they drank tea in the dark tent because they were not showing any light for fear of raids.

343

"They were giving Suda Bay the same, when I was up," Quayle said.

"They're pasting the whole island," the operations officer had come in.

"What's it for?" Tap asked Quayle. He looked in the direction of Tap's voice. There was still the smell of the explosives in the air and Quayle could taste it in his tea.

"Anything. Invasion maybe."

"They're going to have a hard time invading this place."

The operations officer told them they were to stand-by all night. They were expecting something to happen. Recco's over Greece showed that they were massing planes all over the place, and gliders.

"Gliders?" Tap said.

"Yes."

"This will be fine," Tap said. "What the hell are they going to do with gliders?"

"Christ only knows," the operations officer said. "We're standing-by all night anyway."

Quayle was wondering if they'd strafed the camps around where Helen was. He asked the operations officer, who said that Suda Bay itself had been battered around but that was all. Quayle did not like the idea of having so much between Helen and himself. He was cursing all things that had kept Helen on the island and was hoping to Christ to himself that this thing was a balloon and would burst. But so much bombing was going to mean further trouble. He tried to concentrate on what was about to happen, but he could not work it out.

The bombing started again at midnight. It was all over the place now. They could hear it towards the village and in the direction of Suda Bay and sometimes behind them and above, along the mountain. They could see the flashes from one end to the other of the mountain range. The Blenheims had taken off twice to do patrol during the night, but they found nothing, and while they were away the airdrome was strafed and bombed again. The ground fire from the machine-guns brought down another plane, and it burst into flames just above the slit trench where Tap, Quayle and the liaison officer were crouching.

"This ground fire's bloody good," Tap said.

"They're pretty good," the liaison officer said.

"What are they using?" Quayle asked the liaison officer.

"Bren guns. There they go again."

The machine-guns had started again. They kept it up intermittently when the bombing went on. It never seemed to stop, and they tried to sleep in between the explosive groups. There was tenseness unrelaxed, and threat that was a breath continuously drawn in and never expired. And the night was becoming the light water-colour of purple morning waiting for the sun.

"Hell of a lot of chance we've got against this," Tap had said as the bombing started in the pale light. "No planes. Nothing," he said.

"They've asked for more planes," the liaison officer said.

"They could bring all they had and it wouldn't do any good."

"Well, we'll know soon," Quayle said.

"What chance will we ever have against these bastards?"

"It's just a matter of survival," Quayle said.

"That's hard enough," Tap said. They were watching the sky breathe red where the sun was threatening to come up. Quayle was looking for the Gladiator as the light was spreading far enough to see. He could see it still standing, but that didn't mean anything. The whole place was in a mess. The buildings had been flattened, the mess tent had blown away, the field was ugly with a mess of craters that bent over high at the edges with fresh red earth.

They walked through the wreckage of the buildings and picked what they could out of the mess. There was no fire. Some of them salvaged a few pieces of clothing. Tap and Quayle were kicking over the wreckage of their quarters in the dim light when Tap heard the drone, looked up, saw the whole thing.

"Now we're in for it," he said. "Look." He pointed into the dark shadow of the north-west.

"Thousands of them," he said.

As far as Quayle could see there were the black shapes of formation-flying planes. They looked irregular because there were so many. There were an inconceivable number, and they were at less than five thousand feet.

"What the hell is it?" Quayle said, half to himself.

"They'll blow this whole place away. Come on."

There was the general confusion of people running up the slope to the slit trenches and the threat of such a large number of planes causing high shouting and quick carelessness. Quayle was confused too. The nearer they got the less he could understand it, because small concentrated groups of planes could do a better job than this wide-spread-out large group. They were coming directly over, and he was with Tap in the slit trench watching the tracers from the ground machine-guns falling short.

"They're three-engine Junkers," he said to Tap.

"Are they fighters behind?"

"Gliders. They're towing gliders. Christ."

"What's that group way ahead?"

"Junkers."

"Gliders, hell. They must be loaded with bombs or something."

"Or troops," Quayle said. "Maybe this is your invasion."

He had hardly said it when the tail group wheeled off the lead formation and came directly over the airdrome. They were all three-engined Junkers transports as Quayle could see them. He was straining his head back and trying to keep the light of the hidden sun from blotting out the planes. He saw the first group of parachutists suddenly burst white in the sky. Then another group of white bursts, like the white bursts from anti-aircraft . . .

"Parachutists. Here it is, Tap."

"What the hell? Christ, look at that."

The white bursts had suddenly appeared here, there — there, here — over there. They were coming from the down-wind direction directly towards the airdrome. As the Junkers in the tail end of the group passed over, more parachutes burst in the red-blue sky.

They were thick and uneven. There were white, red and striped parachutists, and some fell quicker than others. There was the continuous shriek of machine-guns all around now, and the path of tracers towards the parachutists. As the parachutes got lower, the machine-guns lowered their fire and there was suddenly a complete cross-fire over the whole airdrome.

"Keep down. Those bloody machine-guns are getting low. Have you got a pistol or something?" It was Tap shouting at the top of his voice.

"Come on. Up higher," Quayle said.

"The machine-guns."

"That's the safest place. We'll take a chance. Come on."

They ran higher up through the fire of the machine-guns from the other side of the field. They could see the first parachutists reaching the earth behind the woods, then the next group, one two three four and then two, five, four, hitting the airdrome but not getting up because the machine-gun fire was too deadly and it ricocheted from the field over Tap's and Quayle's heads as they climbed the slope to where they found one of the machine-guns.

"The silly bastards. They'll kill us," Tap shouted.

"That's bloody good cross-fire," Quayle shouted. There was no need to shout but it was automatic because of the threat and the continuous noise of the machine-guns. The parachutists were coming down all around now, but the largest group were coming down on the field and not getting up as the machine-guns poured hell into them. Quayle could hear the crack, distinctive and certain, of rifles, and the short mark of the pistol above the short burst of machine-guns all around.

As they crouched under the noise of the Bren gun, they could see the top row of parachutists coming down and the fire tearing some of their parachutes and some of them catching fire and the black smudge as the figure went hell-directed to earth. Twice, two parachutes came down between them and the air field and Quayle could see the shape of the uniform and the glasses pulled over the German's face and the ammunition around his neck and high boots and the struggle to loosen the parachute when he hit the earth, then the ceasing of his struggles as the rifle cracked and he jerked and lay still.

As the last group came down and the white things were all over the field and caught in the trees, Quayle could see some of the parachutists running to take cover but never getting there as the machine-guns tore them away and apart.

"They haven't got a chance," Tap was shouting again. They had been silent, watching one side, then another, then another group getting killed, then some of them running.

"What happened to the others?" Quayle said.

"They went over towards Canea. There's the gliders now."

Quayle saw the uneven group of gliders coming around in wide sweeps and trying to keep their noses down and coming into heavy nose glides and slow movement and the tracers trying to find them but falling short. Quayle watched a group of three-engined Junkers coming lower.

"Are they going to try and land them?"

"They're crashing them into the mountainside."

They watched a pair of Junkers come low, then level out over an area they knew to be mostly timber with no clearing. They saw the Junkers' flaps go down and the flat sinking as the planes came level over the earth and disappeared.

"Crash-landing them! They must be filled with troops."

Now they were watching the gliders, which were coming in near the airdrome and sloping to land. The first one came down too soon and it slid along the green earth very fast and hit one of the craters and toppled over. There was the mess of men and the crumpling of the plane and the noise. Then the machine-guns pulling up the earth around them and some running and some getting into the craters on the air field. Then the burst of red fire from a machine-gun from one of the Germans in the craters.

"If they get this place we're sunk," Tap said.

"Look at that Gladiator standing out there."

"Look at those gliders coming in now. Look at that."

348

The second and third gliders were flattening out over the field and landed and the black-clothed figures were swarming out. Some made for the edge of the field, others dropped in the craters. There was only the continuous noise of the machine-guns from both sides now. Quayle could see the concentrated fire coming from the timber behind the Gladiator.

"Come on," he shouted to Tap. "We'll head down towards the timber."

"That bloody Gladiator's still there."

"Come on."

They crouched and Tap found running awkward because of his arm. Quayle helped him along. They ran over the uneven ground from under the machine-guns, parallel with the field, to where the road ran into the fuel dump. Quayle could see some of the gliders in flames and the men pouring from them and getting caught in the machine-guns' fire. Some of them were getting into the slopes at the north end of the field.

The two of them fell into the ditch behind the Gladiator near a machine-gun crew who were firing at the dip at the north end where most of those that had escaped from the gliders had run to.

"Keep down," someone shouted to them as the machine-gun bullets splashed the earth. Quayle and Tap crouched into the deep ditch, then crawled along to the Bren-gun crew.

"Who are you?" It was a tall blond Scottish Captain in smock and khaki battle-dress.

"We're from Eighty Squadron."

"Can I see your papers?" He had to shout as they crouched into the ditch as the Bren gun on the high tripod shook with firing.

"What's the matter?" Tap said.

"How the bloody hell do I know you're not parachutists?"

They both showed him their papers. He looked at them quickly and handed them back.

"All right," he said. "Something round is the sign you're not a German."

"Did any of that last lot get away?"

349

"There's quite a nest of them the other end of the field." The Captain spoke abruptly and he was quick and certain in his movements.

"We lost a couple of machine-guns up there," he said. "My name's Mann."

"What's this?" Quayle said. They were looking up as a group of Heinkels came low over the field. They swept from the north end, held their fire until they nearly reached the ditch, then opened with the machine-guns. The Bren gun kept firing at the Heinkels as it strafed them and the woods behind them.

"They must have wireless up the other end," Mann said.

"Where are those Blenheims?" Tap said aloud to himself.

"They ought to be here," Mann said. "I don't know what the hell they're going to do when they get here. Your crowd is in the timber."

Quayle was looking at the Gladiator to the left of them close to the ditch.

"Has anything hit that plane yet?" he said to Mann.

"Nothing. If only you could get it into that timber."

"Why the hell didn't they fill this ditch in?" Tap shouted above the machine-gun again.

They crawled out the other side of the ditch and ran, crouching into the timber. They found the operations officer and some of the aircraftsmen near a small tent camouflaged with leaves and dirt. The Blenheim Squadron Leader named Arnold called to them as they came.

"Are you all right?"

"Yes," Tap said back to him. "When do the planes get here?"

"Any minute. Where were you?"

"Behind the buildings."

"Any parachutists near you?"

"No. Any around here?"

"Some up the mountain. They've got a patrol out for them."

"What's happening?" Quayle asked him.

"The Germans have got a foothold up the north end. There's

isolated parachutists around the whole field but they're no danger. We've still got the road to Canea. A lot dropped between here and the village. They were crashing Junkers."

"What about the Gladiator?"

"I don't know, John. You'll have to wait for the Blenheims. You can't do much on your own. They ought to be here any minute."

"They're going to look nice sitting out there," Tap said.

"That bloody ditch. We could get them here if it wasn't for that."

"Here they are now," Quayle said, looking up. "Did any drop near Suda Bay?"

"Thousands of the bastards. They're everywhere," Arnold said.

Quayle was quickly feeling that this thing was not conceivable yet. He did not believe that so quickly could there be an end to the whole thing. He was trying to think clearly about Helen but he could not because of the intensity of everything around him and he was concerned with the Blenheims now as they came over the field.

"I hope to Christ they come across-wind this way," Tap said.

"There's a signal on the field," Arnold said. They were all watching the Blenheims. There were five of them. They came down in a low sweep and settled in from the north end in singles. The leader chose a section between the craters and the others followed him. The German machine-guns from the north end were firing intermittently at the Blenheims as they came in and taxied to the shelter of where the mountain started from the field near the ditch. The crews got out and one of the aircraftsmen in the ditch stood up and shouted to them. They ran towards the timber. There was no fire from the north end.

"They must have cleared that lot of Boches out," Arnold said.

"What are these boys supposed to do?" Quayle said to him.

"I'm god-damned if I know. Stuart. Are you there? Stuart." A Sergeant came out.

"Get Captain Mann for me, will you?"

351

"It's all right." It was Mann, tall and blond, walking towards them through the light timber.

"Did you clear that lot out from the other end?"

"Yes," Mann said. "We sent in bayonets." Quayle knew that Mann understood what he was doing.

The Blenheim crews came up then. There were fifteen of them. The Flight Lieutenant reported himself to Arnold and said it was pretty hot around here. Arnold told the Sergeant to get the planes wheeled closer into the mountainside and have them refuelled and fitted out.

"What do we do?" the young Blenheim Flight Lieutenant asked Arnold.

"I'm waiting to hear from H.Q.," Mann answered him instead of Arnold.

Working parties had gone out to fill in some of the craters on the field to make a clear runway. Twice they were fired at by snipers in the slopes.

"Is that your Gladiator?" one of the pilots asked Quayle.

"Sure."

"Are you in Eighty?"

"Yes."

"I'm Hickey's brother."

"You are? I'm Quayle."

"So you're Quayle. I heard a lot about you."

Quayle was looking at young Hickey. He could hear the machine-guns on the slopes going intermittently, but it was comparatively quiet now. He was looking at Hickey and seeing how very young he was. Then he was thinking about Helen, and he was trying to get Helen out of his mind because this was what was going on around here and he would have to concentrate. And he was looking at young Hickey to see the facial likeness.

"I'm sorry I didn't manage to salvage anything from his kit," he said to the boy.

"That's all right."

"I had a few things. They were lost."

"It's better that way anyway."

"Yes."

"I'm glad I ran into you," the boy said.

"Yes. We must get together sometime." It ended there.

Quayle was certain, now that the Blenheims were here, that it was going to be difficult doing something about Helen. He knew there was nothing he could do but go over and get her or see that she was all right or that she could get out. But he would have to wait around silently now waiting to be told what to do. It was that sort of situation.

It was silent except for the intermittent machine-gunning and the bombing on the other side towards Canea and Suda Bay. All afternoon it was like that. The quiet was threatening, but towards evening the bombing on the other side became thick and continuous. Quayle heard Mann saying that Suda Bay was getting the hell knocked out of it and Canea was just about surrounded by parachutists. They were watching anxiously for night. Quayle knew that when it was dark enough he would make for Suda Bay. And as the sun started down he reported to Arnold and told him he would like to see about his wife in Suda Bay.

"It's thick with Germans," Arnold said.

"I know. Can we get along the road?"

"There's trucks coming in at dark," Arnold said.

"Thanks. I'll be back in a couple of hours," Quayle said.

He did not tell Tap but walked through the woods between the bottle neck of the mountains. He was continuously challenged but held up the coin in his hand. Then he found the road and started walking until one of the trucks picked him up.

"How far do you want to go?" the driver asked him.

"The olive grove beyond Suda Bay."

"I hope you get there. That was cut off this morning."

"How far can you go?"

"The other side of Canea. I only go to Canea."

"I'll go that far," Quayle said.

At Canea he was challenged continuously by guards and anybody who saw him. He hurried through streets completely flattened by the bombing, and went out along the road to Suda Bay. Another truck came by and he got a ride to the outskirts of the village. It was smashed too, and as he walked he could see the damage all around the place. When he was challenged he could see the nervousness of the men who had fixed bayonets and wore their steel helmets.

He walked clean through the smashed village with the cobblestoned square a scrap heap of craters and stones. There was rapid movement of troops and trucks passing through. He ignored it all and made out along the road leading to the olive grove. He was walking along the middle of it and noticed that there were no trucks on it. He could hear machine-guns ahead somewhere near the olive grove.

He was suddenly challenged.

"Who is it?" he heard the voice. It was an Australian.

"Quayle, Flight Lieutenant."

"Come forward." He stepped out towards the guard he could see dimly with a bayoneted gun held before him.

"I've got a coin here," Quayle said to him.

"All right," the Australian said.

Quayle thanked him and went to walk by him. The Australian called to him. "Sorry, you can't pass here."

"Why not?"

"This is the end of the road."

"I want to get to the olive grove down the road."

"Not this way," the Australian said. "What do you want to get there for?"

"I have my wife down there."

"Your wife?"

"Yes."

"Just a minute. I'll get our Lieutenant." The Australian stepped into the ditch and called someone. Quayle waited and another Australian came up.

"Are you the Lieutenant?" Quayle asked him.

"Yes."

"I'm Quayle, Flight Lieutenant. I'm trying to get to the olive grove."

"You'll never get there. The Germans have it, or most of it."

"What happened to all those women that were there?"

"They were shifted away yesterday morning."

"Where to?"

"I don't know. Somewhere towards Retimo along the coast."

"Can I get there?"

"No. It's all cut off," the Lieutenant said to him.

"Hell. Are you sure?"

"You can walk along the road if you like. You'll last about two hundred yards."

"Is there any communication along there?" Quayle was getting desperate now.

"I don't think so. Not from here anyway. We've been sending out patrols to break through but it's impossible. We'll probably clear the way to-morrow if we don't get more parachutists around here."

Quayle knew then that there was a brick wall. It had all happened too quickly. He should have expected this. He should have got Helen out long ago. But it was not hopeless even if he did not know that she was all right. He did not know whether or not she had been sent back with the other women. He was not sure of anything any more. He was not certain about what he was to do. . . . Perhaps H.Q. has some information. They may have telephone communication with the sector down the coast. . . .

"Where's H.Q.?" he asked the Lieutenant.

"Down the coast. It's cut off too," the Lieutenant said.

"Jesus Christ."

"That's right too," the Lieutenant said. "Your wife's probably all right."

"Yes. Maybe." Quayle did not feel himself completely conscious.

"We'll probably clear it up to-morrow."

"Yes."

Quayle was standing there uncertainly. He turned around and started walking back. He thanked the Lieutenant as he walked away, and he could hear the two talking as he felt the vibration of his feet against the hard road. He had never felt so completely unsure of himself and what he was doing.

He was picturing Helen somewhere and he did not know where. But he could see her with sandals sometimes, and sometimes with two fibre suitcases walking with other women, and sometimes being surprised by German parachutists and shot. He was not certain of anything and he had vagueness about coming back or waiting to get down the coast and whether this invasion would fail. He caught a truck going through Suda Bay and then walked back to the airdrome. It was almost morning when he got there and he could hear the bombing behind him as he walked into the timber.

Arnold was sitting in the dark at the square table outside the tent. There was a guard near him. He challenged Quayle.

"It's me," Quayle said.

"Did you find her?" Arnold asked him.

"No. Is H.Q. cut off?" he asked Arnold.

"That's right. Since about two o'clock yesterday."

Quayle walked to the tent and went in. He lay on the floor and pulled one of the coats near by over him. There were about five others already sleeping there.

He had hardly shut eyes when it seemed he was awakened and there was dim light. It was bombing and he could see the figures running out of the tent. He followed them and made for the ditch near the field. He could see the high Heinkels coming over as he ran. He fell in the ditch as the first of the Heinkels peeled off and apparently came straight for him. He flattened out as he heard the machine-gun and he did not know whether it was the plane or the Bren gun in the ditch firing. Every time he looked up it seemed the smoke was coming from every one of the Blenheims except the one tucked in near the edge of the field near the Gladiator, which was not being touched. It lasted for half an hour, and they were all flat on the earth all the time, it was so intense and so continuous. When it let up he ran back to the timber. Arnold was talking on the phone.

"They just got all the Blenheims except one," he was saying.

Mann was there too. He looked at Quayle. "This is the bloody end," he said. He was angry and quick.

"What happened?"

"That's H.Q.," Mann said. "They've got the wind up. I've got to take my crowd out of here to go defend them."

Quayle felt again that Mann was the man here who knew what he was doing.

"Is that Field H.Q.?"

"Yes. The silly bastards. They're sending a muster of R.A.S.C. drivers here to hold this bloody place. They haven't even fired a rifle before. Of all the bloody things to do . . . If this airdrome goes the whole thing's gone. They'll get planes down and troops and you can kiss good-bye to the whole place."

"When did they get through to H.Q.?" Quayle showed his feelings.

"About an hour ago."

"Is there a passage through?"

"Yes. The Australians broke through about an hour ago."

Quayle was thinking about going with Mann. Then he heard Arnold saying into the phone, "It's hopeless. We haven't got any protection for planes here."

Then silence.

"They should have built a bridge over that ditch."

Silence, then: —

"What the hell. They just came over and picked them off."
Silence.

"You won't hold this place with R.A.S.C. drivers."
Silence.

"All right, sir. Yes, sir. Just as you say. Here's Mann."

"This is Mann," the Scottish Captain said when he took the phone.

"We'll be over in about three hours."

Silence.

"They got here. They got here an hour ago. They're taking over now."

Silence.

"You can kiss this place good-bye," Mann was saying angrily.

Silence.

"That's too bad. All right, then, we'll be over." Mann hung up viciously. "Those silly bastards. Get cut off and now they've got the wind up. If the Germans can land troops it's good-bye to this place. Oh well. That's the way they want it."

"John," Arnold said to Quayle, "you've got to get out of here."

"Where to?"

"Take off. Report to Cairo."

"Leave? Now?"

"Yes. They think it's hopeless with planes here if they get strafed on the ground. It's their own bloody fault for not building a bridge over that ditch."

"But what about the rest of you?"

"We're to stick around. Christ, what a mess."

"I'm going now," Mann was saying. A soldier had taken Mann's rolled army-kit away and Quayle could see the steel-helmeted troops walking through the timber and the trucks taking them away.

"S'long," Mann said to them.

"S'long, Mann," they said.

"I hope you hold out," he said as he turned away.

Quayle was thinking: They've cleared that road. I could get there. Now I've got to get out of here. What the hell. Back to Cairo. I can't walk out of here. How the hell can I get down there? Why the hell didn't they burn up that Gladiator?

"You'd better start moving," Arnold said to him.

"Look. Can't someone else take it?"

Arnold shook his head. "Sorry," he said. "They said you. I

358

know about your wife. I asked them. They said you. Sorry, John. I'll do what I can about your wife."

"What happened to Tap?"

"He went up to Canea last night. He's not back yet."

"Look. Will you do what you can?"

"What I can. Yes. I'm sorry, John."

"It can't be helped," Quayle said. He was thinking: This is it. This is everything. This is like crashing. This is everything. Getting out of here. He was running vacantly towards the ditch where the Gladiator was when he heard the planes.

"Here they come again," someone was shouting. He looked up. He could see the mass of planes. It was the same grouping roughly as that they had seen the first day. There were gliders and Junkers, hundreds of them in large squadrons. They were coming back for another try.

Ahead this time was a group of twin-engined Messerschmitts. They were peeling off already and he ran to the ditch and dived flat as the first one screamed over and he could hear them strafing the timber. He looked at the soldiers around him now. These were the R.A.S.C. drivers. They were all flat. There were no machine-guns firing at the Messerschmitts. There was only one Bren gun at the other end of the ditch. It fired at the second plane, but he could see the tracers way behind it.

"Oh Christ," he said aloud. Then he could see the aircraftsmen coming out from one end to get at the Gladiator. He ran back to the timber. They were all lying flat on the earth as the Messerschmitt came over again.

He could see Tap as they got up.

"John," Tap said.

"Hullo, Tap," he said.

"I hear you've got to get out."

"Yes. For that bloody Gladiator."

"I'll do what I can about Helen," Tap said.

"Thanks."

359

"John. Get that bloody plane off. It's ready," Arnold shouted to him as he flattened out.

"All right," he shouted as the next Messerschmitt came low.

He could see it between the trees. He saw the fire as it came towards them and the high scream of its engine. He didn't flatten out and he stood there and followed it with his eyes and saw the tracers coming through the trees. There was death in the sky in the trees in the shadows and he felt nothing.

He was in a vacuum that was noisy and there was nothing around except the tracers. They were all around him; he could hear the biting and the shouting behind him as the Messerschmitt passed over screaming. He looked around. Tap was on the ground and did not get up. He did not have to look further. He could see the mess of blood and the hanging of his legs and the attitude of Tap's arms.

"He's hit," he shouted to Arnold.

Arnold was already next to him as Quayle got there. They pulled him over. Tap's face was squashed flat into the earth with blood and a mess of flesh.

"Christ. Oh Jesus." Quayle had stood up quickly.

"The bastards."

Quayle could feel nothing any more. This was a greater peak in all their lives than one life reaches and the noise was nothing any more. There was only sight and Tap there squashed into the earth. There was no shouting around him and no chaos and no men running and no Arnold shouting again, "Get that plane off. Here they come." He was not running to the ditch to get in the Gladiator. He could not feel anything until he saw the great splurge of planes coming down.

Gliders, Junkers, parachutists were coming down in a mess and all together. He ran to the Gladiator and got in. He could see the last Blenheim on fire as he ran. Already on the field were gliders and Junkers. There was practically no fire against them. He felt the engine shaking and pushed the throttle.

He did not try to pick a path across the field. He felt the bumps and all around him he could see the mess of gliders and parachutists and above him and on the earth. He had to rip the stick back and climb on nothing as two Junkers came in to crash land. In the whole mess he kept his machine-guns going, and every time one of the Junkers or gliders got into his sights he yelled and pushed the gun button. He had skimmed the edge of the field and climbed around. Below he could see the field almost covered with parachutists, gliders, and crashed Junkers and men running and machine-gun fire.

His look was quick as he dodged between the Junkers and let them have all his ammunition. It was exhausted before the whole thing below him was out of sight.

He automatically set the course for Mersa Matruh on the Egyptian coast. He looked quickly behind, and all he saw was the mountain gradually curtaining the mess of white parachutists, and the crater-pocked field and the whole mess. Everything. And he knew it had all finished. He knew they had the airdrome. He felt the whole thing as he climbed.

The Messerschmitts were way to the right. He climbed and put the throttle wide open, and could think of absolutely nothing except that it was all over. Everything. He had saved a Gladiator. This bloody thing. And all other things were at an end. The whole world might as well stop now. There was nothing more. Nothing.

Chapter 38

He had tried everything. While he was in Cairo he had sat in the square office at the American Legation and tried to have them find Helen. They had tried but they always said the same thing. That they had heard nothing, but that something might come in soon. He had sat in the long room at the British Consulate and heard the native boys outside shouting to each other as he waited. And the British Consulate said they could do nothing. She had no British passport, they said, therefore they could do nothing official to trace her, particularly in what was now enemy territory.

Every time the groups came in from Alexandria that had been evacuated from Crete, he went out to the camps. He wandered through them and looked hard at the women, but he never found her. And he was getting so that he never expected to find her, because she was tangled up with the Crete battle and that had left him with complicated thoughts.

Much as he had mistrusted the army hierarchy before, he mistrusted them more now. He mistrusted them completely. He did not look upon them as individuals any more but as a group who were incapable and inefficient as a whole. Crete had solidified the thing in his mind. He was tangled up because he did not know where to go from there. The doubt he had had before was not complete distrust. It was more isolated disgust. He could go on with his job without thinking much about it. But now it was more.

He doubted the whole thing. He knew that the leadership as a group were incapable of this thing, that they were not the proper group or individuals to run this thing, that they were not even part of it. But he did not know where to go from there. He knew that the distrust interfered with what he was doing. That he didn't want to go back into it all in this frame of mind.

He was physically afraid, with the tangle going on inside him.

The days that he walked along the streets he listened deliberately to the continuous hum of people, the natives, British soldiers, Australians, New Zealanders, Indians, officers with red tabs and perfectly tailored drill shorts and pistols in high brown belts with cords and suede shoes. He looked at it all in that frame of mind. It was tangled up with Helen. But actually the distrust of the leadership was complete and solid. Every time he saw them, or the khaki staff cars, or the tall handsome captains and majors perfectly sun-browned and with sleeves rolled just to where they should be, and the expensive dark glasses and the roadster cars, it only made it worse within him. He hated the tangle because he had never been so badly complicated before. And standing above the whole thing was this desire not to go back into active operations until he knew where to go from this mistrust.

He had lived so completely within the squadron that now when they were all gone he knew nobody, and he did not want to. He lived at the barracks at Heliopolis just outside Cairo. He was training in Hurricanes, because now he was to go into Hurricane squadron work. The actual flying was good for him, except that it depressed him. He knew it was the slide for him to go back into operational work. He wished for the others from Eighty Squadron, because he knew that reacting to them, and how they reacted, had kept him level and with a clear head about what was going on.

He would climb into the Hurricane on the hard sand of the wide Heliopolis airport and automatically give the engine its way. He liked the hard bare feeling of the metal around him. It was cold and solid-looking. He liked the obvious power of the Hurricane and the heaviness of the whole plane compared with the Gladiator. He liked its fast take-off and the fast climb, but there it ended. He wanted tight loops and tight turns like the Gladiator. He knew he could never get them. If he went out in a turn, it was always wide and slow compared with the Gladiator. And he was always blacking-out. Every fast turn he made he blacked-out. His legs got stiff and sore also and the physical strain was greater all around.

And he had no feeling for it any more. He just didn't want to go back into combat. That was continuously there. He mistrusted the whole war as an inanimate thing. He mistrusted the group he felt were misrunning it completely and utterly and with no feeling towards what it was all about. They treated it as a Win if you can, but if you lose, well — too bad. But he could not express it, even to himself, clearly enough. He wanted confirmation from somebody else, from the others around him, that they thought the same. But he knew they didn't, and that tangled it all the more.

There had been the day when he came down after turning a Hurricane inside-out. He had climbed slowly out of the cockpit and allowed the fitter to help him off with his parachute as he leaned against the fuselage. He looked at the fitter and thought of Macpherson who had never got away from Greece. This was a small Cockney with humorous eyes and something of a smile, like Macpherson's. Quayle leaned against the fuselage and watched the fitter throwing the parachute on the wing of the Hurricane. Maybe this one would know. . . . So Quayle made the mistake he had been scared of making.

"Were you in Crete?" he asked the fitter. The boy was surprised when he turned around. He shook his head.

"No, sir," he said. "I've only been out here a short time."

"Well, what did you think of it?"

"Crete?"

"Yes."

Quayle knew that this was being condescending. The fitter looked at him for a moment, then said: —

"Something went wrong?"

"What do you think it was?" Quayle said. He wanted to hear the fitter say what he himself, Quayle, thought. He wanted it confirmed, and the next step told to him.

364

"I don't know. Not enough equipment," the fitter said.

Quayle shook his head. This was not it. This was not what he wanted to hear.

"No?" the fitter said.

Quayle realized he had shaken his head.

"No," Quayle said. "It's not only that. What about the army? What do you think of that?"

"A bit slow," the fitter said. "But it's all right. They do what they're told."

Quayle saw a glimmer in that.

"Do you think they're told right?"

The fitter was being careful with him, and Quayle knew it and cursed again this whole wall, whatever it was, that prevented them from talking openly.

"Sometimes," the fitter said. "They make mistakes like we do, though."

No, Quayle was thinking, this isn't it. This is not what I want. I want the whole thing laid out before me and where to go from here. He nodded to the fitter and made a polite remark and walked slowly to the living quarters. And he knew this was not it. Maybe Helen would know. She would have a rough idea anyway. Christ almighty, a whole bloody war between us . . .

It had gone like that for him all the time. While he walked the streets to go to the American or the British Consulate . . . Or to Headquarters in Garden City, or to the movies which he craved now and would sit in every night — and he was not completely conscious of why he did it. He knew that he didn't like it when they were over, and he went out into the warm streets and the black-out. This was all wrong. But it went on like that, while he went through the Hurricane training and tried to find Helen.

Chapter 39

He had been in Cairo for the heat of June. His face was normal again and his hair had grown where the doctor had shaved it away to put in the stitches. He knew that his Hurricane training was finished, that he was just waiting around now to be posted to another squadron for combat duty. He did not like this feeling of unsureness that never left him alone with clearness. He wanted Helen; or he wanted the whole thing cleared.

He had been told to report to Headquarters at one o'clock that afternoon. He had come in on the Metro from Heliopolis and gone to the American Legation, but there was nothing there for him. Neither was there anything at the British Consulate. He walked slowly down Shareh Soliman Pasha and around the square, and followed the warm throng of people as they moved along the street. He went vaguely towards the Café Parissiana and walked in and sat down at one of the tables with the open front facing the street.

It was warm as the sun came through the open front and he sat there feeling the warmth and thinking of Helen and of lying in the sun on the grass at Crete, and where she was. The waiter put the water on the table and the bread rolls and white butter and gave him the menu. Quayle toyed with it and looked at the boot-black boys fighting to get to two soldiers who had stepped out of a gharry and were going into the cinema next door. It was all pleasant. The noise and the smell of the manure from the gharry horses, and the continuous strange honkings of the ramshackle taxis, and the shouts of the people were all high in the warm lazy air. He leaned his arms across the table and played with the drops of water running down the jug.

He watched two khaki-clad figures walk in the open entrance. They were very different: one tall and blond, the other small and dark. Both were keen-faced with straight noses. He half stood up as he recognized Mann, the Scottish Captain who had been defending the Canea airdrome and then gone to defend Headquarters. That's where Helen had been. Quayle knew the other one too. It was the small American that Lawson had been with at Janina, and Quayle couldn't remember his name. He called to them.

"Mann," he said. "Mann. Can you spare a minute?"

He saw Mann look at him, without recognition. Quayle stood up. Neither of them recognized him. He vaguely thought of his face being normal.

"I'm Quayle," he said.

"Say," Mann said to him. "So it is. Your face . . ."

"Yes," Quayle said. "It's cleared up." The two of them had come to his table. They were all standing up. He shook hands with Mann and then the other one.

"Do you know Milton Woll?" Mann said.

"Yes," Quayle said. "We met at Janina."

"He's a friend of Lawson's," Woll said to Mann.

"Do you know Lawson?" Quayle asked Mann.

"Sure," Mann said.

Quayle let it pass though he did not understand it yet.

"Are you going to have dinner?" he said. He used the English form of dinner for luncheon.

"Sure. Can we sit down?" Mann said.

Quayle said he would be glad. They got chairs and sat down and they ordered when Quayle did. Quayle wanted to ask him straight away whether he had seen Helen, but he waited.

"Where did you meet Lawson?" Mann asked him.

"In Greece. Were you in Greece?"

"No. I was in Spain during the Civil War, that's where I met him."

"You were in the International Brigade?" Quayle asked Mann. He was understanding now.

"Yes."

"When did you get into the army?"

"Oh. Quite early. It's good experience."

"You get around," Quayle said.

Mann only nodded.

"I wanted to ask you about my wife," Quayle said to him. "She was down near Headquarters somewhere in a women's camp. I wonder if you know what happened to them."

Mann shook his head. "No," he said. "I knew there was a camp somewhere there, but I think they were all left behind."

Quayle nodded slowly. They were silent and the waiter brought the bowl of salad and the pot of tea that Quayle had ordered. He poured some of the tea out for Mann. Woll refused and asked for coffee.

"How did you get out?" Mann asked him as they ate.

"I was ordered to fly a plane out. They just took the airdrome as I left."

"That was a mess," Mann said. He spoke quickly and with short words that came with certainness. He leaned forward, and even that was a vigorous motion. "You know," he said. "If they'd left us there the Germans would never have taken that airdrome."

"Things happened when you left," Quayle said.

"All it needed was those machine-guns," Mann said. "The moment we went it was inevitable. What the hell, fancy putting untrained men to hold the one thing the Germans wanted. If I needed convincing, this would convince me."

"Convince you of what?" Woll said.

"That this war's being run by incompetents."

"It's always the same," Milton Woll said. "Look at Spain, and that was a war."

"The incompetents in Spain were the same types that are the incompetents in the British Army. But Spain was different. Christ, they knew what they were doing."

368

"The military mind . . ." Woll said. Quayle could see that Woll was only goading Mann, but this was getting important to him now. Particularly Mann.

"What do you think did lose Crete?" he asked Mann.

"It's not that," Mann said. "Crete was only a sharp example of it."

"Of what?"

"That we fight it, and the Command balls it up."

"The war?"

"Yes."

"It had a lot to do with equipment," Woll said.

Mann shook his head. "They sent us enough equipment to hold off the Germans. All we needed was machine-guns. But what did they do? They sent the guns in one ship and the ammunition in another. One ship goes down, so we have ammunition and no machine-guns."

"Whose fault was that?" Woll goaded. "That's the accident of war."

"Accident nothing. Look at the people in G.H.Q. To be a good staff officer in G.H.Q., all you need to be is a good clerk. A good shipping clerk would have had more sense than to put that stuff separately. But all the clerks are out fighting and men that have never had to count anything in their lives are doing the job in H.Q." And Mann shook his head again.

"Well?" Woll said.

Quayle was slightly suspicious of Mann's outburst. But he knew that Mann felt this thing and was saying what he himself was wanting Mann to say.

"I suppose it will go on here?" he said to Mann.

Mann nodded his head vigorously and gulped some of the tea down.

"It'll keep going to . . ." He stopped, then: "Until they all get bumped off or something happens in England."

"What will happen in England?" Quayle was feeling this now too.

"Anything. It takes time though. After Dunkirk they really

started to get fed up in England. They're a little quieter now, but other things will happen. It's just a matter of survival until they do. Then this bunch will go out."

This is it. This is it. Quayle could hear the confirmation in what Mann was saying. But he was still groping for the whole solid picture.

"Are you talking revolution?" Woll said. He was goading Mann again.

"All I know is that it's a matter of survival until this bunch goes out and then we'll start getting something done the right way."

"Pipe dreams," Woll said. "We thought that in Spain."

"I know," Mann said. "But this is getting too big. Wait until it gets more acute; then we can do something. As it is, we just go on like this. We're not quite sure what we're fighting or what we're fighting for. It's just a matter of survival until we start doing something. The only trouble is that many of the ones that will be needed will get it now."

Woll shook his head but Quayle could see this now. He had not got it clearly but he knew that this was the confirmation he wanted for his own thoughts about it. He did not have this clean-cut like Mann, but there were many things about Mann and what he thought that he did not understand yet. He wanted to hear more.

Mann said to him, "I envy you your flying experience."

"Why?" Quayle was looking keenly at Mann's flushed animated face.

"Because the air force is going to be everything."

Quayle nodded. It was getting above his head now, but this vigour of Mann when he said something or leaned forward was something he understood. He suddenly remembered he had to be at G.H.Q. at one o'clock. He looked at his watch. He had ten minutes to get there. He called for a bill and stood up.

"I've got to be at H.Q. at one o'clock," he said to them.

"Are you working there?" Woll asked him.

"No. I think I'm being posted to a squadron. Look," he said to Mann, "I'd like to see you again. Is it possible?"

"I'll be around," Mann said. "I'm out at Maadi. How about having lunch with me on Wednesday?"

"All right. I'll meet you here. S'long," Quayle said to both of them and went out to catch a taxi.

He was thinking about the confirmation Mann had given him. That this was someone being articulate about what was going on. That there was where he went from here. It was just a matter of survival until it happened. Until what happens? I don't know completely yet, but I will. It's just a matter of survival until it develops. I'll get some more out of Mann. It's just a matter of survival until this develops.

Chapter 40

Quayle did not see Mann on the Wednesday. He was posted to combat duty with a squadron in the desert. He had to leave next day. He did not feel so badly about it because he was getting everything cleared up within him and that was important. He could hear Mann saying that it was just a matter of survival. To survive this stage of it for what there was coming. That was the beginning of it. He would have to think it out beyond that or wait until he could find out a lot more about Mann and from Mann. He wished all the time for Helen. He could get things said to her now that they could not say in Crete, and had tried but failed. He wished that badly.

He caught the train to Alexandria that night. He slept curled up on the polished leather seat of the train apartment as the train created a wind across the desert and a thunderstorm through the villages. He would wake quickly sometimes as the noise of the echo from the wheels was thrown back from a wall, and he would sit up startled with the nervousness that is the lasting effect of bombing. Once he was dreaming wildly about running over a cliff accidentally, all the time looking behind to see if Deus was following with the pistol in his hand, and sometimes he was following and firing at him and laughing. As the light flicked through the window from the red sun rising, he sat up and pulled his boots on and waited for the train to arrive at the station where he would change for the desert.

It was mid-morning when the train eased itself into the junction near Alexandria, and Quayle threw his kit out the window onto the dry dust platform and walked around out of the train. He liked the open feeling of this place because it was right on the edge of the desert, and the dry dust collected pleasantly in the sun. He felt the dry feeling of movement and action and the compactness of the men at the station who were waiting to move up to the front area. He looked at the men as he walked. They had obviously never been up before, and there was slow hilarity between them all. There was no other train in the station and Quayle sat down on his kit to wait for the front train to come in. The other train had already pulled out for Alexandria.

He looked at a small group near him. They were the officers apparently in charge of the reinforcements on the platform. There were a Colonel and three Majors and a dapper young Captain. They all had long white fly-whisks attached to their wrists with a leather thong. The Colonel and the young Captain had expensive suede boots and smartly cut drill shorts and short-sleeved jackets. The Colonel had red tabs on his collar signifying a Staff Officer. They were all talking neatly in exaggerated phrases, and Quayle wondered quickly why in the hell they were not going up in a staff car instead of by train. And he automatically felt the contempt and dislike for this group that he had felt for the same types that were in Cairo.

As his dislike increased, he heard the noise on the opposite platform and saw a group of dun-uniformed soldiers pour in uneven groups onto the platform. They squeezed through a narrow gate, and with great noise and laughing the scraggy group increased in size until the whole platform was full. They were clad in the heavy woolen uniforms of the Greek Army. They all wore the strange overseas cap or dirty steel helmet. Most of them were unshaven, their uniforms crumpled and dirty, their boots low and worn. Some carried blankets across their shoulders, others carried mess tins untidily in their hands or spare boots around their necks. They were just a ragged mass, and Quayle guessed they were some of the few Greeks that had escaped from Greece or Crete.

He looked at them with warm feeling, and was glad they straggled in their natural habit and provided the fantastic contrast to the clean, light-clad British troops around him. He felt fine towards the Greeks. Their dirty unshaven faces peered across the tracks to the side Quayle was on, curious about the large collection of such clean British troops. They shouted to the Britishers, who more or less ignored them. Quayle heard one of the Majors saying, "Good God, what a bunch." The Captain had gone away. The two Majors and the Colonel stood there looking at the Greeks.

"Who are they?" the Colonel said.

"Greeks or something," the smaller Major said.

"Dirty-looking lot."

"Aren't they?"

"Haven't they any officers?" the Colonel said. "They seem to be running wild."

"I think some of our chaps are around somewhere," the taller Major muttered, almost apologetically.

Quayle stood up violently and jammed his hands in his pockets and thought of the day he had seen the Greeks being led away to be shot for killing their officers. He wanted to tell these officers about it, and shock them, and say: "You'd better get away now; they're a wild bunch who shoot their officers because they don't feel the officers are fighting properly."

The Captain who had been with the Majors and the Colonel came back and saw Quayle standing there with his hands in his pockets. He stopped and said carefully: —

"Strange crowd."

Quayle looked at him, and did not say anything. The Captain noticed the D.F.C. ribbon on Quayle's tunic and felt the immediate psychological inferiority.

"Going back?" he asked Quayle.

Quayle was frowning and looking at the Greeks. He nodded casually, without saying anything. The Captain for that flash of a second almost felt Quayle's feelings towards him, and he turned awkwardly and rejoined the Colonel and the Majors.

Then as Quayle stared at the lines of the track, he heard a shout from opposite:—

"Olá. Olá Captain. Is that you?"

Quayle looked up, but saw only the grinning unshaven group directly opposite fighting playfully and laughing at the discomfort of one of them trying to lace his worn boot. Then again:—

"Olá *Inglisi*. It is you. Yes?"

Then Quayle saw him. He saw the dumpy middle-aged figure, dirty and unshaven and smiling widely at him and waving an overseas cap. He groped for the memory of this man to record his identity. He half-smiled at the crumpled figure.

"Ha, Captain," the Greek shouted and jumped down from the platform to the tracks and ran stumbling across them and clambered up near Quayle.

"It is me. You forget? Yes?"

"Georgius!" Quayle remembered in a streak the Australian Greek from Larissa who had sung with Vain that night.

"How are you?" Quayle shouted. They were shaking hands violently.

"Fine. I'm fine," Georgius said. Quayle was smiling. He was happy that the Greek recognized him. He saw the Colonel and the Majors and the Captain staring at him as he still shook Georgius' hand and laughed with him. Quayle felt suddenly elated.

"You're in the Greek Army now?" he asked Georgius.

Georgius nodded, still grinning. "I go in it when the Germans hit us."

"But you're Australian," Quayle said.

"It does not make the difference now. My. You look fine."

"What are you doing here?"

"We come to still fight. Perhaps we will be in the British Army. They have fine uniforms. And what food. We got away to Cyprus. That's where we've been."

Quayle laughed at the gestures Georgius made as he mentioned food and the motion of his hands indicating his stomach swelling, which looked obscene divorced from what he said. It was then that the British officer came up the steps from the other platform. He was walking towards the Colonel when he saw Georgius talking to Quayle. He tapped Georgius on the shoulder with the leather-bound handle of the fly-whisk he carried.

"What are you doing here?" he said in English.

Georgius swung around, startled by the tapping on his shoulder. He looked blankly at the officer, not understanding for a moment.

"You belong over there. Go on," the officer said. Quayle looked quickly at the officer. He could see Georgius suddenly shift his feet and lift himself lightly and with dignity.

"Let him be. It's all right," Quayle said to the officer.

"He's not supposed to be here. They're harder than a pack of kids to keep in order."

"I come to see my friend," Georgius said evenly.

"Is he bothering you?" the officer asked Quayle.

"He's an old friend of mine," Quayle said with rising anger. The officer looked surprised. He did not know what to do. He looked hard at Quayle, then quickly turned and walked towards the Colonel.

"I'm sorry," Quayle said to Georgius. He felt he had to apologize for this impoliteness.

"It is all right," Georgius smiled at him.

"Is he one of your officers?" Quayle asked him.

"Yes. He has brought us from Cyprus."

"He is not pleasant."

Georgius shrugged. "It is the same everywhere with officers. We did not expect otherwise." Then: "I'm sorry," as he realized Quayle was an officer.

"It is all right. I am feeling like that too."

"I will go back," Georgius said, nodding to the other platform. "He is right, we are very wild. But he is the wrong manner. We do not mind if he does not get in our way when we fight. But I will go now."

"Where will you be?"

"I do not know. Nobody seems knowing that. But I will write

for you my name." He had pulled out a dirty small stub of a pencil and was looking absently for a piece of paper. He found a scrap of newspaper and laboriously wrote his full name in Latin lettering and "Greek Army" after it. He handed it to Quayle with the pencil. Quayle wrote his name and number and gave it to Georgius.

"Perhaps we will meet within the war." Georgius had held out his hand and was smiling again. Quayle felt the natural warmth towards him that he felt for Nitralexis and Mellass and the tall Greek and the little Greek. He felt the sanity of this little middle-aged man, and it overwhelmed the anger he felt at the stupidity and foppishness of the British officer and those standing over there laughing with stupidness. He knew quickly that this sanity of Georgius and the others was why he knew he could go on doing what he had been doing. It would always outweigh the hopelessness that he felt when he became disgusted with the incompetents.

The two shook hands firmly, and the train that Quayle was to take came in with the great noise of engine steam, and they had to shout.

"It is fine seeing you," Georgius said loudly.

"And you," Quayle said.

They both held their hands out again and gripped warmly.

"S'long Georgius!"

"S'long . . ." Georgius looked at Quayle's name on the newspaper, then said, "S'long John!" — and smiled broadly.

As Georgius stumbled across the tracks, Quayle looked once and smiled very happily, picked up his heavy kit and got into the train which quickly filled. But he felt anger again when he saw the Colonel and the three Majors walking along with five soldiers behind them carrying their bulky kit for them. They went to two compartments kept clear for them. He heard the young Captain laughing with exaggeration and it was only drowned by the train blowing a head of steam and jerking its way out of the station towards the desert.

Chapter 41

As the slow train dragged over the desert, he was glad to have seen Georgius. He remembered the Jesus Christ Greek and the little Greek vividly again and knew that he could go on flying a plane even though survival was everything. He was trying to work it out from what Mann had said to him. He saw much of the illogic in taking an instant dislike to that officer group at the station. He suddenly included the thought that one of them or all of them might be feeling the same way he did, and some of those back in Cairo might feel the same way he did. It was not just officers. They represented something and even though he didn't know if they did feel as he did, he was bound to be antagonistic towards them.

He never considered for a moment that he was in the same category, technically. The acuteness he felt, in the division between himself and the incompetents, and the warmth and sanity he saw as part of Georgius and the Jesus Christ Greek and the others who went into the mountains, were all tangled with his feelings about the vacuumatic attitude of that type in the next compartment. And he wondered again about Helen. He always considered her alive, and wondered what would be the way she would do what she had to do in the situation.

At Mersa Matruh there was a station wagon waiting for him. He threw his two small suitcases in the back and the driver put in the heavy bed-roll and the green canvas bed. It was new because he had replaced all his kit while in Cairo. They went out along the coast road, over the asphalt road, then up the escarpment and to the south, to Bir Kenayia. The station wagon took him up to the square wooden hut and the driver said this was the operations room and the Squadron Leader was in there, and that he, the driver, would take the Flight Lieutenant's things to the tent. He pointed out the tent at the other end of the field. There were ten to fifteen Hurricanes on the field, and a small motor refuelling tank.

Quayle walked into the operations room. There were the clerks and the officer with the three stripes on his sleeve and a D.F.C. ribbon on the shirt, and Quayle smiled at that.

"I'm Quayle," he said. He handed over his movement order to the Squadron Leader.

"Hullo, Quayle," the Squadron Leader said and they shook hands. "I'm Scott," he said.

"How're you?" Quayle said stiffly.

The Squadron Leader was standing up and unfolding the paper. He put it in one of the wire baskets and walked around the rough table.

"I'll take you over to the mess. Most of the boys are there now," he said.

As they walked to the other square wooden building that had been painted the same colour as the rusty desert, Scott asked Quayle about Crete and Quayle answered him noncommittally. They stepped into the square building with a linoleum floor, and the nine or ten pilots who were sitting around reading or drinking at the rough bar looked up.

He took Quayle to each of them and introduced them by their surnames, which Quayle forgot the moment he heard them because this was like going to school for the first time. They all crowded him to the bar and asked him what he wanted to drink, and Quayle had to conform and he said whiskey-and-soda, so the aircraftsman behind the bar poured it out. They all drank to Quayle and he drank back, alone, to them.

He got away from them an hour later, and went to the tent to get his kit laid out. It had already been done. He was re-sorting it when the tent flap was pushed back and someone walked in. It was evening and Quayle could not see who it was.

379

"Quayle?" the voice said.

"Yes."

"John. It's me. Gorell." It was young Gorell who had been wounded that day in Larissa and shifted back to Egypt.

"Gorell! How are you? Are you in this squadron?"

"Yes. I thought it must be you." They shook hands.

Quayle fumbled around and lit a lantern. He saw the clear face with little or no expression and the blond hair.

"How's your neck?" he asked the boy. Gorell fingered the slight scar and half-turned to show it to Quayle.

"It's gone now," he said. "It was too bad about Hickey and Tap and the others."

"Yes."

"Did you know Finn never got to Crete?"

"No, I didn't."

"Yes. I asked for him. He just didn't arrive."

"What happened to South?" He was the other one left from Eighty Squadron.

"You're taking his place. He got it about a week ago," young Gorell said.

Quayle shook his head and sat on the camp bed but it threatened to cave in so he stood up again. He did not know what to say to young Gorell. He knew how to talk to him when the others were around and he did not have to be careful, as he had to be now because they were strangers.

"I heard you got the D.F.C.," young Gorell said to him.

"Yes." Quayle nodded and rubbed his unshaven chin.

"That was pretty good," young Gorell said. "The others too."

They talked for a while about Hickey and Tap and the others. Then young Gorell said how about going over to the mess for some dinner because it was dark and getting late. Quayle said he would wash up first and he would be over in a minute. Young Gorell went out and Quayle poured some of the water from the petrol tin into the canvas basin on a three-legged stand and unrolled the khaki washing kit. He washed his face without taking his shirt off, combed his hair. Then he walked across the dark airdrome to the mess building. He could not find it at first because of the complete darkness. When he did, he went in and the others were already eating. He sat down in the vacant chair next to Scott, the Squadron Leader, and he was introduced to the others who had not been in the mess building when Quayle was there before.

When they had finished, the Squadron Leader told them they'd better get to bed early, there was a patrol in the morning. He looked at Quayle.

"Do you want to go?" he asked Quayle.

"Sure," Quayle said. He knew he might as well start.

"They'll call you," Scott said. "Good night."

"Good night," they said as Scott went out.

"I think I'll follow him," Quayle said. He said he was tired and if they didn't mind . . . They all said they didn't, so he said "Good night" and walked over to his tent and went to bed.

It was four o'clock when the Corporal woke him. He got up in the cold dimness and lit the lamp. He hurriedly shaved in the cold water and pulled on the old shorts and khaki shirt and the new sheepskin-lined boots over his long stockings. He hunched his shoulders in the cold and put his hands in his pockets as he walked across the dry airdrome. The sun was lighting its way before coming up, and Quayle heard the engines of the Hurricanes crawling into warmth as he went into the mess building.

Young Gorell and four others were there. They greeted him casually and he sat down and ate the bacon and eggs and thick tea. Then they got up together and went across to the operations room. Scott was there with his great-coat on over his pyjamas. He told them to make for Mersa Matruh, patrol at fifteen thousand in the given area for an hour and come back. They all went out pulling on their helmets. Quayle was shown the plane he was to fly, and he took one of the parachute harnesses from the operations room and walked into the morning light towards the Hurricanes.

They took off with Quayle leading the boxed V-flight. The sun was over the horizon by the time they were at five thousand feet. Quayle got the habit again, crouched in the narrow cockpit and looking behind, or as near behind as he could crane his neck, and he could feel the strangeness of being back in combat. He was not completely comfortable, and he was thinking about Mann and Helen again and turning around until his neck was sore and his head ached from the blur he got every time he twisted it.

Sometimes he thought he saw other planes, but it never developed. For an hour it was just patrolling and keeping the formation and keeping his eyes strained and feeling the cold and wishing he had put a jacket on, then heading back to the airdrome and putting down into the high morning. It was like that during all the patrols. They did not run into anything. But he was getting the feel of things back again now, even though he heard Mann. *It's a matter of survival.* And that's what it was to him now. He knew that. Before, you survived if you could. Now, it was a deliberate matter. He mistrusted everything around him and what he was doing. He was careful with the others and quieter and seldom smiled or relaxed the puckering in his forehead. The others left him more or less alone. Sometimes he wanted to talk with young Gorell but his restraint would not let him.

He was used to the desert again too. It was hot because it was June. The sand spread low across the airdrome and the wind picked it up and sometimes filled everything as it had before. And if it wasn't the dust it was the sweat and the flies, and the wet nights and cold morning. The flies and the sweat were the same too, like the dust and the heat. If you got rid of the flies, you figured you wouldn't sweat. The wet feeling of humid sweat mixing with dust to a paste on your face was unpleasant. The wet irritating grittiness of your shirt against your back was continuous even when you took your shirt off. And the patrols went on, and the war was quiet, making them heavy on the mind because of their dullness and strain. When he landed he missed the collectiveness and exchange of feelings that had gone on in Eighty Squadron, even after a dull patrol.

Once he came in on the belly of a Hurricane because the undercarriage or the oleo legs had stuck. He brought the plane in fast, and as it ripped and vibrated across the stony desert he caught something of the old excitement. When the ground crews and other pilots had rushed over and helped him out and talked excitedly about it, he felt no part of it because they were strangers. As he walked away from the plane he caught up with young Gorell, hoping that maybe there would be some feeling here.

"Funny," he said to him as he caught up in the same stride.

"Hullo." The lad was not sure of himself with Quayle.

"You know, it's not like piling up a Gladiator," Quayle went on.

"They're heavier," young Gorell said. "Hurricanes, I mean."

"No," Quayle said. "I mean I don't get that feeling of waste. Gladiators used to be precious."

"More than Hurricanes?"

"You remember in Greece, the day we lost three at Larissa?"

"That was the day I got it in the neck."

"That's right, you didn't stay."

The boy shook his head.

"It's a pity," Quayle said half to himself.

"Yes," young Gorell said, merely to indicate he was listening.

"Yes." Quayle was quiet again; then: "Did you get on with them?"

"The Greeks?"

"Yes."

"All right," the boy said.

"I suppose they feel mad at us now."

"Yes." Young Gorell kicked a dry bush across the 'drome and watched the brown curling dust catching his boots as he walked into its cloud.

"What do you think they'll do now?" It was not the sort of question Quayle usually asked, or ever asked, young Gorell was thinking. What's happening?

"I suppose they'll knock the Germans around some," the boy said naïvely.

"Yes." Quayle was pulling off his helmet. "They were going into the mountains when we left." Quayle looked at young Gorell's simple face and accepted the obvious honesty of the boy, and was glad he had talked to him, even though he wouldn't know what it was all about — though why shouldn't he? But Quayle rejected it even as he said: "They know what it's all about." And was surprised when young Gorell said boyishly: "They certainly do."

Quayle plunged again. "They make it clearer," he said.

"What?"

"They make you rather fed up with some of our bunch."

Quayle was finding it difficult, but he knew he was desperate in his feelings again, and he did not expect any help from the lad in exercising them by speech.

Young Gorell dismissed it with a buoyant: "There's good and bad anywhere. It's not a matter of whether you're Greek or not."

"I know," Quayle said. "They distinguish it better than we do."

"They make mistakes too. But they'll do me."

Quayle was not ready to believe that young Gorell could mean more than he was saying in this simple way, and he would not accept the idea that he was being careful.

"They're all right." And Quayle was musing again.

"You know," young Gorell laughed, "they're really like us."

"Well, they know what they're doing better than we do." And Quayle knew this was the critical moment.

"Why?" Gorell talked highly. "We make mistakes too. But they had a cheap bunch of officers. But they'll have to make a change, like we will have to."

"You think so?"

"Don't you?" the boy said cheerfully, and he could only say it that way because he had seen, just as suddenly, and with equal surprise, that Quayle wanted to talk about this; and young Gorell lost some of his slight awe and juniority, and reluctance to disturb

384

Quayle's reserve. And he was surprised when Quayle quietly said "Yes," without reserve.

They had almost reached the building where Quayle would put in his report, and as they approached it Quayle took a quick look at Gorell again and he wanted to find out all in one piece how much he thought and what he knew; and he did not want to be reserved now, but knew he would be careful because he could not drop the restraint he had used for so long.

"What changes?" he asked quickly. They were standing there now and just not just making conversation as they walked.

"Oh. Get in some new talent," young Gorell said. And he knew he was taking a chance too. "Give anybody a break, and I don't only mean in the army."

Quayle knew that was what he wanted, and he thought it out quickly. . . . He is not simple. He feels as I do. There must be others. It's inevitable we know who feels this way. We automatically get together. Mann, me, Georgius, Gorell, and the Greeks. . . . Quayle knew he had wanted this surprise reminder that within his own orbit there was someone who felt the same, and he was no longer feeling like an oddity. They were still standing there, then suddenly Quayle felt the responsibility of remaining to talk, and fell back on his restraint and said awkwardly: "I've got to put in a report."

"Yes." Young Gorell was awkward too.

"Well—" Then Quayle paused. "How about a drink later on, before dinner?"

And the boy was surprised and as pleased as Quayle was about it, and said: "Sure," and went away, as Quayle did, with the feeling of loneliness gone.

As he opened the door to the operations room, Quayle was feeling glad that this was not an oddity. That this feeling was cumulative and was collective and the more this went on the more there would be in it, and even if you did get it in the neck there were plenty of others around and they must all get together some day. It was just a matter of time before they got together and it all changed. Mann and his matter of survival. Now me and a matter of

385

time. It's working out. Time and survival; that's what matters; that's it; I'll leave it at that for the moment while I do this report.

It was later that day that Quayle had been watching them jack up the Hurricane. He had been standing there as the slight wind caught the dust in contagious swirls. A station wagon came up with a warm blast of moving air. The khaki-clad figure next to the driver got out and walked towards him.

"Hullo Quayle." It was Lawson.

"Well—Lawson," Quayle said. "You're always turning up somewhere."

"That's my job. How're you, anyway?"

"Fine," Quayle said. "Come on over to the mess."

"I hear you got the D.F.C.," Lawson said politely, as they walked.

"That was a long time ago. In Crete. When did you get out of Crete?" he said as they walked.

"I didn't. Not with the British."

"Helen didn't, either," Quayle said.

"I know. That's why I came out to see you," Lawson said. Quayle stopped walking and puckered his forehead.

"Is she all right?" he said quickly.

"Yes. She's all right. She's with her mother in Athens."

"Look," Quayle said. "We'll go over to my tent. It's better there."

They walked the other way across the hard airdrome in the hot sun.

"I've been moving hell to find her," Quayle said. He was slightly buoyant now that he knew about her. "She's all right?" he said again.

"Sure," Lawson said. "I went from Crete to Athens with her."

"What happened?" he said as they went in the tent. Lawson turned the chair backwards and sat down with his arms leaning on the back of it.

"She was caught in that house. The Germans took her to the camp

386

behind Canea after the British left. That's where I was caught. Do you remember the little Greek officer in that house?"

"The owner?"

"Yes. He told the Germans that Helen was the wife of an English officer, so they kept an eye on her all the time."

"They didn't do anything to her?"

"No. They annoyed her some. But they only kept her for a while. When we got back to Athens they let her go out to her mother."

"I'm glad of that," Quayle said.

"Did you know they took Stangou?"

Quayle shook his head.

"Sure," Lawson said. "They had him chalked up. They took him about the second day after the Germans took over. They don't know where he is."

"That's tough," Quayle said. "Did Helen give you a letter or something?"

"No. They watched her too much. They didn't like my going out there, either. She couldn't give me a letter, because when the Germans let me leave Greece they took all my papers. I knew they would, so we couldn't risk it. She just said to tell you that she was all right and that it didn't look as if the Germans would let her out."

"Is there any chance of her getting out?"

Lawson shook his head.

"They won't let her out," he said. "I tried to get her out with me across Turkey. But the Greeks wouldn't give her a passport. The Germans said she couldn't go anyway."

Quayle was excited now and he stood up and walked up and down as Lawson spoke.

"She said you'd both have to wait until all this is over. She said she'd get out if she could, but she'd live with her mother until it was all over if she couldn't get out."

"How was she taking it?"

"Pretty badly at first. But when she saw how her mother felt when Stangou was taken away, she pulled up a bit. She's all right, though. They haven't much food, but they're all right."

Quayle could think of nothing to say.

"She gave me this for you." Lawson held out a small, thin silver ring.

"Thanks."

"She still had that big silver one you gave her."

Quayle pushed the small ring onto his little finger and looked up as young Gorell walked in.

"We've got to go," the boy said. "Hullo," he said to Lawson.

"What's up?" Quayle asked him.

"Something's heading for Mersa Matruh. We're in a hurry. The C.O. wants you."

Quayle looked around for his helmet, sat down and pulled on the sheepskin boots.

"Look," he said to Lawson. "I've got a job to do. Can you wait till I come back? They'll look after you over at the mess. Come on over with me."

"Sure," Lawson said. "I'd like to stay around here to-night anyway."

"Fine. You can put up in my tent."

They hurried across the airdrome to the operations room. Quayle got the orders, and told Scott about Lawson, and he said it would be all right. Then he came out again and hurried to where the five Hurricanes were warming up. Lawson walked over with him.

"Helen said something about you going to England," Lawson said.

"I was thinking about it. It's different now," he said.

"Is it because of Helen? She said, don't stay for her."

"It's a bit of everything," Quayle said.

"Yes. I guess it's all the same war," Lawson said.

Quayle nodded as he pulled on his helmet. "It's just a matter of survival," he said.

"Well, I'll see you later," Lawson said. He stopped, because they had reached the Hurricane and were shouting above the slow roar of the engine.

"Thanks a lot for coming!"

"That's all right. Say, and she told me to tell you the baby will come about February."

Quayle looked around quickly at Lawson. Baby . . . Helen . . . Baby . . . Great Christ. Me. Baby. Helen. With a baby. Survival . . . Lawson saw it all in his look.

"I thought you knew," he said.

Quayle shook his head.

"Thanks anyway," he said vacantly as he turned and climbed onto the wing of the Hurricane and lowered himself into the cockpit and pulled up the door. He revved the engine automatically and buckled the harness. He unlocked the chassis, still thinking Helen, baby, Helen, me, baby. He looked around at the others; plugged in the phones then.

"Let's go," he said and pushed the throttle with his left hand until the plane moved, gathered speed across the field. Lawson waved a hand to him, but he didn't see it. He automatically watched the other planes behind him as he lifted the plane off the ground.

He pushed the undercarriage lever to up, and by the time he had it up he had trimmed the tail and set the climb. He looked behind him at the steady flight of the four planes with young Gorell directly behind him at the right. They were climbing rapidly, and he twisted the gun button catch on the control column to FIRE and half relaxed to think as he kept his head turning. It was all confusing. Everything was confusion.

But he was too tense to give it much thought now. They were to intercept an enemy formation heading for Mersa Matruh. It ought to be almost over Mersa Matruh by the time they could catch it, Quayle was thinking. Then . . . Helen, baby, me, matter of survival. Fancy young Gorell.

They came over Mersa Matruh at fifteen thousand. It was clear, and below was the rust of the desert. They were all straining around to see where the bombers were.

Young Gorell saw them first. He shouted into the phones.

"Right underneath us, John," he said.

Quayle pulled the flight around in a steep bank and saw the group of bombers with the fighter escort a little behind and above them.

"Messerschmitts. Look at their wing-tips," young Gorell said into the phones. Quayle could see the square wing-tips and he shouted "Head on" into the phones as he came around in a turn. He had a rough count of them. There were about ten or fifteen. He was tense now and he was opening the throttle to get the speed in level flight before winging over. He was seeing Mann, Georgius, Gorell in quick face flashes.

"Here we go," he said into the phones. He pulled the stick over and pushed hard with his left foot. The plane whipped into a slip and over on its back, losing height rapidly until he was in glide shape again and helling towards earth with the Messerschmitts suddenly before him and breaking up. A Messerschmitt suddenly got in his sights, and he pressed the small button and felt the jerk of the machine as he pulled out and tried to break the dive. He whipped past the Messerschmitt and he swung his head around to see it as he roared by. He could only see another Hurricane, probably young Gorell, coming down and flattening out behind a Messerschmitt.

Quayle cursed the fact that he couldn't tight loop and come straight back into it. Instead he came around in a wide climbing turn and looked for any of the Messerschmitts that had broken formation. He caught a glimpse of the bombers way ahead. He was easing over to go after them when he saw the Messerschmitt coming up below him. He saw the mess of white and yellow tracers all around him and he winged over and rolled off his level flight and came onto the tail of the Messerschmitt. The Messerschmitt was giving everything it had, and put its nose down in a climb. But Quayle came quickly across in a beam attack and held his finger on the button as the Messerschmitt went into a glide. Quayle went after him until it was far enough and he was certain he had it. Then he climbed again in a wide loop looking around as he went up.

He could see a Hurricane with a Messerschmitt on its tail just behind him and he climbed high enough to meet it as it came along. He got its white belly in his sights and sprayed the cone of white metal into it. It broke away before his eyes and he saw the pieces flying from it and the whole thing burst in black smoke. He automatically ducked his head as the black smoke came straight towards him in a rush. He pulled his head up again. But it was too late.

It was all an accident. The split second, when his head had been down, mattered. A Messerschmitt suddenly lurched straight in front of him.

He knew he couldn't stop it. The two planes screamed together. He knew he couldn't stop it but he pulled the stick back hard and yelled. He was ripping towards the Messerschmitt. They were two powerful engines on the same track hurling towards each other, cars on a race track, hell's thunderbolts clashing, great atoms a million miles an hour head on. He could feel it. Oh Christ, look at me now. Look. Helen, baby, matter of survival. Get up on the seat, jump. This is everything, baby, Helen, matter of survival, get up, quick, quick, this is it, get up, matter of survival, hell, this is it, this is it, this is it.

They were hurling towards each other. Young Gorell looked below and saw it. He saw the inevitable. He saw the great ripping, tearing scream and he felt it all himself. He saw the pieces, the blot in the sky.

Quayle saw the immediate blackness of the thing as it hit him. His thoughts were high in a spiral that was not singular any more but in great complication at an apex. There was the great rushing, the physical strain, speed, inevitable, matter of survival, Helen, survival, and the quick jerk of his head and terrific rushing and himself screaming.

Gorell saw the green and yellow flame as the pieces ripped. The high black explosion boiling in the sky. He saw the blackness of it and the entire nothingness. He looked around desperately for the white burst of parachutes. They all did. The pilots of the Messerschmitts and the Hurricanes were one. They were waiting for it, the white burst of parachutes. They waited.

But there was none. None. None.

There was only the white cloud in the blue sky.

THE END

1/11 - 43